Praise for

Heidi Swain

'A summer delight!' **Sarah Morgan**

'Sweet and lovely. I guarantee you will fall in love with Heidi's wonderful world' **Milly Johnson**

'A little slice of joy' *Heat*

'So full of sunshine you almost feel the rays' *Woman's Weekly*

'The queen of feel-good' *Woman & Home*

'A true comfort read and the perfect treat to alleviate all the stress!' **Veronica Henry**

'A story that captures your heart' **Christie Barlow**

'Sparkling and romantic' *My Weekly*

'A delightfully sunny read with added intrigue and secrets' **Bella Osborne**

'A wonderfully uplifting story with a picturesque setting you'll wish you could visit' *Culturefly*

Also by Heidi Swain

The Cherry Tree Café
Summer at Skylark Farm
Mince Pies and Mistletoe at the Christmas Market
Coming Home to Cuckoo Cottage
Sleigh Rides and Silver Bells at the Christmas Fair
Sunshine and Sweet Peas in Nightingale Square
Snowflakes and Cinnamon Swirls
at the Winter Wonderland
Poppy's Recipe for Life
The Christmas Wish List
The Secret Seaside Escape
The Winter Garden
A Taste of Home
Underneath the Christmas Tree
The Summer Fair
A Christmas Celebration
The Book-Lovers' Retreat
That Festive Feeling
The Holiday Escape
Home for Christmas
Best Summer Ever
All Wrapped Up

Heidi Swain
Walking on Sunshine

**SIMON &
SCHUSTER**

London · New York · Amsterdam/Antwerp · Sydney/Melbourne · Toronto · New Delhi

First published in Great Britain by Simon & Schuster UK Ltd, 2026
Copyright © Heidi-Jo Swain, 2026

The right of Heidi-Jo Swain to be identified as author of this work has been asserted in accordance with the Copyright, Designs and Patents Act, 1988.

1 3 5 7 9 10 8 6 4 2

Simon & Schuster UK Ltd, 1st Floor
222 Gray's Inn Road, London WC1X 8HB

For more than 100 years, Simon & Schuster has championed authors and the stories they create. By respecting the copyright of an author's intellectual property, you enable Simon & Schuster and the author to continue publishing exceptional books for years to come. We thank you for supporting the author's copyright by purchasing an authorised edition of this book.

No amount of this book may be reproduced or stored in any format, nor may it be uploaded to any website, database, language-learning model, or other repository, retrieval, or artificial intelligence system without express permission. All rights reserved. Enquiries may be directed to Simon & Schuster, 222 Gray's Inn Road, London WC1X 8HB or RightsMailbox@simonandschuster.co.uk

Simon & Schuster Australia, Sydney
Simon & Schuster India, New Delhi

www.simonandschuster.co.uk
www.simonandschuster.com.au
www.simonandschuster.co.in

The authorised representative in the EEA is Simon & Schuster Netherlands BV, Herculesplein 96, 3584 AA Utrecht, Netherlands. info@simonandschuster.nl

Simon & Schuster strongly believes in freedom of expression and stands against censorship in all its forms. For more information, visit BooksBelong.com

A CIP catalogue record for this book is available from the British Library

Paperback ISBN: 978-1-3985-3873-3
eBook ISBN: 978-1-3985-3874-0
Audio ISBN: 978-1-3985-3875-7

This book is a work of fiction. Names, characters, places and incidents are either a product of the author's imagination or are used fictitiously. Any resemblance to actual people living or dead, events or locales is entirely coincidental.

Typeset in Bembo Std by Palimpsest Book Production Limited, Falkirk, Stirlingshire

Printed and Bound in the UK using 100% Renewable Electricity
at CPI Group (UK) Ltd

This book is dedicated to anyone who is looking for the courage to follow their heart

Chapter 1

I already felt like I had negotiated my fair share of challenges since Dad died eighteen months ago – funeral arrangements, probate, the family house sale, the sharing of Dad's possessions between me and my older brother, Zack, and my thirtieth birthday to name a few – but now I was in the midst of what I considered to be some Even Bigger Ones.

Having had my fill of the nine-to-five routine, working as an HR manager for a business that would have been far more successful had the owners been truly invested in the welfare of the staff I had helped them recruit, I had worked my notice period and, with my worldly goods, along with most of Zack's, all safely in storage, I was now heading to the village of Willowell in the Suffolk countryside to complete a task that was destined to feel like yet another ending, ahead of flying to Spain to spend a few restorative weeks of the summer with my brother.

'Tilly!' Zack's familiar voice filled the car as I pulled into a convenient lay-by and answered his call. 'I'm so sorry.'

'I should think so, too.' I pretended to scold him as I turned off the engine. Though actually, I was genuinely a little frustrated that he'd gone off grid right at the point when I needed his brand of brotherly encouragement and rousing pep talks the most. 'I really could have done with you these last few weeks.'

'I truly am sorry for disappearing,' he said sincerely. 'You know what my work environment can be like. But you have done it, haven't you? You have finally left that job you'd long fallen out of love with?'

'I have,' I confirmed, feeling proud that I'd stuck to my guns, stopped fretting about the loss of a regular pay cheque and made the break even without his rallying cries from the sidelines of my life. 'And I'll never have another like it again. I'm done with being stuck in an office for forty-plus hours a week.'

'Good for you, Sis!' Zack laughed. 'But it hasn't *really* been that long since we last spoke, has it?' He sounded unsure.

'Yes, Zack,' I said patiently. 'It has. Check your bank account if you don't believe me. The last time we were in touch was the day we received the money from Dad's estate. Three weeks ago, today.'

So much had happened in those twenty-one days that it felt like even longer to me.

'You know, I'm still not comfortable—'

'Yes,' I quickly cut in before he got into his stride. 'I do know you're still not comfortable about it, but it's what Dad wanted. What I wanted, too. A split of everything he left shared equally between us.'

Zack hadn't been happy with Dad's will from the moment it was read. He thought that I, having been the one who had looked after our father because he worked and lived abroad and had done for years, should have received the lion's share of the money, but Dad hadn't wanted that and neither had I.

It was Zack, five years older than me, who had helped Dad pick up the pieces after Mum had died when he was in his teens and I was still at primary school, and that, as far as I was concerned, meant between us we'd done our bit. Heartbreakingly, we had lost both our parents to cancer but we'd done everything we could, and that our ages and circumstances allowed, to emotionally support one another through the trauma of it.

'But—'

'Never mind but,' I cut in sternly. 'Now, tell me exactly where you're calling from. You are still in Spain, aren't you?'

He was silent for a second.

'Zack?'

'No,' he confessed, and I could tell he was grimacing and feeling guilty because he was only now getting around to filling me in. 'I'm not. You haven't booked your flight yet, have you?'

'Funnily enough,' I told him, because I was used to him relocating at a moment's notice, 'I haven't. I thought I'd better wait in case you moved again. So, where are you now? And more importantly, can I still come and see you?'

'I'm on my way back to Bali, and yes, you can still come and see me.'

I let out a breath and had a quick think. Bali was a world away from Spain and I wasn't sure I was in the mood for a long-haul getaway.

'Remind me again what the project in Bali is,' I stalled, while I tried to reconcile my mind with joining him there.

'Mangrove restoration,' he said concisely. 'The project is well underway, but I've been asked to go back and check its progress. I'm going to be there for at least a couple of months.'

'I've heard that before,' I teased, surprised he'd be staying in one place for more than two seconds together.

When Zack and I were growing up, we'd both been adamant that our adult jobs would revolve around spending as much time out of doors as possible. Zack had caught the horticultural bug from Mum, and our annual summer camping trips to Willowell with Dad, which were classic Enid Blyton-style adventures, had inspired me, and we had both dreamt of pursuing our passions into adulthood.

Zack had succeeded admirably and travelled the world setting up and monitoring a whole host of plant-based conservation projects. I, however, down to a need for security which I now wondered if losing Mum at such an impressionable age could have accounted for, had set my childhood dreams aside and as an adult made completely different choices. Unlike my brother, I had settled for the reassurance of structure and routine.

I could see now that losing Mum hadn't impacted on Zack in the same way as me; he hadn't lost his ability to make brave choices, but then we weren't the same person and the age difference between us probably explained a lot. However, thanks to a couple of things that had serendipitously happened to me during the last year and a half, I was finally, slowly making my towards the life I'd always secretly wanted, but for a long time, hadn't had the courage to embrace.

'I know,' Zack sighed. 'But I mean it this time. I'm staying put for as long as I can.'

'Of course you are.' I nodded.

'I'm tired, Tills,' he said, and I realised he genuinely sounded it. 'And I can't bear to even begin tallying up my carbon footprint. All these flights . . .'

'Just keep focusing on all the good you're doing,' I encouraged him as his words trailed off. 'And if it'll make you feel any better, perhaps I won't come out. That'll be one less trip to add to our combined number of miles spent traversing the globe.'

Not that I'd done all that much criss-crossing. Not compared to him, anyway.

'No, you must,' he insisted. 'Now you've jacked in your job and have finally remembered how amazing it feels to spend more time outdoors than in, I want to help you keep going. Were they upset to lose you at the charity you'd been volunteering with?'

'They were, actually.' I swallowed, thinking of the wonderful people and the beautiful place I'd left behind at the wellbeing charity, Woodland Adventures. 'Those woods and the people connected to them are what I'm going to miss now I've moved on. My weekends won't be the same without them.'

Along with everything else, I'd also given up my room in the house I'd short-term shared with two other people, but never really bonded with, after the house I'd lived in with Dad had been sold. So, along with my HR job and the colleagues there who I had little in common with, and my partner, Lee, who I'd parted company with when it became obvious that the rediscovered outdoorsy me wasn't the version he wanted to be with, my ties to my old life were well and truly cut.

With the nest egg from Dad sitting safely in the bank, I now had space in my life to embrace a new adventure, and it was that that I forced myself to focus on, rather than feeling upset about leaving the team at Woodland Adventures behind. The end of my romantic relationship had been no loss – I had no desire to squeeze myself back into a shape that had never been the right fit, and especially for a man who couldn't accept the new me – but the day I left the woods for the last time had broken my heart a bit.

'It's time for a new adventure,' Zack said stoically, astutely echoing my thoughts as he often did, but I wondered if he meant just for me or both of us. 'And at the risk of sounding like a cracked record, I'm sorry I can't be with you this week.'

'It's fine,' I said, as I glanced at the packed cardboard box on the passenger seat. 'We'll be fine.'

'Tell him I'm really sorry, won't you?'

'You can tell him yourself, if you like.' I smiled. 'He's right here next to me.'

'Seriously?' Zack laughed.

'It didn't feel right putting him in the boot,' I said, shifting a couple of things so that I could check that the wooden box containing Dad's ashes hadn't become dislodged.

It was packed in with a hat, a couple of small photo albums and childhood holiday journals that I hadn't wanted to put into storage and had been planning to take to Spain.

'That feels weird,' Zack said, but I could tell he was smiling. 'Though if I was transporting him, I daresay I would have let him ride shotgun, too.'

'Of course you would.'

'Are you going to let him go tonight?'

'Yes.' I swallowed. 'I don't want to put it off and as it's the solstice, it feels fitting.'

'Crikey, the solstice,' Zack sighed. 'The mid-point of the year. Where are the months going?' He sounded wistful again. 'I really should have been back more . . .'

'I keep telling you, it's okay,' I reminded him, because I didn't want him feeling even worse. 'Honestly. But this is the right time to do it, isn't it?'

'Absolutely,' Zack confirmed. 'The solstice is the perfect time for transitions and change, so ideal. And I'll raise a glass to us all, wherever I happen to be tonight, your time.'

'Oh, Zack,' I whispered, as I felt a lump form in my throat and the prickle of tears that were still quick to gather, even though I was moving on with my life.

'I'd better go,' he said, and I could hear his voice was thick with emotion, too. 'Let me know how you find Willowell, won't you? I hope it hasn't changed.'

We'd decided together that Willowell was the perfect place to scatter Dad's ashes. The three of us had slowly healed there during our holidays after Mum had died. Dad, with the best of intentions, had moved us out of the family home, which had once been the heart of us, and in lieu of it Willowell had come to feel like our special place. Our time there had benefited us all. As I'd reached adulthood, along with my love of the outdoors, I'd slowly lost sight of what the village and countryside there had once meant to me, and I was excited to discover if it was going to reclaim its hold on my heart.

'It always felt like home, didn't it?' I smiled.

'Yes,' Zack agreed. 'More home than where we ended up. If that makes sense.'

'It does.' I swallowed.

It suddenly dawned on me that I currently didn't have a home and that if I didn't fly to Bali to stay with Zack, once my time in Willowell was up, I had nowhere to go. Even though

I was determined to embrace my newfound freedom, it did feel a little unsettling to have no base at all.

'I'll let you know about the village,' I promised, keen not to get bogged down with worry. 'I know there's a village store there now, because the cottage I'm staying in is attached to it, but beyond that, I've no idea.'

We ended the call once we'd made a plan – in so far as I ever could make a plan with my brother – to speak again in a couple of days, and as I climbed out of my car for a breath of air and a stretch, I realised he'd never told me the reason why he'd recently been off-grid. Classic Zack.

I opened the passenger door to pick up my phone to message and ask him and a sudden gust of wind rushed through the driver's side open window and whisked Mum's cherished but rather battered ancient straw hat out of the box next to Dad's ashes and away. Almost before I had realised what had happened it had blown halfway down the dusty lay-by and was in danger of being lost over a hedge.

'No!' I shouted, as I slammed the door shut and set off after it.

The tatty old thing that Mum used to wear when she was gardening was showing its age and was of no financial value, but I would have been devastated to lose it. Fortunately, that didn't happen, because there was a very sleek black car parked quite a way back from mine, and the driver, on spotting the unfolding drama, jumped out and set off in pursuit.

Being that much closer than I was, he was able to lunge for it and turned around grinning, with the hat clasped tightly in his grasp. Most people wouldn't have bothered, but he hadn't hesitated to help. What a hero!

'I take it this is yours?' he smiled, as I came to stand in front of him and felt my breath hitch and a rush of heat flood my face, and not because of the unexpected chase and fear of losing Mum's hat.

'It is.' I swallowed as I took in his impeccably cut suit – something I had never before been impressed by, but couldn't help noticing because he wore it so well – thick dark hair, kind deep brown eyes and enviable lashes. 'Yes, it's mine.'

'Here you go, then,' he said, dusting it off before handing it over.

'Thank you,' I said, taking it and holding it tight. 'It was really kind of you to come to the rescue like that.'

'It can be my good deed for the day.' He smiled as his eyes met mine. 'I always aim to get in at least one.'

Thoughtful, kind and the most handsome man I'd ever laid eyes on. This guy had it all going on. Unless of course, it was just a line, but his smile, which made his eyes crinkle attractively, looked completely genuine, so I didn't think it was.

'I hope that didn't sound as cheesy as I think it did.' He then groaned and wrinkled his nose which made me laugh because he looked rather silly.

'It didn't,' I said, willing my cheeks not to flush even deeper. 'And you've truly surpassed yourself with your deed for today, because this grubby old hat has great sentimental value and I would have been devastated to lose it.'

'In that case, I feel even happier to have helped save it.' He smiled again. 'Even if it did prompt me to say something cringey.'

'You really didn't.' I laughed again. 'I'm truly grateful. Thank you.'

That should have been the moment that I turned and walked away, but my feet felt rooted to the spot, and I would have given anything to find something else to say that would have prolonged our conversation, but the truth was, the interaction had run its course.

A sudden blast from the horn of his car made us both jump and I then realised there was a woman sitting in the passenger seat and she looked rather peeved as she tapped the face of the watch she was wearing.

'I'd better go,' the guy said, gesturing over his shoulder with his thumb towards the car.

'Yes,' I nodded, as I took a step away, 'I should be off, too. Thanks again for rescuing my hat.'

'Anytime,' he grinned.

I broke eye contact before he did, and as I walked back down the lay-by, I wondered if it was his partner in the car. I hoped not, because unless my imagination had been completely carried away by his luscious looks, he was giving off a flirtatious vibe and that would have been entirely unacceptable, wouldn't it?

I caught sight of myself in the rearview mirror as I put Mum's hat more securely in the box, then settled into the driving seat, adding yet more creases to my oversized sea green linen dress with mismatched wooden buttons. My long, wavy, dark hair was escaping the knot I'd tied it up in and I wasn't wearing a scrap of make-up. My freckled face was bright red and my neck looked rather blotchy. Um . . . the flirtation was definitely wishful thinking on my part then.

My libido had lain idle since I'd split with Lee, and if I was being completely honest, for a while even before that, so it must have forgotten how to interpret the signals. How embarrassing.

I hoped the stranger hadn't thought I was flirting with him, but then I wasn't likely to ever see him again, so I don't suppose it really mattered, did it?

'Right then, Dad,' I said, as I pulled on my seatbelt, started the car and put the encounter with the handsome stranger out of my mind. 'Let's go and have one last adventure in Willowell, shall we?'

Chapter 2

It had been a long time since either Zack or I had visited the picturesque Suffolk village of Willowell but as I drove along the narrow road through it, I could see that I was very happily going to be able to tell my brother that it hadn't changed all that much at all. The pretty river still meandered its way through the heart of the village, which was reached, via the approach I took, by crossing a stone bridge which looked the same as I remembered it from the many times we had played Poohsticks there.

Lots of the houses had classic pink-washed walls and quite a few were thatched. The majority had prolific roses and wisteria growing around the doors and windows and, with barely another car in sight, it felt like I'd stepped back in time. This was a feeling that I'd also experienced when visiting Willowell in the past and I was delighted it remained. Everything looked picture perfect, and I was so happy to be visiting again at last, even if it wasn't for long and it was for a sad reason.

That said, I knew that between us, Zack and I couldn't have settled on a better final resting place for Dad, and I also felt that he would have been very happy with our decision that I should bring him here. We might only have spent a few weeks a year in Willowell, but each of us felt settled and at home right from the moment we crossed the bridge and set up our simple camp in an obliging farmer's field to one side of the river just beyond the edge of the village. Our time here had genuinely healed us all and I suppressed the urge to berate myself for leaving it so long to come back.

Following the instructions issued by the Airbnb owner, I carefully pulled through the narrow gateway set between what was now the village store and the property next to it, and parked my car in the gravelled courtyard, in front of what I recognised as the tiny cottage I'd booked for the next few days.

'Well, I hope you won't, Kaya,' were the first words I heard as I walked around to the store and through the open front door, which was flanked by boxes of seasonal vegetables and buckets of fresh flowers. 'Because it's summer now and you know it'll be even busier in here soon and I'm going to need your help with the cottage on changeover days, too.'

The woman talking was wearing a pale pink apron dress and her abundant blonde hair was tied up in a scarf of the same colour. She was standing with her back to me and had the other woman, who I guessed was Kaya, not spotted me, I would have stepped outside again.

'Customer,' the assumed Kaya said and then quickly ducked through a door at the back.

'Hi.' I smiled as the other woman, who looked to be around my age, turned around. 'I'm Tilly. I've booked the cottage. I hope I'm not too early?'

She immediately replaced her frown with a smile and put down a basket which was full of handmade bars of soap with dried flowers pressed in the tops.

'Tilly, hi,' she beamed. 'I'm Melody, the cottage owner, and no, you're not early at all. It's all ready for you.'

'Fantastic.' I nodded.

'Just give me two secs and I'll grab the key.'

I walked back around to my car and lifted my small suitcase and rucksack out of the boot. I didn't have much in the way of luggage because I was only staying a few days and then, potentially, jumping on a plane.

'Can I give you a hand?' Melody offered when she appeared again.

'Thank you. If you could take the rucksack, that would be great. There's not much in it, so it's quite light.'

I decided to leave the box containing Dad's ashes and Mum's hat, among other things, in the car for the moment.

'Here we are then,' Melody said, opening the door and letting me in ahead of her. 'Welcome to Rose Cottage.'

The interior looked even smaller than it had on the website, but I didn't mind that because I was planning to be out and about every day as opposed to in it for all that long.

The ground floor was open plan with a sitting room and minuscule kitchen, featuring Cabbages and Roses classic floral pink fabrics, and I knew the bedroom and bathroom were decorated similarly because I'd seen them online. The pretty aesthetic and pared back furniture made the most of the bijou space, and given the colour of Melody's apron and headscarf, I guessed pink was her favourite.

'It's beautiful.' I smiled as I drank in the scent of the old-fashioned roses which were arranged in a spongeware jug on the coffee table in front of the sofa.

'Thank you.' Melody smiled back. 'There's a folder full of

local info and some foodie treats in the kitchen, along with milk, tea, coffee and so on.'

'Perfect.'

'I would offer to show you around, but I'm not sure where my sister's disappeared to and there's no one else in the store.'

'It's fine,' I reassured her. 'I know where you are if I need you.'

'Okay,' she nodded. She was almost out the door when she turned back. 'I'm sorry if you heard us arguing when you arrived,' she said, looking embarrassed. 'That was absolutely not the welcome I'd envisaged giving you.'

'I only caught the tail end of it,' I reassured her, 'and nothing horrendous.'

'Okay,' she said again, and I noticed her shoulders relax. 'My younger sister, Kaya, has trouble staying in one place for more than five seconds together. She's only just back from one trip abroad and already wants to book another.'

'I have a brother like that.' I grinned.

'Really?'

'Yes,' I told her. 'Zack. I never know where in the world he'll be working from one day to the next. This morning for example, I thought he was in Spain, but now I've discovered he's en route to Bali.'

Melody laughed at that.

'Well, if you want to compare notes on travelling relatives, you know where to find me,' she offered. 'I hope you're soon settled in here.'

'It feels like home already,' I said, looking around again.

'That's Willowell for you.' She smiled in response and headed back to the store.

She was certainly right about that.

It didn't take many minutes for me to unpack, and I rather restlessly whiled away the afternoon, counting down the time until I walked down to the river. The weather was hot, but the intensity was tempered by a welcome covering of light cloud. I could have headed out and explored the village and stocked up on more treats from the store straightaway – the scones I'd already demolished had been as light as air – but I didn't want to undertake anything else until I'd completed the task I'd come here to do.

Curled up on the sofa, which would have been only just big enough for two, and with Dad's ashes and Mum's hat now on the table with the jug of roses in front of me, I looked through the photograph albums and holiday journals and lost myself in a sea of happy memories as the clock ticked on.

There were a couple of places and landmarks which featured in our photos every year but didn't have dates attached. The only way I could tell when they were taken was by paying attention to how much Zack and I had grown during the intervening months, and I thought it would be fun to seek out those familiar and much-loved spots and photograph them again.

I was certain Zack would appreciate making the comparisons between now and then as much as I was going to, and I wondered if he remembered how we had always said that visiting them made us feel like we were 'walking on sunshine'. Our holidays in Willowell had been truly halcyon in every conceivable way and those three words had become a much-loved catchphrase of ours while we were here.

'Right,' I said, as the afternoon began to fade into evening and I was checking the clock almost as often as I blinked, 'I think it's time, Dad.'

After I'd unknotted my hair, so I could wear Mum's hat, I carefully put the wooden box into the bottom of my rucksack then, having checked the lid couldn't work loose, I set off.

The walk out of the village was as pretty as I remembered and the drop in temperature as I ducked under the trees and switched to the footpath that ran along the side of the river was something I was accustomed to, too. However, at that point my steps started to slow down, and my heart began to weigh heavy in my chest.

Even though I had come to Willowell with the intention of saying goodbye to Dad, it was still hard. I'd pictured the moment it would happen – and where – multiple times, but now it came to it, now the sun was setting on the solstice, it suddenly felt like it was going to be the hardest thing in the world to achieve. Even more difficult than when the three of us had scattered Mum's ashes, and I guessed that was because this time I was saying goodbye to mine and Zack's very last physical connection to them both.

The path along the river felt a little different to how I remembered it, but only because the trees that bordered it had grown. It wasn't all that much further on before I reached the sweeping bend in the watercourse and then a few steps beyond that, I reached the spot Zack and I had settled on.

'This is it, Dad,' I said on an out breath as I knelt on the grass and looked at the house that was built some way back from the river on the opposite side.

It was a traditional, detached Georgian property, set in stunning gardens that rolled right down to the river, and it had its own wooden jetty and a gentle, pebbled slope into the water. I had always adored the house and fantasised about living there and swimming in the river every day, through the summer at least.

We had spotted otters here and the occasional kingfisher too, and I thought now, as I had then, that it was the most beautiful place I had ever seen. Willow trees dipped their leaves into the gently flowing water, and in the shallowest points further along, we'd watched cows venture in to drink and cool off, and locals gather to paddle or picnic.

'Do you remember how I used to come and look at this place every day, Dad?' I whispered. 'We used to pitch our tent in that field behind me and then you'd turn me and Zack feral for the next two weeks and I'd be endlessly drawn to look at this house.'

It felt a long time since I had enjoyed that sort of heady freedom, but I was slowly starting to make my way back towards it now, or towards as much of it as I wanted. I didn't think I'd sacrifice a regular shower or properly brushing my teeth again, but Zack had been right about me feeling better for rediscovering the feel of fresh air on my face on a regular basis.

The light began to properly fade, and I realised that the reminiscing and harking back was all well and good, but it was unhelpfully enabling me to put the moment off. I took a deep breath, then quickly lifted the box out of my rucksack and loosened the lid.

I felt panic rise in my chest, and I didn't think I'd be able to get any further, but then someone in the house began to play the piano or listen to a recording. Astonishingly, they'd chosen 'Clair de Lune', a piece of music that Dad had loved and listened to on such a regular basis that we'd picked it as one of the pieces for his funeral.

Having received such an obvious and beautiful sign that this was the moment, I didn't hesitate further. I lifted the lid properly off the box, then carefully leant forward and slowly let Dad's ashes slip away. Some drifted into the river and some were carried up and away on the breeze.

By the time the music had finished, I had tears pouring unchecked down my face and Dad was gone. Or his ashes were. As I dried my eyes, I knew he was still with me in some way, just as he had been since the day he died, but he was with Mum now, too, and there was a feeling of comfort and completion in that.

When I looked up at the house again, the doors leading out to the garden had been closed, and after taking a moment to settle my emotions, I took that as my second cue and made my slow way back to Rose Cottage where I would message my brother and let him know how beautiful parting with Dad had been.

Chapter 3

Feeling grateful that the most emotional part of my trip to Willowell had been successfully completed and that it had happened in such a beautifully poignant way, I slept soundly, and from the following morning, began to explore the surrounding area and take photographs of all the places that I knew Zack would love to see again.

The next catch-up we'd arranged hadn't lasted beyond a few minutes because he was in an area with practically non-existent phone signal or internet, but I had just enough time to describe in more detail how releasing Dad's ashes had gone and later I sent him an email with photo attachments that he would be able to view when he visited somewhere more geared up.

My time in and around Willowell and chatting with Melody, who was so open and welcoming, flew by and, with just a couple of days suddenly left, I realised I had made a new friend, but I still hadn't booked my flight to Bali. Now, as well as feeling uncertain that I wanted to make the trip or pay the gargantuan last-minute change of plan parking charges that I hadn't previously factored in, I really didn't want to leave the village I'd fallen back in love with, either.

'I don't suppose,' I said to Melody, as we sat on the bistro set that belonged to the cottage in the courtyard one evening while sharing a bottle of wine and a bowl of olives, 'there's any chance of extending my stay here, is there?'

We'd already talked about the reason behind my return to Willowell as well as the joys of having a relative who disappeared off the face of the earth on a regular basis, and I knew that situation was harder for her because whenever Kaya came back she always promised to help with the store and cottage but rarely delivered. As absent as he was, at least Zack never made promises he didn't then keep.

Melody had reached breaking point with her sister's lack of support a couple of days prior to our current conversation and told Kaya that she was planning to take on someone from the village to help her for the next few months.

Thankfully, that appeared to be the wake-up call that was required. Kaya needed to refill her travel fund if she wanted to head off again, and being blessed with the means to work through the summer right on her doorstep, she was now knuckling down and earning her keep. It wasn't a total sibling relationship transformation, but enough of one to put the smile back on Melody's face.

'I'm afraid not,' she sighed. 'The cottage is booked right through the summer season now, which is brilliant on the one hand, but I'm gutted on the other because I would have loved it if you could have stayed in it for longer.'

I wasn't someone who generally clicked easily with people, but Melody and I had hit it off right from the start and I felt she was someone I would definitely want to keep in touch with when I left.

It was a surprise to acknowledge that I'd recently said goodbye to colleagues I'd worked with for years without so much as a backwards glance and yet here I was, feeling so fond of someone I'd only very recently met. I supposed that was how life and friendships worked out sometimes. Perhaps, now I was finally discovering my real self, I'd also find myself drawn to my true tribe.

'I would have loved that, too,' I said as I refilled our glasses. 'I don't suppose you know of anywhere else local that might be available, do you?'

She gave the question some thought but didn't come up with an answer.

'Oh well,' I said. 'Bali it is then.'

'You could sound a bit happier about that.' Melody laughed. 'Kaya would trade places with you in a heartbeat!'

'Now there's a thought.' I smiled as I popped an olive into my mouth. 'I'll stay here and do Kaya's job, and she can fly to Bali and keep my brother company. I bet they'd get on like a house on fire!'

'I'm sure they would, too,' Melody laughed, 'but I know my sister's finances won't run to it, so let's not even mention it as a joke, okay? Because otherwise she'll be nagging me to fund her flight on yet another vague promise of one day paying me back.'

'Fair enough,' I said, as I clinked my glass against hers. 'I won't say a word.'

The weather had been generally sunny and hot since I'd arrived, but the next day was cloudy and felt cool in comparison and so I decided to set out a bit further from the village on foot. I walked a route that I was fairly certain would take me past the front of my dream house, a view of it I hadn't seen before, and as I got closer, I felt excited to discover if it really did look like the solid and symmetrical typical child's drawing of a house that I'd always imagined.

Unfortunately, I wasn't destined to find out because there was a curved drive leading down to it and huge oak and beech trees further screening the view, so I didn't get to catch a glimpse of even so much as a chimney. I was disappointed about that but happy to admire the towering old trees and I did at least discover the name of the house.

'Fernside,' I said aloud, as I read the sign set on the side of the road next to a pair of open and ornate wrought iron gates.

The name felt highly appropriate given that much of the back garden was shaded and from my favourite vantage point along the river I had seen huge ferns in both pots close to the back of the house and planted in the sweeping borders right down to the riverbank.

Still feeling slightly sad not to have had my curiosity settled, I hoisted my rucksack higher on my back and carried on walking. When my tummy started to growl a few paces on, I decided to head back to the cottage along a different lane which I felt confident would be a helpful shortcut.

Melody had saved me a slice of the quiche she had made and sold in the store and I thought it would be just the thing for my lunch with a locally grown apple. I was still doing my utmost to ignore the fact that I really should start packing, when I spotted something that put the upsetting prospect right out of my head.

'Hey, Kaya,' I panted, as I breathlessly rushed into the store a few minutes later.

She looked at me and raised her eyebrows in that way of hers that made me feel about two inches tall.

'Have you been for a run?' she asked.

Her tone suggested that she thought that was highly unlikely even though she'd asked the question.

'Almost,' I said, as I slipped off the rucksack and squeezed the stitch in my side that the speedwalk back to the village had induced. 'Tell me, what do you know about the woods up the road?'

'Which woods?'

'The ones in that direction,' I vaguely pointed, 'with a for sale board hammered to the gate next to them. There's no number or agent listed on the board. In fact, I think it looks hand painted and I'm not entirely certain that it's genuine.'

'I don't know anything.' Kaya shrugged, using a tone that suggested I should have known she wouldn't. 'I wasn't even aware there are any woods up that way, let alone that they're for sale. I didn't move here when my sister did, so I don't know the area like she does. I'm only ever really passing through. And now chained to this place, of course.'

'Perhaps Melody might know something then?' I suggested, hoping she'd fetch her sister in lieu of her lack of knowledge.

'I daresay,' Kaya huffed. 'She knows everything else, doesn't she?'

'Did I hear my name?' Melody asked as she stepped into the store from the stockroom and gave her sister a look.

I hoped Kaya didn't talk to customers like that. Melody might soon end up regretting giving her a front of house role if she did.

'Yes.' I nodded, still trying to catch my breath. 'You did. You don't happen to know anything about the woods that are up for sale, do you?'

'The ones that way,' chimed in Kaya as she added my vague arm wave in the general direction for good measure, which in turn set the many bangles she wore jangling.

I narrowed my eyes at her but didn't comment.

'If you mean the patch of woodland a mile or so out of the village in that direction,' Melody pointed more accurately, 'then yes, I do. They belong to Constance Clarke.'

'Constance Clarke,' I repeated.

'Word on the street is that she doesn't really want to sell them, but folk are saying there's work that needs doing on the house, expensive work, and Constance hasn't got any money to do it.'

She stopped then and turned bright red.

'Melody!' Kaya unkindly pounced with relish.

'I know,' Melody winced, sounding flustered. 'I shouldn't have said that because it might not even be true. I don't do gossiping. I wasn't gossiping.'

Given that she ran the local store, which historically was as much a focal point for gathering news of neighbours as the village well and watering pump had once been, she was bound to occasionally slip up and repeat what she'd heard, wasn't she?

'Of course you weren't gossiping,' I reassured her. 'You were just filling me in, weren't you? So, it is a genuine for sale sign then?'

'Yes.' Melody nodded.

'And where would I find this Constance Clarke?' I asked.

'You're in the market for buying some woods, are you?' Kaya asked, sounding amused again.

Melody and I both ignored her question. Melody because she doubtless didn't want to come off as being as nosy as her sister, given what she'd just said about gossiping, and me because I didn't know the answer, even though the prospect did hold huge appeal.

'At Fernside,' Melody told me, and I felt my heart kick again even though I'd stopped walking a while ago. 'Constance lives in a house called Fernside.'

I thanked her for the info, quickly made my excuses and headed to the cottage to have the lunch I then felt like I needed more than ever, along with a very long think.

By the end of the evening, I'd decided that the next day, my penultimate one in Willowell, would include a trip to meet Constance Clarke who lived at fabulous Fernside. Not only would I be able to ask her about the woods she had for sale, I would also get a proper look at the exterior of the house. Possibly even the inside if she asked me in.

Had Kaya popped up and asked me again if I was in the market to buy some woods, I still wouldn't have known how to reply, but I didn't think there was any harm in checking them out and settling my curiosity, especially when the viewing potentially killed two birds with one stone.

Scattering Dad's ashes had been made possible by a serendipitous nudge from Fernside, so it might just be conceivable that what I decided to do next with my life might come to light via there, too . . .

'What have you got planned for today, Tilly?' Melody asked, as I walked around to the store the next morning just as she was refilling the buckets with yet more beautiful bunches of fresh flowers. Abundant and locally grown, they seemed to be one of her bestsellers. 'Anything exciting?'

I'd barely slept and was feeling rather jittery about the idea that I had been brave enough to allow to take root during the long hours of the night. Whereas before I had been wondering if, after my trip to see Zack, I could become a part of something that already existed workwise, now I was considering the possibility of becoming the sort of person who set up their own something and became a business owner myself.

It was a huge leap, even though it was only happening in my head, and because it was all still just a daydream (or a wide awake in the middle of the night dream), I didn't feel ready to share the details. Not that Melody had asked for the ins and outs, but if I didn't get anywhere with Constance, it wouldn't have been worth explaining, anyway.

'I thought I might pop down to Fernside,' I said casually, sticking to the bare minimum. 'Introduce myself to Constance and ask her about the woodland.'

'So, you really are interested in buying it then?'

Melody looked as wide-eyed at the prospect as I did.

'No,' I blagged, while fiddling with the strap of my rucksack so I didn't have to look at her. 'Not buying it. I'm just interested in the . . . trees. You know, what species grow there, that sort of thing. I used to volunteer in some woods, and I've developed a bit of a passion for woodland in general. I'd love to have a look around, but not without permission, so I'm going to ask if I can walk there.' I hoped that was going to be enough information to satisfy her curiosity. 'Do you think she'll mind me dropping by unannounced?'

Melody cocked her head. 'She might,' she said. 'She's a bit of a character.'

'Right.' I sighed, wondering then if I had the courage to risk it. I didn't want to get off on the wrong foot with Constance Clarke, but there had been no phone number or contact details on the for sale board, so other than just turning up, I wasn't sure how else to get in touch.

I suppose I could have asked Melody to do it on my behalf, but as I didn't want to divulge that I really was thinking about buying the woods, it didn't seem likely that Constance would welcome me, a stranger, into her home, on the pretence of simply talking trees.

'But if I phone to tell her that I'm sending someone along with the grocery order she phoned through last night,' Melody then suggested, solving the conundrum, 'she's bound to be more amenable. And you'll be doing me a favour because I'll either have to get Kaya to take it for me later or leave her to run the store while I go over there. And neither option fills me with glee.'

'In that case,' I said, as I turned around and rushed off before I lost my nerve. 'Consider me your delivery driver. I'll go and start the car.'

The lane leading to Fernside felt far narrower in my car than it had on foot and I drove down it with my fingers crossed in the hope that I wouldn't meet anything coming from the opposite direction. Unfortunately, luck wasn't with me.

'Damn,' I muttered, as I spotted a car in the distance and no obvious place for either of us to pull very far over.

My attitude changed, however, when I saw who was behind the wheel. He had the biggest smile on his face and no passenger today.

'I recognise that hat,' grinned the most gorgeous guy on the planet as we drew level.

'I bet you didn't really believe that I wore it, did you?' I laughed.

'I did wonder . . .'

'Well, here's the proof.'

'In all its glory,' he said, biting his lip.

'Hey,' I objected because he clearly didn't think it was glorious. 'Don't be down on the hat.'

He went to say something further, but another car pulled up behind him.

'I'd better move,' he said, as he glanced into his rearview mirror and put his hand up to the person waiting. 'It was nice to not quite meet you again.'

'Likewise,' I said, then breathed in nervously as both cars squeezed by with just a couple of inches between us.

I refocused on the lane and pulled my attention back to the task in hand, but I couldn't help smiling that our paths had crossed again. Forgetting further about his previous passenger, I wondered if a third time really might be a charm . . . With any luck, if we did see each other in the future, I might even be wearing something other than Mum's old hat and a bright red complexion!

A little further on, I turned off the lane, through the gates, and drove down the drive to Fernside.

'I don't believe it,' I gasped, as I looked at the front of the house for the very first time.

It was exactly how I had always imagined it would look. Four chimneys, five multi-paned sash windows, three above, two below, equally spaced and with a tiled and ivy-covered entrance between the bottom two. The front door was painted green and on either side of it stood two huge pots filled with yet more overflowing ferns. The gravelled drive swept right around the house, and it had a large closely cut turf circle at its centre.

It all looked very grand and very beautiful and there were no obvious signs of the work that Melody had mentioned needed doing.

As I parked up and then lifted Constance's grocery order off the passenger seat, I wondered if she was going to be as grand as her home. I should have pumped Melody for details to help me make a decent first impression. I quickly put the box down on the drive, left Mum's hat on the passenger seat, ran my fingers through my hair and smoothed down my baggy shirt.

'Well,' I muttered as I picked the box up again, 'I'm here now and I'll have to do.'

I waited for what felt like an age after knocking before I heard someone moving about behind the front door.

'Who is it?' came a voice that didn't exactly exude a warm welcome.

'I've got your groceries from the store,' I responded because my name, unless Melody had supplied it, wouldn't have been any use.

'You should know to come round the back by now. I don't use this door. The gate's unlocked as usual.'

I took a step back and, having worked out which way I needed to go, I struggled through the gate, along the side of the house and around the back to where an elderly woman wearing a floral-patterned dress and leaning on a walking stick was waiting. My eyes wanted to take in the extensive garden and the back of the house, but knowing that would have been rude, I kept my gaze on her and offered a cheery smile.

'Hello, Miss Clarke,' I said, still smiling. 'I've got your—'

'So you said,' she interrupted. 'But who are you? You're certainly not Melody or that flighty sister of hers.'

'I'm Matilda,' I explained. 'Tilly. Melody said she was going to call and let you know I'd be dropping your shopping off on her behalf today.'

'Well, she didn't,' Constance Clarke huffed, drawing her lips together into a thin line.

If I'd been asked to age her, I would have put her in her mid-eighties, though she was not particularly frail. I wouldn't have been at all surprised if she opted to give me a whack with her stick if she wanted to see me off her property.

'Or perhaps she did call.' She frowned and looked suddenly less fierce. 'I think I did hear the phone ring, but Melody should know better than to call when I'm listening to my news programme . . .'

My arms felt like they were going to drop off with the weight of the shopping I was holding.

'Well,' I said, with an effort to keep smiling, 'here's everything you ordered. Where would you like me to put it?'

She looked at me for a long moment, and I got the impression that she was weighing me up. I wished she'd do it a bit quicker. The box was starting to slip and so was my smile.

'I suppose you'd better bring it into the kitchen,' she said eventually and headed back inside. 'And I prefer to be called Constance, not Miss Clarke. I'm not a schoolmistress.'

'Sorry,' I apologised, even though I felt it would have been presumptuous to have called her by her first name.

'Melody usually unpacks the shopping for me, but I suppose I'll have to see to it myself today.'

'I don't mind doing it,' I said, my eyes darting everywhere as we went first through a large, untidy, plant-filled sunroom and then turned left into a chaotic kitchen. The interior of the house, or the little I'd now seen of it, didn't look how I had expected it to, at all. 'That is, if you'd like me to,' I added, hoping to get into her good books.

'I won't pay extra for it,' she grumbled. 'And Melody makes me a pot of tea to go with the cake before she goes. She hasn't forgotten the cake, has she?'

I set the box down on the only part of the table that wasn't covered in newspapers, crockery and piles of clothes. I wondered if there was anyone looking after Constance but then banished the thought because what looked like disorder to me might well be how she happily kept house. Each to their own and all that.

'She said she'd sent everything you asked for, and I think it looks like there's a cake box on the top,' I pointed out.

'Put it in the fridge, would you?' Constance asked, waving her stick in the direction of an ancient looking refrigerator. 'And there should be some cheese to go in there as well.'

Under Constance's staccato instructions, I soon had everything put away in the rather empty fridge and cupboards, and the pot of tea made. There had been an uncomfortable moment when I had asked if she liked her milk in first, but I'd glossed quickly over it by admiring the profusely flowering orchid on the windowsill.

'Looks delicate,' Constance had sniffed, 'but it's pretty tough, that one.'

I wondered if anyone had ever thought or said that about her.

'It's very pretty,' I said again as I tried to work my way up to mentioning the woods. The longer I'd been there, the further my courage had ebbed away. It was now or never though. 'I was wondering—' I began.

'Yes, yes,' she cut in. 'You can get off now. Tell Melody I'll settle up with her as usual, at the weekend after my appointment with the hairdresser.'

I was dismissed, but I hadn't achieved what I came for and stood dithering in the doorway.

'That's what we always do,' Constance said, assuming that I wasn't sure about the payment arrangement. 'You don't need to worry about the bill.'

'No,' I said, stepping right back into the kitchen again. 'It's not that.'

'What then?'

'I was wondering if I could ask you about the woods?'

'The woods?' She frowned.

'Your woods,' I gabbled. 'Willowell Woods, I think they're called. That's the patch of woodland that you've got up for sale, isn't it?'

'Who told you about Willowell Woods?'

'No one. I just happened to see the sign when I was out walking.'

'Well, what about it?' she asked sharply. 'There's already been a lot of local interest, you know. In fact, I'm certain someone is about to put in an offer. You're not local, are you?'

'Not exactly,' I confessed.

I got the impression that as a non-resident, she didn't think

I had any business being interested in her woods and I also surmised that the make-do-and-mend sign had been put up with a view to only attracting local interest. Most people in the vicinity would know who the land belonged to, so a name and number wasn't necessary. Incomers beware!

'You haven't been up there already, have you?' she then scowled.

'No,' I said quickly. 'I just saw the sign and asked Melody who the woods belonged to. It's clearly private property and I wouldn't have dreamt of trespassing.'

Constance nodded. 'Right,' she sniffed. 'Well, plenty would, so I appreciate that you haven't done that.'

'But would you mind if I *did* go and take a look?' I asked politely. 'You guessed right in that I'm not really a local, but I holidayed here every year when I was growing up. My dad used to bring me and my brother, Zack, and we camped in a field next to the river. With the farmer's permission, of course.'

'Did you now?'

'And I might never have lived here, but I've always felt at home in Willowell. More home than home,' I added wistfully, remembering what Zack had said. 'It's such a special place. So special in fact, that I came back this time to . . .'

'You came back this time to what?' Constance sounded intrigued when I didn't finish the sentence.

'My brother and I decided this was the perfect place to scatter our dad's ashes,' I said croakily. 'It's where we've always felt happiest and where we wanted Dad to be.'

'I see.' Constance swallowed, looking a little choked herself, which I wouldn't have predicted.

'We'd had it planned for quite a while,' I continued, 'and I knew I would be doing it alone because my brother is abroad, but when it came to it the other night, I didn't think I was going to be able to see it through. Then, right at the crucial moment, someone in a beautiful house on the other side of the river to where I was sitting started to play or listen to "Clair de Lune", our dad's favourite, and I managed it in the end.'

Constance opened and closed her mouth.

'We had it played at his funeral,' I added.

'The music was coming from here, wasn't it?' she sighed.

'Yes,' I confirmed, then explained. 'It was and it made me so happy because this house was always my favourite to stop and look at on our walks. I used to endlessly drag Dad and my brother along the riverbank to admire the back of it.'

I felt my face flush.

'And now you're inside it,' said Constance as she looked around. 'I won't ask if it lives up to your expectations.'

'I think it's perfect,' I responded, and she looked surprised.

'And what about your mother?' she asked.

'Sorry?' I blinked.

This seemed to be turning into something of a soul-baring first encounter. She was finding out a lot about me, yet I knew practically nothing of her. Though, I supposed, given that I was the one asking something of her, that was fair enough.

'You've mentioned your brother and father, but what about your mother?'

'Mum died when I was ten,' I told her. 'And we started to holiday here after she had gone. Willowell very quickly became our happy place. I think it helped that we hadn't been here with her. It was somewhere completely new to us, and we made memories here that were entirely our own . . .'

I hadn't considered that before.

'My goodness, she must have been young herself,' Constance calculated, then immediately apologised. 'I'm so sorry. I didn't mean to pry. You must think I'm being incredibly nosy.'

'No,' I said. 'Honestly, it's fine, and you're right, she was young. I find it harder talking about Dad dying though, what with it happening not all that long ago.'

Constance nodded in what appeared to be understanding and I wondered if there had ever been anyone in her life who she now struggled to talk about.

'Well,' she said, her tone much softer than it had been when I first arrived, 'I don't suppose there'd be much harm in you going and having a look, would there?'

'Really?' I said, one hand moving to my chest to settle my heart.

'Yes,' she said. 'Though I can't imagine why you'd want to. Are you actually interested in buying it?'

'I might be,' I said as she appraised me again. 'But I won't know until I've seen it.'

If Kaya and now Constance's reactions were anything to go by, I obviously didn't look like the wood-buying type. Perhaps I wasn't. Time would tell . . .

'Well, the asking price is eighty thousand,' Constance said bluntly, sounding more like her former self. 'Not a penny less.'

So far, I'd only got as far as imagining what the figure might be, but the price was roughly around what I had been expecting.

'If I think I might be interested, shall I come back and tell you? Or should I telephone instead? I could ask Melody for the house number.'

'Come back and tell me,' Constance said, a flicker of a smile playing around her lips. 'But before you go, you can get that cake box out of the fridge again. All this talking has made me hungry.'

Chapter 4

Feeling elated that I'd now not only seen the front of Fernside, but also inside a small part of it, I left Constance delicately devouring a chocolate éclair and drove back to the gated entrance of the woods, which was just a short distance away from the house drive.

I hadn't really paid any attention to it when I'd spotted the for sale sign, but there was an area next to the boundary of the woods that was hardstanding and large enough for at least half a dozen cars to park on. Constance had informed me that I could park there, and I hoped it was also included in the sale. It needed clearing and tidying, but it would be a genuine bonus if it was. I had been worried about parking, but this off-road area would be more than adequate and a big tick on the list I'd started to mentally make.

I had so much adrenaline coursing through my system that my hands were shaking as I adjusted the straps on my rucksack, and my heart was beating hard again as I climbed over the locked gate that I hadn't thought to ask for the key to. I stopped for a moment and pulled in a deep breath.

These woods, set in the very part of the country I loved most, had the potential to help fulfil both my childhood dream *and* the brand-new business idea I'd dreamt up during the night, so I needed to assess them objectively. However, the fluttering feeling in my chest suggested that was going to be tricky because my heart, as well as my head, was already trying to talk me into buying them, no matter what I now discovered.

I planted my feet to help me feel more grounded, closed my eyes and began to breathe in for three and out for six while my senses slowly tuned in to what I could smell and hear. There was a fragrant scent of wild honeysuckle on the breeze which stirred the leaves of the trees, and a blackbird melodiously singing somewhere. Given the heat of the day, it wasn't a surprise that I couldn't hear more birds, but I had a feeling they were there, watching me from afar and no doubt wondering what I was doing on their patch.

'Okay,' I said softly as, feeling a bit calmer and certainly more connected, I opened my eyes again and blinked. 'Let's see what you've got, shall we?'

As always when I ventured into woodland, it didn't take many moments for my heart rate to further settle and a sense of tranquillity to descend. I hadn't been sure my heart was going to behave on this occasion, because there was so much at stake, but it was soon tamed. The air beneath the trees felt marginally cooler than on the road, and the sunlight, which was dappled thanks to the dense green canopy, was a soothing and gentle balm to my excited jitteriness.

I was desperate that Willowell Woods would turn out to be what I hoped for, but I couldn't afford to be blinkered if I came across any issues that suggested it wasn't the best place for me. I resisted the urge to cross my fingers and carried on exploring, mindful that there were already tendrils of connection reaching out to me that went way beyond the usual contentment I felt when walking in woods such as these.

The first thing I noticed was the most obvious; the wonderful variety of established trees. Some of the oaks, with their huge, gnarled and twisted trunks, looked almost ancient, and there was beech, hawthorn, hazel, holly and elder, too.

I pressed my hands to the bark of one of the tallest oaks and thought about all the changes in the landscape, and indeed the world, that would have occurred since it was an acorn. It was miraculous that it had survived, and as I looked up into its branches, I wondered how many species of insects, birds and mammals a tree of such magnificence supported in its lifetime.

Along with the trees I also noted an abundance of wildflowers. Some varieties were in flower, while others were waiting to bloom or already had. Cow parsley, ragged robin, toadflax, vetch, foxgloves, oxeye daisies and common knapweed flourished and there were other plants I didn't know the names of. There was evidence of squirrels and foxes, and I could only guesstimate the number of birds flitting about. There were probably bats, too, and perhaps even a badger sett tucked away somewhere.

On the surface, it all looked idyllic, but I could see that the woods weren't perfect. Practically all the paths that were man-made were impossible to clearly make out, and impassable in some places because of the encroaching nettles and brambles, and there were a few tree limbs that needed taking down. And ivy, left unchecked, was rampant. A couple of the trees appeared to be all but strangled by it, and a large pond, located roughly at what I guessed was the centre of the woods, was stagnant. Where there could have been irises and dragonflies in abundance, I spotted nothing more exciting than the odd fly.

'Coppicing and brush cutting,' I muttered as I moved on, adding more things to my mental checklist as I ran my hands lightly over the bark of the trees and looked up into the canopy, 'and repairs to the owl boxes.'

The list was becoming extensive, but nothing was beyond salvaging or, for me at least, detracted from the beauty and magic of the place. Once the tasks were completed and some light made its way back in, every bit of the woods would start to flourish again.

The entire area had obviously been loved once, so what had happened? I remembered again what Melody had let slip about the Fernside finances. If Constance didn't have the coffers to make the, so far unseen, repairs to the house, she certainly didn't have the money to maintain the woods, did she?

'But I might,' I whispered, as I continued to explore.

The set-up that I was dreaming of wouldn't be easy to achieve. I already knew that getting approval to run a business in woods wasn't a walk in the park and there would be the issue of gaining planning permission to erect some sort of building that I would want to use as a base to contend with, too. Nothing would be straightforward, but the connection I felt to both the village and now the woods that bore their name made the prospect of the challenge worth fighting for.

'I'd better engage warrior mode and start polishing my shield.' I smiled as I made my slow way back towards where I thought I'd parked my car. 'There could be a battle ahead.'

I must have walked off course at some point, thanks to the

overgrown paths, but it didn't matter, because what I discovered completely took my breath away.

'I don't believe it!' I gasped, as I rushed through the undergrowth, ignoring the sharp scratch that tore through my cotton trousers. 'Why did Constance not mention this?'

Positioned ahead of me and in its own clearing – or what would be a clearing when the area was managed again – was a large wooden cabin-style building with a chimney in the roof. The windows were covered in a thick coating of grime on the outside and dust on the inside, but I rubbed at one of the panes with a tissue from my rucksack and, shielding my eyes from the light, peered inside.

I could make out a large open space with a log burning stove in a cage at its centre and possibly a separate room, or even two, towards the back. The whole place was dusty and covered in huge cobwebs, but depending on what it had been used for before, it might just be the fulfilment of the wish I hadn't even yet dared to properly make.

A building, put up with the proper planning permission, already on the site, would make Constance's asking price far too low, but if a business of some sort had been run from it in the past, then it might potentially cut through a whole lot of red tape.

'I need to talk to Constance,' I gulped. 'Now, where did I park my car?'

I didn't bother with the front of the house but slipped through the gate and quietly knocked on the back door. It was far later than I had realised once I'd finally made my way out of the woods where the birds were chattily settling down for the night and, not knowing if Constance went to bed early, I didn't want to startle or disturb her. I needn't have worried though, because she snatched open the sunroom door practically the moment I'd appeared.

'I'd all but given up on you,' she tutted. 'I thought you'd had your look around and left.'

'I had my look around,' I told her. 'But I got a bit lost trying to find my way out.'

'Lost?' She frowned, as if the idea was absurd. 'What's happened to your leg?'

I looked down and found the scratch I'd received when bowling towards the wooden building had run deep and my trousers, as well as torn, were now bloody.

'I had an argument with a bramble.' I winced, feeling the sting of it now I knew it was there.

'You should have stuck to the path.'

'Easier said than done,' I muttered, as I tried to pull the fabric away from where it had stuck to my skin.

'What was that?' Constance demanded.

'Never mind.'

'Well, come in,' she said and walked back into the house. 'You can clean your leg up and put the kettle on again.'

I insisted my leg was fine when Constance couldn't locate her first aid kit and my tummy growled as I made another pot of tea, but dinner would have to wait. The only evidence I could see that Constance had consumed more than the éclair I'd left her eating was a jammy spoon and a whiff of toast in the air. Even though it wasn't my business, I wondered again if she was being looked after or was able to properly look after herself.

'So, how did you find the place?' she asked, as I handed her a cup and saucer containing properly made tea without instruction, this time.

She was settled in an armchair that had lost most of its stuffing and she looked much smaller cocooned in the depths of it than when she was standing up, and she wasn't overly tall then.

'Beautiful,' I told her as I sat at the table. 'Stunning. Some of the trees looked ancient.'

She smiled at that.

'They're not quite that old,' she told me. 'But a fair few of the oaks have seen many more winters than I have.'

It was my turn to smile then.

'The woods aren't without their issues,' I went on. 'But overall, they were wonderful.'

'Issues?' Constance frowned and I realised I'd offended her.

'There are just a few remedial bits and pieces that need seeing to,' I said quickly and airily, my tone hopefully suggesting that it could all be sorted in a day because I didn't want to further upset her.

'What sort of remedial bits and pieces?' she asked sternly.

'Just a bit of brush cutting and path clearing,' I said, and she looked at my leg again.

'Anything else?'

'Maybe tidying around the pond and taking down a couple of tree limbs that have been damaged, probably by the wind.'

I didn't want to name it all.

'What about coppicing?' she asked nonetheless.

'Yes,' I agreed, 'that would be great. Getting more light on the woodland floor would encourage more wildflowers, not that there aren't a lot already.'

'That all sounds like quite a lot of work to me, rather than bits and pieces,' she said. 'And you seem to know your stuff.'

I realised her suggestion of coppicing had been a test.

'I used to volunteer with a charity in a woodland close to where I previously lived,' I told her. 'And I took a couple of practical courses to learn about woodland management at the local horticultural college.'

'I see,' she said, sounding surprised. 'Good for you.'

'I really enjoyed it.'

She was quiet for a moment and had a faraway look in her eyes.

'I can't say that I'm not upset to think that the place has got a bit out of hand, but it has been a while since I managed to get down there to look at it myself.'

If I did buy it, I'd make sure it was accessible for her and take her there as soon as I could, because her tone suggested she missed spending time in it.

'I won't be knocking any money off the asking price because of the state of it though,' she said shrewdly, which made me feel slightly less sorry for her.

'I wasn't expecting you to,' I smiled. 'But as I was viewing the site with an eye to buying it, I needed to make sure I took the time to look around properly and factor into my calculations any work that might need doing.'

'Very wise,' she said and took a sip of tea. 'And how did you find the plant centre? Was that in a state, too?'

'Plant centre?' I frowned.

'Yes,' she said. 'The building and all the beds and cold frames set up around it. My younger sister used to run a woodland plant nursery from the cabin and the space in front of it was where she grew and displayed the plants. That's why there's a car park next to the road.'

My heart leapt at her words. Knowing there had been an

established business on the site really could make it easier for when I wanted to apply for permission to set up a new one. I felt my cheeks flush, but I reined myself in. I was already dreaming that I was going to forge ahead with my idea, but there was still a lot to consider. I couldn't afford to get carried away this early in the proceedings.

'People used to come to her for gardening advice and a walk around the woods and then head off with a boot full of wonderful woodland and shade loving plants,' Constance continued wistfully. She sounded proud as she reminisced. 'Grace was a well-known expert in her field.'

I wondered what had happened to Grace because Constance's tone suggested perhaps more than the usual sadness at losing a relative and, given how the site had deteriorated, I knew it had been a long time since it had been a nursery. I was also curious to know if Grace had been the person responsible for planting the Fernside ferns.

'And she had the perfect setting there in the woods to showcase her knowledge,' I commented.

'Indeed, she did,' Constance sighed. 'Willowell Woods have been in our family for as long as anyone can remember and I was immensely proud of what Grace achieved there.'

'Well, the building looked as though it needed a good clean but was otherwise fine,' I said. I decided not to mention that I hadn't spotted any outside beds or cold frames which might further spoil Constance's memories of the place. 'Though I didn't go inside, obviously.'

'I should have given you the key,' Constance sniffed, before blowing her nose on a tissue from her dress pocket. 'I didn't think.'

'I managed well enough without it. And it's good to know that there's been a business on the site before.'

'You'll want to run something there if I agree to you buying it then, will you?' she asked shrewdly.

She was as sharp as a packet of pins.

'Well,' I said, 'I know we're a very long way from that at this point, but yes, if I did become the owner,' just saying the words felt thrilling, 'then yes, I would need to run a business there to generate an income. I wouldn't be able to take the woods on if I didn't think I'd be able to get permission . . .'

But how was I going to establish the likelihood of that without taking the plunge and buying it first? It was quite a conundrum. I wondered if the local resident who had also expressed interest in the site was buying the woods for pleasure rather than business. If that was the case, Constance would surely favour them over me because it would be so much easier to sort out.

'I see,' she said.

'I have lots of thinking to do and so many enquiries to make . . .' I said, biting my lip.

And how on earth was I going to do that and encourage Constance to think seriously about my offer when I was in Bali? Especially if the location Zack was still staying in had intermittent Wi-Fi.

'And this venture you have in mind wouldn't be anything that would bring harm to the woods, would it?'

'Absolutely not,' I said passionately. 'It would involve people coming to visit, but only in small groups at a time. What I have in mind would be both physically and mentally beneficial to the visitors and the fee I'd charge them would in turn enable me to keep the woods in the healthiest possible condition and eventually pay me a wage.'

I knew I had so much number crunching to do, but I'd been shown the financial ropes by the manager at Woodland Adventures and what I had in mind for Willowell Woods wasn't all that different.

'Well, I'm intrigued.' Constance nodded and I felt pleased to have piqued her interest.

'I haven't thrashed out all of the details yet,' I admitted, 'but as soon as I have, I'll be able to fill you in.'

Again, the potential difficulties of trying to work it all out overseas and then somehow let Constance know filled my head. I couldn't imagine she was email savvy and a letter could take a while to arrive. Perhaps I'd have to telephone, though not when her news programme was on, of course, because she wouldn't pick up!

'The sooner the better,' she said, and I wondered again if she was thinking about the other buyer. 'Do you have a timeframe in mind?'

'Not yet,' I said, 'and before I work that out, I think we need to discuss the price.'

'I'm not coming down,' she snapped. 'There might be some remedial whatnots to see to, but I think the asking price is fair.'

'I was going to suggest you put it up,' I laughed.

'Oh.'

'Have you had it independently valued?'

'Well, no,' she said and shifted in her seat.

'You should,' I insisted. 'You might want to avoid selling through an agent and paying their fee, but you must add into the asking price the fact that there's already a building on-site. And will the car park be included, too?'

'Of course. Why would I want to keep that?'

'I just wanted to be certain,' I told her as my heart raced again. The place was perfect. 'You really need to find out the true value of the woods and everything that comes with it,' I encouraged her.

'I suppose . . .'

'And I'm assuming there was planning permission granted when the cabin went up?' I asked and the look she gave me was withering. 'Of course, there was. Sorry.'

'Eighty still seems like a decent amount.' She shrugged. 'But perhaps you know best.'

'I wouldn't want to make an offer without knowing the true value,' I insisted again. 'And the other interested party shouldn't either.' Constance didn't comment on that. 'Anyway, I promise I'll come back to you as soon as I can. Unfortunately, my time staying in the village comes to an end tomorrow, but I'll try not to—'

'You're leaving the village,' she cut in.

'Yes.' I swallowed.

I hoped I hadn't just handed the woods to the other buyer by saying that, but I could hardly not tell her, could I?

'Are you going home?'

'No,' I said. 'I don't actually have a home at the moment.'

'No home?' she said, with a sharp intake of breath.

'Nope,' I confirmed, feeling my tummy gurgle again, but this time not from hunger. 'No fixed abode. My home was sold after Dad died and I've just given up my room in a houseshare along with my job.'

Saying it out loud, on the back of my sleepless night, made me feel giddy. Sometimes it did all feel like an exciting adventure, but at other times, such as now, it was a bit overwhelming. I might have had my heart set on embracing something new with the security of Dad's legacy behind me, but it was still a massive difference to the life that I was used to.

The fact that I'd stuck at a job I hated for the sake of a regular salary for so long was proof that my current situation was a complete change to all that had gone before, and even though I'd wanted to do it, it was a lot to process and get used to.

'No home *and* no job,' Constance gasped.

'That's right,' I told her, trying to sound like the carefree person I was striving to be. 'My job was slowly pummelling the heart out of me, and with Dad's estate settled, I thought it was the ideal time to embark upon a new voyage.'

'Well,' Constance said, sounding astonished, 'I do admire you. I am sorry about your family home, though. I'd be devastated if I had to leave Fernside.'

I didn't tell her that it wasn't the one I'd spent my early years in or that Dad's best efforts to make the one that came after it homely had never really worked. Once Zack had left, it had felt even emptier and Dad and I both knew it, even though we'd never talked about it. Willowell truly was the place I felt at home, but I didn't want Constance to think I was spinning her a line if I said that.

'I'm not surprised,' I said instead, as I looked around. 'It's beautiful.'

'Thank you.' She smiled. 'I was born here, you know.'

'Wow!' It was my turn to sound amazed then.

That meant she'd potentially lived her entire life under the same roof. What a thought that was!

'So, where are you heading to then?' she asked.

'Bali,' I sighed.

'In that case, I won't expect to see or hear from you again very soon.'

She sounded rather upset about that. As was I.

'Between you and me,' I said, 'I don't really want to go. I might try and find a Premier Inn or Travelodge that's reasonably near to here. At least while I'm thinking everything over about the woods . . .'

I wondered if Zack would be upset if I didn't immediately join him.

'A place like that would be a far cry from Bali!'

'I know,' I agreed, thinking the contrast between an East Anglian town stopover spot and the Indonesian archipelago couldn't have been greater. 'But my heart feels like it needs to be here for longer now. I feel like I need to stay as close to Willowell and the woods as I can while I get everything straight in my head. I'd change the plan to fly out for good if I thought my brother wouldn't mind . . .'

'The brother you used to holiday here with, along with your dad?'

'Yes, that's right, Zack. That's who I'm supposed to be visiting. It was originally going to be a trip to Spain, but his work has relocated him.'

'How exotic.'

'He's always jetting about. I wouldn't have minded Spain, but Bali feels a bit far, especially now. It's partly a childhood dream of mine that I'm trying to recapture along with this new business idea and Willowell feels far more suited to helping me make it happen than an island on the other side of the world. Even though it is a beautiful one.'

'Yes,' Constance said. 'I can understand that, and you know,' she added thoughtfully, her next words suggesting that she had warmed to me far more than I realised, 'I think I might have the answer, if you really don't want to go.'

'Oh?'

'You could move into my garden apartment,' she smiled. 'But only, as you say, if your brother wouldn't mind the change of plan.'

Her offer of accommodation, assuming I'd heard her right, had tripped off her lips as easily as if she was offering me another cup of tea. Surely, I must have misheard.

'Your garden apartment,' I parroted, feeling rather dazed.

'Yes,' she nodded. 'It's at the back of the house. A little self-contained place. I'm certain you'd be able to give your idea more thought there and with the added benefit of being practically on the doorstep of the woods.'

'Are you being serious?' I frowned.

'I am,' she laughed. 'I mean it. I wouldn't have suggested it otherwise.'

'Constance, I don't know what to say.'

The thought of living at Fernside even for just the shortest amount of time was a total dream come true. A prospect my much younger self would have immediately jumped at. And it felt wonderful to be so trusted, especially given that Constance and I had only just met, but should I accept?

'The arrangement would benefit me, too,' Constance pointed out, which helped me start to make up my mind. 'I really do think that I want to seriously consider selling my woods to you, Tilly, and I'd appreciate the opportunity to get to know you better ahead of properly deciding. Parting with them isn't just a whim and I want to be completely sure that I've established the right impression of you before going ahead.'

'But what about the other interested party?' I reminded her. 'The local poised to put in an offer.'

She shrugged and looked mischievous. 'Doesn't exist,' she confessed. 'A ruse. I initially assumed you didn't know anything about Willowell and wanted to put you off, so I made them up.'

'I don't believe it!' I laughed, feeling the air leave my lungs and a sense of relief descend.

'So, what do you think?'

Her generous offer had come completely out of the blue, but then so had the well-timed sound of 'Clair de Lune' the night I'd scattered Dad's ashes and then later spotted the Willowell Woods for sale sign. Maybe this was all meant to be . . . Written in the stars . . .

'What do you say?' she asked again, hopefully.

'All right.' I swallowed, and I felt my heart rate rocket at the prospect. 'You're on. Thank you, Constance. Thank you very much indeed.'

'Don't thank me until you've squared it with your brother.' She smiled. 'Or until you've seen the—'

'Yes,' I said, as I quickly jumped up from the table and fumbled for my phone. 'I'll do it now.' I nodded, punching in the security code to unlock it. 'I'll go and call him right away.'

'Even before you've seen the accommodation I'm offering?' she laughed.

'Yes,' I laughed with her. 'It's an apartment here in Fernside, so it's bound to be perfect, isn't it?'

Chapter 5

I didn't wait for Constance to ask again if I wanted to view the apartment before I burnt my bridges on the imminent trip to Bali but instead rushed outside to the garden and walked back and forth, taking in nothing of my lovely surroundings, until I landed on a spot which had a halfway decent phone signal. I had felt calm and grounded as I walked around the woods, but now I was practically spinning!

'Zack!' I shouted when he finally picked up and as I wilted with relief that he was currently somewhere with enough signal for the call to connect.

I was standing close to the side of the house and felt quite dazed. The heady combination of Constance's out of the blue offer and my lack of dinner was taking its toll and I leant against the wall for support.

'Tills!' he shouted back. 'How are you getting on?'

'Brilliantly!' I told him, my excitement making me almost trip over my words. 'I'm still in Willowell and you won't believe what's happened!'

'Tell me,' he laughed.

'Before I do,' I said, as I pulled in a calming breath. 'Can you tell me if you would be terribly upset if I didn't fly out to join you? At least not yet. And please be honest,' I hastily added.

If he said he would be disappointed, then I'd tell him about the woods, but not about Constance's accommodation offer. If he was going to be upset that I was bailing, then I wouldn't let him down, even though, as selfish as it felt to admit it, I would much rather stay in Willowell and get to grips with the potential next chapter of my life.

'To be honest,' he finally said, 'given how things are working out here, I was going to suggest you didn't fly out and if you've got another option, you should take it.'

'What's going on?' I frowned, my excitement quickly taking a backseat. 'Has something happened with the project?'

'It's not the project,' he said eventually, sounding completely unlike himself. 'That's all fine. In fact, I have no idea why my bosses wanted me to come and check it.'

'So, what is it then?'

'It's me,' he sighed. 'There's something going on in my head and it is to do with work, but I can't put my finger on it yet.'

'You didn't really sound like yourself the day you told me you were heading out there,' I said, thinking back. 'I'm worried about you, Zack.'

'Don't be, please,' he insisted. 'I daresay it's all the travelling catching up with me. I'm going to try and take a bit of a break. Which I know probably sounds absurd, given where I currently am.'

'It doesn't sound absurd,' I quickly reassured him. 'You're in Bali for work, not play. You're always dismissive about taking holidays because of where you're located.' I couldn't remember the last time he'd had a proper break. 'You should take some time off. You deserve it and you mustn't get burnt out, especially when you're on the other side of the world!'

I remembered that when I'd confirmed that I'd left my job, the day I came to Willowell, Zack had mentioned it being time for a new adventure. I had wondered then if he had meant just for me or for both of us but hadn't asked. Perhaps now it was time for him to also consider making some big changes. So far, I was predominantly thrilled with what I'd managed in such a short space of time, and I hoped a break would give my wonderful brother the headspace to achieve something similar.

'I'll see what I can do,' he promised. 'I'm sorry to put a downer on things. You sounded so excited when you called. Tell me what's happened.'

'Only if you stop apologising.'

'All right.' I didn't say anything. 'Come on,' he said. 'I mean it. Tell me.'

My heart kicked again as I zoned back in to where I was standing and why.

'Oh Zack,' I smiled. 'You were right. I sounded excited because I am. I really am!'

'Good!' he said sincerely. 'Now, tell me why.'

'Can you brace yourself? Because it's pretty monumental.'

'I'm locked and listening.'

'Okay,' I said. 'Here goes.'

I then explained how I'd come across Willowell Woods, who they belonged to, how I'd met Constance *and* that I'd been gifted a look inside Fernside. I saved the news that the woods were up for sale for the biggest reveal once Zack had processed all of that.

'Crikey, Tills!' he said in amazement. 'That sounds like all your childhood dreams rolled into one. Finding woodland in Willowell *and* getting to look around your dream home. But how come discovering the woods took you to Fernside? Were you asking for permission to walk in them or was it just an excuse to have a nose?'

'Well . . .' I said, dragging the word out. 'I did come to Fernside to ask for permission to walk in the woods.'

'And have you been? How did you find them?'

'I have been. And they're practically perfect. So wonderful in fact,' I squealed, 'that I'm thinking about buying them!'

'Say that again,' Zack requested, after a beat had passed. 'I think the signal must have dropped out. I thought you said you were thinking about buying them.'

'I did!' I told him. 'The woods are up for sale, and I want to buy them and set up a business in them.'

My declaration was heartfelt and sincere, and I was back to feeling giddy again.

'Do you mean it?' Zack gasped.

'With the whole of my heart,' I told him. 'I'm not sure exactly what I want to do yet, but most likely something similar to the set-up at Woodland Adventures. There's some remedial work to sort out first, but there's so much potential, too.'

'You're more than qualified to do it,' Zack said keenly, and I was grateful that he hadn't waded in with a note of caution. That would have contradicted his laidback personality and might have made me doubt myself. 'And in your dream setting. This is so amazing!'

'It really is,' I agreed.

'Your excitement is more than justified,' he laughed, and I

was delighted he thought so. 'Are the woods well established? Are they old?'

'Pretty old and very established. There are some huge oaks.'

'Oh wow.'

He sounded wistful and I guessed it had been a long time since he'd seen trees in a woodland setting in the UK for himself.

'And there's so much wildlife and so many wildflower varieties and birds,' I said. 'It was impossible to count them all on just one look around.'

'It sounds idyllic.'

'It is.'

'Though you know,' he thoughtfully pointed out. 'That level of diversity might not be in your favour Tilly, because it isn't going to be easy to get permission—'

'There's already been a business on the site,' I happily interrupted him. 'And I know that doesn't guarantee that permission would be granted again, but it's a help, isn't it? And there's a building, too. A big cabin, legally erected and all ready to go.'

I knew that was a slight exaggeration, but once the cobwebs were brushed away, the dust vacuumed up and the chimney swept, the cabin would be all set. It wasn't a huge undertaking.

'And parking?' Zack asked.

'Hardstanding for at least half a dozen cars just the other side of where the woods start and that's included in the sale, too.'

'Crikey,' he whistled. 'So, all the time I've spent worrying that you'd be stressed about what you were going to do next has been wasted, because you've already got to grips with it!'

'I sure have.' I smiled, though I didn't like the thought of him worrying about me, especially when he had concerns of his own. 'I've made a decent start, anyway.'

'And what about the finances?' he asked. 'Have you got into that side of things yet?'

'Just a little so far but I'm aware that I can't rush in and buy the woods on the assumption that I'll be able to do what I want with them. You don't need to worry about me leaping in feet first where funds are concerned.'

'I wasn't worried about that,' Zack laughed. 'That's far more my style than yours. You've never been a feet first kind of person, have you?'

'Hey!' I objected.

'That's not a criticism. Especially not in this situation.'

'Good,' I said back. 'And Constance is happy to wait while I get my ducks in a row. She's keen to get to know me before we progress any further because the woods have been in her family for ever and she isn't willing to let them go to just anyone.'

The fact that she'd already tried to put me off by making up a local buyer was proof enough of that. How lucky was I that she was willing to consider that I might be the right fit?

'Do you know why she's selling them?' Zack asked.

'I don't,' I told him because all I'd heard was gossip and I wasn't going to share that. 'But she's not had the site properly valued and is currently seriously underselling it. I've suggested a formal valuation before we finally settle on a figure.'

'Yes,' Zack said seriously. 'You must get that sorted. What's she like?'

'I've only spent a few minutes in her company so far so I

can't really say, but I'm going to get to know her much better extremely quickly now.'

'How come?'

'Because she's invited me to move to Fernside while we move things forward.'

'You're joking?' Zack sounded as flabbergasted as I had been when Constance had offered me the garden apartment. 'She's asked you to move in?'

'She has,' I laughed. 'There's an apartment here and it's that she's offering me.'

'Crikey,' Zack laughed. 'That sounds ideal. Does she live in Fernside on her own?'

'As far as I know. She mentioned it was her younger sister who ran a horticultural business from the woods, but as Constance talked about her in the past tense, I can only assume that she's died.'

I felt emotional as I took in the size of the house. It was a huge place for one person to rattle around in and, if she was entirely on her own, I wondered if she might be feeling lonely and whether that could have also prompted her to ask me to move in.

'So,' Zack said, once he'd taken a moment to further process everything. 'You're moving to Fernside.'

'Yes,' I smiled. 'I am. I don't know how long for, but I can't imagine there's a better place for me right now, can you?'

'I can't,' Zack responded. 'Willowell has always been such a special place for you, me and Dad, and now you get to stay there for longer than a holiday.'

'It's a dream come true.'

'What's the apartment like?'

'I have no idea,' I confessed as I glanced at the time. 'I haven't seen it yet. I rushed out to call you as soon as Constance mentioned it. She'll be thinking I've abandoned her!'

'You'd better get back to her then,' Zack laughed. 'And good luck.'

He was gone before I could say the same to him, and I realised we'd been talking for ages. I still had to pack my things at Rose Cottage and have something to eat, but first, I wanted to see my new home.

'So?' Constance asked, as she stiffly stood up when I went back into the kitchen. 'What did your brother have to say?'

'Plenty,' I smiled. 'But most importantly, that he's happy for me to stay put.'

I was thrilled that Zack had been so understanding, but I wasn't so caught up in my own fresh start that I had forgotten that something was amiss with him. Going forward I would try, even though it wasn't easy with the internet issues, to keep in touch more. There were only two of us in our family now and we needed to support one another more than ever.

'Well, that's marvellous news.' Constance nodded as she rubbed her hip with the hand that wasn't holding her walking stick. 'Grab that set of keys with the oak leaf keyring and we'll go and look at the apartment. I haven't been in for a while, so I don't know what sort of state it's going to be in. I hope I haven't offered you a dud.'

I held my breath as I turned the key in the apartment door, but I needn't have worried. Constance's concerns were completely unfounded and, aside from needing an airing, the place seemed to be in a better state than the house.

'It's called the garden apartment because it overlooks the

garden,' said Constance, who I had helped down the three steps to reach the door, which had a small, sunken patio leading up to it. The door opened straight into a little lobby with coat pegs and shoe storage and then a compact cream and sage green kitchen. 'Which I suppose is stating the obvious.'

'And it's perfect,' I told her, as I flicked on a couple of table lamps and looked around. 'Ideally proportioned.'

It was bigger than Rose Cottage, but not by much and the soft glow from the lamps made it look and feel so cosy.

'Don't say that until you've seen the rest of it,' Constance insisted.

There were French doors in the sitting room, and they opened out onto the patio which was filled with pots of hostas and ferns and, joy of joys, I could hear the river from there, too.

'I can hear the river,' I smiled at Constance.

'Lucky you,' she smiled back. 'I think I need to get my hearing aids adjusted.'

I didn't point out that she wasn't wearing any.

'There's one bedroom,' she explained as we continued the tour, 'and no shower in the bathroom, I'm afraid, just a bath. I suppose the decoration is a bit old-fashioned for a young woman like you.'

'Not at all,' I was quick to say, because I loved it. The dark woodwork and practical jute carpets made it feel snug. It would doubtless be a comfortable den in the winter with a fire blazing in the grate. 'Are these Sanderson curtains?'

The floral fabric was beautiful and the cushions on the sofa and two armchairs were made from the same material.

'Could be,' Constance said vaguely. 'The bedroom is all Laura Ashley, I think. The whole place hasn't been touched for years.

You'll have to have a look through the kitchen and see if there's enough crockery and cutlery. You can always nab things from the house, and I won't mind you using my washing machine because there isn't one of those here, either. We might as well turn the fridge on while we're here. It should be all right. It looks like the door has been left ajar since it was last turned off.'

I felt a wave of emotion wash over me as I looked around again.

'This is extremely generous of you, Constance,' I struggled to say, because of the way I was feeling. 'Opening up your home to me like this, even if it is with a view to working out if you want me to buy your woods.'

I had been about to carry on and ask if she was all alone in the house, but she fixed me with a look, and I stopped.

'It's not just about the woods,' she said. 'The larger part of my offer is, but there's the other thing, too.'

'The other thing?' I assumed she was going to say she was lonely.

'I can tell . . .'

'Tell what?'

'That you need a rest,' she said, taking me completely by surprise. 'It seems to me that you've been through quite a time of it. And even though some of it, such as giving up the job that you said was grinding you down, has been exciting, it's all been a challenge as well as a risk and that takes a toll on a person, doesn't it?'

I was determined not to cry, but it was a struggle to keep the tears trapped behind my eyes, rather than rolling down my cheeks. I don't know why, but I hadn't expected her to be so empathetic and keyed in.

'It would have been selfish of me to notice this in you and then withhold an offer to help,' she said, as if offering such assistance was the most natural thing in the world and something she'd do for every stranger who crossed her path. 'I recognised in you what I experienced in myself when . . .'

'When?' I croaked.

'You can rest here for a while,' she carried on, putting the spotlight firmly back on me. 'Then decide what you want to do about the woods. Consider your time here as a bit of a holiday, to start with, at least. I'm truly in no rush.'

I looked around at the heavy old-fashioned furniture, which looked solid and safe. The apartment already felt like a cosy hidey hole from the world with the beautiful garden in front and the sound of the gently flowing river beyond, and I knew that spending some time here to get myself more together and keep moving forward on my new path was going to be a wonderful thing.

'Does that sound all right with you?' Constance asked softly.

'That sounds absolutely perfect.' I swallowed, as one traitorous tear made its slow way down my cheek and I quickly brushed it away. 'But on one condition.'

'What's that?' she asked, sounding suspicious.

'That you let me pay you rent.'

She looked appalled. 'I didn't offer you the apartment with a view to—'

'I know you didn't,' I cut in. 'You offered me the apartment with the very kindest of motives, as your caring words have just proved, but these are my terms. Rent, I'll stay. No rent, I'm off to Bali.'

Constance wasn't happy, but she eventually relented.

'You can keep the key,' she said, once I'd checked the fridge was working, turned off the lights, locked the door, and helped her back up the steps. 'That way you can let yourself in in the morning, or whenever you're ready to move in.'

'If it wasn't for having to pack up Rose Cottage,' I told her, 'I'd stay longer tonight.'

'You think you'll be happy here then?' she asked, her gaze fixed on mine.

'Ever so,' I told her. 'This is literally a long-held dream come true, but with the addition of wonderful Willowell Woods thrown in for good measure.'

Constance looked as thrilled about that as I was.

Chapter 6

Having briefly touched on more of the practicalities, such as where I would find bed linen, towels and so forth, and in spite of the huge changes the day had delivered, I practically skipped back to Rose Cottage that afternoon. Or I would have done, had I not been driving.

As I started to repack my few things with more haste than care, I thought that rent wouldn't be the only thing I would give Constance while I was staying in the apartment – she had informed me it had been used as extra guest accommodation in the past – but I would have to be discreet about it.

I might not really know her yet, but I had already deciphered that she was a proud woman, and she might not take kindly to me doing domestic things around her house because it would infer that I felt she wasn't keeping on top of it all herself.

It was obvious she had no support in the house because no housekeeper would let the ironing pile grow to the extent of the teetering tower in the Fernside kitchen, so perhaps I could ask if I could iron my own clothes in the house because the apartment kitchen was too small to put a board up and then do Constance's, too.

If she took offence, I'd apologise and say I'd got carried away. And, as I would be using her washing machine, I could perhaps put some of her laundry in with mine on the pretence of making up a full load. I'd soon find ways to do my bit without her realising it, because I really thought she could do with a helping hand.

I didn't expect to sleep that night, but as soon as my head hit the pillow, I went out like a light and didn't wake until the sun streamed through the bedroom curtains the next morning.

'One key to the cottage,' I said, putting it down on the counter in the village store. 'And I've stripped the bed and piled the sheets along with the towels I used and left them just inside the front door.'

'You're a star,' said Kaya, who seemed to have found her manners along with a much-improved mood. 'Thank you, Tilly.'

'You're keen to be off,' Melody observed sadly.

'Not quite off.' I smiled.

She raised her eyebrows and I went to explain, but she stopped me.

'Why don't you go and see to the cottage now, before we get busy in here again?' she said to her sister.

'All right,' Kaya willingly agreed, and I tried not to let my mouth fall open. She was completely tamed. 'I'll just grab the cleaning stuff. Bye, Tilly.'

'Is she for real?' I mouthed to Melody and she put a finger to her lips.

'Don't,' she whispered. 'You might jinx it.'

I swallowed down a giggle.

'Won't be long!' Kaya called from the back door and headed

across the courtyard weighed down with cleaning paraphernalia and an empty wash basket.

'So,' I laughed, once I was certain she was out of earshot. 'What is going on?'

'She's turned over a new leaf.' Melody beamed.

I was agog. 'How did you manage that?'

'I didn't,' Melody confided. 'She was already getting there, unexpectedly throwing herself into and suddenly loving her domestic duties, but now my friend Rick is back from his holidays, looking even more tanned than usual and fitter, too, and she's seeing the extra attraction of a summer spent in Willowell with her sister.'

'Tell me more,' I laughed.

'He's a local Kaya hadn't previously met *and* the only guy on the planet who comes back from a holiday with the lads looking healthier than when he went.'

'And that's impacted on Kaya, how exactly?' I grinned, potentially guessing the reason, but enjoying her telling me anyway.

'It can only be that she's got the hots for him, can't it? And even though she was settling down already, clearly the thought of spending a few weeks flirting with Rick, while she replenishes her travel fund, has put a very happy spring in her step.'

'Ah, right,' I laughed. 'I see.'

'It's not going to happen, though.'

'How come?'

'Rick's gay.'

'And you haven't told her?'

That was a twist I hadn't seen coming.

'You know I'm not one to gossip,' Melody winked.

'Melody!' I laughed louder. 'You do know this will come back to bite you, don't you?'

'I do,' she nodded. 'But for now I'm enjoying some sisterly harmony. Anyway, what's going on with you? I didn't think you'd be in such a rush to vacate the cottage. In fact, I had the feeling that I was going to have to full-on evict you. I'm going to miss having you nearby to talk to and share the occasional bottle of wine with.'

'No,' I said, barely able to keep a lid on my excitement and feeling surprised that she had forgotten my previous hint, 'you're not.'

'I am,' she insisted. 'I know we haven't known each other for five minutes, but—'

'What I mean is,' I cut in, 'you won't get the chance to miss having me nearby because I'm only moving up the road. Barely to the outskirts of the village!'

'What?' she gasped. 'How come?'

'Well,' I said, 'to cut a long story short, yesterday was pretty monumental . . .'

'Go on,' she nudged, because my words had trailed off as I started to think about it all again.

'Sorry.' I blinked. 'Okay, well, as you know, I went to Fernside with the groceries for Constance and as a result of a subsequent chat, she kindly gave me permission to visit the woods, which are stunning by the way, and then . . .'

'Go on,' Melody urged again, more impatiently that time.

'When I went back to the house, I said . . . I said that I wanted to think about buying them.' Melody's eyes were on stalks. 'And *then*,' I carried on, 'when I explained that I sadly had to leave Willowell today, Constance asked if I'd like to move into this little apartment that's attached to Fernside, rather than go to Bali, so I could do my thinking there!'

'No way!'

'And I said yes!' I nodded enthusiastically. 'And it's going to be so much easier to make plans and sort things out if I'm here rather than on the other side of the world.'

'Of course it is,' Melody agreed.

'So, what do you think?'

'I think you've made my day and it's not even lunchtime!' she exclaimed, pulling me in for a hug. 'And,' she grinned, when she let me go, 'it also explains the phone call I had from Constance yesterday when I guess you must have been walking around the woods.'

'Oh? What did she want?'

'Just to ask what I knew about you. Obviously, I couldn't tell her your entire life history, and I didn't share anything I didn't think you wouldn't want me to, but given what you've just told me, I reckon she must have been sizing you up as a lodger practically from the moment you turned up!'

'She's canny, isn't she?' I smiled, thinking how Constance had been a step ahead of me the whole time we were together the day before.

'Oh yes,' Melody agreed. 'I might not know all that much about her private life, but I've gleaned enough to know that nothing gets past her. She doesn't miss a trick and my guess is she's keeping you close to see if you come up to snuff before she lets you buy the woods. Which,' she added, 'is something we absolutely have to talk about!'

'Up to snuff!' I guffawed. 'Have you swallowed the *Downton* box set or something?'

'It's always on in the hairdressers!' Melody giggled. 'I must have picked it up in there. But you know what I mean.'

'Yes,' I grinned. 'I do. And you're completely right. Constance said that's exactly what she had in mind when she offered me the apartment.'

I didn't mention how she'd also keyed into the fact that I needed a bit of respite after all the changes that I'd recently made to my life.

'And so . . . the woods?' Melody mentioned again. 'You just made out that you were interested in the trees when you headed to Fernside yesterday.'

'I am interested in the trees,' I said, sticking to the story I'd previously used.

'And that you just wanted to walk around without trespassing,' Melody probed further.

Clearly, she wasn't going to be fobbed off, and I could hardly blame her. I would have been intrigued myself if she'd done something similar. Wanting to buy a patch of woodland wasn't your usual, every day kind of purchase, was it?

'I *did* want to walk around without trespassing!' I laughed.

'You never so much as hinted that you were really interested in buying them though.' She tutted. 'Even when Kaya asked you outright. What on earth would you do with them?'

'Now I'm not leaving Willowell,' I pointed out, 'we've got plenty of time to discuss that. In fact, once I'm ready to share what I've got in mind, you'll be one of the first to know and you'll soon be sick of me rattling on about it.'

'I very much doubt that,' Melody contradicted me. 'But if you do buy them, does that mean that you'll also be thinking about permanently relocating here?'

'I'm not sure relocation is an option when you haven't already got somewhere to live.'

'But you have, haven't you?' she nudged. 'The apartment at Fernside. I didn't even know the house had one.'

Again, I felt my pulse race at the mention of my dream home, my current home. If you'd told me even just two days ago, that my next address would begin with the name *Fernside*, I never would have believed it. That said, it wouldn't do to get carried away. If I did buy Willowell Woods, then I was going to be seriously stretched when it came to funding the purchase of my own home to eventually move into. Constance was right, setting about this slowly and steadily was the right way to go.

'I've got the apartment for now,' I said thoughtfully. 'And I can't give you a better answer about the woods or where I'm going to live permanently if I do buy them, because I'm only just at the very beginning of considering my options and trying to work it all out.'

'That's fair enough,' Melody accepted. 'It's exciting though, isn't it?'

'So exciting!' I clapped. 'And I'm setting off to move in right now. Not that it'll take me long, because I've only got enough stuff to tide me over for a long holiday abroad.'

I hoped the British summer was going to be kind and that I'd be able to manage with the few clothes I'd originally packed for my trip to see Zack in Spain because every other outfit I owned was currently in storage along with everything else. If the weather changed, I'd have to order a few things online or beg and borrow from Melody. We looked to be pretty much the same size. Though I might not be for long if I carried on eating her quiche and scones at the current rate.

'Travelling light is liberating,' said Kaya, who then appeared with a basket full of laundry and caught the tail end of the conversation. 'Has Rick been in?'

'No sign yet.' Melody smiled at her sister and I gave her a conspiratorial look. 'You'll meet him soon, Tilly,' she added, turning her attention back to me. 'He looks after the gardens at Fernside.'

I thought it was interesting that Constance paid someone to look after the garden when the house needed work doing to it. I wondered if that was because it was perhaps her sister's legacy or if Constance valued plants above bricks and mortar. I'd most likely soon find out, but given that Fernside was literally her for ever home, and one she was obviously attached to, I didn't think that could really be the case.

'You've been telling Tilly about Rick, have you?' Kaya said, as she looked me over, but she didn't ask why Rick being Constance's gardener would mean anything to me.

As far as she knew, I was supposed to be leaving the area that day.

'Don't worry, Kaya,' I said. 'He doesn't sound like my type.' Melody flashed me a look. 'And even though I'm staying now, I won't have time to be thinking about—'

'You're staying?' Kaya interrupted.

'I am,' I confirmed. 'And I'm going to be far too busy to factor in a summer romance.'

The image of a very handsome man dashing down a lay-by to retrieve Mum's hat popped into my head. I would have had time for him, but it was unlikely I was ever going to see him again, so I didn't need to worry about time management where he was concerned.

'Probably just as well,' Kaya smiled. 'I'll go and get this lot in the wash. I'm pleased you're staying, Tilly. My sister has mellowed a bit since she's had you to moan to about me.'

I laughed at that and Melody shook her head.

'I thought you were going to drop me in it then,' she whispered, as she began to fill a couple of the jute bags which had the store name printed on them.

'You made your bed,' I shrugged. 'So, you can lie in it, but I'll be standing at the sidelines with a fire extinguisher, ready for when the bomb goes off.'

I was playing along, but I did wonder if Kaya's smile at my mention of romance was a hint that she already knew about Rick.

'It won't be that bad.' Melody grinned as she carried on adding things to the bags. 'Here, these are for you.'

'What?' I said. 'No way, Melody. I don't need all this.'

The bags were full of foodie treats and basics like milk, bread and eggs, along with products from the natural bathroom range she stocked and a bunch of flowers from the bucket outside the door.

'Moving in present,' she insisted and hooked the handles over my arms. 'And I thought you could warm up the chicken and leek pie I made yesterday for a celebratory dinner with Constance. I do worry she doesn't eat enough . . .'

Given that I was certain she'd had just toast for her dinner the evening before and that there had been no sign or smell of a hot lunch having been eaten earlier, I thought Melody was right, but it wasn't my business to say.

'Well,' I said, 'that's extremely kind of you, Melody. Thank you. I'm sure we'll both enjoy it and the apartment will look even lovelier with these homely touches.'

'Good,' she said, as a couple of customers arrived. 'Now go and get settled in and we'll catch up as soon as you're free.'

It was too busy, and my arms were too weighed down, to hug her again, but as I set off on the short journey to Fernside, I felt very loved and truly blessed to have found such a good friend during what had previously been planned as a brief visit.

As predicted, I quickly settled into the garden apartment. The first thing I had done, having arrived quietly so as not to disturb Constance, was open the windows and prop open the door, which allowed the soft summer breeze to sweep through. I had always been an advocate of having windows open in the early morning and truly felt that I was more prepared to face the day, once the old air and energy had been blown away and some fresh, welcomed in.

The fridge was doing its thing, though the shelves were currently a bit sparse, and I found all the linen in the cupboard Constance had described. The scent of lavender filled the bedroom as I shook out the sheets, and when I went back into the sitting room the flowers Melody had given me had perfumed the air in there, too.

'Anyone home?' I heard Constance call from the top of the steps a short while later and just as I finished giving the place a quick dust.

How lovely did that word sound? I'd only been here a couple of hours and already Fernside felt more like home than the houseshare I'd endured ever had. I could feel a halcyon time coming as I settled into life in the safe and snug sanctuary.

'I am, Constance.' I smiled and rushed out to see her. 'Would you like to come and look at what I've done with the place?'

'No, no,' she said, leaning heavily on her stick. 'I don't want to disturb you.'

'You're not disturbing me,' I said, hopping up the steps so I could see her properly.

She was wearing the same dress she'd had on the day before and her shoes were on the wrong feet. She did have her hearing aids in, though.

'And before you think I'm completely dotty,' she said, also looking at her footwear. 'I know they're the wrong way round, but they took so long to get on, I couldn't be bothered to change them.'

I supressed a smile. Or I thought I had.

'It's not funny,' she scolded me. 'Getting old is no fun. I don't recommend it.' A look of pain then crossed her face. 'What a wicked thing to say,' she tutted. 'It might not be fun, but it is a privilege.'

I didn't know what to say to that. Mum had been so young when she'd died and Dad had been no age either, not really, so I already knew we should be grateful for every day. However, it felt like far too gloomy a conversation for such a happy occasion, so I changed the subject.

'Now I'm unpacked,' I said, 'I thought I might have a look at the garden and perhaps eat my lunch down by the river, if that's all right?'

'Sounds lovely,' she said and looked down the sloping lawn towards the jetty.

'Would you like to join me?' I asked. 'I haven't got much in to eat, but I'm sure we could cobble a picnic together between us, and Melody has provided a moving in celebratory dinner that I'll warm up for us tonight, if you'd like that, too.'

Constance looked taken aback. 'Oh, well . . .' she began, but didn't get any further.

'Unless you've already got plans?'

'I haven't had dinner plans since nineteen eighty-nine,' she chuckled.

'That settles it then.' I nodded. 'We'll spend the day together. I'll be on my own, otherwise. And you did say you wanted to get to know me better before we went any further with the woods, didn't you?'

'I also said, there's no rush,' she pointed out.

'We'll keep things purely social then,' I promised. 'What do you fancy for lunch?'

'I don't know,' she said, shifting from one foot to the other. 'I don't usually bother with a meal at midday.'

I was appalled but tried not to let it show.

'Leave it with me and I'll put the pie in your fridge, shall I? I thought we could eat in the Fernside kitchen this evening as there's more room. And would it be all right if I borrowed some powder and put a wash on?'

'Is it one of Melody's pies?'

'Chicken and leek, fresh from her oven just yesterday.'

I had no idea how Melody found the time. The store was always busy and yet somehow, she kept the fridges stocked with the loveliest things.

'My favourite,' said Constance, smacking her lips, and I could have sworn I heard her tummy rumble. 'And it's fine to put a wash on. There might be a few things of mine in the machine, so just chuck those back in the basket.'

Here was an opportunity to help beyond filling her belly for the day.

'I've only got a few bits, so I could do it all together, if you like.' She gave me a sharp look. 'It would make more sense to do one full wash than two part-loads, wouldn't it? It would save energy and water.'

'I suppose,' she relented. 'Yes, that would be best.'

'Great,' I said, going to head back inside. 'I'll sort it now and then make our lunch.'

'Are you always this bossy?' she called after me.

I reappeared again, carrying a garden chair from the apartment patio.

'Not usually,' I grinned, 'but I do find an inadequate breakfast a great motivator when it's almost time for lunch.'

She chuckled at that and leant on my arm as she lowered herself into the chair.

'I'll sit here while you organise us then, shall I?' she said, a touch sardonically.

'I won't be long,' I responded and whizzed off.

True to my word, I'd made cheese and chutney sandwiches, grabbed a couple of apples and some slightly soft biscuits from her cupboard and put a wash on in record time. Constance had swapped her shoes over and was dozing when I returned to her, so I slipped by and, forgoing the exploration of the garden, headed straight down to the river that I was longing to get properly reacquainted with.

It all looked rather different from this side of the bank, but it was still utterly beautiful. And cool, too, I found when I slipped off my sandals and dipped my toes in. I wouldn't be able to wait much longer before I took a swim.

'I'm not sure I'll get down there, you know!' Constance called as I popped a couple of bottles of water into the river and secured the string around their necks with a big pebble to keep them cool.

'Of course you will,' I said, as I straightened up and readjusted my dress. 'It's only a few steps. I'll carry the chairs first and then you if necessary.'

It didn't come to that, but it did take a few minutes for us to get settled on the wooden jetty. Not because Constance couldn't manage the walk, she was fine so I didn't know why she had doubted herself, but because we kept stopping on the way so she could do some deadheading or tell me the history of some plant or other.

'I can't remember the last time I sat down here,' she said wistfully, once she'd eaten her share of the sandwiches and biscuits, but declined the apple on account of the new denture she was 'bedding in'. 'I'd forgotten how lovely it is.'

'It's truly idyllic, isn't it?' I sighed drowsily.

If I didn't pay attention, I thought I'd soon be asleep. The sound of the river was soporific, and I could feel my eyelids growing heavy.

'Wake up, Tilly,' Constance said, what felt like seconds later. 'You just missed the water vole. Didn't you hear him plop out of his hole and into the river?'

My eyes snapped open and I sat up straighter. I seemed to have slipped down the chair, and my head had lolled to one side. What scintillating company I was for Constance!

'Oh no,' I moaned. 'I missed him.'

'Don't worry, he'll be back.'

'I always assume a water vole is male, do you?'

'Yes,' she nodded. 'That's years of reading Grahame for you.'

'I love *The Wind in the Willows*.' I swallowed. I couldn't help wondering if Dad was somewhere listening. I kept trying not to think about how I had scattered his ashes from the other bank just a few days before, but now I couldn't help it and really, it wasn't an unhappy memory. 'I used to bring my copy to Willowell every year and Dad would read it to me and Zack in the evenings.'

'What a wonderful tradition to have.' Constance smiled. 'And how funny to think that you were one side of the bank listening to the tale and I was the other reading it aloud, possibly at exactly the same time.'

'That is funny,' I agreed. 'Who were you reading it to? Was it your sister?'

'Sometimes,' she said evasively.

I was tempted to ask if there had been anyone else but thought the information would be best coming unprompted from her, rather than me forcing her hand.

'I rather wish I hadn't put my copy into storage now,' I sighed.

'You can always borrow mine.'

'Thank you, Constance. That's very kind.'

'Perhaps you could read it to me sometime?' she suggested.

'I'd love to,' I promised, and then, despite my former thought about prying, my curiosity got the better of me. 'I take it there's no one else who would read to you?'

'No,' she said bluntly. 'No one now.'

'In that case,' I quickly said, keen not to ruin the mood, 'we could sit down here in the evenings when the weather allows, couldn't we?'

'We could,' she agreed.

I didn't get my swim that afternoon because we chatted and

dozed the entire day away. I popped back to the house to sort the laundry and make cups of tea and refill the water bottles and we talked about all sorts of things, but not Constance's family or her past, and I respected her privacy and didn't ask again.

By the end of the day, when the pie had been reduced to crumbs and the washing up was drying in the rack, I felt like I'd already been staying at Fernside for weeks rather than just a single day. Falling asleep, with the gentle sound of the river babbling away in the background, came as easily as turning off the light, and as I drifted off, I knew that Constance felt as content as I did, because she'd already told me.

Chapter 7

Waking in the Fernside garden apartment that first morning, it felt like all my Christmases had come at once. Moving day – I felt justified in calling it that even though it had only involved one suitcase, a rucksack, a box and a few bags – had been perfect, and the best thing was, Constance was as blissfully happy with our arrangement as I was.

'Time to swim,' I said excitedly, as I stretched out in the bed and pushed back the light summer floral sprigged duvet and opened the matching curtains.

I was still extremely keen to forge ahead with my plans for the Willowell Woods, but my new landlady had insisted more than once the evening before that I should take a break before I got further into it and, deeming it would be rude to upset her, I was going to wholeheartedly embrace her suggestion.

'Cold,' I gulped, as I stepped into the river. 'Really, really cold!'

I'd got my water shoes and shorty wetsuit on – knowing I was coming to Willowell and that I might enjoy some wild swimming here, I hadn't put these things into storage and had planned to leave them in my car when I left the country – but the chilly river temperature still took me by surprise. I'd also got my tow float, and I'd told Constance that I would be taking an early dip every morning. Dad had drummed it into me from an early age that when it came to swimming, safety always came first and especially if you were swimming alone.

The water felt silky soft against my skin, and having dipped my shoulders under, I let the river gently carry me further downstream before swimming back. The slow flow meant that the return strokes to the Fernside jetty weren't a stretch, and I took my time and the opportunity to admire the overhanging willow trees that gracefully bowed and dipped their leaves into the water. I could see right to the bottom of the riverbed, and it was a joy to know that the water was as clean now as it had been when I was growing up. However, that hadn't helped me to persuade Constance to take an early morning swim with me.

'You must be joking!' she had protested when I suggested it. 'I've got better things to do of a morning than take a cold bath.'

'Such as?' I blinked, as I bit the inside of my cheek to stop myself from laughing at her shocked expression.

'*The Times* crossword, for a start. That's taking me far longer to complete now than it used to.'

That had been the end of the topic, but the look on her face when I'd offered to find her bathing suit was still making me smile.

'You don't know what you're missing, Constance,' I said aloud, as I climbed out of the river, wrapped myself in my changing robe and then sat with my feet dangling over the edge of the jetty while I started to dry off.

'You do know this is private property, don't you?' said an

irate voice behind me that didn't belong to Constance, but did make me jump.

I twisted around to see who sounded so put out and found myself in the presence of a sun-bronzed god. What was it with this part of Suffolk? I'd had interactions with just two men – not including my brother – since I'd arrived and they were both stunning to look at! This one was tall, blond and, if his calf muscles were anything to go by, very toned.

'I do know that,' I said, shielding my eyes from the sun as I looked up at him. 'Do you?'

The sun had created a sort of halo around him, which further emphasised his god-like appearance. It was then that the penny dropped.

'Oh, you're Rick, aren't you?' I squinted. 'The gardener.'

'Yes.' He frowned down at me. 'That's me. But how do you know my name and who are you?'

'Melody in the store mentioned you when we were talking about . . . Well, never mind what we were talking about,' I backtracked. 'And I'm Tilly. I'm renting the garden apartment from Constance.'

I kept my explanation simple and didn't mention my interest in the woods.

'She never said the apartment was up for rent,' Rick frowned, looking back towards the house.

'I don't think it was officially,' I told him. The subject of what I was going to pay was one I needed to broach with Constance again. 'It was a spur of the moment thing, really. I needed somewhere to stay and Constance offered.'

'Crikey,' he said, sounding surprised. 'You must have made quite an impression.'

'What do you mean?'

'Well, Constance is a very private person,' he said, running a hand through his golden hair, which was slightly curled, collar length and ruffled. 'And she's fiercely protective of Fernside, so she wouldn't open it up to just anyone.'

'She must have decided that I'm not just anyone then, mustn't she?' I smiled.

'I guess so,' he said, as he looked me over again.

'And don't worry,' I told him when it became obvious that he was as protective of Constance as she was of the house. 'I'm not secretly planning to sell Fernside out from under her or anything like that. I'm completely trustworthy. Though,' I added, 'I do appreciate that someone untrustworthy would say that . . .'

Rick laughed at that.

'What's the temperature like?' he asked, with a nod to the babbling river, having decided that I wasn't intending to make off with the Clarke family silver. Assuming there was any.

'Chilly to start with,' I said, as I wrapped my robe tighter around me. 'But not unbearable. Fine once you're in and swimming about.'

Before I knew it, he was pulling off his boots, stripping down to his trunks and wading in.

'Shit!' he shouted and I inelegantly snorted and laughed as he bobbed up and down. 'It's not fine, it's bloody freezing!'

'It is not.' I laughed harder. 'Just keep moving and you'll soon warm up.'

'Are you coming back in?' he asked playfully and splashed my legs.

'No,' I said, lifting them up and tucking them under me. 'I'm not and don't soak me because I've only just got dry.'

'Aah!' he shouted again as he floated like a starfish on his back. 'When will it get any warmer?'

'Like I said before, as soon as you—'

'Richard Brown!' a voice suddenly bellowed from further up the garden and cut my instructions off.

Had I not turned around and seen Constance standing there, I never would have believed the sound could have come from her.

'I do not pay you to frolic in the river with young women,' she scolded. 'I pay you to tend to my garden. Now, get out of there and get on.'

I stuffed the sleeve of my robe into my mouth to stop myself from laughing as she turned back to the house.

'That was your fault,' Rick said as he nimbly jumped out and shook his wet hair all over me.

'How do you work that out?' I protested at both the accusation and the soaking. 'Don't!'

'Because if you hadn't lied about the temperature of the water, I never would have been tempted to go in.'

'Well, I didn't think it was *that* cold,' I shrugged. 'So, I definitely didn't lie.'

'Lend us your robe,' he said, pulling at a corner of it.

'No chance,' I said, wrapping it even tighter around me. 'Run about in the sun for a bit like you probably did when you were a kid, that'll soon dry you off.'

He stuck his tongue out and I shook my head. He was hilarious.

'Unbelievable!' he shouted after me as I stood up and walked back towards the apartment, but he was laughing and so was I.

I ran what I had intended to be a quick bath, but then

found myself lingering in the bathroom which, though old-fashioned, was very beautiful. With Laura Ashley wallpaper above the waist height tongue and groove panelling and a deep cast iron bath on feet, it was a huge step up from the shower room I'd previously shared with housemates who had far lower hygiene standards than me. The thought of keeping this wonderful room with its nostalgic decoration, just for me, felt like a total luxury.

As the water cooled, I realised how long I'd been in, so I pulled the plug, got dry and dressed and headed to the sunroom where I spotted Constance sitting with a newspaper folded on her lap. There was no sign of Rick, which was probably just as well. I wouldn't have wanted to get him in trouble again. Not that I thought the first time had been my fault.

'Good morning, Constance.' I smiled. 'It's going to be another beautiful day.'

'Though perhaps not a peaceful one,' she said, looking at me over the top of her glasses.

'I'm sorry about that,' I quickly apologised, because she looked fearsome.

'You're not the one who should apologise,' she tutted. 'It was that boy. It's always that boy.' Her expression softened despite the admonishment. 'But that's just his way,' she said and shook her head. 'He's always been the same.'

'Have you known him for long?'

'Since he was born and he's always been one for getting into mischief. His father was the gardener here before him and he also used to do the tree work in the woods.'

'Is Rick an arborist, too?' I asked, my mind suddenly working overtime even though it wasn't supposed to be. 'He might be able to make a more detailed assessment of what needs doing in the woods than I can, if he is,' I pondered.

'He is,' Constance confirmed. 'And I suppose we could consider that.' I rather liked how she had said *we* instead of *you*. 'But he doesn't come cheap. I can barely afford to keep him on here . . .'

Her words trailed off and I switched to talking about breakfast, though I wouldn't forget that Rick might be able to make himself useful in the woods at some point.

'Do you fancy some eggs and bacon?' I asked, holding up the packet of local streaky that Melody had given me and which I'd grabbed from the fridge on my way out. I had roughly totted up the cost of her welcome care package, and I definitely owed her. 'I know you've got eggs in the kitchen, so it can be a joint effort. I'm ravenous after my swim and long bath.'

'Was the bath all right?'

'Utter bliss, thank you. It's such a pretty room. So, how about this breakfast?'

'Well, I've already had my yogurt,' Constance commented, and again I was appalled by her lack of sustenance, 'but that does sound tempting.'

'I'll get it started then,' I said, before she could change her mind, 'and after we've eaten, would it be all right if I did my ironing in your kitchen? There's more room in Fernside.'

'Yes, that will be fine,' she nodded.

I thought it would be easy to include her pile in with mine but didn't say that was my plan in case she objected.

'Perhaps Rick might fancy a bacon sandwich?' I suggested instead. 'Got to keep the workers happy.'

Constance looked at me. 'What did you make of him?' she asked. 'He's not your type, is he?'

'Constance,' I laughed. 'What are you like?'

'Well, is he?'

'He's certainly easy on the eye,' I said, as he suddenly appeared from the shed, pushing a lawnmower and still looking a little damp around the edges.

'Well before you fall completely in love with him,' Constance said, leaning on my arm as she levered herself out of the chair, 'I should tell you that as well as being wickedly attractive, he's also gay.'

'Does that mean you think he's easy on the eye, too?' I risked asking, as I wondered how far I could push her sense of humour.

Quite far as it turned out.

'Anyone with a pulse would think he's a beautiful man,' she said seriously, and I laughed again and so did she.

'What are you two cackling about?' Rick stopped to ask.

'Never you mind.' Constance smiled and gave my arm a conspiratorial squeeze.

'Eggs and bacon in around half an hour?' I offered Rick.

'Count me in,' he grinned. 'I hope you're staying for the whole of the summer, because I don't usually get offers like that!'

I hoped I was going to be there that long, too, but not so I could supply him with breakfast on a regular basis.

The rest of the day flew by, even though I didn't seem to do a lot. Once the breakfast things had been cleared and the ironing done (stealth mode was a total success), I explored more of the garden which, compared to some other places I had seen in the village, was still looking verdant. I guessed that was because of the shade the tall trees surrounding it offered.

There were ferns, fatsias and hostas in abundance and, in the long beds closer to the house which got more sun, salvias, delphiniums and roses thrived. There were lots of other plants I didn't recognise and I thought I should ask Constance to teach me on a daily tour. Rick was certainly keeping it all in tiptop condition, so he was worth whatever she paid him.

I had already started to suss a few things out and one of them was that Constance might not have been particularly active for a while and that her sureness, when she was on her feet, had taken a knock because of that. Her reluctance to walk down to the river the day before had felt more like a confidence issue than inability and I wondered if her sore hip was the result of not being used rather than being worn out. I hoped my presence at Fernside might help with that, if it was the case.

'I thought I might walk down to the village and stop at the store,' I told her, when I popped into the sunroom towards the end of the afternoon and found her dozing in a chair. 'Can I pick anything up for you?'

'I hope it isn't too quiet for you here?' she asked, which took me by surprise. 'You aren't bored, are you?'

'Absolutely not,' I asserted forcefully. 'Fernside is perfectly peaceful. Exactly the sanctuary you cleverly worked out that I needed.'

She looked pleased about that.

'Well, that's all right then,' she nodded. 'There used to be a television in the sitting room, but I had it taken away when I realised how long it had been since I'd last watched it.'

'Who needs television when you've got this garden?' I sighed dreamily, looking out at it and noticing how many birds were flitting about. 'And Rick told me while we were washing up that you've got quite a library, too.' I hadn't seen the house beyond the kitchen. 'Reading and birdwatching, that's enough entertainment for anyone, isn't it?'

'I certainly think so and I'll have to introduce you to my blackbird. I haven't seen him yet today, but that's probably because of the furore Rick caused this morning.' She said it with a smile in her tone. 'He comes with his whole family sometimes.'

'Rick does?'

'No,' Constance laughed. 'The blackbird, as you well know.'

'And what about the piano?' I asked. 'I didn't know if I was listening to a recording or someone playing, the evening I scattered Dad's ashes. Is that your entertainment here, too?'

She didn't answer for a second.

'Something like that,' she said ambiguously. 'What are you picking up from the store? I could do with some milk, but I'm not sure you'd want to carry that all the way back.'

For some reason, she didn't want to fill me in on the piano situation, and remembering how she'd cut me off the evening before, I didn't press her about it. I did however think that it must have been her playing the evening I scattered Dad's ashes because had she been listening to a recording that would have been simple enough to say, wouldn't it? I wondered why she didn't want me to know.

'I can pick up some milk,' I said. 'How much do you need?'

In the end, I decided to drive down because between us there were quite a few things we wanted.

'Tilly!' Melody greeted me. 'How are things? How are you settling in?'

'Very good and wonderfully,' I was thrilled to be able to tell her. 'The apartment is a dream and I'm spending quite a bit of time with Constance, too. She's so lovely.'

'I bet she's enjoying that,' Melody said. 'I've often wondered how she copes rattling around in that huge place on her own. It must be lonely at times, even if she'd most likely say otherwise.'

'So, she is completely alone then?'

'I've never heard any different,' Melody shrugged.

'It does seem like a lot of space for one person,' I said as I roughly guessed the size of the house beyond the kitchen, 'but then as she's lived there her whole life, she probably doesn't think anything of it.'

'We know you've been swimming in the river,' Kaya, who had been listening, then chimed in. 'Because Rick filled us in when he was in here earlier. He thought you were mad.'

'Did he?' I laughed. 'Well, that's probably because he didn't enjoy his impromptu skinny dip as much as I enjoyed my swim with the right kit on.'

Kaya's mouth fell open. 'Was he completely . . .'

'No,' I told her. 'He kept his trunks on.'

'And how did he, you know . . . look?'

'So,' Melody loudly interrupted as a customer came in, 'what can I get you, Tilly? You can serve Mrs Benson, Kaya.'

We moved further towards the back of the store.

'Any more thoughts on buying the woods?' Melody asked as I handed her the list of things that Constance wanted.

'Not yet,' I said. 'But I'm hoping you've got some notebooks.

I could do with one to start jotting down my thoughts and plans in.'

The first thing I'd make a record of was Rick's name as he might just be the right person to help assess the state of the trees in the woods.

'Going old school.' Melody smiled. 'I like it. I've got a few,' she added and led the way. 'They're over here.'

She stocked more than I would have expected and left me to choose one while she found the things on Constance's shopping list. All the notebooks were lovely. The handmade, hemp covered selection were perfect for my project and I picked up a green one and then treated myself to a beautiful hand-turned wooden pen to go with it.

In the past, I'd favoured pencil over pen when starting a new notebook for fear of making a mistake, but those days were over and I was attempting to embrace the ethos that there are no such things as mistakes.

'I think that's everything,' I said, once I'd filled two baskets with enough food to see me through the next few days. At some point, I was going to have to visit a supermarket, because the store didn't carry a couple of things I was going to need. 'I don't suppose there's a cashpoint anywhere in the village, is there?'

'Sadly not,' Melody confirmed. 'You'll have to go to town if you need a bank and then I daresay you'll be hard pushed to find an actual branch.'

'I just need some cash,' I told her. 'But I might have to go to my bank at some point. I'll look online to find out where the nearest one is.'

'I'll tell you where you can go around here without having

to look it up first,' said Kaya, who had now finished serving Mrs Benson and had even helped load her shopping into her car.

'Go on.'

'The pub,' she grinned. 'We're heading down to The Greenman tonight. Why don't you join us? You can fill us in properly on Rick's swim session.'

I ignored that suggestion.

'How did I not know there's a pub in the village?' I frowned.

'Didn't you read about it in the cottage welcome pack?' Kaya tutted. 'I told you that thing was a waste of time,' she said to her sister. 'You put in far too much information.'

'I didn't look at the pack,' I quickly said, because Melody looked hurt, 'because I'd come to Willowell with a task to do and my time was accounted for. I'm sure the pack's fine.'

'Well,' said Kaya, 'the pub details are in there, but as you missed them, I'll give you directions.'

'It's a bit off the beaten track and slightly out of the village,' Melody said, letting her sister's criticism go, 'but totally worth looking for.'

As well as directions, the pair also drew me a map.

'How does it survive?' I asked, as I tried to fathom the route. 'If it's this hard to find, it can't have many customers.'

'Oh, it has.' Melody smiled as she turned the paper around in my hands, so I was looking at it the right way up. 'Word of mouth is a wonderful thing and it's always packed in the evenings.'

'Once found, never forgotten,' Kaya laughed. 'And of course, it's the only place to get a pint for miles, which gives it an obvious attraction.'

'Right,' I said, thinking it sounded rather interesting, especially now I'd worked out the track I thought it was up and had more of an idea of the location. 'Well, I don't think I'll make it tonight, but I'll visit at some point.'

I took out my card to pay my bill.

'I've put Constance's bits on her tab,' Melody told me and keyed in what I owed.

'No,' I said. 'Don't do that. Stick it all on my bill.'

'She won't like that,' Melody winced.

'Well, we won't mention it then,' I shrugged. 'And if it does come up, I'll say I hadn't realised or something and she can give me her amount in cash.'

Melody was reluctant to go ahead and I realised that, what with sorting the laundry and already cooking extra meals, perhaps I was overstepping.

'On second thoughts,' I said. 'You're right, I will just pay for what I've got.'

'And as you can't come to the pub,' Kaya asked, as I gathered my bags together. 'Does that mean you've already got plans?'

'I have,' I grinned. 'A hot date.'

'Surely not with Rick?' she gasped.

'No,' I told her with a wink, as I walked out. 'With my brand-new notebook.'

Chapter 8

I was still mindful of the fact that I was taking my time and settling in as Constance had kindly suggested, but having unpacked her groceries and said goodnight, I then couldn't resist the lure of the new notebook and sat up on the patio until late in the evening, scribbling away and further developing the plans for what I envisaged I could set up in wonderful Willowell Woods.

Some of the ideas were pie in the sky, but what was life without a little imagination? That was something else Dad had always said, and I realised that part of the reason why I already felt so settled was because I could sense that he was here at Fernside with me. There was no doubt in my mind that he would have heartily approved of the adventure I was considering and there was someone else who wanted to be kept up to date about it, too.

I was just about to turn off the lamp next to my bed when my phone buzzed with an incoming call from Zack.

'Hey, Tilly! How are you getting on?' he asked, the second I answered. 'The photos you sent look so good!'

'I'm having the best time,' I told him. 'And the apartment

is perfect. It's so cosy and compact. I've been swimming in the river, too, which is the most wonderful feeling, and I've met Rick, the gardener. He's hilarious . . . Zack?'

'I'm so . . . been ages since . . .'

'Zack?' I said again.

The call cut off because of the reception on his side of the world and seconds later a message landed. It was just three words.

'Potential love interest?' I read the question out loud and laughed, then spent the next couple of minutes composing an email response which set the scene of my introduction to Rick and declared that he was definitely not love interest material. Not for me, anyway.

Zack knew all about how Lee, my ex, had ended our relationship when he realised I was turning into someone who would rather spend a Sunday out in the woods wearing waterproofs as opposed to watching TV from the sofa indoors, and my brother still worried that I had been hurt as a result of the rejection.

I had tried to reassure him multiple times that I was confident in myself, fine following the split, had in fact fallen out of love long before it, but his protective big brother gene had overridden all and he was intent on vetting anyone else who came along. Even though he was having to do it from the other side of the world. And as much as I didn't want him to fret, it did feel wonderful to be so loved.

'Can I help you?' I asked, when I spotted a woman I didn't recognise peering through the gate on my walk back up the garden after my swim early the next morning.

There was no sign of Rick, and as the sunroom door was still closed, I hadn't caught a glimpse of Constance, either.

'I'm looking for Miss Clarke,' the woman said primly. 'She knows I'm coming because I have an appointment, but she isn't answering the front door.'

She sounded rather cross about that.

'Constance doesn't use it,' I told her, from my side of the gate. 'If you tell me your name, I'll go and see if I can find her for you, if you like?'

I didn't open the gate to let her in because it wasn't my place to.

'Miss Lyons,' she said in a crisp tone. 'And you are?'

As I didn't know the purpose of her appointment, or why Constance hadn't responded to her knocking on the door, I didn't feel obliged to explain who I was.

'I'll only be a minute,' I said instead and walked around to the sunroom. The door was unlocked, so I slipped inside and then into the kitchen. 'Constance?' I called, but there was no answer.

The kettle was warm, so I knew she was up and had made a drink, but with no sign of her, and Miss Lyons impatiently waiting, I felt I had no choice but to open the door that led into the rest of the house and call her again.

'Constance!' I shouted, as I tried not to be distracted by the dusty state of the large circular entrance hall or the thick motes my opening the door had caused to dance. I could see doorways into the rest of the downstairs rooms but didn't venture further. 'Constance, are you there? You've got a visitor.'

The air felt heavy, unaired and smelt slightly musty. There was a beautiful mahogany table in the centre of the hall, along with piles of newspapers precariously stacked near the unused front door, a jumble of shoes and racks groaning with coats, and from what I could see of the stairs, something on practically every step that was probably waiting to be carried up.

It was a literal incline of trip hazards and things to hinder the smooth and safe movement of the stairlift that I could see parked at the top. It all looked as chaotic as the kitchen had when I first arrived and I wondered if the whole of the rest of the house was in a similar state.

I had started to discreetly tame the clutter in the kitchen and Constance could now walk safely, rather than shuffle around the room. I would have to think carefully and shrewdly if I wanted to help in the rest of the house, because as I was staying in the garden apartment, it wasn't my place to have knowledge of or worry about anywhere else.

'Any luck?' came a voice behind me and I realised that Miss Lyons had not only let herself through the unlocked garden gate, she'd also made her uninvited way into the house.

What a cheek. I had no idea who she was, so I certainly wouldn't have given her entry without Constance's express permission.

'No,' I said crossly, as I loudly closed the door behind me. 'And I think you should wait outside.'

'Miss Clarke won't mind,' she said, putting the briefcase I hadn't noticed she was carrying on the kitchen table. 'It looks better in here, I must say. Has she finally got herself a cleaner? We did talk about the state of—'

'Thank you, Miss Lyons,' Constance snapped, as she stepped into the room behind her. I'd no idea where she'd sprung from. 'I have no desire to hear you discussing my business with anyone other than me. And, if I'm being honest, not even then.' The woman did at least have the grace to blush. 'How did you get in? The sunroom door was shut.'

'I didn't ask her in,' I said quickly. 'She was on the other side of the garden gate when I came in to find you.'

Constance nodded. 'Thank you, Tilly,' she said. 'I think we'd better keep that gate locked from now on. Why don't you go and get dry before you catch your death, my dear? And you,' she frowned at Miss Lyons, 'can wait in the sunroom. Half past we said and it's nowhere near that yet.'

'Would you like me to come back when I've got changed?' I asked Constance.

'No,' she said, 'but thank you. I'll be fine. She won't be staying long.'

'All right,' I reluctantly agreed, 'but I will come back later if that's all right because there's something I'd like us to discuss?'

'I'll see you in a while then.' Constance smiled and I left her and Miss Lyons to it.

I had wanted to eat breakfast outside on the patio, but when I opened the apartment doors, I could hear voices, tense and slightly raised, and quickly closed them again for fear of overhearing a conversation slash argument I wasn't supposed to be privy to.

'Knock! Knock!' I shouted, when it was almost lunchtime and once I was certain that Miss Lyons had left and I had given Constance long enough to compose herself or work off her temper. Or both.

'Come in, come in,' she called back, sounding like her usual self. 'My unwanted visitor was sent off with a flea in her ear a while ago and with any luck she won't darken my door again.'

'I really am sorry she just walked in,' I apologised. 'Had I realised she was likely to intrude—'

Constance wouldn't hear of it. 'Not your fault,' she said, waving my apology away. 'Though I'm pleased she saw you because you've rather saved my bacon.'

'Oh?' I frowned. 'What have I done?'

'We'll get into that in a minute,' she said, with what looked like a mischievous smile. 'First you can tell me what you've got under that tea towel?'

'Egg and ham salad,' I said, as I followed her into the cool kitchen and put the plates on the table, 'and before you tell me off for making one for you, the ham needed using up. There were too many slices for me to eat and I hate waste.'

'As do I,' she said, as I had known that she would. 'Are they for now or tonight?'

'I thought we could have them now if you like. Are you hungry?'

'I am rather,' she said, rooting through a drawer for some cutlery. 'Going to battle always gives me an appetite.'

She sounded positively gleeful.

'I thought I heard raised voices.'

'We didn't disturb you, did we?'

'No, I went back inside so I didn't hear anything I wasn't supposed to.'

'Probably just as well given that your name came up. You might have inadvertently ruined the ruse if you'd interrupted.'

'Did my name really have anything to do with saving you from Miss Lyons and whatever she was here for?'

'It had *everything* to do with it.' Constance smiled as she sat at the table.

I wasn't sure if it was my imagination, but she seemed to sit down without so much as a wince and I noticed she was wearing some jewellery, too. A lovely string of pearls. I hadn't spotted those earlier.

'Go on then,' I said. 'Tell me.'

'Fetch the salad cream and then I will.'

I did as I was asked, but a strong vinegary scent assaulted my nostrils when I opened the lid and set me off coughing.

'Crikey, Constance,' I spluttered, 'we can't eat that. However long have you had it?'

She looked thoughtful.

'A while,' she conceded. 'You best put it in the bin if it's as bad as all that.'

'I've got some mayonnaise in the apartment; shall I get that instead?'

'No, thank you. Not unless you want it?'

'All I really want is to hear about how I've somehow saved the day for you.'

Constance picked up her knife and fork and after a few mouthfuls, set them down again and dabbed her lips with an embroidered linen napkin.

'Miss Lyons,' she began, injecting the name with some force, none of it positive, 'is from the local social services and she's been a thorn in my side for a few months now.'

'Social services?'

'Yes, apparently, my . . .' She took a moment before continuing. 'Some . . . busybody reported to them that I was living here on my own and couldn't cope and they've been hounding me ever since.'

'Oh, crikey.' I grimaced, imagining how much she would

hate that. 'I suppose it's good, that they've made the effort to follow up.' She gave me a grim look. 'But I can understand why you're upset about it.'

'There's been talk of all sorts,' she huffed. 'From meals on wheels to assisted bathing and even, horror of horrors, the suggestion of me actually selling up and moving into some sort of home.' She shuddered at the mention of it.

That sort of set-up might suit some, but I knew it wouldn't be for Constance.

'But who would do that?' I frowned. 'Who would report you to them?'

Surely, it could only have been someone who had been inside the house and from what I had already made out, Constance didn't have many visitors.

'I do know who it was,' she glowered. 'But that's by the by. It doesn't matter now because the situation has been completely resolved. Neither they, nor Miss Lyons, will be bothering me again.'

I was dying to know who the culprit was, but she had made it very clear that I wasn't going to find out.

'How can you be so sure that she won't be back?' I asked.

'Because you're here.' Constance winked. 'I've told Miss Lyons that you're my live-in housekeeper.'

'Constance!' I gasped, my fork suspended halfway to my mouth. 'You have not!'

'Well,' she shrugged, 'it's not all that far from the truth, is it?'

'What do you mean?'

'You're already feeding me up,' she said, with a nod to the lunch I'd prepared, 'and you've made yourself handy in here, too.'

I felt my face flush.

'Don't think I haven't noticed how much tidier this kitchen is,' she went on. 'Or the fact that the ironing pile is diminishing.'

'So much for being discreet,' I tutted.

'Nothing gets past me, but you don't have to do any of it, you know. I can manage just fine. Not that I'm not grateful.'

'It's as easy to do for two as one,' I told her. 'And I like the company.'

'Yes,' she smiled. 'I like that, too.'

'Though there is one thing I don't like,' I said.

'Oh?'

'The fact that we haven't decided how much rent I should pay you yet. And we haven't looked into getting the woods properly valued either, have we?'

'All in good time about the woods and you know I'm not happy about you paying rent . . .' she began but stopped when I gave her the sort of look she'd earlier bestowed on me.

'And knowing that it hasn't taken any time to turn the kitchen around, I was wondering if there was anywhere else in the house that you'd like me to have a quick sort through. Given that I'm here as your live-in housekeeper,' I said, making air quotes without putting down my cutlery, 'it's the least I can do.'

'No, thank you,' Constance said, as she drew herself up. 'That I really wouldn't be comfortable with, even though the house is getting a bit dusty and untidy in places . . .' she then conceded.

From what I'd now seen of the hallway, that was putting it mildly.

'In that case,' I suggested, feeling clever, 'how about you use the first lot of rent I pay you to get a firm of cleaners in and let them have a bit of a blitz? That way, once it's done, we could, or you could, I mean, keep on top of it far more easily going forward.'

She looked to be giving that idea some thought, so I carried on eating while she mulled it over.

'Or I could get it blitzed and then perhaps use part of your future rent to pay someone to come in for a couple of hours or so every week, couldn't I? I admit I've never been a huge fan of the domestic side of life . . .'

That sounded like a very good idea to me, and I liked the thought of being with her long enough to see that funded, set up and running.

'In that case,' I nodded, 'that would work brilliantly. Though I am happy to do my bit. And there's no reason why we can't carry on doing the laundry together and sharing a few meals, is there?'

'I don't see why not,' she agreed willingly, which made my day. 'I've no idea what the going rate would be to rent the garden apartment, but you're not paying full market value,' she then stubbornly added. 'And I promise we will get the woods valued but only when you've had more time to settle in.'

'I had a feeling you were going to say that about the rent,' I tutted. 'So, what will you let me pay?'

'And once the house is in a happier state,' she said thoughtfully, once we'd finally settled on a figure, 'I might feel more inclined to invite people back in . . .'

'That would be wonderful,' I encouraged. It was heart-warming to hear her say that and I felt emboldened to ask her what had been running through my mind. 'And I've been wondering if you'd be open to me inviting Melody, Kaya and maybe Rick around one evening for a picnic in the garden. They wouldn't have to come into the house.'

'That sounds almost like the old days.' Constance beamed. 'Parties in the garden with friends throughout the summer used to be a regular treat here, you know.'

'Did they?'

'You sound surprised.'

'I suppose I am,' I confessed. 'It's hard to imagine now because it's so quiet.'

Constance smiled at that. 'When Grace and I were growing up,' she reminisced, 'it was far from quiet. Fernside was the place *everyone* wanted to be invited to. We had some very raucous escapades here, especially when my parents were away. Though Grace was considerably younger than me, so didn't always get up to quite the same amount of mischief. That said, I remember one particular night in the shrubbery . . .'

'Go on,' I giggled, as she turned red.

'Let's just say,' she said with diplomacy, 'that a couple of guests had to go home wearing rather less than they arrived in.'

'Constance! I'm seeing you, and Fernside, in a completely different light.'

'Oh, my dear,' she chuckled, 'you have no idea . . . But enough about that.'

'No,' I said. 'I want to hear more. Much more.'

'One day, perhaps,' she said firmly. 'Another time.'

'Fair enough,' I reluctantly agreed. 'But is it a yes to my rather tame picnic supper suggestion?'

'Why not?' she beamed. 'That would be fun.'

'Thank you.' I smiled. 'And I'm planning a trip to Sudbury

tomorrow, so I can get you the first lot of rent in cash then, can't I?'

'And maybe also help me find a decent cleaning company?'

Everything was coming together wonderfully.

'Absolutely,' I promised.

With our next steps settled, I asked Constance if she would mind if I went back down to the woods later that day.

'I know there's no rush to officially do anything, but there are a couple of things I'd like to look at again,' I explained.

'That sounds to me like you've been giving your ideas greater thought,' Constance observed.

'I have,' I confirmed. 'But not with any sense of urgency. More mulling it all over and seeing what develops. I had been trying not to, but I can't seem to get the wonderful place out of my head now.'

Constance looked pleased. 'It is wonderful, isn't it?'

'Utterly,' I agreed.

It saddened me to think that she was potentially parting with the family woods for financial reasons as opposed to because she wanted to or was ready to, but her reasoning wasn't my business, even though I was becoming fonder of her by the second.

'So, does that mean that you're ready to tell me what you're planning?' she asked.

'Even though there's no rush?' I grinned.

'Well, you've piqued my curiosity now,' she smiled back.

'I'm almost ready,' I told her, as I thought of the notebook I'd started to write in and the feeling of excitement it filled me with.

'You know, now you're living here, you don't have to ask if

you can go to the woods,' Constance said kindly. 'Just pop down as and when you want to.'

'Thank you.'

'And you might as well have the keys to the gate and the cabin,' she carried on. 'They're on the leather fob in the shape of an oak tree. And while we're sorting keys, take one for the garden gate, too. Rick has already got one and we really should keep the gate locked to ward off any other unwelcome visitors.'

'Are you expecting more?' I frowned as I sorted the keys.

She didn't answer for a moment and when I looked over at her, I couldn't read her expression.

'No,' she said then, seeming to rally, but I couldn't help thinking her words didn't ring true. 'Not now. Unless for some reason,' she added, 'Miss Lyons takes it upon herself to check up on us.'

'I don't think she'd dare,' I said with a wry smile.

With the keys in my pocket, I tidied the lunch dishes, grabbed my notebook and headed back to the woods. I couldn't unlock the rusted padlock, so left my car in the parking area and climbed over the gate again instead.

It was another hot day, but I'd opted to wear a long-sleeved shirt and full-length trousers. I had no desire to leave with more scratches and snags from the brambles following my second walk around.

'You first, I think,' I said to the cabin, having negotiated the overgrown path and easily found it again.

I had originally planned to leave it until last, but the lure of the key in my pocket proved too much and I held my breath as I turned it in the lock. It twisted around easily, but the door had warped and needed a hefty shove before it would open. I hoped I'd be able to get it closed again.

'Aren't you just perfect?' I said happily a few minutes later, as I looked around more and inhaled the smell of warm wood.

Along with the wood burning stove, there was a tiny kitchen and cloakroom at the back, which had compost style loos and another small room that must have been an office. There were a few curled up plant catalogues on the windowsill in there, but nothing else.

Much of the interior was large, open, empty and airy and offered endless arrangement opportunities. I could easily imagine it set up for what I had in mind. The cabin had the potential to be both a refuge if the weather was too inclement to be outside and a cosy sanctuary during the chilliest weeks of the winter. I imagined conversations being had around the fire and, for some reason, a dog's presence featured, too . . .

'Anyone home?'

'Damn,' I gasped, as my feet practically left the floor. 'Where did you spring from?'

'Heaven,' Rick grinned. 'According to the guy I met on holiday.'

'For pity's sake,' I tutted. I didn't want to smile but couldn't help it. 'What are you doing here?'

'I could ask you the same thing,' he said, looking around.

'I asked first.'

'Fair point. I was just passing, and I saw your car, so I thought I'd better stop and check you were okay.'

'That was kind.'

'I am kind.' He smiled. 'When I'm not being full of myself.'

I rolled my eyes at that. At least he was self-aware.

'Your turn,' he said then.

'What do you mean?'

'Your turn to tell me what you're doing here.'

Knowing that I was, at some point, going to ask him to assess the tree work that I thought needed doing, I figured I might as well tell him sooner rather than later that I was planning to buy the woods from Constance.

'I'm here,' I ventured, 'for another look around, because I'm going to buy the woods. Though I'd appreciate it if you'd keep that to yourself.'

He had been standing side-on to me and fiddling with the cage that covered the fire, but shot around to fully face me once he'd heard my explanation.

'Really?'

I tried not to be offended that he sounded so shocked. I supposed my declaration was a bit out of the blue.

'Really.' I nodded. 'I've got an idea for a nature-based business and Willowell Woods is the perfect spot to turn it into a reality.'

'Crikey,' he said and puffed out his cheeks. 'And Constance knows about this?'

'Of course she knows about it, you twit,' I laughed. 'Who do you think gave me the key for the cabin? And the gate, too but I couldn't shift the padlock on that.'

'I see,' he said.

He sounded unusually serious and it unsettled me a bit.

'What is it?' I frowned.

'Well,' he said, drawing the word out. 'Probably nothing, given that you and Constance already have an agreement, but I heard a rumour in the pub last night that—'

'If it was about someone local having already made an offer,' I cut in, 'that was something Constance was previously putting about, to put incomers, like me, off.'

'Oh well,' Rick laughed and pointed at the keys in my hand, 'that's worked, hasn't it?'

'Like a dream.' I smiled. 'I take it that is what you heard?'

'Pretty much,' he shrugged.

'Can you tell me exactly what it was that you were told?'

'Just that Constance has accepted an offer, and that the woods are officially sold,' he told me. 'I had no idea that it was to you, though.' He grinned then. 'Fancy that.'

'I'm delighted to have amused you,' I tutted.

Chapter 9

Despite my best efforts to shrug off what Rick had said he'd heard, I decided that for clarity's sake and my own peace of mind, I would mention it to Constance. Deep down I knew we were on the same page, but I didn't want to carry around an unnecessary niggle when a tactful conversation would rid me of it.

'Constance!' I called, as I arrived back at Fernside and heard her walk out of the sunroom. 'Are you there?'

My voice was louder than I had realised, and it made her jump, which wasn't the best of starts.

'What is it?' she asked, as one hand flew to her chest. 'What's happened? Is there something amiss in the woods? Or is it the cabin?'

'Sorry,' I hastily backtracked on panicking her. 'No, it's nothing like that. Everything's fine.'

I shifted from one foot to the other, wondering how to broach the subject without her thinking that I was questioning what she'd previously said, which of course, was exactly what I was doing.

'Spit it out then,' she said. 'For heaven's sake, you've got me imagining all sorts now.'

So much for being tactful and keeping the situation light.

'It's nothing bad,' I finally began. 'I saw Rick down there . . .'

'Oh well, I don't mind him having a wander and if it's nothing worse than that?'

'He said something,' I continued awkwardly. I seemed to be making more of a hash of it with every word. 'And I just thought I should mention it. Even though I know it isn't . . .'

'Oh, for goodness' sake,' Constance tutted. 'Will you just get on with it?'

'He said there's a rumour going about that you've already accepted an offer on the woods,' I blurted.

'I see,' she said.

'And given that we haven't gone public with our arrangement yet . . .'

I knew Melody wouldn't have mentioned anything to anyone because she hated gossip.

'You wanted to check there wasn't some truth in it and find out if I was intending to play you off against someone else in a bidding war, is that it?'

She sounded both angry and appalled and I felt every bit as bad as I deserved to.

'No,' I said and hung my head. 'No, of course not. I'm sorry. I should never have said anything.'

'I wish you hadn't,' she snapped. 'I appreciate that you might not be used to village life, Tilly, but this is part of it. Gossip and rumours are always rife and the sooner you learn what to do with both – I recommend doing nothing – then the happier we'll be.'

After the harsh but justified telling off, I could feel tears gathering behind my eyes. 'I didn't mean to upset you,' I apologised.

'Well, you have upset me.'

'I'm very sorry,' I said sincerely. 'Can we please pretend I never mentioned it?'

I hoped I hadn't done our relationship any lasting damage. Her reaction had been unexpectedly sharp.

'I think we'd better had,' she said, and I felt marginally relieved.

'I promise I'll never question you again,' I told her.

'Good.'

'Shall I go and put the kettle on?'

I just wanted us to get back on the friendly footing we'd been enjoying before.

'No, thank you,' she said and turned away. 'I have some telephone calls to make.'

'I'll see you later, then,' I said, as she walked off.

She didn't answer and I hoped I hadn't shaken her faith in me. The next time I saw Rick, even though what had just happened wasn't really his fault, I would tell him to keep any rumours he heard about the woods, village or Fernside strictly to himself.

I didn't see Constance for the rest of the day or the following morning. Knowing that I had a few jobs to do in Sudbury and wanted to set off early, I didn't go for my early swim and left feeling unsettled. I didn't like missing the swim and I hated not seeing Constance for breakfast and having the opportunity to completely clear the air between us.

I'd been staying at Fernside no time at all, but the comfortable pattern of my mornings was already set, and as I joined the faster and busier roads that took me away from the lanes around Willowell, I realised how happy I was to no longer be subjected to a daily commute and what a luxury it was to be able to organise my time in a far more relaxed way.

Going forward, assuming I hadn't blown my chances of buying the woods, when I launched my business, I would make a point of setting my days up how I wanted them to run. My current laidback schedule was holiday mode, but there was no reason why I couldn't adopt a more stress-free approach to work once everything was organised.

'You're looking at . . . well . . . at least a couple of hours,' the mechanic in the third garage I later stopped at told me. 'Maybe even a bit longer than that.'

During the hot and sticky journey to town, it had become increasingly obvious that the air con in my car needed gassing, and having finished my errands at the bank and my few bits of shopping, including buying some more clothes, I decided that I'd see if I could get it sorted on spec. Third time was looking likely to be a charm, even if I was going to have to wait around.

'That's fine,' I said. 'I'm just grateful that you can do it. I don't suppose there's anywhere I can get something to eat around here, is there?'

'There's a burger van round the corner.' I didn't much fancy that on such a hot day but needs must. 'Or a pub further up the road. It's a bit of a walk, but the grub's half decent.'

'I'll try there,' I said, unlocking my phone to search for it. 'I really appreciate you fitting the car in.'

'It won't be done very quickly, but if you leave your number with my mum, who's covering the desk today, she'll message you when it's ready to pick up.'

'Brilliant. Thank you so much.'

The mechanic's mum, Cath, was just heading out to another

garage to pick up a part and, hearing that I was walking to the pub, kindly offered me a lift as she was going to be driving practically past the door.

'I won't be about to take you back,' she said, 'but you've got your brolly so you should be okay to use that for a bit of shade.'

'Thanks again,' I said, as I climbed out with my bag and the umbrella I would later use to shield me from the heat on the return journey. 'At least I'm nowhere near as hot now as I might have been if I'd had to walk.'

She laughed at that. 'You wait until you're my age,' she smiled. 'You'll always be hot then!'

I waved her off thinking that was something to not look forward to, and when I walked into the pub I felt even more grateful that I hadn't arrived looking like a hot mess, or not too hot a one anyway, because I immediately spotted the hat retriever sitting at a table with a guy opposite him. How fortuitous was that?

They were talking intently and looking at some paperwork and, as I slipped discreetly by and made for the loos, I thought it was a shame that I hadn't brought the hat with me, because I might have been able to use it as a conversation starter as well as wearing it on the walk back to the garage.

'What are the odds?' I smiled at my reflection, as I washed my hands, then touched up my lip gloss.

I hoped we might have an opportunity to at least say hello. My faux pas with Constance and the guilty, tummy churning feelings it had evoked were temporarily forgotten. That said, my tummy did still feel fluttery, but for an entirely different reason.

I sat at a table tucked just around the corner from hat man – I really needed to find out his name if we were going to keep bumping into each other – and as I first drank a thirst-quenching Coke and then tucked into a crisp and fresh chicken Caesar salad, I wondered if he'd left and I'd missed my chance to chat. Though that said, he might not have even recognised me, and I could have just been saved the humiliation of being met with a blank expression when I said hello . . .

I tried to put him out of my mind and was thinking about whether to order some ice cream to spin the time out further when I looked up to ask the server if I could have another minute to decide and found it wasn't the server standing next to my table.

'Hello.' I smiled at the guy, who hadn't left after all. 'Are you here to take my order for two scoops of strawberry and chocolate ice cream?'

'I'm not.' He laughed and looked around. 'But I'm sure I can find someone who will.'

'No,' I said. 'You're all right.'

'I thought it was you,' he smiled down at me.

'And I thought it was you.' I smiled back, hoping I didn't look as hot as I suddenly felt. His shirt sleeves were rolled up, and his tanned forearms were a sight to behold. 'But I didn't want to interrupt.'

'Just a bit of business,' he explained, and I noticed he didn't have the paperwork he and the other man had been looking at.

'Do you conduct all of your business out of pubs on the edge of industrial estates?'

'Not as a rule,' he grinned. 'This was my first time.'

'And how have you found it?'

'Time will tell, but the steak was decent.'

'Did you have dessert?'

'I did not.'

'Well,' I said, looking at the server who was now approaching, 'I'm about to. Would you like to join me?'

The question took me by surprise as I wasn't the sort of person who usually made such a forthright offer, but my flash of confidence was rewarded when he pulled out the chair opposite mine and sat down.

'So,' he said, once we'd ordered, and as he looked around the table and on the floor. 'No hat today?'

'No,' I confirmed, as our eyes met. 'And that was a mistake, but then I wasn't expecting to have to take my car into the garage and have a long walk in the hot sun. I have my umbrella for the trip back. The mechanic's mum gave me a lift here, so . . .' My words trailed off. 'So, no. No hat.'

He smiled and nodded, and I felt my cheeks start to flame. Rambling *and* feeling hot, I must have been making a glorious impression. So much for the flash of confidence. That had obviously upped and left.

'Do you live in the area?' he asked, before I had gathered my wits enough to fire a question at him.

'No,' I said. 'Well, sort of. No . . . not really.' *Oh god.*

'Are you not sure?' he frowned.

'I'm staying in the county temporarily,' I tried again, having taken a breath. 'But with a view to a permanent move to the Suffolk countryside if certain things happen as I hope they will.'

'I see,' he said. 'Or I sort of do, and I know I'm biased because I grew up here, but you couldn't have picked a more beautiful place to move to.'

'You're a fan?'

'Die hard,' he smiled. 'I love it. Though I don't get to visit as often as I'd like to, which is a shame because I find the countryside you're hoping to settle in a real tonic.'

He didn't say what it was he needed a tonic for.

'It is beautiful,' I agreed, thinking of Willowell woods, Fernside, the river and beyond.

'So,' he asked next. 'What is it that you're hoping will work out?'

'Oh. It's too complicated to get into,' I said, waving the opportunity to explain away. 'Why don't we start with something simpler?'

'Okay,' he agreed.

'I'm Matilda,' I told him, finally getting around to the basics. 'Though everyone calls me, Tilly.'

'That was my favourite Roald Dahl book,' he said, sounding wistful. 'And film. The Trunchbull used to terrify me though.'

'Me too,' I agreed. 'Though my parents were nothing like the Wormwoods. If anything,' I continued, my tone sounding as reflective as his, 'Mum was more Miss Honey.'

'Was?'

'Yes,' I said, as I reined in the emotion that thoughts of Mum reading the book to me at bedtime had stirred. 'She died when I was ten.'

'Oh crikey, Tilly,' he said. 'I'm so sorry.'

'Thank you.' I swallowed.

'I lost my mum when I was eighteen and that was tough enough to negotiate, I can't imagine what it was like at ten.'

'In that case, I'm sorry for you, too.' I sighed. 'My dad was the greatest support, and my brother, who's a few years older than me, was amazing, too.'

'That must have helped.'

'It really did. Though we lost Dad too, a short while ago. What about you? Do you still have your dad?'

'I never knew him,' he said. 'But I do still have a Miss Honey of my own. Or a similar version of her . . .'

'Lucky you,' I smiled. 'About having a Miss Honey, I mean.'

'I am lucky. Or I have been. Unfortunately, she's had a bit of a personality change of late and has morphed into something more akin to The Trunchbull.'

'Oh dear.' I grimaced.

'Oh, ignore me,' he said and sat up straighter. 'I'm just being dramatic. She's not that bad. Just a bit stubborn and set in her ways, I suppose.'

'I know someone like that,' I said, thinking of Constance.

From what I'd experienced of her so far, her personality was a blend of the two, too. Miss Honey had invited me to stay at Fernside and The Trunchbull had seen off Miss Lyons! I hoped she wasn't going to only show that side of herself to me now that I'd upset her.

'And I'm James, by the way,' the guy said, striking his forehead. 'I've just realised I didn't say. I got sidetracked talking about favourite childhood books.'

There were far worse things to be absorbed by and I could already feel myself being captivated by this guy.

'As in *James and the Giant Peach*?' I ventured and he laughed.

'Yes, I suppose so. We've both got our names in the titles of Dahl's books, how funny is that?'

'It is a coincidence,' I said, biting my lip. 'But our upbringings don't seem to have been anything like our namesakes'.'

'Quite so,' he grinned.

He looked right at me and I felt my insides melting faster than the ice cream we were about to eat.

'So,' said James, as we tucked in. 'You're staying in the area with a view to moving permanently to beautiful Suffolk, your car is currently off the road and you have impeccable taste in hats, or your mum did. Tell me more?'

He really had been paying attention if he'd remembered the hat he'd rescued had belonged to Mum. He got even more Brownie points for that.

'The car isn't really off the road,' I explained. 'It's just having the air con sorted.'

James rolled his eyes. 'I meant tell me more about you, not your car. Tell me, what makes Tilly tick?'

That felt like a rather intimate question, but then we'd kicked things off with explaining that we both no longer had our parents, so . . .

'You're very inquisitive for a stranger.' I pretended to frown with disapproval.

'I'm a barrister.' He shrugged and licked his spoon, which made my tummy feel a bit funny again. 'It's my business to get into your business.'

'A barrister who conducts *his* business in a pub?'

'Not all my business,' he smiled. 'Today was an exception. It was a meeting about a new pro bono case I'm considering taking on. Coming here for an informal chat worked best for the client and I was happy to oblige.'

'Pro bono?'

'Free,' he explained. 'Pro bono work is stuff I do for free.'

'A barrister who works for free.'

'You sound amazed,' he laughed.

It was true I had made certain assumptions about him based on the way he looked and the car he drove, but I was quickly recalibrating those now. The shift in opinion made me like him even more.

'I am a bit,' I admitted. 'Do you work for free very often?'

'More than my boss wants me to,' he told me. 'Far less than I'd like to, but the details can wait for another day.' I was delighted there might be one. 'I believe everyone should be entitled to the best legal representation, no matter what their income,' he said. 'Don't you?'

'Of course,' I agreed.

Swoon!

'So, come on,' he nodded in encouragement. 'Tell me what's tempted you to my beloved home county. Assuming it isn't also yours?'

'It isn't where I grew up, but I'm following a childhood dream which came about thanks to holidays spent here,' I told him. 'It's something I lost sight of for a long time but when Dad died, I started to make my way back towards it and now I'm inching closer to potentially achieving it.'

Or I would be if Constance could forgive me.

'That sounds amazing.'

'It is,' I smiled. 'I've given up my job, put my possessions in storage and returned to the place where my heart has always felt at home . . . to . . .' I hesitated to say the words.

'To?'

'To find myself, I suppose. And I know that's a total cliché—'

'No,' James cut me off. 'No, it isn't. Well, it is in the sense that the phrase has been overused and misapplied, but I can tell that's not what you're doing, Tilly. You're taking the time to truly discover what makes you *you* and that should be a part of everyone's life journey, shouldn't it?'

'You don't think I'm mad then?' I asked.

'I think you're amazing,' he said, pinning me again with his beautiful brown eyes. 'I envy you.'

'You envy me?' I echoed.

As far as I was concerned – and granted my deductions were based on the time it took to eat two scoops of ice cream – James seemed to have life licked. He was professional, compassionate, kind and a great listener. But then I remembered how long I'd been masking my way through life, doing a job I despised and sticking with a relationship I felt no passion for. It wasn't all that long ago I'd been in turmoil, but no one around me had a clue. Other than Zack, but that was because I'd outright told him. Was James in turmoil?

'Why do you envy—' My phone started to ring, and I reached for my bag. 'Okay, that's great,' I said, when I answered the call. 'I'll start walking back now.'

'Car sorted?' James asked as he pulled out his wallet and then a bank card.

'It is,' I told him. 'And I'll get this. Your ice cream's on me.'

'Well, thank you,' he said, treating me to another full wattage smile. 'That's very kind. I'll give you a lift to the garage if you like.'

'Don't you need to get back to work?'

'Not until I've seen you safely back to your car and we've exchanged numbers,' he grinned.

'Oh really?' I smiled back.

'Because I mean,' he said, 'if you don't yet know anyone

around here and you have car trouble on the way home, who are you going to call?'

'It was an air con fix.'

'Even so,' he shrugged. 'Who would you ring if disaster struck?'

'My breakdown provider?'

'Oh dear,' he said, wrinkling his nose. 'Have I pushed my luck?'

'That depends,' I told him, thinking it was a bit late to bring it up, but at least I hadn't entirely forgotten. 'The first time we met, you had a passenger in your car . . .'

'A work colleague,' he said, looking me dead in the eye. 'Who hasn't got a hat to her name, which was why she was so grumpy.'

'Right,' I laughed. 'But just for clarity's sake, are you single, James?'

'Absolutely.' He smiled. 'Very much so. Have been for ages. You?'

'Absolutely.' I grinned and held out my hand for his phone. 'Very much so. Have been for a while and suffered no heart-break in the break-up.'

His smile grew even wider. 'Yet another story for another day,' he laughed.

'I'm not sure it is,' I also laughed. I didn't think I'd want to talk to him about Lee. 'I'm sorry that you have to work with a grumpy, non-hat-wearing colleague.'

'So am I,' he grimaced. 'But if anyone asks, I didn't say that.'

Once we'd exchanged numbers, I quickly paid, and we walked out to the car park and James made for a vehicle I didn't recognise.

'This is my car,' he told me. 'The fancy one you've seen me in before belongs to my boss.'

'Ah, right.'

'I could never spend what he does on cars,' he tutted as he pressed the fob, and I found myself liking him even more. 'My money goes to a far more worthwhile cause.'

'Which is?'

A loud blast from a car horn behind me cut our conversation off.

'I got held up!' It was Cath, the mechanic's mum. 'I can give you a lift back to the garage if that's where you're heading now?'

I looked from her to James.

'That's the garage owners' mum,' I explained. 'As she's here, I might as well go back with her.'

James looked disappointed and I felt it too, but it would be silly to turn her down and then drive the distance to pick up my car right behind her.

'Sure?'

'It would be rude not to, wouldn't it?'

'Yes,' he agreed. 'I suppose it would. Can I message you?'

'Message, call, whatever you like,' I said, as I went to walk away. 'You've got my number now.'

'It was very nice bumping into you again,' James smiled.

'It was very nice bumping into you again, too,' I smiled back.

'Friend of yours?' Cath asked as I slid into the passenger seat.

'You know what,' I said, as I waved out of the window and James waved back. 'He might just be.'

Chapter 10

I'd had my share of dates and relationships over the years – some short, fun and sweet, others longer and rather more serious – but none of them had ever started in the same way as my connection with James. Yes, it had been fun and flirty, but it had felt intimate, too.

Considering we were only just on first name terms, I had shared a lot about myself over that bowl of ice cream. It had been a revealing encounter and initially I wondered if that was the result of the barrister in James coaxing things out of me and making me say more than I usually would, but then I realised that hadn't been the case because he had shared just as much as I had. As first conversations went, it certainly felt . . . unique.

Even though meeting James proved to be a distraction, the closer I got to Willowell and then Fernside on the journey home, the further thoughts of him drifted away, and in their place my last conversation with Constance began to play out in my head again. I felt wretched to have upset her and hoped that she really would be able to forgive and forget, as she so distressingly had phrased it, the upset I had caused.

'Tomorrow then,' I whispered when I arrived back and found both the sunroom door and the one beyond it closed. 'I'll talk to her tomorrow.'

Having forgone my early morning swim the day before, I was up with the lark and in the river extra early the following day. My continuing concerns about how much I'd hurt Constance meant I hadn't slept well. My tossing and turning in the increasingly hot bed matched the thoughts toing and froing in my head, and I hoped that the dawn swim would cool me down and help me get some perspective on the situation. I was also mindful that I hadn't heard from James, but then I hadn't messaged him, either . . .

The river was refreshingly cool and restorative and, in my body at least, I was feeling almost back up to speed when I later went in search of my dear new friend. I had heard the sunroom door open while I was eating my breakfast and I found Constance sitting in her usual chair, with the paper in her lap and a pen between her teeth. Her brow was furrowed in concentration, and I guessed the crossword was proving extra tricky that morning.

'Tetradecagon,' she triumphantly said aloud as she filled a word in.

'A fourteen-sided shape?' I ventured, hoping the memory of my high school maths was correct.

She looked at me over the top of her glasses. 'Oh dear,' she sighed.

'Was that not right?' I grimaced. 'Maths was never my strong suit.'

'No, you were right,' she said, setting the paper aside. 'What

I meant was, oh dear, look at the bags under your eyes. They almost match mine.'

My swim had perked me up a bit, but the river didn't have magical healing properties and Constance was right; I did look tired.

'I didn't sleep well,' I told her.

'Me neither.' She smiled. 'I didn't like our quarrel.'

'Neither did I, Constance,' I said and rushed over to sit on the small sofa next to her chair. 'I'm so sorry I even mentioned that wretched rumour.'

'And I'm sorry that I didn't see your upset for what it was.' Constance tutted and reached for my hand.

It was a kind show of affection and one I immediately returned.

'Which was?'

'That you were scared that you were going to miss out on buying the woods, of course,' she said, giving my hand a squeeze.

For someone of her age she had a surprisingly strong grip and I returned the gesture, though not with too much force.

'Can we really put it behind us?' I asked.

'Of course we can,' she said stoically as she let go of my hand. 'I've already given Rick a piece of my mind. He should have known better than to take heed of gossip. My advice is, listen to it if you can't resist but always go straight to the organ grinder if you want the facts.'

I took a moment to consider that.

'Like I did, you mean?' I said softly.

It was Constance's turn to think then.

'My goodness, Tilly.' She gasped. 'You're right. You did, didn't you? You came straight to me, and I was so cross I told you off! I'm so sorry.'

'We're both sorry,' I said.

I had the strongest feeling there wasn't any substance to the *Fernside needs work and that's why the woods are up for sale* gossip, but given we'd only just cleared the air, I wasn't going to mention it.

'We are,' she agreed. 'I think we should carry the lesson forward but let the upset that it taught us go. Tea will help. Why don't you go and put the kettle on?'

'And I'll leave this in the kitchen, shall I?'

I held up the envelope I'd got for her.

'What is it?' she asked.

'The rent I promised you. And we're going to look for a cleaner today, aren't we?' She suddenly didn't look as on-board with the plan as she had before. 'Someone who will keep Miss Lyons and her crew off your back?' I reminded her.

'Yes, I suppose so . . .'

'Or, like I suggested before,' I pushed harder, 'I could do the whole place myself. I really wouldn't mind and it would save you—'

'Absolutely not,' she objected loudly. 'Put the envelope in the Quality Street tin in the cupboard above the kettle and bring the parish magazine back out with the tea. There's bound to be some firm or other in there that we can try.'

'Right you are.' I smiled, knowing that I'd won that battle, at least.

The tin turned out to be stuffed with cash, mostly five-pound notes, but it was a substantial amount, and I had a job to squeeze the envelope in with it.

'Do you know how much money you've got in that tin, Constance?' I asked her, when I rejoined her with the tea tray and the magazine she'd asked for.

'No idea,' she shrugged. 'I haven't been able to reach inside that cupboard for quite some time, but I hadn't forgotten the money was there.'

'Well, there's quite a lot. I could barely get the lid back on.'

'My father always said you should keep some cash in the house,' she told me. 'He didn't trust the banks and always kept a tidy sum in various hidey holes about the place.'

'Well, you're clearly following his advice,' I told her. 'You haven't got any more tucked away, have you?'

'No,' she said, but she didn't sound sure. 'I don't think so. I'll have to have a think before we get the cleaners in, won't I?'

'You will,' I agreed as I picked up the magazine and flicked through it. 'Now, let's have a look at the domestic section, shall we?'

An hour later we'd long emptied the teapot *and* exhausted the list of cleaners and cleaning firms offering their services locally. Constance had raised some objection to all of them. Some were 'too big an outfit' while others fell into the 'I haven't trusted that family since the grandfather was discovered scrumping our gooseberries' category.

'Oh Constance,' I grumbled. 'This is impossible.'

'Well, I've got to have someone I can trust, haven't I?' she sniffed.

'Yes,' I said, tempering my frustration, but only just. 'Especially if you've cash hidden all over the place.'

'It won't be much—' she started to say, but my phone pinged

loudly, and I made a grab for it, knocking over my empty cup and dropping the magazine in the process.

'For goodness' sake, Tilly!' Constance scolded, as I read the message that had landed. 'Steady the buffs.'

I had no idea what that meant, but her tone told me I was in trouble.

'Sorry,' I blurted, but I knew I didn't sound it because I couldn't stop smiling.

'You don't look very sorry. Good news?'

'Ever so.' I blushed.

The message was from James. An apology for not yet ringing and a succinct explanation that he had been caught up in an unexpected meeting in Sudbury and was now reading some case notes he'd had to quickly get to grips with. Apparently, his boss hadn't been impressed that he'd taken so long over the pro bono meeting and not made it back to London. He would have been raging if he knew how long James had lingered over dessert!

'Is it a love note from your amore?' Constance asked. 'Do you even have an amore? I can't believe I've never asked.'

'It's a message from a friend,' I told her. 'Someone I've only recently met.'

'Oh,' she said, her eyes twinkling. 'Tell me more.'

She settled further back while I explained how I had bumped into someone because of Mum's runaway hat and that we had then met again by fluke, but for longer, the previous day. I didn't say that the person was drop dead gorgeous, because I didn't want Constance to think that I was shallow, but as I described our chance meetings, I felt myself dazzled again by James's beguiling brown eyes and wonderful smile.

'That sounds very much like what you youngsters call a meet-cute, doesn't it?' Constance grinned, once I had finished.

'I suppose it does,' I laughed. 'But I wouldn't have expected you to have heard of that expression, Constance!'

'Rick keeps me up to date,' she laughed. 'Sometimes in a little too much detail. The things that boy gets up to! I'd love to see him find the right man and settle down, but something tells me he still has wild oats to sow. If that phrase applies . . .'

'Constance!'

'Well, it's true,' she laughed. 'And I'm sure he wouldn't mind me saying it. In fact, he'd be thrilled to know that the topic of his rampant love life had formed a part of our morning conversation.'

Knowing what a show-off and how full of himself Rick could sometimes be, even if it was tongue in cheek, I didn't think Constance was wide of the mark in saying that.

'You're right,' I laughed, too. 'And what about you, Constance?' I got swept along and asked.

'Me?'

'Yes,' I nodded. 'I've shared, now I want to hear about your love life.'

'I haven't had one of those for a very long time.'

'Am I rude to ask?'

'Not at all.' She smiled and sighed. 'I was in love once. Very much in love, and I truly believed I always would be, but they left me for someone else. I suppose I never really got over it. I certainly never sought out another relationship again. I've been on my own for well over half a century now.'

'I'm so sorry.' I swallowed, trying to get a handle on how it must feel to have been alone for that length of time.

'It's all right.' She shrugged. 'I'm used to it now. In fact, I rather like it because, in case you hadn't noticed, I'm a little set in my ways.'

I didn't comment on that.

'Well, I'm still sorry and I didn't mean to pry,' I said. 'He was a fool to leave you.'

'She,' Constance corrected me. 'She was a fool. But the world was a very different place back then, so I do have some understanding of why she did it, even if I was raging at the time. She married and moved out of the county, which I suppose was a blessing of sorts.'

'A double betrayal,' I whispered.

'Yes,' Constance agreed. 'It was, rather. But now, let's get back to your young man.'

Clearly the subject was closed, but I felt honoured Constance had shared her past with me, even if it was a heartbreaking story.

'What about him?' I smiled.

'Are you going to message him back?'

'I'm off to the pub with the gang in a bit,' I told her. 'But I will reply before I go.'

'Good,' she said firmly. 'Life's too short for playing games and what is it now . . . ghosting, especially when you're obviously smitten. No point in playing hard to get when you've already been caught.'

'Constance!' I laughed, and she did, too.

'And as you're going to see everyone, you can ask them if they'd like to come to supper here later in the week, can't you?'

'Are you sure? The house won't be cleaned by then,' I reminded her.

I hoped the prompt might make her think twice about ringing, or letting me call, someone listed in the parish magazine, but it didn't work.

'We can stick to the garden then,' she shrugged. 'And just use your place if someone needs the loo.' I liked the garden apartment being referred to as my place. 'And if you haven't got beyond messaging your meet-cute by then,' she winked, 'Rick's tales of seduction will soon have you yearning for love, or something like it, and meeting up with him again.'

'I can't believe you said that! You really are the limit!' I grinned.

'I know,' she giggled. 'You wouldn't think it to look at me, would you?'

'No,' I laughed back. 'You really wouldn't.'

I messaged James before I headed out that evening but didn't get anything back, which was fair enough, given that I knew he was working. I hoped his boss wouldn't expect him to put in too many extra hours to get caught up. Personally, I would have been proud to employ someone who had such a philanthropic attitude, but I could tell James's employer had different priorities. The expensive car was a bit of a giveaway, as was his annoyance over the time James had been away from the office.

I felt rather amused that I was so ready to spring to James's defence. I barely knew him and yet I would have stood up for him against his boss. When Lee had left me, I had told myself that I wouldn't get involved with another suit, but James, with this pro bono work and love of the Suffolk countryside, was already shaping up to be more my type than Lee ever was. Not that James and I were involved, but it felt wonderful to imagine what a potential relationship with him could look like . . .

'You are a love to come and pick me up,' I said to Melody, when I met her at the end of the drive. 'I'm really looking forward to sampling a pint of this local bitter you and Kaya keep going on about.'

'Better stick to a half,' she grinned. 'It's potent stuff. You look lovely, by the way. That's a gorgeous dress and your hair really suits you left loose. I had no idea it was so long.'

'Thank you.' I blushed as I pulled on the seatbelt. 'The dress is new. I picked it up in Sudbury. What with only having enough clothes with me for an extended beach holiday, I thought I'd better get a couple of extra outfits.'

'Well, it looks great. Really light and cool.'

'I love your dress, too,' I told her. 'We need cool clothes in this heat, don't we?'

'Tell me about it,' she agreed. 'I was baking in the store today.'

'You must be mad!'

'I meant hot,' she laughed, as she set off and negotiated the narrow lanes more expertly than I so far had. 'Not literally baking.'

'Thank goodness for that!' I laughed back. 'You should come down to Fernside in the evenings and cool off in the river. Constance wouldn't mind. In fact, she's asked me to invite you, Kaya and Rick to supper in the garden one evening this week.'

'Oh, I'd love that,' Melody said. 'I've heard a couple of older Willowell locals talking about the old days when Constance and her sister used to have parties, but I've never known her to entertain since I've lived in the village. What have you done to her?'

'I'm not sure,' I smiled. 'But I'm happy she's getting her mojo back, whatever's prompted it.'

'You've prompted it,' Melody said with emphasis as she turned the car onto an even bumpier lane. 'You're suiting each other, Tilly, and that's lovely to see.'

'We really are.' I sighed happily and looked up at the canopy of trees above our heads which practically met in the middle. I wondered if deliveries to the pub had to come this way. 'Here's hoping that will continue when I tell her what my plans for the woods are.'

'I'm sure it will,' Melody said kindly. 'And I'd love to come to supper. I'm sure Kaya would, too. She's already at the pub with Rick, so you can ask them at the same time.'

'And you'll swim with me in the river?' I asked.

'Probably not,' Melody sighed. 'Kaya's the mermaid, not me. I'll dangle my feet off the jetty and paddle a bit, but I'm not a strong swimmer.'

'Would you like to be?'

'Maybe,' she shrugged. 'Now, here we are. What do you think?'

The Greenman pub was situated on the right-hand side of the lane we'd driven down, and I could see a sheltered outdoor seating area behind it and a small patch of woodland beyond that. The pub itself was covered in parts with Virginia creeper which made it meld seamlessly into the landscape, and the mullioned windows and chimney doubtless made it feel cosy in the winter.

'I love it,' I said, as we crossed the lane on foot and Melody stepped into the dark interior ahead of me.

'I knew you would.' She beamed as I followed her in and looked around. 'I had a feeling it would be right up your street.'

The inside was shady and cool and decorated in a palette of dark brown and mossy green, with framed photos on the walls. It put me in mind of Tolkien's Shire. I wouldn't have been at all surprised to find Rosie Cotton serving behind the bar, but in her absence, I was introduced to the landlord and owner, Carter Cox.

'Carter, meet Tilly,' Melody smiled. 'Tilly this is Carter. Pub owner, basket weaver and bushcraft expert.' Carter raised his eyebrows. 'And expert beer keeper, of course,' she quickly added.

'I was hoping you were going to mention that, Melody.' Carter winked at her and then smiled at me. 'I'm pleased to meet you, Tilly.'

His Suffolk accent was pronounced, and his voice was deep.

'I'm pleased to meet you, too,' I smiled back.

Thickset and with a greying beard and hands the size of hams, he was quite a few years older than me, probably nearer forty than thirty. He was a handsome man with a weathered complexion who, just like his pub, fitted perfectly into the Suffolk countryside and, given his broad range of talents, might be someone it would be useful for me to get to know properly.

'And don't take any notice of Melody,' he advised, rather dampeningly. 'She's bigging up my bushcraft skills. I haven't had an opportunity to practise them for quite a while.'

'But they're not the sort of thing you forget, are they?' I ventured.

'That's true,' he agreed as he rubbed a hand over his beard and glanced at a beautiful handmade basket next to the currently unlit fire. 'Skills for life.'

'So, Tilly, is bushcraft the sort of thing you're planning—' Melody began but stopped when I gave her a look. 'Never mind.'

'Come on,' I said quickly. 'Let's get the drinks in. I'll go for a pint, please.'

'Sorry,' Melody said, while Carter sorted our order. 'I shouldn't have said anything, but with Carter being such an expert, I got a bit carried away.'

'It's fine,' I said. 'You haven't said anything to anyone else though, have you?'

'No,' she promised. 'Not a soul.'

Kaya then appeared, so I couldn't ask if Melody had heard the rumour Rick had mentioned, too.

'Here you are!' Kaya called from just inside the doorway that led out to the seating area behind the pub. 'I'd all but given up on you two. Come on. We've got pizza.'

'I'll bring the drinks outside,' Carter offered.

'Rick's flirting with the guy cooking the pizzas and it's been such a bore,' Kaya moaned, adding a theatrical and very loud fake yawn for dramatic effect.

'She knows then?' I whispered to Melody.

'Has always known apparently,' Melody laughed. 'But she's forgiven him because he's so lovely to look at.'

'That's big of her!' I laughed.

'And so shallow!'

I daresay she'd say the same about my blatant attraction to James, but we did have things in common that went beyond his good looks.

'Thank you, Carter,' I said, when he arrived carrying a tray full of glasses. 'What do I owe you?'

'I've set up a tab, and you can all settle up at the end of the night,' he said, handing me a half, rather than the full pint of bitter I'd requested, and which, I then remembered, Melody had said I shouldn't go for. 'First one's on the house.'

'And that's not the reason it's a half,' commented Rick, as he came over carrying yet another pizza.

How much did he think we could eat? Though they did look good.

'Thank you, Carter,' I said, raising my glass and taking a long sip. 'Wow,' I sighed, as the rich and earthy flavours danced across my tongue. 'That's delicious.'

'And brewed just up the road,' he told me. 'Now, I'd better get back inside. It's going to be busy tonight.'

'I'm sorry I caused trouble,' Rick said, bending to drop a kiss on my cheek the moment Carter had gone.

'It's fine,' I said, with a shrug, because I just wanted to forget about it. I hadn't liked the way the rumour had sprung back into my mind the moment Melody had put her foot in it and nearly said too much. 'Water under the bridge.'

'Oh god,' said Kaya, standing with her hands on her hips. 'What's he done now?'

'Nothing worth talking about,' I said quickly and changed the subject. 'But there are a couple of other things that are.'

'Go on then,' Kaya encouraged, as she sat down and picked up her glass.

I extended the invitation Constance had sent me with and was delighted when all three of them confirmed that they'd love to come along.

'So, all really is well at Fernside,' Rick smiled. 'You're bringing Constance right out of herself; do you know that Tilly?'

'That's what I said,' commented Melody.

'I'm not sure it really has anything to do with me,' I modestly told them both. 'But I do know one thing that's not so great.'

I took another drink and Melody nudged one of the pizzas towards me.

'Drink *and* eat,' she grinned. 'Otherwise it'll hit you faster.'

'It's only a half,' I laughed.

'A potent one,' Kaya winked.

I picked up a slice and folded it before taking a bite. It was as tasty as the bitter.

'So, come on,' Rick said impatiently. 'What's amiss?'

I finished my mouthful before telling them.

'Constance needs a cleaner for the house,' I sighed. 'But it's proving tricky to find one. And before you say it, we've been through the local directory and she's not happy with anyone listed. And she won't let me do it, either.'

'I'll do it,' Kaya piped up.

I looked at Melody.

'She's really good,' Melody praised and Kaya looked chuffed.

'I do the cottage, and I've got a couple more local jobs now, too,' Kaya expanded. 'The bigger the challenge, the more I'm loving it.'

'Well,' I said, 'Fernside, or the little I've seen of it, could be a good fit for you.'

Was this the beer talking? I hoped Constance wasn't going to be offended that I'd mentioned that she was looking for a cleaner or that I'd suggested that the house needed a good sort out. All I really wanted was to find her some help. And if Kaya was genuinely keen to take the work on, then I'd already found it.

'There's nothing more satisfying than seeing the messy before and sparkling after,' Kaya said and sounded like she meant it. 'And it's keeping me fit while I can't afford to go to a gym, too. I'd be glad to take it on.'

'In that case,' I said, thinking it really would be a bonus to have someone Constance already knew cleaning the house and potentially coming across any cash she'd hidden, 'leave it with me. I'll talk to Constance and come back to you.'

'Great,' Kaya smiled, clinking her glass against mine.

With that settled, we ordered more drinks, tucked into the pizzas and enjoyed the slowly darkening evening and the pretty strings of solar lights that lit up The Greenman garden. I asked Carter, who had managed to spend a decent chunk of time with us, to take a photo of us all smiling like loons. I sent it to Zack in the hope of reassuring him that all was well in my world and to stop him worrying about me. I hoped all was well with him too, but I wasn't sure it was. His emails were becoming less frequent, and I wasn't sure that was all to do with the lack of Wi-Fi.

'Are you sure you can find your way inside?' Melody whispered, when she dropped me back at the house. 'You were a bit wobbly when we left the pub.'

I'd ended up drinking almost two pints of the extra potent bitter and had felt wonderful, until it was time to leave.

'I'm completely fine,' I said, as I climbed out of the car and tried to make my legs behave. 'The drive back with the windows open sobered me right up.'

The massive hiccup I then let escape suggested otherwise and we both put our hands over our mouths to contain a fit of the giggles.

'I'll ring you tomorrow,' I promised, once I'd composed myself. 'Now go, otherwise you'll be too tired to open the store in the morning.'

'Not an option,' Melody smiled. 'Okay. We'll chat tomorrow.'

She drove off and I slipped inside the gate, having eventually remembered that it was locked and I was going to need my key to open it. As I locked it behind me, the sound of piano music drifted across the garden, and I thought how lovely it was that Constance was listening to or playing it again. She'd never confirmed either way when I'd broached the subject.

I had no intention of making her jump or interrupting her evening and crept quietly around to the sitting room and peeped through the open French doors. It was just as well that the music was quite loud because the tipsy gasp that escaped me would have been easily heard, even by someone with Constance's reduced hearing.

'Well, there's my answer,' I whispered, and I watched in awe as her fingers danced quickly and lightly over the keys. I was so mesmerised, I didn't think to take in any of what the rest of the room looked like. 'So, it was you, Constance. You're the musician.'

She was completely absorbed and had no idea that I was there, and I was grateful for that, because for some reason, she obviously didn't want me to know about her talent. I crept silently away, carrying her musical secret with me.

Chapter 11

I hadn't been convinced the bitter really was all that strong, but the following morning I woke with a headache, dry mouth and zero desire to admire the sunlight that was keenly finding its way around the bedroom curtains. Ergo, I had a hangover – something I hadn't experienced in years, and it was a feeling I couldn't wait to see the back of.

'No swim for me this morning,' I croaked. My throat felt dry as I carefully swung my legs out of bed and gingerly set my feet on the floor. 'Nope, definitely not,' I breathed as the world shifted on its axis and then reluctantly resettled.

A trip to the river would have been foolish, so I washed down a couple of painkillers with a pint of water, made myself some sympathy tea and went back to bed. I didn't go to sleep though, because as I slowly resurfaced, I began to think in more detail about the trip to the pub and its landlord, Carter Cox.

I added his name to my notebook. Having talked to him alone a couple of times before my second pint, then admired some of the baskets he'd made and looked at the framed photos of him applying his bushcraft skills that were hung around the pub, I had surmised that he was a genuine man of the woods with loads of experience behind him. He had sounded full of disappointment that he didn't currently have opportunities to practise his crafts, and I wondered if, once everything was up and running, he might be interested in playing some sort of part in my business.

Feeling both inspired and reminiscent, I scrolled through the most recent additions to the Woodland Adventures Insta account and imagined what a business grid of my own could look like. Meeting Carter felt like another serendipitous nudge, and along with suggesting that Kaya might be the perfect cleaner for Constance, I also knew that the time had come to share my vision with her.

I had a bath, then, because it was late, breakfasted alone. I enjoyed the perfect bacon sandwich, enhanced by a smattering of brown sauce, and it perked me up no end. I was just about to leave the apartment when my phone rang. It was a video call from James!

A quick glance in the mirror showed that I didn't look as bad as I'd earlier felt and with a wide smile lighting up my face, I propped up my phone, sat on the sofa and answered the call before it rang off.

'Morning, Tilly,' he greeted me, his own smile matching mine. 'How are you?'

'I'm good,' I nodded. 'Really good.'

I wasn't going to mention the hangover.

'I'm sorry I didn't manage to call you yesterday,' he said.

'That's no problem. You sounded hard at work.'

'I was.' He seemed tired, in spite of his smile. 'And I had a lot of thinking to do, following the unexpected meeting.'

'Nothing too taxing, I hope?'

I had assumed the meeting was to do with the case he was in Sudbury to discuss, but now I wasn't so sure.

'Ever so taxing,' he said distractedly. 'But never mind that now.'

'Well,' I said, wondering what it had been about, 'I was pleased you had enough time to message.'

'You were?'

'Yes,' I smiled. 'I was.' As Constance had said, there was no point playing hard to get when I was already caught. 'So, are you back up to speed now? Have you processed the case notes your boss landed on you?'

'Pretty much,' he told me. 'My phone was a bit of a distraction while I was trying to read them though.'

'How come?'

'Because I kept checking to see if you'd messaged again after you replied to what I'd sent,' he confessed.

I was thrilled that he had wanted to hear more from me.

'You did say you were working,' I pointed out. 'And I didn't want to disturb you.'

'Well, I'm not working now,' he smiled. 'So, when can I see you again?'

'Hang on,' I laughed. 'Aren't you already in trouble? You can't go playing hooky today. Isn't your boss cracking the whip after your late finish yesterday?'

'He is, but I'm dodging it. I've decided I'm going to hang about for the day and travel back to London tonight. Are you free?'

'I've got work plans this morning,' I told him because I didn't want to put off talking to Constance about the business. 'But I'll be free later this afternoon.'

'That works for me,' James grinned.

'Great,' I smiled back. 'So, where shall we meet?'

'I have a wonderful place in mind,' he said instantly. 'It's somewhere I love, but,' he added, 'it won't appeal if you're not an outdoorsy type.'

I knew he loved the Suffolk countryside, but I hadn't been expecting that.

'Well, luckily for you,' I told him, 'I am an outdoorsy type.'

'You've got walking shoes?'

'I have.' I was intrigued. 'Have you?'

'Never travel without them.'

'Okay,' I said as I continued to recalibrate my thoughts about him. 'I have a rucksack, too, if we need to carry anything.'

'Perfect,' he said and gleefully rubbed his hands together. I had mentioned it as a joke, but he sounded thrilled that I came so well equipped. 'You can carry the Kendal mint cake.'

'Where on earth are we going?' I laughed.

'You're not a long way from Sudbury, are you?' he asked, without telling me.

'No, not far.'

'Great,' he said, but then his phone started to bleep with an incoming call. 'Bugger.' He tutted. 'Tilly, sorry I have to go. I'll send you the postcode and a time. Just message back if you don't fancy it or if the time's no good for you. Sorry.'

'No worries,' I said quickly, but he was already gone.

I waited a few minutes to see if James's message was going to land, but when it didn't, I decided to continue with my plan for the morning. I flicked through my notebook, took a deep breath and headed over to the house.

'Oh Constance!' I gasped, when I found her struggling to make tea while wearing wrist supports on both hands. 'Here, let me do that.' She relinquished the kettle without either of us getting scalded. 'What have you done?'

'It's nothing,' she said dismissively. 'Just a bit of arthritis. The splints help.'

I then remembered that I had seen her playing the piano the night before. I had been so caught up curing my hangover and then immersed in the call with James that I'd forgotten all about that.

'Honestly, Tilly,' Constance said more forcefully, when she noticed me staring. 'It's nothing.'

She obviously wasn't going to mention the piano and neither was I. I didn't want her thinking I'd been sneaking around, but I was intrigued to know why she kept her playing a secret. I knew she didn't play all that often because I would have heard her, but was that because of the physical pain it caused her or something else?

'Shall we drink this in the sunroom?' I suggested, inviting myself to join her. 'It's turned chilly since the sun went in, but it'll be warm in there with the door closed.'

It was a snug spot and, thanks to the orchids and various other houseplants Constance was always misting, the air smelt deliciously green and fresh. There was a large jasmine growing there and I couldn't wait to breathe in the scent of that in the spring. Assuming I was still living in the apartment or visiting Fernside then.

'So, how did you get on last night?' Constance asked, as I set her teacup within easy reach on the table next to her chair. 'I noticed you didn't swim this morning.'

'I had a great time,' I told her. I wasn't going to mention the bitter being the reason I hadn't swum. 'It was a late night, and I met some interesting people. One guy in particular has got me thinking this morning.'

'Oh?' She smiled. 'What about your meet-cute? Are you still thinking about him, too?'

'I am thinking about him,' I told her, but didn't say more because I didn't want to get distracted. 'And I didn't mean I'd met someone as in romantically met them. I meant I'd been introduced to someone who has inspired additional thoughts about my business.'

'Oh, I see,' Constance nodded. 'I know you're settling in as I suggested you should, but I can't wait to hear about it. I'm already feeling excited and I don't know what it is yet!'

'Well,' I said, producing my notebook with a flourish, 'today's your lucky day.'

Constance clapped, then winced because she'd forgotten about the splints. 'I'm all ears,' she said, sitting forward.

'I haven't got it *all* worked out yet,' I felt it was important to point out, 'but I thought it was time I shared the gist of it with you.'

'Share away.'

I began by explaining how it was a bee and butterfly covered buddleia growing out of a car park wall that had given me the wake-up call I hadn't realised I needed.

'It was in the car park that belonged to the building that housed my office,' I expanded. 'And when I came out of work one day, I noticed it was covered in butterflies, and it smelt amazing. I watched the insects at work for ages and felt totally soothed before the drive home as a result.'

'How lovely.'

'It was,' I agreed. 'And it made me realise how long it had been since I'd noticed something green and growing. I'd fallen into the all too familiar routine of driving from home to work and back again during the week and then to the supermarket on a Saturday and with nothing else in-between. Or nothing that got me properly outside anyway.'

Lee and I had been in such a rut, but it turned out he was very happy to stay there, whereas I was soon eager to break out. I didn't mention him to Constance because he was consigned to the past and no longer relevant.

'I see,' Constance said.

'And when I talked to some of my colleagues,' I continued, 'I discovered they were in exactly the same situation, but hadn't realised it, either.'

'As are so many other people, I would imagine,' Constance sighed. 'Work isn't just about the hours you're paid to do something, is it? There's often a lengthy and stressful commute to endure before and after it, too.'

'Exactly,' I agreed wholeheartedly. 'And with that in mind, I talked my boss into letting me organise a trip for some staff to visit the local woods. He thought it would be a waste of time, but it wasn't, especially not for me. That excursion, arriving right when I needed it, further reignited my passion for green spaces and kicked so much off.'

'What did you all do there?' Constance asked keenly.

'Oddly enough, given the timing of the trip, *I* shouldn't have been doing anything.'

'What do you mean?'

'When the date for it came through,' I explained, 'I was on

compassionate leave after losing Dad. I was struggling with my grief and nowhere near ready to go back to work. However, staff illness meant that I ended up going, and ultimately I was so grateful that I did because the experience literally brought me back from the brink of this darkness I felt trapped in. It opened my eyes and gave me the fresh start I needed.'

'Oh, Tilly.' Constance sniffed and I felt rather tearful, too.

'We did all sorts,' I said, as I pulled my focus back. 'Shelter-building, fire-lighting, foraging, some outdoor feasting, whittling.'

'That all sounds fun.' Constance smiled and blew her nose.

'It was,' I nodded. 'Everyone achieved something and it helped me so much that soon after, I started to volunteer in the woods myself. My brother and I had made this pact when we were holidaying in Willowell,' I said, filling her in, 'that when we grew up, we'd have outdoor jobs. He's always succeeded in making that happen and now, after a very long hiatus, and I suppose you could say because of my grief, I'm following in his footsteps.'

'I recall you telling me that you'd done some studying and training involving woodland, too,' Constance remembered.

'That's right,' I nodded. 'I'm qualified now to do all of the things my colleagues and I were introduced to on that fateful day, as well as offering guided forest bathing and workshops on how to create nature journals.'

'And as I recall, Carter Cox knows about that sort of thing, doesn't he . . .' Constance said thoughtfully.

'He does,' I confirmed. 'And that's who I've been thinking about this morning.'

Along with James.

'So, is this the sort of business you're planning to set up in Willowell Woods? Something that will offer people the opportunity to try their hand at the things you've learned how to do.'

'That's exactly it,' I confirmed. 'I want to offer as many people as possible, of all ages and abilities, the opportunity to reconnect with nature, relax in it and relearn some long-forgotten skills. I would love to see more people embracing the changing seasons and understanding how breathing in some fresh air and watching green things growing can benefit their mental health. And,' I finished up as I caught my breath, 'I think Willowell Woods will be the perfect place to enable them to do it.'

It sounded like the perfect pitch to me, but then I wasn't the person who had the family connection to the place and generations worth of history attached to it, was I?

'No wonder you were so pleased to hear about Grace's nursery having been run from there in the past,' Constance said ponderously as she seriously took my flushed face in. 'And the building still being in place is a bonus, too.'

'And the car park,' I reminded her. 'That's a huge plus. So, what do you think?'

She was quiet for a few agonising seconds as she drank her tea.

'Opening the woods up for people to explore . . .' she said, once she'd put her cup down again. 'Opening the gate and letting folk back into the place.' I wasn't sure what conclusion she was going to come to, and I could feel my cheeks turning even redder as I held my breath. 'I think . . .'

'Yes?'

I was sitting so close to the edge of my seat, I was poised to fall off it.

'I think it sounds like the most wonderful idea anyone could have possibly come up with!' she finally said, and I couldn't decide whether to laugh or cry.

In the end, I expressed my relief, excitement and gratitude by having both a joyful laugh and shedding a few happy tears.

'Are you sure you mean it, Constance?' I asked, once I'd wiped my eyes, blown my nose and almost composed myself. 'You don't want to think about it a bit longer?'

She smiled and handed me another tissue. It was lucky she always had a pocketful.

'I do not,' she said with conviction. 'This is the ideal next adventure for Willowell Woods. The thought of selling them didn't initially sit comfortably with me, but I soon came to realise it was for the best and knowing that you're going to be the person who buys them is the best possible outcome. I hope I'll be able to come and see it all once you're up and running.'

This was really going to happen!

'I'm intending to get you there a lot sooner than that, Constance,' I told her eagerly. 'Path-clearing is going to be a priority and then you'll be able to wander around the place without a care in the world.'

A shadow fleetingly crossed her face. It happened so quickly that I wondered if I had imagined it, but I hadn't. It was gone in an instant but the sight of it troubled me for a minute.

'I shall look forward to that,' she said. 'And why don't you get Rick to survey the trees and gives us an idea of the cost to carry out the work? I'd like to get that done before you take the place over.'

'I'm happy to pay for that,' I said firmly. 'Along with the right price for the woods once you've had them properly valued.' She began to look mutinous. 'That's non-negotiable.'

'Oh, all right,' she relented. 'And while all this gets going, you should start making enquiries as to the likelihood of getting permission. I haven't forgotten that you said you wouldn't be able to take the woods on if you couldn't make them work for you.'

I reached for my notebook and started making a new list. Now that Constance had given me her seal of approval, I could begin to set the wheels in motion. I refused to allow any doubts to worm their way in. This was an amazing moment and I was full of optimism and determined to embrace it.

My vision nonetheless clouded with unshed tears, as I wished that there was some way I could have shared with Dad what was happening. I still talked to him on occasion and I would certainly be thanking him again for making this a financial possibility, but how I wished I could show him around and make him a part of the venture.

'Penny for them,' Constance said softly, as I sat with my pen poised over the page.

'I was wishing that Dad was here and could be a part of this.' I swallowed. 'Though if he was, I wouldn't have the money to do it.'

'And I was just thinking how much I'd love Grace to know what was going to happen, but then if she was here, her nursery would be too.'

We looked at one another, both bright-eyed again and missing relatives who had meant the world to us.

'Dad always said he thought it was unfair that he got to live so much more life than Mum did and I suppose I feel a bit that way myself about him now. He wasn't all that old when he died . . .'

'But if he hadn't gone, my dear, your trip to Woodland Adventures might not have been as impactful,' Constance suggested tenderly, 'and you wouldn't now be creating something to benefit so many other people.'

'You're right,' I said stoically. 'And I owe it to him to live my very best life, don't I?'

Constance looked at her hands and nodded. 'Yes,' she said croakily. 'We shouldn't forget how lucky we are to still be here. And we should strive to make the most of our talents, even if it is hard sometimes . . .'

I suddenly realised that she had felt guilty about exercising her musical talent ever since Grace had died and that was why she kept her piano playing a secret and only indulged in it every now and then.

'We have to live life to the fullest, don't we?' I said.

'We do,' she agreed. 'I'm finally coming to terms with that and now we've got you sorted, if I can find someone to get the house shipshape, I might find myself ready to expand my horizons, too.'

'Oh, for pity's sake,' I tutted. 'I can't believe I forgot to tell you! I've found you a cleaner, Constance.'

'You have?'

I remembered then what she had said about Kaya being flighty. I hoped her impression of Melody's sister wouldn't put her off.

'Yes,' I said. 'Kaya would love to take it on. And apparently, she loves a challenge. Melody says she works wonders in Rose

Cottage on handover days and she's got another couple of local employers now, too.'

Constance gave that some thought. 'On the occasions I've met her, Kaya's always seemed a rather capricious young woman,' she said eventually, and I thought I'd failed, 'but she's full of energy and if Melody's happy with her work, then I think we'll give her a shot. It would be a comfort to have someone else working here who I already know.'

'We'll have to give her a heads up about your hidden cache.' I smiled as my phone pinged. 'And put another loot tin in the kitchen for her to put it in if she finds any.'

'Good idea,' Constance agreed. 'Would you mind having a word with her and seeing if she can make a start before the supper party?'

'Leave it with me,' I said, as I surreptitiously read the message. It was from James, and it made my eyebrows shoot up. 'I've got to go out this afternoon, but I'll talk to her first thing tomorrow.'

'Going anywhere nice?' Constance asked, with a nod to my phone.

'I'll let you know when I've been,' I beamed.

Chapter 12

Having keyed the details James had sent me into my satnav, I set off towards Sudbury with one eye on the weather. The day had started sunnily enough, if a little on the cool side, but I could see dark clouds gathering and that didn't bode well for the location he'd picked for our . . . date. Was it a date? I had no idea, but whatever it was, it was probably now going to be damp. I hoped that wasn't a portent related to our decision to meet again.

I had just pulled into a space in the town's leisure centre car park when the first few drops of rain hit the windscreen and I got the feeling that my lightweight jacket wasn't going to be enough to keep me dry on the walk around the local water meadows.

James had wonderfully but unexpectedly suggested The Meadow Walk, which was part of the longer Gainsborough Trail, but perhaps I shouldn't have been surprised about his choice given that he'd got excited about walking shoes and a rucksack.

'I can see you,' he said, when I answered his call.

'Do you have any idea how terrifying those four words are to a woman on her own?' I pointed out, as the rain began to drum more noisily on the car roof.

'I realised that the second the sentence left my mouth. Sorry,' he groaned. 'What I should have said was, have you arrived yet? I just saw a car pull in and I think it might have been yours.'

'That's more like it,' I said, looking around and spotting where he'd parked. 'And I can see you, too.'

'Now *I'm* freaked out,' he said, and I laughed. 'Stay where you are and I'll come over.'

He was only a matter of seconds, but in that time the rain started to hammer down harder and there was a distant rumble of thunder. It was hard to hear it clearly over the noise of the rain, but it was undeniably thunder.

'Ah!' James hollered, as he yanked opened the passenger side door, jumped into the seat and slammed the door shut again. 'Where the hell has this come from?'

'Hello, James,' I said, deadpan, as he stuffed a bag in the footwell in front of him.

'Hello, Tilly,' he responded breathlessly and laughed. 'How are you?'

'Considerably drier than you.' I smiled and handed him some sheets of kitchen towel.

'Why have you got kitchen towel in your car?'

'For moments like these, of course,' I told him. 'And aren't you grateful that I have?'

He rubbed the sheets over his face, round the back of his neck and through his hair, making it stand up on end.

'Yes,' he said, as he screwed it up. 'I am and I'll make sure to carry some in my own car from now on.'

'And a rubbish bag, too,' I said as I took the towel from him and stuffed it in the bag I also kept in the car for such occasions.

'Are you always so organised?' he grinned.

'You're a fine one to talk,' I teased. 'You said earlier that you've got a stock of Kendal mint cake.'

'But I was joking about that,' he said. 'Though I do have supplies.' He pointed at the Waitrose bag he'd brought with him as another rumble of thunder, louder that time, rolled overhead. 'I thought we might want something to eat and drink after our walk, but I'm not sure if you're going to want to get out of the car now?'

'Are you?' I laughed. 'In this.'

We'd been having to practically shout to make ourselves heard, but suddenly and thankfully, the cacophony quietened a little.

'No,' he sighed and bit his lip. The action made the temperature in the car spike. Or perhaps that was just me. 'I suppose not and I was really looking forward to it.'

'You're full of surprises, aren't you?' I said, because he was.

'What do you mean?'

'You're a barrister who prefers to work for free,' I reeled off. 'The day we first met, you were wearing an extremely expensive looking suit and today you're wearing . . .'

'TK Maxx,' he said, plucking at the fabric of the damp shirt. 'This was an excellent find in TK Maxx.'

'You drive a mid-range car and your idea of a first . . . date,' I hesitated to say the word out loud, but he didn't baulk at it, 'is a walk around some water meadows.'

'Are you disappointed?' he asked earnestly.

'Absolutely not,' I declared. 'If anything, I'm relieved and I think you're great. A conundrum, but a great one.'

'Well, that's all right then,' he said, settling deeper into the seat, 'because I think you're great, too.'

I could feel my cheeks starting to flame and cracked the windows a little. They were steaming up as much as I was.

'So,' I said. 'What made you pick here rather than a pub or café?'

'I'm back off to London later,' he reminded me, then surprised me again by adding, 'and I needed a green space top up before I'm chained to my desk again. I grew up in a very outdoorsy family, and I've never kicked the habit. I go a bit stir crazy if I don't get outside and look at a tree or a patch of grass every day, and I know London has parks and so on, but not near where I work.'

I'd never met a more perfect man.

'I'm the same,' I told him and, unable to suppress my feelings, I could feel my smile was as wide as my face.

'That's makes us a match then,' he beamed in response. 'My last partner ditched me because I wanted to go camping in the Lake District rather than spend a fortnight poolside somewhere scorching hot. Sorry.' He looked mortified. 'That was ages ago, and clearly I'm out of the dating habit. Who brings up an ex on a first date?'

He sounded mortified which made him even more endearing.

'If it makes you feel any better,' I consoled him, 'I can talk about my ex, too. He dumped me because I'd transformed back into an outdoorsy type who didn't want to spend her weekends watching sport on TV.'

'I do feel better,' James nodded. 'Thanks for sharing that. Not that I'm happy about your break-up, of course. Though if you hadn't broken up . . .'

It struck me then that he might have been feeling a bit nervous.

'All in the past,' I smiled. 'And that's enough about exes. Why don't you tell me why you didn't pick an outdoor career as you're such a fresh air fiend? I can't imagine there's much scope for open air courtrooms.'

'Can you imagine?' he said and ran a hand through his hair. 'That would be amazing.'

'You'd end up cloud watching and losing your thread in an argument.'

'You're so right,' he said and ducked his head. 'And I know this explanation will probably sound really corny, but the truth is, I had this urge after Mum died to do some good in the world and striving for justice felt like the right course to take.'

'Does it still?' I asked and he twisted in the seat so he could properly look at me. 'From what you've said before, I've got the impression that you're not currently enjoying your work. Or some of it, anyway.'

'You're right,' he sighed. 'I love the pro bono stuff, that's where my heart is, but the rest of it . . . I've only been with this firm for about eighteen months, but I knew I'd made a mistake within days of moving to them.'

'What were you doing before?'

'Practically all pro bono work with a practice on the Essex–Suffolk border.'

'And why did you leave?'

'Money,' he said bluntly.

'Oh.'

'Money and ego.'

'That doesn't sound like the guy I thought I was getting to know,' I frowned.

'It was completely out of character,' he quickly explained.

'But I found myself needing to make a lot more money and the boss of the firm I've now moved to was both persuasive and very determined to poach me. He said all the right things and made me an offer I simply couldn't turn down.'

'You must be very good at your job if he was so keen to have you.'

'I get by,' he said self-effacingly. 'And the money is great, but he also promised I could spend twenty per cent of my time continuing with the pro bono work.'

'But you're finding that isn't enough?' I asked, as I flicked the window wipers on.

The sky was completely grey, and it was still pouring with rain.

'It isn't actually anywhere near the twenty per cent he promised and now he's pressuring me to do less and less all the time.'

'So,' I sighed, 'you're finding the money isn't worth it.'

'The money definitely isn't worth it,' he repeated. 'But I still need it.'

I was curious to know what he was doing with it.

'Would it offend you if I asked why?' I ventured. 'Do you have a shocking secret lifestyle to fund?'

'It's nothing like that,' he said seriously and I knew he was being honest with me. 'There are no skeletons in my closet or bad habits, either.'

'So, what is it then?'

'There's something precious that belongs in my family and by topping up the collective coffers, I'm helping to keep it there.'

'So, this job is an entirely selfless trade-off then,' I said, saying it as I saw it. 'You're doing something you're not happy to do, but for the greater good.'

'You make me sound like a saint or something,' James protested. 'I'm not that, but I'm doing, and will continue to do, everything I can to keep things as they are. Even when temptation is thrown in my path . . .'

'Temptation?'

'The unexpected meeting I mentioned was with my former boss. He called me up out of the blue and, when we met, he told me he wants me to go back and take the job I had before.'

'So, you *could* go back to doing what you love full-time?'

The expression in his eyes was heartbreaking.

'I could,' he said, 'but at the expense of losing the very thing I've been fighting to keep.'

'Oh, James,' I sympathised and laid a hand on his arm, 'that's so unfair.'

He placed his hand over mine, and even though we were having a heartfelt conversation, I felt my pulse quicken and my temperature rise. It continued to escalate as our eyes locked and neither of us looked away.

'It's the pits,' he sighed and I felt myself leaning towards him.

'What are you going to do?' I swallowed.

'The only thing I can do, carry on.'

His gaze dipped to my lips, and I found myself looking at his. Without a word, we began to move closer and then the loudest crack of thunder ripped through the sky and we sprang apart. On reflection, it was the oddest moment to lean in, but I found he was like a magnet. We'd barely spent any time together, but I knew I could fall fathoms deep for him if I let myself.

'I think that's Thor's way of saying you're a valiant man, James,' I said, once I'd caught my breath. 'And I'm in complete agreement with him about that.'

'Thank you,' he smiled.

'Now, come on,' I nudged, to give us a moment to recover. 'Tell me what you've got in that bag?'

He had put together a wonderful picnic, and as we munched our way through it, the windows misted up to the point where I had to turn the engine over to clear them.

'I wasn't sure we'd want all of that,' James said, once we'd put the rubbish in my bag and as he used the hand wipes I also kept in the car. 'But I'm pleased I picked it up.'

'I was hungrier than I thought,' I told him, 'so it was appreciated. Thank you.'

I hoped Constance had bothered to have something. I'd check on her when I got back.

'So,' said James, 'you've listened to me moaning about my work, now tell me something exciting about this childhood dream you're following.'

'I can understand why you said you envy me now,' I sighed, as the penny dropped. 'But if it wasn't for the money Dad left me, I wouldn't be pursuing my dream. I'm not the sort of person who makes massive life changes without a plan and some security.'

James grinned.

'What?'

'The kitchen towel, wipes and rubbish bag were a bit of a clue,' he quipped.

'Are you teasing me?' I pretended to huff. 'You've needed all three of those things this afternoon.'

'I'm not teasing you,' he said, putting his hands up. 'I'm grateful. And I think we're probably similar in lots of ways we haven't even mentioned yet.'

'I take my time when it comes to making big decisions and I need to feel safe before I jump.' He nodded in agreement. 'I'm more laid-back than I used to be, but I do still like to know I've got some security,' I explained.

To any outsider looking in, my unusual business idea might have seemed at odds with what I'd just said, but if it wasn't for the financial security Dad had given me, I wouldn't even be considering pursuing it. And even now, if it didn't look like I'd be able to secure permission, I wouldn't buy the woods on a whim. Not that I wanted to think about the possibility of failing.

'I'm the same,' James nodded. 'I'm all for security, too. The pro bono work didn't fund anything like the lifestyle I could be leading now if I didn't have other commitments, but it was steady and regular and enough.'

'I'm pleased to hear you say that about the comfort of security,' I admitted. 'Because I was wondering if you might think I was totally boring.'

'Far from it.'

'Pursuing my childhood dream might sound impulsive, but it's all planned out. It's not a whim. My brother on the other hand,' I reflected, 'is the total opposite. He's all for flying in feet first without a care for the future.'

James shuddered.

'Exactly.' I applauded. 'I'm more chilled than I used to be, but my brother's way of going about things is still anathema to me.'

'And me. So, how is it coming on, this carefully thought-out plan of yours?'

'Slowly,' I nodded. 'I only presented the idea for the first time this morning to the person who will have an influence over whether it comes off.'

'That's a huge step though, Tilly,' James cheered. 'A massive leap. How was it received?'

'With much enthusiasm,' I was thrilled to be able to tell him. 'A green light all the way.'

'So, you're off and running then?'

'Not quite, because there's loads to do before I launch. It will take months, but I've made a very good start.'

'Tell me then, what is it you want to do?'

'Let's just say,' I said mysteriously, 'it's something very outdoorsy.'

'Is that really all you're going to tell me?'

'For now.'

'When you know I'm a . . . what did you call me . . . a fresh air fiend!'

'Sorry.'

'Well,' he said, as he reached for my hand and stroked the back of it, causing the air to rush out of my lungs. 'At least I know it's something I'll be able to get excited about. Outdoorsy is definitely my thing.'

'Something fundamental we have in common,' I said happily. It felt wonderful to share that passion, but it was awful that James couldn't follow his heart, especially when he'd been offered another chance to. 'Are you really going to have to turn your old boss down?' I asked sadly.

'I am,' James sighed. 'I can't do anything else, but at least I can live vicariously through you, Tilly. Follow your dream for me.'

'I will,' I promised, 'but I'm sorry you can't have what you want, too.'

'So am I,' he agreed, 'but it's worth it. And that's what I mustn't lose sight of. I have to keep reminding myself that I'm doing this job with good reason. Very good reason.'

He gently let go of my hand to check his phone, which had just beeped, and I thought he must love his family very much. I noticed he was wearing a Rolex as he picked the phone up. A vintage Rolex.

'Damn,' he muttered.

'What is it?' I frowned.

'A traffic alert. It looks like I'm going to have the journey from hell back to London.'

'That's the last thing you need,' I tutted.

'It's never pleasant. I think I'd better head off.'

'Okay,' I nodded. 'Will you let me know when you're safely back?'

'I will,' he said and leant over to lightly brush my cheek with his soft, full lips. 'I'm sorry the weather has let us down.'

He hadn't moved more than an inch, and I could feel the heat between us.

'I'm sorry you didn't get your green space top up,' I whispered.

'Next time.' He smiled and moved to pick up the bag.

'Next time,' I echoed, and with another heart stopping smile, he was gone.

Chapter 13

Constance was keen to know how my trip had gone when I popped in to see her early that evening, but I didn't fill her in. Instead, I cited the weather as scuppering my plans and I didn't mention what I'd been up to. Nor did I mention it to Melody the following day when I went to tell Kaya the good news about Constance wanting to take her on.

James and I had shared a few messages since he'd arrived back in London, and even though I knew I had good friends now to confide in, I wanted to hug whatever was developing between us to myself for a little bit longer. If things progressed further, then I'd talk about him. Perhaps even invite him to Fernside. How wonderful would that be? Swimming with him in the river would be a total treat and I got the feeling Constance would appreciate a man with principles and a strong sense of family loyalty.

'So, Kaya, what do you think?'

'I can't wait to get stuck in,' she clapped. 'I've only ever seen the house from the other side of the river, but it looks pretty big.'

'I've only seen the kitchen and hall myself,' I told her, 'so I can't tell you exactly how much there is to do. It might be a general tidy up or it could be a massive mucking out.'

'Fingers crossed for the latter,' she said, as she rushed off to check her cleaning supplies.

'If you'd have told me that my sister would find her vocation on the end of a feather duster, I never would have believed it,' Melody chuckled, as she watched her go.

'I might not know her all that well,' I joined in, 'but it would have taken me by surprise, too.'

'Fancy joining me for lunch?' Melody offered.

'Thanks, but not today. I thought I might head back to the pub.'

'You're a glutton for punishment!' She laughed again. 'Did you have a hangover?'

'A tiny one,' I confessed. I didn't add that talking to a guy I'd recently met in the intimate setting of my car during a thunderstorm had completely cured me of it. 'But I'm not going for the bitter. It's Carter I want to see.'

'Oh really,' she said in a sing-song voice. 'He's single, you know.'

'No,' I said, playing along. 'I didn't know, but that is interesting.'

'I knew he'd be your type,' Melody winked. 'What with that whole "man of the woods" thing he's got going on. I had a feeling you two would click.'

I realised then that she'd thought I was being serious and when I considered Carter's interests aligning so well with mine, I could understand why.

'I was only joking,' I said, hopefully nipping her desire to matchmake in the bud. 'It's true I do like a guy with a passion for the great outdoors.' An image of James and I walking hand in hand around Willowell Woods sprang to mind. 'But Carter's not my type, Melody.'

'Give it time,' she smiled. 'From tiny acorns and all that.'

I didn't even try to think of a comeback for fear of being told the lady doth protest too much.

'Tilly!' Carter warmly greeted me when I arrived at The Greenman. 'What can I get you? A whole pint or a half?'

'Ha, ha. Very funny,' I smiled. 'That stuff should come with a warning. Tastes delicious but has one heck of a kick.'

'To be fair,' he reminded me, 'we did try to warn you.'

'Um,' I conceded. 'That's true and next time I will take more notice.'

'So, there'll be a next time then?'

'Definitely,' I grinned. 'But today I'll have lemonade, please.'

'Very wise.'

'It's quiet in here,' I observed, while he poured my drink and added a slice of lemon and lots of ice.

'It's always like this until early evening,' he said, looking around. 'Sometimes I wonder if it's worth opening during the day.'

'What would you do if you didn't?'

'I dunno,' he said, keying the amount I owed into the card reader.

'Maybe you could brush up on your bushcraft skills again,' I suggested.

'I suppose I could,' he nodded. 'Perhaps we could find somewhere to do it together. You said it was something you were keen on too, didn't you? What do you think?'

I took a sip of my lemonade. It was fizzy and cold, the perfect combination because now the storm had cleared out it was hot again.

'I am keen,' I told him. 'And in fact, I already have the perfect place in mind to do it.'

'Go on,' Carter encouraged.

'Willowell Woods.'

'Willowell Woods?' He frowned. 'They're up for sale, aren't they?'

'They were,' I corrected him. 'But they're off the market now because the owner, Constance Clarke, has agreed to let me buy them.'

'Really?'

'Really.'

'Well, I never.' He was agog and I wondered if he was thinking about the rumour that had been discussed in this very bar.

'She loves the sound of what I've got in mind for them and, as long as I can get permission to set the business up, it'll be all systems go.'

'A business?' Carter questioned, sounding even more surprised. 'What sort of business?'

'Can you keep a secret?' I asked him.

'I'm famous for it,' he said proudly.

'I hope you mean that,' I said seriously.

'I do.' He nodded. 'I hear all sorts in here, but I never comment and I never pass anything on, either.'

'Well, in that case . . .'

As there were no other customers requiring his attention, I was able to fill Carter in with the same details I had shared with Constance. He asked lots of sensible questions and made a few noteworthy suggestions, too.

'Crikey,' he whistled, when I'd finished telling him, and after I had added some of the things he'd said to my notebook. 'That sounds amazing. I haven't seen the woods myself, but with a car park and cabin on-site, you've already got everything you need.'

'I can't deny it's a relief to hear you say that,' I puffed. 'Constance knows that a business works there, because her sister had a very successful woodland nursery on the site years ago, but you've got experience of the skills and crafts I want to offer, and you also think it's a good idea.'

'I think it's an excellent idea,' he said vehemently. 'It would be amazing to have something local that offers this sort of thing. I've heard of nothing else like it for miles.'

Carter's opinion was worth its weight in gold and his enthusiasm for the idea prompted me to take the conversation a step further.

'And would you possibly consider helping out?'

'What do you mean?'

'When the business is up and running, would you be interested in offering a few classes in the crafts that you're most experienced in? I'm not looking for a huge commitment at this point, obviously, but it would be good to know if it's something you'd be open to considering.'

'Well now,' he said, after he'd looked intently at one of the photos he'd hung behind the bar. In it, he was standing in the middle of a woodland clearing, leaning on a carved stick and smiling at the camera. 'I'd have to give it more thought before I said a resounding yes, but I am keen, Tilly. I'm very keen.'

'I hoped you would be,' I grinned. 'But there's no rush. There's plenty of time for you to mull it over.'

'I already am,' he chuckled. 'In fact, do you know what? I'm going to get back on it this week and start honing my skills straight away.'

I had obviously ignited a spark and not the sort Melody had been hinting at.

'Fantastic.' I beamed and raised my glass to toast him. 'I'm so pleased you're interested and all I ask is that you keep what I've told you completely to yourself.'

'Of course.'

'Once things are a bit further down the line, I'll be happy to go public, but it's too early yet.'

'You can count on me,' Carter promised again and I had the feeling that he was someone I could genuinely rely on.

'I am planning to tell Melody, Kaya and Rick soon,' I told him. 'But that's it. Close friends only.'

It felt wonderful to have some.

'Good plan,' Carter agreed. 'And if there's any arb work that needs to be done, Rick's your fella for that.'

'There is,' I told him, 'and funnily enough, Constance and I have already thought of asking him.'

'Of course you have,' Carter nodded and smiled.

'We're having a supper party with the others at Fernside soon, and we'd love it if you could come along, but I don't suppose you'll be able to get away, will you?'

'Is this when you'll be sharing your news with the gang?'

'It is.'

'In that case, leave it with me. I'll be there.'

'Fantastic.'

'What a great day this is turning out to be!'
'I couldn't agree more,' I very happily assented.

I arrived back at Fernside in an ecstatic mood. Not only had I secured Kaya as Constance's new cleaner, I'd also now got Carter properly fired up about refreshing his bushcraft skills and potentially helping me out in the woods. It would be good to occasionally have someone else for the visitors to work with and I believed we would each bring something different to the table.

'So, isn't that fabulous news?' I again said to Constance who seemed less enthused than I had hoped she would once I'd filled her in. 'Kaya is as keen as mustard and Carter is really excited about the business,' I repeated.

'That's wonderful, dear,' Constance said, but I could see she was preoccupied. 'I've already said I'm thrilled.'

She hadn't quite put it like that.

'Has something happened?' I frowned.

'What do you mean?'

'Well,' I swallowed. 'It's just that I thought you'd be as fired up as I am, but if you're having doubts about it all, you can say—'

'No, no.' She quickly cut me off and patted my hand. 'It's nothing like that . . .'

'But there is something?'

'Nothing for you to worry about,' she said unconvincingly. 'Now, if you don't mind, I think I'll head upstairs for a little nap. It's rather warm again, isn't it?'

I headed back to the apartment and whiled away a bit of time adding to the notes I'd made in the pub. By the time I'd finished mapping out phase two of the venture, I was feeling in a buoyant mood again and decided I'd ring Zack and fill him in.

It had, I realised, been an age since we'd talked properly and I had a horrible feeling that I'd been rather self-absorbed since I'd moved into the garden apartment. So much for my intentions about us keeping in closer touch. I supposed old habits die hard, but that was no excuse, especially when Zack had been hinting that something was amiss.

I tried and failed to get through to him at least half a dozen times, but worryingly with no success. Before I started to spiral into a panic that he wasn't picking up, I reminded myself that he was in Bali, in a remote rural area with little connection to the rest of the world and that doubtless accounted for his inability to respond to my reaching out.

Following the pep talk, I still needed a distraction to stop me fretting and thought I'd try James.

'James! Oh, I can't see you. Is your camera off?'

'Tilly,' he said, sounding tense. 'Yeah, yeah it is. Hi. I'm driving and sometimes the camera plays up. How's your day been?'

He sounded blunt as well as tense.

'Good.' This was a dramatic understatement because the last few hours aside it had been fantastic. 'Really productive. You?'

'Um,' he said and I thought I heard a horn honk. 'Pretty much the worst. I don't think my day could have been more of a disaster.'

'Oh.' I swallowed. 'I'm sorry to hear that.' He didn't respond. 'Was it a work-related thing or—'

'Nope.' He cut me off. 'Something else. A family thing.'

'Right,' I said. 'I see. Sorry.'

I couldn't say more than that because other than knowing his mum had died and he'd never known his dad, I was clueless about who else he was related to and why they'd be giving him grief. Perhaps it was something to do with the thing he was working so hard to keep in the family, but as he was in a bad mood and driving, I didn't ask.

'Look,' he sighed, 'I'm the one who's sorry. You've just caught me at a really bad time. Can I call you later and apologise for being so grumpy, when I'm not feeling so . . . grumpy?'

'Of course,' I said. 'I shouldn't have called.'

'Don't apologise,' he groaned, 'because that will make me feel even worse. I'm the one in a mood and you sounded so happy when you rang. Do you want to tell me about your day?'

'I do,' I said. 'But it'll keep.'

'Sure?'

'Totally.'

'You aren't going to ghost me after this, are you?'

'Um,' I said in a sing-song tone. 'Not sure. Maybe.'

He laughed at that.

'Well,' he said, 'I wouldn't blame you if you did. I'll catch you later, yes?'

'Perhaps,' I smiled.

'Maybe,' he said, and with that, I rang off.

Chapter 14

Not being able to contact my brother, combined with the distracted and grumpy moods Constance and James had respectively been in, rubbed off on me a bit and the resultant dip in my own outlook rather took the shine off what should have been the happiest day, as did the fact that James didn't call back. So, after a restless night spent mostly tossing and turning, and following my regular river swim, which felt nowhere near as restorative as usual, I headed to the place that I knew was guaranteed to cheer me up.

With a packed rucksack, and the keys Constance had given me, I drove back to the woods. Having missed out on a second proper look around the day Rick had found me in the cabin, I intended to take a walk with a view to nourishing my soul, rather than thinking about my business plans.

Thwarted again by the rusty padlock on the gate, I climbed over and set off in the direction of the pond. It took me a while to get there and not only because of the brambles and nettles that barred my way and had to be negotiated.

'A nuthatch, treecreepers and a great spotted woodpecker,' I recited, as I added the birds I had seen to a page in the back of my notebook. 'And that's on top of the blackbirds, thrush, robins and wrens.'

The tally was impressive considering I'd only been in the woods a few minutes and I thought that birdwatching trips would make an interesting addition to everything else I was intending to offer. So much for not thinking about my plan . . . not that thinking about it took anything away from the pleasure of walking around the woods, connecting to the earth and grounding myself again. I defied anyone to come here and not feel better about life by the time they left.

I'd just set out a blanket and my breakfast when my phone started to ring. I thought I'd misheard for a moment because under the branches of the largest oak tree I'd so far discovered was the last place I would have expected to pick up a signal.

'I'm a horrible, miserable ogre and I'm sorry,' were the words that greeted me when I answered it.

'Hello, James,' I laughed.

'How did you know it was me? My number gave me away, I suppose.'

'No,' I said as I eased off my walking trainers, sat down and folded my legs underneath me. 'I didn't see that.'

'What then?'

'You were the only horrible, miserable ogre I was waiting to hear from. Everyone else in my life is perfectly delightful.'

Apart from Constance. She hadn't really been an ogre the day before, but she hadn't been her usual self either. I'd go and see her once I'd finished my breakfast and felt further soothed by my time among the trees.

'Oh great,' James pretended to huff. 'So, everyone else's perfect behaviour has made mine look even worse.'

'And the fact that you didn't ring back last night like you said you would hasn't done you any favours, either,' I batted back lightly.

'Ah now, actually,' James said, and I could tell he was smiling even though we didn't have our cameras on, 'I did you a favour there because my filthy mood continued right throughout the evening and almost to bedtime. Consider my silence a merciful act. I spared you from more of my grumpiness.'

'Almost to bedtime,' I repeated pensively. 'Did the situation resolve itself by then?'

'Sadly not,' James informed me. 'That's still unresolved.'

'So, what or who did cheer you up then?'

I found myself hoping it was a what, rather than a who.

'My buddy,' he said simply.

A who then, but not necessarily an overly friendly one.

'Well, thank them for me, will you?' I requested. 'Because I'm breakfasting in a beautiful spot this morning and I would have hated you to call still in a grumpy mood and spoil it.'

'Where exactly are you?' he asked.

I looked around with my rose-tinted spectacles sat firmly in place. They ensured that the state of the pond and the abundance of brambles barely registered.

'Paradise,' I breathed. 'An outdoor paradise.'

'Sounds nice,' James huffed. 'I'm jealous.'

'Nice is such an insipid word,' I tutted. 'Glorious is a far better description.'

'Are you alone?'

'I am. Not a buddy in sight. Are you really feeling better?'

'Yes and no,' he said. 'Quite a lot has happened since our car picnic.'

'Such as?' I asked and sat up straighter.

'Well, for a start, I can't help thinking about the job offer from my old boss.'

'I'm pleased to hear it, but I thought that was a non-starter.'

'I did too, initially,' he frowned. 'But seeing how fired up and excited you are to follow your heart has cast a different light on my determination to carry on regardless.'

'I'm not sure I'm comfortable with the sound of that,' I told him. 'I'd hate to be responsible for inadvertently encouraging you to make another decision you might regret. You're carrying on regardless for family, after all.'

'Family who are currently doing themselves no favours where I'm concerned,' he sighed. 'But don't worry, like I said, I'm still just thinking about it, rather than acting on it.'

'Well, that's good,' I said. 'We do like a plan, don't we?'

'We do,' he agreed. 'I can't wait to see you again,' he said, after a moment of quiet.

'Likewise,' I said, smiling. 'But there's not much chance of that now you're back in London,' I pointed out.

'I'm not going to be here more than a couple of hours.'

'How come?'

'My boss took umbrage that I was away longer than I said I'd be and is sending me to Cambridge. There's a case there that he wants me to take on at short notice.'

'Another one?' I frowned. 'He sounds like a right piece of work.'

'He's that and more,' James laughed.

On the one hand, I was sorry that he'd annoyed his boss who I knew was already unhappy with him, but on the other, Cambridge wasn't all that far away.

'I'll be working through the case notes with my colleague tomorrow and from then on immersed in the trial until it comes to an end,' he said.

'And what about this afternoon?' I asked. 'I could drive over to Cambridge and meet you if you like. It's not far.'

'Really?'

'Really, but only if you haven't already made plans.'

'I haven't had time to make plans, and even if I had, I would have cancelled them for ones that involved spending time with you again, Tilly.'

That declaration caused a blush to bloom and more than justified the journey. Given that going forward I was going to be occupied with my own plans and James was going to be in court, I thought we owed it to each other to make the most of an unexpected opportunity to see one another again.

'That's made my morning,' I smiled.

'Good. It was meant to.'

'So, where shall we meet?' I asked. 'I don't know Cambridge at all.'

'How about the botanic garden?' he suggested, and I felt my breath catch. He must have heard it, too, because he then said, 'Or don't you trust the forecast? It did rather let us down before, didn't it?'

'Oh, I don't know,' I laughed. 'I very much enjoyed our car picnic, and I would love to see the gardens. I've never visited. Have you?'

'Many times,' he told me, and given what I now knew of his passion for spending time outdoors, I wasn't anywhere near as surprised as I would have been to hear him say it the day we first met. 'There's a lovely café in the grounds, so we could grab a bite to eat there once I've shown you all my favourite spots and you've discovered some of your own.'

'Fantastic,' I smiled. 'That sounds wonderful.'

'I couldn't agree more.'

'Okay, well, it's almost eight now,' I said, checking the time, 'so when do you suggest we meet?'

'We want to make the most of the day, and as I'm ready to set off now, how does half eleven at the garden entrance sound? Is that too soon for you?'

A quick look at the route confirmed that I could be there for then.

'No, that works for me, but will it give you long enough to get sorted when you arrive?'

'Plenty of time,' James confirmed. 'I'm staying quite nearby so as soon as I've dropped my stuff off, I can walk straight there.'

'All right,' I said, feeling my tummy fizz with excitement. 'I'll see you there at half eleven.'

'And wear those shoes of yours that are comfy to walk in,' he advised, before he rang off. 'Because there's miles to cover and loads to see.'

'I love that you sound so excited,' I laughed.

'I am excited,' he told me. 'I'm meeting *you* in one of my favourite places!'

I was lucky not to get indigestion given how fast I bolted my breakfast. I had known the time in the woods would soothe me, but I hadn't expected James to play such an important part in the recovery of my mood, too.

'You've just missed her,' Rick informed me, when I arrived back at Fernside and knocked on the locked sunroom door to check Constance was okay.

'Missed her?' I frowned.

'Hairdresser day,' he grinned. 'She's just gone. I'm surprised you didn't pass her on the drive. She has a taxi pick her up and ferry her back.'

'Oh, right,' I said. I felt disappointed to have missed my friend but pleased that she felt happy enough to have her hair done. 'Did you speak to her? Was she okay?'

'Seemed fine to me.' Rick frowned. 'Why, what's up?'

'Nothing,' I shrugged. 'She just seemed a bit distracted yesterday, and I was worried about her.'

'Well,' he said, picking up the wheelbarrow he'd been pushing when I arrived, 'she was happy enough to have another go at me about listening to gossip, so I'd say normal service has been resumed, no matter what was vexing her yesterday.'

'That's good then,' I said, biting my lip.

'Not for me,' he laughed. 'She's like a dog with a bone. Almost put me off wanting to come to supper.' I rolled my eyes at that. 'I don't suppose you fancy giving me a hand, Tilly, do you? I've got at least three hours work to do here and just two hours to do it in.'

I got the impression that Rick charged Constance for far fewer hours than he worked, but I couldn't help him that morning because I needed to get ready and go.

'On any other day,' I told him.

'Yeah, yeah. I know,' he moaned.

'I'm not making excuses. I'm about to head out,' I said. 'I've got a date.'

Rick put the barrow down again and the look on his face made me instantly regret my unguarded explanation.

'A date?' he beamed. 'With Carter, by any chance?'

'No,' I frowned. 'Not with Carter. Have you been talking to Melody?' I added suspiciously.

'No. Why?'

I felt cross with myself then. Melody didn't gossip, so she wouldn't have mentioned to Rick her previous attempt at matchmaking.

'Never mind,' I tutted, as much at myself as him, and strode off.

'Enjoy your date!' Rick called after me.

There was no sign of him when I left, so I was thankfully able to slip away without my outfit – a floaty floral dress from Zara and the nondescript but comfortable walking shoes – being scrutinised and commented on.

I'd looked online for the best places to park and was running a couple of minutes late by the time I'd found my way from the park-and-ride drop-off to the garden entrance. Feeling slightly out of breath, I took a moment to readjust my dress and check my reflection in the pocket mirror from my bag. Slightly pink around the edges, but not too flushed, which was a relief. My hair, which was trying to escape its bun, was a bit mad though . . .

'You look beautiful,' said a voice behind me.

'James!' I gasped and spun around. 'I didn't see you.'

Wearing knee length shorts and a linen shirt, with a pair of sunglasses tucked into the unbuttoned collar, he again looked as little like the guy in the impeccable suit that I'd first met as it was possible to. I have to say, I much preferred the casual version, and he looked comfortable with it, too.

'Well, I saw you,' he said and lightly brushed my cheek with another soft kiss. Whatever aftershave he was wearing was intoxicating. 'I hope you've got your mum's hat with you. We are heading into a garden, after all, though you won't be weeding today.'

'No hat,' I told him, as I slipped the mirror back into my bag. 'I ended up leaving in such a rush, I completely forgot about it.'

That was partly Rick's fault.

'Oh well,' he smiled. 'We'll just have to share this one, won't we?'

From behind his back, he whipped out a straw hat that he'd kept hidden.

'Where did you get that?' I laughed, as he plonked it on his head.

'Online,' he grinned as he attempted to straighten it, but as it was slightly too snug a fit, he couldn't adjust it all that much. 'I thought one day we might have the chance to match.' I was even sorrier to have left Mum's hat back at Fernside when he said that. 'Do you want to wear it first or shall I?'

'Thanks for the offer, but I'll be too hot with my hair down,' I told him. I'd piled it up to keep it off my neck and didn't want to change it. 'You should wear it though.'

I didn't expect him to, but he did. He looked rather comical, and I found myself liking him even more for that. Lee had always taken himself far too seriously, so I appreciated a man who didn't, and James was shaping up very nicely to be that kind of guy.

'Come on then,' he said. 'I can't wait to show you around. I love this place, and I know it like the back of my hand, so if I'm getting on your nerves still going on about it in ten hours' time, just tell me to shut up, okay?'

'Will do.' I laughed as his excitement made him almost trip over his words.

'Have I thrown you by picking this place?' he asked, while we queued to buy tickets.

'Given that you had us meet at a water meadow for our first date?' I nudged. 'Not really. To be honest, it's a thrill to know that there's so much more to you than the sleek and suited man I first met.'

'I really haven't gone down in your estimation?'

'Absolutely not,' I said firmly. 'Like we agreed before, with our love of the outdoors, we're a match. And it was your kind actions that appealed to me most the day of the hat rescue, not the car and your clothes.'

'So, I'm doing all right? I pass muster today?'

'Let me just check,' I said, taking him in again. 'Crumpled shirt, ruffled hair under the hat *and* a garden lover. You're far from wanting.' I approved. 'Right up my street, actually.'

We moved a step forward in the queue.

'Lucky me,' he smiled seductively. 'And I hope you know, Tilly that's a two-way street, because you're perfect for me, too.'

I'd never been called that before.

'Lucky me too, then,' I said back breathlessly.

James quickly checked the time, and I noticed he was wearing the Rolex again.

'I hope this queue soon goes down,' he sighed. 'I want to make the most of this visit.'

'Me too,' I said. 'And I notice you're not entirely averse to the finer things in life,' I added, with a nod towards his wrist.

'The watch? Oh, I didn't buy this. It was a present from my wonderful mum. An investment piece, she called it.'

He looked fondly at it again and I couldn't help thinking that he was becoming more desirable with every second.

'You need to be careful, James,' I said, as I fanned my face with my hands, 'otherwise I might find myself . . .'

'Yes?'

Our eyes met and I knew it would be the easiest thing in the world to fall for him, but I could hardly confess that, could I? We'd barely had any time to get to know each other yet.

'Well, that's a relief,' he said, taking my hand and giving it a squeeze when I didn't finish the sentence, 'because I could also easily find myself . . .'

'Yes?' I swallowed and looked intently at him.

'Two adults?'

Neither of us moved and the person behind us huffed.

'Just the two adult tickets, is it?' the kiosk operator asked again.

'Er, yes, please,' said James, when I finally looked away. 'Two tickets. Thanks.'

Once we were through the gate, he took my hand again and it felt like the most natural thing in the world to walk around the beautiful gardens, through the tropical glasshouses and along the bee borders with our fingers entwined.

James hadn't been exaggerating when he said he knew the gardens well and he was quite the horticultural expert, too. Something I would never have expected of a young barrister, but I'd learned my lesson now. Assumptions, of any kind, weren't allowed.

'What's next?' I asked and my tummy gave the loudest rumble.

'Lunch, I think,' James smiled. 'I'm really hungry, too.'

I lifted our hands so I could see the time on his watch. 'And no wonder,' I laughed. 'It's well gone two!'

Fortunately, the lovely café was still well stocked, and we packed a tray full with delicious food and more bottles of water, then found a table in the shade to eat at. It felt reminiscent of our first picnic, though the setting was a million times lovelier.

'What's been your favourite thing so far?' James asked.

We'd talked of nothing other than the garden, both of us lost in the magic of the day and not wanting the bubble to burst by bringing in real life issues like James's work conundrum and my trepidation over getting permission to set up my business. Our Cambridge date was halcyon in every way.

'Well,' I said, having mulled the question over, 'I've loved everything, and I know there's still the lake to look at, but so far, I think I like the Palm House the best.'

'Steamy,' James grinned.

'It was unlike anything I've ever seen before. So many exotic plants, and yes,' I agreed, 'very steamy. What about you?'

'All of it!' he grinned. 'The autumn garden is glorious, though obviously not in the middle of the summer. We'll have to come back later in the year to admire that.'

I didn't respond immediately and James frowned.

'Am I being presumptuous?' he asked, sounding genuinely worried.

'No,' I said, pinching a triangle of sandwich off his plate as quickly as he then nabbed one from mine. 'You're not. I'd love to come back and see the autumn garden with you.'

I was already seduced by James's company and his enthusiasm for green spaces, which he said were a soothing balm for jaded spirits – an ethos I fully endorsed myself – and now the suggestion that we could come back to the beautiful garden later in the year only deepened the feeling.

'Good,' he smiled and offered me some crisps.

The rest of the afternoon seemed to be over in a blink and

having admired the lake and walked what was beginning to feel like double the amount of recommended daily steps, I checked the time and realised I needed to collect my car.

'I can't believe I'm going to say this,' I sighed, 'but I need to go.'

'No,' James objected.

He gently pulled me towards him, and I had no desire to resist. We were in a secluded spot, many of the day's visitors had now left, but we lingered, neither of us apparently wanting the trip to end. As I pressed my body close to his, I knew I certainly didn't.

'How about we get your car and go out for dinner?' he suggested, as he tucked a strand of hair behind my ear. The feel of his fingers lightly touching my skin caused a rush of heat to course through me. 'You could drive back to Suffolk later tonight, couldn't you?'

I was longing to, but with the supper party happening the next day, I felt like I needed an early night to make up for the previous restless one.

'I really need to get back,' I whispered with regret. 'I've got things I need to see to, and you've got this case to get to grips with, haven't you?'

He let out a long breath. 'Yes,' he said and moved so that his mouth was just an inch from mine. 'You're right. But next time you come here you can travel by train, so we won't have to think about your car.'

'That sounds like a wonderful idea,' I whispered and completely closed the distance between us.

Our first kiss was perfect. Initially tender and soft, it increased in intensity, just the right amount, and when I touched James's tongue with my own, he responded as I had known he would.

'Or you could come and visit me,' I said breathlessly, when we finally broke apart.

I could easily imagine James at home in the garden apartment, which was just big enough for two. I wondered how Constance would feel about overnight guests.

'I'd like that,' he smiled and we kissed again.

He walked with me, back to the bus pick-up point and we kissed for a third time, but not as passionately as there were other people queuing around us.

'Would you mind if I called you sometime to talk about my career dilemma?' he asked, as the bus came into sight and the queue shuffled into more of a line. 'I didn't want to mention it today, but I would appreciate your input while I'm still thinking about it.'

'If I can help,' I told him, 'I will.'

'And I'll see you again, soon. Yes?'

'As soon as you've won this case,' I said, subtly reminding him that he needed to focus on what he'd come to Cambridge for.

He kissed the back of my hand and held on to it until the very last second. I waved as the bus pulled away and he waved back with the hat in his hand. As I turned to face the front, I noticed the woman sitting opposite me was smiling.

'Is he a keeper?' she asked.

As second dates went, that was the most perfect one I'd ever had. More than worthy of a romantic Hollywood blockbuster.

'Absolutely,' I laughed, as my phone pinged with a message from him, thanking me for the most wonderful day. 'No doubt about that.'

Chapter 15

I thought about the details of our date – the perfect location, the perfect hat *and* the perfect kiss – all the way back to Suffolk and then for much of the night. My initial visit to Willowell and then the move to Fernside had already been wonderful, but the addition of James, who was both handsome and had the most glorious hidden depths, felt like the cherry on life's cake. I had no idea where our relationship, if it wasn't too early to call it that, was headed, but given that we felt so in tune with each other already, I had every intention of enjoying finding out.

I didn't see Constance before I went to bed, but I knew she was back from the hairdressers and feeling okay because she, or Rick acting on her behalf, had slipped a note under the apartment door, suggesting we get together early the next morning to talk about plans for the supper party which was happening that evening.

Having checked the weather forecast on more than one app, I was keen for us to eat in the garden, perhaps on the jetty, but that would mean lots of fetching and carrying, so I'd be guided by my friend and how she had organised previous parties she'd held.

James and I messaged for a while once I'd let him know I was safely home, but then he had to focus on his case notes. Conversely, I felt so lightheaded in that besotted way that lands right when you're at the start of something special that I couldn't focus on anything. If only my absent brother would now magically call then literally everything would be idyllic.

'Hello,' I croaked sleepily as I answered my phone at what turned out to be just after four in the morning. 'Hello.'

'What am I looking at? Have you turned your phone torch on? Is that the inside of your ear?'

I sprang up in bed and flicked on the bedside lamp.

'Zack!' I shouted, as I grappled with my phone. 'Oh my god, where are you?'

'You know where I am,' he laughed, but then his face fell. 'And I've just realised what time it is for you. Shit, Tilly. Sorry. Go back to sleep.'

'No way,' I said, as I plumped up the pillows and got comfy. 'Who knows when you'll call again.'

'I'm sorry,' he repeated. 'I know I've been even worse than usual at keeping in touch since I landed here.'

'Well,' I conceded. 'You did say you were pretty remote, didn't you?'

'I did,' he said, 'and I was, but I've moved now.'

'Already?' I couldn't believe it. 'Where to this time?'

'I'm still in Bali,' he informed me, 'but I'm taking a break from work. I've gone on sabbatical to . . . think about things.'

'No way.' I gawped, my mouth falling open in surprise. 'You've done it.'

'I have.'

'So,' I quizzed, leaning closer to the screen to get a better look at him. 'What things need thinking about? Are you okay?'

I felt utterly amazed that he was taking the break I'd long said he needed.

'Very okay,' he told me, and given how well he looked, I couldn't dispute his pronouncement. 'It was that photo of you and your new friends in The Greenman that kicked things off. You looked so happy, Tilly. Pursuing your heart's desire clearly suits you and it has prompted me to think about mine.'

'Well, that's good,' I said. 'Though I did think following your own heart was exactly what you were doing . . .'

'I was,' he shrugged. 'But things change. People change.'

I couldn't argue with that, either.

'So, do you have a plan?' I asked, and he gave me a look. 'No,' I smiled. 'Of course you don't.'

'I'm going to hang here for a bit,' he said and showed me the cerulean view. 'And see how I feel in a few weeks.'

'There are worse places to hang.'

'That's what I thought.' He nodded as he looked around.

'Well,' I smiled, 'I'm relieved to hear from you, and I'm so pleased you're taking a proper break. I'm sure you'll feel loads better for it, no matter what you decide to do next.'

'I thought you'd be happy, but I'm sorry I woke you. It's lunchtime here.'

'What's on the menu?' I yawned.

'Fish probably. I'll send you a photo.'

'And will you be able to keep more in touch now?'

'It depends where I end up.'

'I thought you said you were hanging there!'

'I meant hanging in Bali,' he said as if I should have realised. 'Not necessarily in this exact spot. I might go off grid again . . .'

'You're incorrigible,' I tutted. 'But thank you for keeping me in the loop. Now, go and catch your lunch.'

'I love you, Tilly.'

His face filled the screen and I felt a lump forming in my throat. 'And I love you, too,' I told him. 'I'll see you soon.'

'You never know, you might!' He laughed and signed off.

I slumped back against the plumped up pillows. It was a relief to have heard from him, but I couldn't help wishing he was going to be one of the guests at the supper party that evening.

'Good morning, Constance!' I waved cheerily as I walked up the lawn following my swim. Zack had sent me a photo of his lunch and it had put the smile back on my face. I'd wanted to hear from him, and now I had, I could stop fretting. 'I'll be with you as soon as I'm dressed.'

'Good morning, my dear.' She beamed back from her chair in the sunroom. Her former distracted mood had apparently been replaced with a far sunnier one and my own lifted even higher to match it. 'I think we're going to be in luck with the weather.'

'It wouldn't dare rain today,' I smiled, then veered off to get dry and changed.

I took my Willowell Woods notebook to the house, because I carried it practically everywhere now, and a smaller one where I could write down anything relevant for the evening we were poised to host.

'Knock, knock,' I said aloud when I found her chair empty

and headed to the Fernside kitchen. 'Oh Constance, your hair looks lovely.'

She'd been a little distance away earlier, so I hadn't been able to see properly.

'Thank you.' She nodded and patted the side of her head. 'It was certainly in need of a trim. Come on, let's go back to the sunroom and get things going while the day warms up.'

In the past, I had always organised any event or trip I was involved with, with weeks to spare, so the fact that we were only now discussing preparations for something that was happening that evening felt like another leap into the unknown for me. However, I knew Constance would have it all in hand, so it wasn't a daunting one.

'There's a lot to do,' I couldn't stop myself from saying as the list grew.

'And it's all covered,' Constance said confidently.

'Are you sure?'

She began to reel everything off.

'I've got Rick coming to move tables and chairs and Carter's sorting out the drinks. Melody and Kaya will bring flowers and the food I asked Melody to prepare when I was in the village yesterday, and we'll sort crockery, cutlery and glasses this afternoon. What else is there to fuss over? Aside from adding a few candles, blankets and cushions . . .'

'Oh Constance!' I laughed, having added a neat row of ticks next to everything in my notebook. 'You've really got it all under control, haven't you?'

'Of course.' She winked. 'What's the point of spending time with friends if the preparations are such hard work? There's no pleasure in that. And when I mentioned it yesterday, everyone offered to chip in.'

'Oh well, in that case,' I said, closing the notebook. 'I'll leave them to it, though I would like to contribute something more than making it look pretty and pouring drinks.'

'Carter will pour drinks,' Constance corrected. 'What have you got in mind?'

'Perhaps a couple of simple dishes,' I said, trying to think of tasty extras. 'What's Melody bringing?'

I wouldn't want to end up making the same thing.

'One of her trademark quiches, new potato salad and dressing and a pudding,' Constance responded. 'And she's bringing all the green stuff too, so that will need prepping.'

'In that case,' I said, 'I'll go and collect the salad this morning, so we can have it ready in advance, and I'll see if she's got the ingredients for me to make some onion and goat's cheese tarts and my favourite no bake strawberry cheesecake.' Constance's tummy rumbled loudly. 'But first, I'll make you some breakfast.'

'I was going to try and hold out,' she started to say, 'but your talk of tarts and cheesecake has scuppered that idea.'

'I thought you were having three meals a day now, even if we don't always eat together,' I frowned at her.

'It's a hard habit to break,' she confessed. 'And before I forget, Kaya will be starting her big house clean after the weekend. As she was in the store with her sister yesterday, it was the ideal time to get her pencilled in and she was fully booked before then.'

I would have liked to say more about Constance forgetting her breakfast, but as she'd moved the conversation on, I decided not to. I shoved away the urge to ask what had distracted her the day before, too. Everything seemed to be back on an even keel now, so there was no point rocking the boat, especially on such an exciting day.

'That's wonderful,' I said breezily, echoing her positivity. 'What do you fancy to eat?'

'Melody had saved me some double-yolk eggs,' she said, with a smile. 'One of those, fried in a bit of butter in a sandwich with a dollop of brown sauce, would go down a treat.'

'One egg sandwich coming up,' I smiled back.

The hours flew by, and I didn't get a chance to ask Rick not to mention my date because in the time I'd been to the store for the salad and ingredients, he'd arrived at Fernside, shifted the garden furniture entirely on his own and left again.

I'd no idea how he'd managed to do it all so quickly, but there was now a large table and two smaller ones and a collection of chairs at the bottom of the lawn, close to the jetty, and, in the sunroom, Constance was gathering blankets, throws, lanterns and cushions in jewel colours to add some luxurious but comfortable touches.

It didn't take long for me to bake the tarts and make the cheesecake in the Fernside kitchen. It was better equipped and had a larger oven than the garden apartment, and with Constance keenly watching, making suggestions and sampling anything I left unattended, it was an enjoyable way to spend some of the day and kept my mind from straying too often back to James and our time together in Cambridge.

Not that time spent thinking about him was a problem, but it did make me hanker to feel his lips on mine and enjoy the seductive sensation far sooner than they were likely to.

'Just a couple more lanterns, I think,' Constance said, a short while before everyone was due to arrive. 'Then we'll be all set.'

I didn't say anything. I was too taken aback by how beautiful it all looked. Nothing matched in the area we'd set up to eat and relax in and none of it looked put together, or styled and agonised over, because it hadn't been.

It had been wonderful to watch how Constance effortlessly and casually set everything down with such artistic and bohemian flair. There had seemed to be no effort on her part and that, I then realised, was because Constance herself was unconventional. It made me want to see more of the house and I hoped any future supper parties might happen indoors as well as out. If this was how she could make an impromptu party look, the house she'd lived her entire life in was doubtless going to be a glorious discovery.

I hoped again that I might be able to invite James to Fernside. He had the same sort of laid-back, posh but not, demeanour as Constance . . . but then it wasn't the moment to start mooning over him again because our guests were almost due.

'Right, come on,' Constance said as she clapped her hands and pulled my thoughts properly back to the gathering at hand. 'Let's go and dress. I've aired my favourite kaftan for tonight. We can carry the rest of the lanterns and candles down with us once everyone's arrived. And don't forget your little speaker thingy for the music, too. Have you decided what you're going to wear?'

'I have,' I told her. 'I picked up a patterned floaty top hemmed with tiny gold bells in Sudbury, and I thought I'd wear that with some cotton shorts and my leather sandals.'

'Oh,' she smiled. 'I like the sound of that.'

As it had been such a hot day, everyone turned up with their swimming gear on under their clothes, and once hellos had been said and the food and drink put in the kitchen, they raced down to the river and stripped off. Kaya and Rick noisily jumped straight in, while Melody sat with her feet dangling and energetically splashed them if they got too close or her sister threatened to pull her in.

'No chance of seeing the kingfishers now,' Carter, who had held back to walk Constance down the lawn, commented, while I followed on behind with the extra lighting and my speaker which was already quietly playing my James Quinn playlist courtesy of Spotify. The tiny gold bells on my top tinkled melodiously and added a magical sound to the already enchanting scene.

'You're quite right, my dear,' Constance agreed, as she slipped her arm through his. She looked fabulous in the purple, jade and teal kaftan and with strings of jet necklaces of different lengths draped around her neck. 'But that will give you an excuse to come back another day, won't it?'

She turned and smiled at me and I hoped she hadn't jumped to the same conclusion as Rick and even Melody – that Carter and I might make a romantic match. Given that she knew all about my thrilling meet-cute, she couldn't think I needed another man on my radar. But then I hadn't told her anything had come of my lay-by encounter, so she might.

'I'd like that,' Carter smiled. 'And maybe an otter will even grace us with its presence. The birds and wildlife are my favourite things about this stretch of the river and seeing your view of it, Constance, it looks even lovelier.'

'Thank you,' Constance said graciously.

'An otter sighting would be amazing,' I agreed. 'And there's a water vole that's often about, too.'

'You're not trying to play cupid, are you Connie?' Rick shouted in a sing-song tone, as he climbed out of the river and looked at the three of us.

Constance shook her head and tutted, but it wasn't the matchmaking suggestion she was initially objecting to.

'My name is Constance, dear. No one has ever called me Connie in my life.'

'Sorry, Constance, dear.' Rick grinned and flicked river water over Melody, who yelped. 'But you do all know that Tilly is already spoken for, don't you?'

I could have floored him.

'I didn't know,' Melody said, grabbing Rick's leg, but he shook her off. 'But that's probably because she didn't want me, or anyone else to.'

'Is she now?' Kaya commented, as she joined Rick on the jetty and ignored her sister's subtle suggestion that the subject wasn't up for discussion.

Melody's words were confirmation that she'd taken the hint that I wasn't romantically interested in Carter and that would have been a relief had Rick not now annoyed me.

'She had a hot date yesterday, didn't you Tills?' he blundered on. I threw him the fiercest look I could muster and his smile faltered.

'You're a nuisance, Rick,' I said crossly. 'Do you know that?'

'I wondered where you were when I got home and you weren't here,' Constance commented and I felt my face flush at the thought of my time with James becoming the hot supper party topic. 'But as you didn't mention it earlier, I decided not to ask. Rick needs to take the hint and also mind his own business.'

'Hear, hear!' Carter agreed with Constance.

She didn't appear to have a matchmaking agenda and I was thankful for that, but still cross with Rick for sabotaging the start of the party by mentioning my date.

'Quite right,' Melody chimed in and threw Kaya a look. 'And you should know better.'

'Sorry.' Kaya looked suitably embarrassed.

'And I'm sorry, too,' Rick spoke up, looking equally chastened by Constance's telling off.

'No, I'm not having that. I'm cross with you Rick,' Constance said fiercely. For the sake of the party, I would have accepted his apology, but she was really rattled. 'You take things too far. Now go up to the apartment and change. You can come back when you've given some proper thought to people's boundaries and privacy.'

Rick flushed red and scooped up his clothes. I might have expected him to laugh the scolding off, but Constance's crossness had hit its mark. He was in real trouble, and I knew I wouldn't have wanted to find myself on the sharp edge of her tongue. Not that he didn't deserve it.

'I'll come with you,' Kaya said, as she picked up her abandoned dress. 'You won't tell everyone about your date while we're gone, will you?' she added tactlessly.

'For pity's sake,' Melody muttered. 'Sense the tone, Sis.'

'The only thing I have any intention of talking about is what I've got planned for the woods now Constance has confirmed that she's happy with the idea,' I told her, and Rick's mouth dropped open.

'Finally!' Melody clapped, while Kaya and Rick shot off up the lawn.

'In fact,' I shouted after them, 'I think I'll start now, so if you don't want to miss out, you'd better hurry up.'

'She means it!' Carter bellowed. 'She's telling us right now!'

Laughing, Kaya tripped Rick up and quickly overtook him.

'If I'd been a little sprightlier, I would have tripped him up myself,' Constance commented mischievously, and Melody, Carter and I laughed. 'Now, my good fellow, see me settled and then the three of you can go up to the kitchen and start carrying down this fabulous feast you've all played a part in preparing.'

There were tealights in jewel-coloured holders running down the length of the table, so the food looked as good at it tasted and the mismatched crockery and different coloured glasses added to the aesthetic. It took far less time to devour the dishes than it had to put them together and every mouthful was delicious. There was something magical about sharing a meal out of doors as the heat of the day slipped away, the sun set and the natural light gradually dimmed.

Being in the company of my new friends made it even better, and as I went around and lit more candles and offered blankets to warm up cooling shoulders, I again felt like my luck had landed in the biggest possible dose. Rick might have wound me up on more than one occasion, but even he was lovely, really. He just got a bit carried away sometimes.

'So,' said Constance softly, who was sitting in a chair on the lawn and feeding the blackbird who had come to visit now the noise had quietened thanks to full bellies and hearts, 'if Tilly does now tell us what her plans are for the woods, can we trust you Rick to keep them a secret or are you going to go blabbing all over the village?'

'Yes,' I challenged, as I looked over at where he was stretched out on one of the blankets, 'because if you're going to be even the slightest bit tempted, you should leave now because I'm not ready to go public yet.'

'Scout's honour, I'll keep it to myself,' he promised as he sat up.

'Me, too,' Kaya, who was sitting cross-legged next to him, said quietly.

'I bet you were never in the Scouts, Rick,' Carter chuckled, and the blackbird cocked its head at him, but didn't fly off.

'But the sentiment is sincere,' Rick said, holding up two, three, then four fingers in an attempt at the salute, which made Carter shake his head. 'I truly am sorry for before, Tilly.'

'I'm not sure you should risk it,' Carter said to me. 'That's nothing like the salute. An abomination really.'

Rick yelped and threw a piece of pastry crust from Melody's delicious quiche at him in protest. Carter caught it, crumbled it up and slowly held out his hand. Constance's blackbird wasted no time in hopping over and taking it from him.

'You can tell a lot about someone by how birds and animals react to them,' Constance nodded. 'You've done the right thing asking Carter to get involved with your venture, Tilly.'

'Aha,' said Rick, and the blackbird squawked and flew off. 'Sorry,' he whispered. 'But my guess was sort of right, there is something going on between you, isn't there?'

'There is, but not what you've assumed Rick,' Carter smiled. 'Put him out of his misery, Tilly, before he jumps to more unfounded conclusions.'

I waited while Melody refilled everyone's glasses again. We had soft drinks as practically everyone was driving and, even though I wasn't, I wanted to share my plans with a clear head.

'Crikey!' Kaya was the first to comment, once I'd talked about my idea for turning Willowell Woods into a sanctuary where visitors could connect with nature, along with the ways I, and eventually Carter, would help them achieve it. 'That all sounds amazing.'

'You really think it's a good idea?' I asked seriously.

'A phenomenal one,' Melody agreed with her sister. 'And I love that you'll be playing a part in it, Carter.'

'Me too,' he nodded. 'I've already been out in the woods behind the pub and started brushing up on my skills again.'

I was delighted that he was so keen.

'As long as I can secure permission,' I reminded everyone, 'it will be great.'

'Having had a business there in the past is bound to make a difference to that,' Rick sensibly pointed out. 'And it's not like you're planning to alter anything in the woods, is it? You're not going to cause any harm to the trees or strip the site with a view to getting permission to build on it at some point down the line, are you?'

'Far from it. Aside from taking down any dangerous branches, little will change. And what does, such as reinstating the paths and clearing the pond, will only enhance the woodland. The diversity down there is phenomenal, so nothing is going to happen that could endanger that.'

I was looking forward to making a night-time visit to look for bats, owls and moths.

'I'm happy to check the trees,' Rick offered. 'Unless acting the fool has put you off letting me loose with a chainsaw . . .'

'Not quite,' I said. 'I was going to ask if you might come and make an assessment of what needs doing.'

'And if there's anything really pressing that needs seeing to,' Constance said to us both, 'I'd like you to deal with it right away. I feel ashamed that the woods haven't been properly maintained, so anything that will be for the benefit of the trees needs to happen before Tilly has taken ownership.'

'I didn't know there'd been a business there before,' Melody said, before I had the chance to suggest we could split the cost. 'What was it and will you be able to build an office or something there, Tilly?'

The explanation and further discussion went on long into the evening. The candles had burnt low and were casting long shadows before we'd finally exhausted the topic. Constance hadn't said much about her sister's business, and sensing that she didn't want to talk about Grace, I quickly carried the conversation on when Melody and Kaya expressed their sympathy for her loss. I had assumed that everyone would know about Grace but then remembered that the sisters were relative newcomers to Willowell.

By the time we were stifling yawns, we'd explored every aspect of the business, the bottles of drink were empty and there was nothing beyond a few crumbs on the plates.

'Well,' said Constance, once most things had been carried back to the house and as we waved the others off into the star-filled night. 'I think that was a roaring success, don't you?'

I slipped my arm through hers and lightly rested my head on her shoulder. It was only then that I realised how tiny she felt. Her quick wit and mental sharpness often made me forget her real age and diminutive size.

'I do,' I agreed, and lifted my head again. 'Though it felt a little self-indulgent to talk about the woods and what I'm hoping to do with them for so long. I rather monopolised the conversation, didn't I?'

'Not at all,' Constance objected and turned back towards the gate. 'Everyone, aside from Kaya, because she's likely going to be leaving again, is going to be involved, so they were happy to listen and incredibly excited, too. Self-indulgent, my eye,' she tutted.

She was right. Kaya didn't have a part to play because she was considering leaving in the autumn, but Rick and Carter had roles and so did Melody now. She was going to supply the snacks and lunches I would serve in the cabin.

It felt wonderful to be drafting in local businesses and I wondered if there was anyone else I could involve. Supporting already established enterprises and making the most of Willowell residents' skills could only strengthen my cause when the time came to apply for permission, couldn't it? Not that that was my real motivation for doing it.

'Thank you, Constance,' I said, giving her arm a gentle squeeze. 'I'm really beginning to think that this is going to happen now, aren't you?'

'I *know* it's going to happen,' she said firmly, going through the gate ahead of me. 'There's nothing that's going to get in your way.'

I hoped we were right to be so convinced, because I was finding it increasingly difficult to imagine my future without Willowell Woods being one of the biggest things in it.

Chapter 16

For the next few days, life at Fernside continued as contentedly as it had for practically the entire time since I'd arrived. Constance and I regularly enjoyed breakfast together after my early morning river swims and then also saw each other at various points throughout the day.

Rick, who was properly behaving, continued to squeeze the garden work into his regular maintenance round and sometimes in the evenings everyone came to swim, chat or both, and quite often these impromptu gatherings were enhanced by some leftover bakes Melody treated us to from the store, or by me reading us a chapter from Constance's beloved copy of *The Wind in the Willows*.

Stretched out on blankets and with the lanterns softly flickering it was as enchanting as our first get-together, and I often found myself wishing the summer wouldn't end, even though I adored the colours of autumn and snuggling up in a cosy sweater. And this year, there'd be James to cosy up with, too. What a seductive prospect that was.

Constance hadn't yet offered to play the piano for us, or even mentioned that she could, but I was secretly hoping for rain when Kaya finished cleaning, so we could move inside, because then she might. If my mention of Dad, Zack and I coming to terms with living a fuller life beyond the loss of Mum had got her thinking about enjoying music when Grace wasn't here to enjoy the woods, then she might consider sharing her talent. I hoped she would because her playing was beautiful.

James was so busy working we didn't have an opportunity to meet in person, but every evening we chatted on the phone. I felt like I had known him so much longer than I really had and when I mentioned that to him, he said he felt the same way about me. He also told me he was a few steps closer to deciding about his career but didn't tell me which way the pendulum had swung. I had my own opinion about that but kept it to myself.

'Have you heard any more from your brother?' Constance asked one morning after we'd finished our breakfast. 'Is he still on sabbatical?'

I brushed the crumbs off my hands and unlocked my phone to show her the most recent photos he'd sent. Despite the technical challenges, Zack had been messaging much more than before and the sight of him standing in front of a waterfall with a lush green forest behind him and a huge smile on his face filled my heart with joy.

'Oh, my goodness,' Constance sighed dreamily. 'Isn't that exquisite?'

'It certainly is,' I agreed.

'Are you sure you're not regretting staying here rather than flying out to join him?'

'Absolutely not,' I told her. Given that it was the photo of the gang in The Greenman that had kicked his soul-searching off, I was even happier to have stayed put. 'I'm more than content.'

It was interesting that Zack and I seemed to have switched roles to a certain extent in recent weeks. Whereas I was usually the cautious one who needed endless plans and lists to keep my life running how I liked it, I'd found myself becoming a bit freer and easier since the move to Fernside. The casual evening gatherings were evidence of that.

Zack, on the other hand, had now stopped long enough to think a few things through and get to grips with the possibility of planning some changes. When James and I had previously talked about our approaches to life's challenges, I had mentioned the vast differences between my brother and I, but this summer we seemed to have borrowed a bit from each other and the balance was proving the right way to go for both of us.

'Well, that's all right then,' Constance smiled. 'I'm very happy that you're so happy to be here.'

'Though I wouldn't mind having the opportunity to give Zack a huge hug.' I sighed as I looked at the photo again.

'Family is precious,' Constance said wistfully. 'Especially when there's so little of it left to go around.'

I put my phone away again and looked over at her.

'I'm so sorry you haven't got family now, Constance,' I said softly. 'I can't imagine being entirely on my own.'

The thought of something happening to Zack was one I never allowed to linger, though since losing Dad, it did occasionally rear its ugly head. Poor Constance.

'I do have one relative left in the world.' Her admission of this floored me.

'You do?' I frowned. 'I don't believe it. Why have you never mentioned them or—'

'Because we don't speak,' she briskly interrupted. 'We've cut ties and have nothing to do with each other now.'

'But family is—'

'Yes,' she cut in again. 'Precious. I completely agree, but not the sort who report you to social services and pit themselves against every important decision you attempt to make.'

She sounded very bitter, but given the upset Miss Lyons had caused, I didn't think I had a hope of talking her around or facilitating a reconciliation. Not that I had any grounds to. That would have been interfering on a scale that went way beyond doing some ironing.

'I've recently discovered,' she carried on more calmly, 'that found family can mean as much, if not more, than those connected by blood that you once held so dear but have become estranged from.'

'Oh Constance.' I swallowed over the lump in my throat as I nonetheless wished, despite my former conviction not to get involved, that there was something I could do to help. 'That's such a tragedy. Who is this relative? A cousin or—'

'Now listen,' she said sternly, and I heard a car arriving on the drive. 'Here's Kaya, so we'd better get cleared up.'

'But—'

'I mean it Tilly,' she said firmly. 'I don't want you to say another word to me about this. Or anyone else for that matter. Promise?'

She clearly regretted that she'd mentioned the situation and wasn't going to elaborate whether Kaya was there or not.

'Promise,' I reluctantly pledged.

'Here she comes,' she nodded towards the back door as the sound of singing met our ears and Kaya unlocked the gate. 'Let's get these plates in the sink, quick.'

We'd had kippers that morning, with thick slices of buttered toast, and eaten them outside so as not to stink the whole of the house out too much, but Constance obviously had a feeling Kaya would object.

'How's she getting on?' I asked, in lieu of the other questions I really wanted to ask.

Constance was still refusing to let me or anyone other than Kaya see further inside than the kitchen. She said she wanted the whole place spick, span and polished before she opened it up again and Kaya had been sworn to secrecy as to what any of the rooms looked like. I was itching for her to finish but she wasn't the sort of housekeeper to cut corners.

The amount of stuff she'd carried out for Rick to cart away would have justified having a skip and given that Kaya had found a few hundred pounds hidden about the place, Constance could have afforded one!

The only things Kaya had shared with me was that there was a room upstairs that Constance had asked her not to go into and that she'd seen no evidence of the rumoured repairs that needed doing. I speculated that the issue might be in the mystery room, but if there wasn't a problem, what was it that had really prompted Constance to put the beloved family woods up for sale?

'She's getting on very well,' Constance told me. Her tone suggested that she was happy with Kaya's progress and that she had now completely moved on from the former topic of conversation. 'She's working hard and seems to be enjoying it, which is a bonus.'

'Morning folks!' Kaya greeted us. 'Hey! Oh yuck. What's that smell?'

Her smile had instantly disappeared.

'Kippers,' Constance told her. 'Tilly cooked them for our breakfast.'

'Well, I hope the kitchen doesn't smell like those plates. We'd better have all the windows open if it does. What's the point of me freshening everywhere up for you to stink it out with smoked fish?'

It was a brave woman who told Constance off.

'We made sure the kitchen door was shut when I cooked them,' I quickly told her. 'So, it shouldn't have wafted too far.'

'That's all right then,' she said. 'And I'm sorry I'm a bit late.' We hadn't realised she was. 'Only, the people who checked out of the cottage left it in a right state and as there's another guest going in this afternoon, I had to sort it.'

'Shame on them,' Constance tutted.

'Um,' Kaya sniffed. 'I'll spare you the worst of the details, but we'll be lucky if the make-up stains come off the towels. Now, I'd better crack on. There's still plenty to do.'

With the upstairs rooms now back to the standard Constance said her parents and sister would have expected, Kaya was going to work her magic on the landing and stairs, then move into the ground floor rooms.

'As soon as the office is clean,' Constance told me, once Kaya had gone, 'I'll dig out the folders Grace kept the nursery paperwork in. She was a stickler for keeping details and some of it might be useful.'

'Anything you can pass on will be helpful,' I thanked her. I might have chilled out in some respects, but where the business was concerned, I was still all . . . well, business. 'I want to have all my ducks in a row, right from the off.'

Constance approved of that.

'No one prepares to fail,' she began.

'They only fail to prepare,' I finished. 'One of Dad's favourites.'

I remembered him telling me that Mum was the laidback one and he was the list maker. Zack and I had assumed that my brother favoured Mum, and I was more in Dad's camp, but now I wondered if we were each more of a combo of the two.

'Wise man,' Constance nodded. 'Now, let's clear up and then you can get on with your day.'

'You sound like you want to get rid of me,' I ventured.

'Not at all, but I would imagine you have a lot to do.'

She was right and I was going to need a distraction to make me forget what she'd formerly said. Or at least, not fall to thinking about it for too long.

Some of my day consisted of me looking up local consultants and agents who might be suitable for valuing Willowell Woods. It hadn't escaped my notice that Constance hadn't broached the subject again, but I hadn't forgotten. I might not have a bottomless financial well to draw from, but I wasn't going to pay her a penny less than the woods were genuinely worth, even if it did mean I ended up living in a shoebox for a while.

I'd settled on two firms by the end of the day and was just about to go and suggest them to Constance when James called.

'Hello you,' I smiled at the screen as the call connected. 'How are you doing?'

'Oh, I'm all right.' He smiled back, but the expression didn't reach his eyes, which had dark smudges under them.

'I'm not sure you mean that.'

'No,' he said, stifling a yawn, which made him look even more exhausted. 'I'm not sure I do either. This case is really taking it out of me. The client is a total nightmare, and I just know my boss set me up with them as punishment for taking on the extra pro bono case in Sudbury.'

'That wouldn't really have been their motivation, would it?' I frowned. 'That kind of behaviour would be ridiculous.'

'Well,' he sighed. 'That's how it feels.'

'I'm sorry, James.'

'Me too,' he agreed, then sat up straighter and I could see more of the space around him. I realised he was calling from an office, so was obviously still at work even though it was late. 'But it's not all doom and gloom,' he carried on.

'Oh?'

'I'm relieved to say that, after much deliberation and a *very* early walk along the river this morning, I've finally reached a decision about my dilemma.'

'Go on,' I encouraged him.

Given that he'd made the decision with the help of some time outside, I had a feeling I already knew what he was going to say. He was finally putting himself first and I immediately got carried away imagining him in his new role and potentially being closer to me on a full-time basis.

'I've decided to stick with what I've got.'

'Good for you!' I clapped. 'Wait . . . what?'

'I'm staying where I am,' he repeated.

That was the worst decision ever given that it meant continuing to work for the boss who was currently making him suffer for doing decent work.

'But why would you decide that?' I blurted out. 'You're so unhappy there, James.'

'I know,' he said, trying to sound certain he was doing the right thing, but not quite managing it, 'but this way, the family silver stays in the safe and ultimately, that's what matters most.'

I knew he'd taken his time and given his decision serious thought, so it wasn't my place to attempt to talk him out of it, but I really wanted to.

'Is it really silver that you're protecting?' I asked, even though I knew it wouldn't be.

'No,' he said, with a small smile. 'It's something far more precious than that.'

'Well, I hope I get to see it one day. I'd love to know what it is that's putting you through all of this and decide for myself if it's worth it.'

'I'm sure you'll see it,' he said. 'And I know you'll love it.'

'And I hope I get to see you again soon, too,' I said.

'Me too.' He smiled and this time his eyes did light up.

'I can't wait to pick up where we left off.' I smiled back.

'In the botanic garden, you mean?' he asked, feigning ignorance. 'It would be good to see it again as the summer inches towards its end . . .'

'You know exactly where I mean,' I laughed.

'Yes,' he said. 'I do.' Our eyes locked and then there was a loud knock on his office door. 'Damn,' he said. 'I have to go.'

'All right.' I swallowed, wishing I was there to kiss him goodnight, or even better, that he was sitting on the apartment sofa with me. 'Don't work too hard.'

'I'll try not to,' he promised. 'Bye.'
'Night. I hope you sleep well.'
'You too.'

With thoughts of mine and James's wonderful kisses still filling my head, I decided to have an early night. However, when I turned off the lamp, my mind began replaying my earlier conversation with Constance. It was extraordinary to think that she had a family member out in the world somewhere. I knew I'd promised that I wouldn't mention them again, but I would have loved to see them reconciled every bit as much as I was finding myself falling in love with James.

Chapter 17

Early the following morning, I woke with a start and lay for some seconds before I worked out what the sound I was listening to was.

'Rain, rain, go away,' I muttered as it splashed against and then ran down the bedroom window with some force while I snuggled deeper under the covers in response.

I might have been hoping for some rain to prompt Constance to potentially entertain us with her piano playing, but Kaya hadn't finished cleaning yet, so rather than moving our evening gathering into the sitting room, it would have to be cancelled rather than relocated.

'There'll be no treats tonight,' I sighed, thinking of Melody's baking when it became apparent that I wasn't going to go back to sleep, even though I didn't now have to get up.

I wasn't a fair-weather adventurer, but my planned walk around the woods could wait because there was no point in getting soaked for the sake of it. With a yawn, I pushed back the duvet and swung my legs out of bed. At least I'd be dry in The Greenman. I was going to see Carter later to ask how him brushing up on his bushcraft skills was coming along.

A knock on the door as I was drinking my first coffee of the day revealed Rick standing in the rain and looking a bit fed up about it.

'Hey,' I said. 'Do you want to come in?'

I opened the door wider, but he stayed outside.

'I'll only soak your floor,' he said considerately, as the water ran off the bottom of his waxed coat and puddled around his boots. 'Constance has just sent me along to say don't worry about joining her for breakfast because she's got to pop out.'

'In this weather?' I frowned. 'Did she say where to?'

I had hoped to run the names of the firms I'd found to value the woods by her, but that would have to wait now.

'Oddly enough,' Rick said, rather sardonically, 'she didn't share the details of her destination with me, she just asked me to tell you.'

I wondered if she was avoiding me following her relative revelation and I also wondered if Rick knew anything about the mystery person. He was local born and bred, after all. It was on the tip of my tongue to ask him, but remembering the promise I'd made to Constance that I wouldn't discuss it, I couldn't bring myself to break it.

'I suppose this will be a day off for you then, will it?' I asked instead and peered out at the rain again. 'I'm off to see Carter later. You can come if you like. It might be handy for the three of us to talk together.'

'No day off, I'm afraid.' Rick shivered and I guessed he was only wearing a T-shirt and shorts under the soaking wet coat. 'Though I'm heading to a place with a huge glasshouse, so at least I'll be working under cover.'

Mention of the glasshouse made me think again of my trip

to Cambridge and the steamy kisses James and I had shared. I gave a little shiver, but a different one to the kind Rick had just experienced.

'Where did you just go?' he grinned. 'I lost you there for a minute.'

The smile on his face suggested he had an inkling of an idea that I wasn't now thinking about the weather.

'Never mind,' I said, as the beginnings of a blush started to bloom. 'Thanks for the message. I hope you dry off soon.'

'So do I,' he said and flapped the coat in my direction.

'Don't!' I squealed. 'That's really cold.'

'See you later,' he grinned and walked off.

I shivered again. The temperature had dropped but the garden was looking lush. The lawn appeared to be three shades greener already, not that it had turned very brown because it was well shaded, but the ferns and hostas were sitting up higher in their pots and along the border. I supposed I could forgive the forecast if it was doing such wonderful things for the natural world. Just so long as it didn't give renewed vigour to the brambles and nettles covering the paths through Willowell Woods.

'Hey, Tilly,' Carter greeted me later that morning.

'Hi,' I smiled as I pulled off the jacket that hadn't turned out to be as watertight as the label promised. Thank goodness I hadn't ended up having to rely on it the day James and I should have walked around the water meadows. 'What a day!'

'What a day indeed,' he said, looking out of the door. There was now what looked like a bubbling stream running along the side of the lane. 'Isn't it typical? The one night I can get away to join you all at Fernside this week and the heavens open.'

'I know,' I sympathised. 'What are the odds?'

'Slim to none,' he chuckled. 'But I suppose there'll be other nights, won't there?' I'd already sent a message to our WhatsApp group, so he knew this one was off. 'What can I get you to drink?'

Given the temperature, I asked for a coffee, and I could see the few customers – mostly drenched walkers who had made a beeline for the cosy pub – were of the same mind.

'You're quite busy this morning,' I commented. 'At least the rain's good for business, but are you going to be free to chat?'

'I can't really stop,' Carter said, as another customer rushed in. 'But here's some good timing. You could do worse than strike up a conversation with this customer.'

'Oh?'

'Hang on,' he said and headed off to greet the woman.

She was in her forties and wearing a coat that had repelled the rain far better than mine. She was also sporting a waxed cap, and when she pulled it off, she ran her fingers through her cropped hair to tease it out a bit. She looked over at me and caught me staring because I was wondering what Carter was saying to her and who she was.

'Come and say hi,' I heard Carter say and the pair then came over. 'Tilly, this is Helen Harper. Helen, this is Tilly.'

'Hello, Helen.'

'Hello,' she said and looked briefly at my coat, which was draped over a barstool and starting to drip on the floor. 'The weather caught you out too, did it?'

'It did,' I nodded. 'Though you seem to have fared rather better than me.'

'Helen works for the council,' Carter said. 'She's a planning officer.'

'Oh,' I said, feeling suddenly on the back foot. 'Right.'

'Carter was just telling me how you're keen to get people to reconnect with the natural world,' Helen smiled.

'I didn't say more than that,' Carter said, as my gaze swung back to him. 'I thought I'd leave the rest to you. Assuming you want to.'

'Oh dear,' said Helen, sensing my discomfiture. 'Has he put his foot in it? If it makes any difference, I'm all for getting folk outdoors, too.'

'You are?'

'God, yes,' she said, while Carter made her a coffee. 'If it was down to me, fresh air and forest schools would be on the curriculum from nursery education onwards. Kids really miss out if they don't get taken on nature walks or have a birdfeeder in the garden, and that means they often grow up without knowing the benefit of it, too.'

Her words were music to my ears.

'I couldn't agree more,' I said earnestly.

'And I also think we desperately need the opportunity now to plug the gap that lack creates,' she went on. 'It's a pet topic of mine, so forgive me for running on, but I'd love to see more people exploring green spaces on a regular basis, wouldn't you?'

A deep rumble of thunder cut my answer off.

'Though perhaps not today, hey Tilly?' Carter smiled.

'Not in a thunderstorm,' I agreed, as lightning flashed and the pub lights flickered, 'but on every other day, certainly.'

'So, you really are a fresh air ambassador, too?' Helen smiled.

'A fully paid-up member of the club,' I told her. 'The benefits to physical and mental health as a result of getting outdoors are second to none so the more time spent doing it the better. But I obviously don't need to tell you that.'

'So, what do you think can be done to inspire more people to do it?' she asked.

I looked at Carter, and he nodded in encouragement.

'I'm not sure this is the right time or place to get into it,' I faltered.

'Let Helen be the judge of that,' Carter urged.

'You don't think I should let Helen be the judge when I apply to the council for permission?' I asked him pointedly.

'Well, this sounds serious!' Helen nudged. 'You have to tell me now.'

'Go on,' Carter nodded. 'Tell her. Don't buy her a coffee though, because that could be construed as a bribe. Do you have your notebook with you?'

'Yes.' I swallowed and held it up.

'Come on then,' said Helen. 'Let's go and have a chat.'

Two cups of coffee later, the storm had rolled away, and I had taken Helen through pretty much every aspect of the plan that I had come up with so far. It had been thrilling to fill her in and the fact that she might well end up being one of the planners who had a hand in deciding both my fate and that of the woods made her enthusiasm even more encouraging.

'And there's already been a business on the site?' she asked again, adding a few more words to the notes she'd made on a page torn from the back of my notebook.

'That's right,' I reiterated. 'And the wooden building, which was built for that business, already sits wonderfully in the landscape and it won't need changing. Unless it needs adapting for wheelchair access and conveniences.'

'So, all you really need from the council is a yes?'

'That's right,' I confirmed. 'There's some tree work to carry out, but not a huge amount.'

'Safety first.'

'Always. And I'll keep group numbers small when I do open, so every visiting adult can enjoy the ambience and get the most benefit from their time in the woods.'

'And limiting numbers would ensure you didn't end up with cars parked along the lane, too . . .'

Helen was familiar with the location and the entrance to the site.

'That's right. No extra parking would be required.'

She put down the pen Carter had lent her and sat back on her chair. She steepled her fingers while she mulled everything over.

'I'd love to come and have a look at the place,' she requested eventually.

'That can easily be arranged,' I told her, and I thought my heart was going to beat out of my chest. 'Constance has given me the keys to the gate so I can come and go as I please.'

I didn't mention that the padlock was currently rusted shut. Helen looked spry enough to clamber over the gate in the same way that I was currently gaining access. Though perhaps bolt croppers and a new padlock and chain would be a better option when it came to impressing her.

'And she approves of what you have in mind?' she asked.

'Completely,' I confirmed. 'The only reason we haven't yet moved further on with the sale is because she needs to have the site properly valued and I need to try and establish the likelihood of getting permission to run the business there.'

'Well,' Helen said, as she glanced over her notes again and tapped a polished and manicured nail on the table, 'I personally can't think of a single objection to what you have in mind.'

'Really?' I squeaked.

'Really,' she smiled. 'Obviously, that's only my opinion, but you've answered every one of my questions and even though it would have to go to committee level because it's a business in a woodland, the fact there's been one there before will stand you in excellent stead for getting approval for another. Especially of the kind you're proposing.'

'I don't know what to say,' I gulped, as my eyes filled with very happy tears and I blinked hard to stop them escaping. I was trying to come across as a seasoned professional after all. 'I can't tell you what a weight this is off my mind . . .'

'But remember,' Helen cautioned, 'this is only my opinion.' However, she then thrillingly added, 'But the rest of the planning team will get this through. I know they will.'

'I wish I knew you better Helen,' I sniffed, becoming completely unprofessional then as I got carried away, 'because I'd give you the biggest hug.'

She laughed at that and Carter sidled over.

'So, am I forgiven?' he asked tentatively, with a sheepish grin. 'The smile on your face suggests I might be, Tilly.'

'You could say that!' I beamed and jumped up to hug him because I had to hug someone.

'You've been talking for ages,' Carter said, when I eventually let him go.

'Oh crikey,' said Helen, in response to the mention of the

time. 'I've just seen how late I am! I'm supposed to be in a meeting in twenty minutes.'

'That's my fault,' I grimaced. 'I'm so sorry.'

'Do not apologise,' she told me. 'This has been a breath of fresh air, and the local and wider community are going to benefit so much from what you're going to be offering.'

'And local businesses, too,' Carter pointed out.

'Oh yes,' I said. 'I can't believe I forgot. Melody, from the Willowell Store, is going to supply food, Carter here will be occasionally running some courses and Rick, a local gardener and arborist, will be carrying out the tree work.'

'Wow!' Helen commented as she pulled on her coat, which looked far drier than mine. 'This just keeps getting better.'

'And I'm sure there'll be other people who'll come on-board once we're up and running,' I puffed, feeling slightly out of breath.

'I might have a couple of suggestions myself,' she said ponderously, as she put her cap back on. 'I'll get Carter to give you my email and you can get the ball rolling as soon as you and Constance have sorted the sale. Keep in touch, yes?'

'Super,' I said, as she made for the door. 'And yes, I will. Thank you, so much.'

She stopped and looked back. 'You're very welcome,' she smiled. 'And would that tree guy that you mentioned happen to be Rick, as in—'

'Yep,' said Carter. 'That's the one.'

'I thought it might be,' she said mysteriously, and was gone.

There had been a lull in the rain and the rest of the customers had left by then, which was just as well given the happy squeal and subsequent silly dance I did around the bar.

'And not a glass of bitter in sight,' Carter laughed, as he watched me. 'I know you wanted to throttle me when I introduced you, but I knew there was no one better for you to talk to.'

'And you were right,' I applauded him. 'I take it Helen knows who Rick is?'

'Um,' Carter winced and rubbed a hand around the back of his neck. 'He had a bit of a thing with Helen's son, Tobias, and it didn't end well.'

'Bloody Rick!' I groaned, assuming it was him causing the heartbreak, which Carter then confirmed it was. 'If being connected to him scuppers this for me, I'll brain him.'

'It's all water under the bridge,' Carter said quickly. 'And besides, Helen is far too professional to let something personal influence her.'

'Thank goodness for that!' I snorted, feeling excited again.

Chapter 18

I headed back to Fernside in the happiest mood. I felt even more ecstatic than when Constance had agreed to me buying Willowell Woods because then my excitement had been tempered with the fear that I wouldn't get permission for the business, and my dream wouldn't come true. Now, however, I was feeling far more optimistic!

I knew what Helen had said was only her opinion, but she was so keen and convinced that her colleagues on the planning committee would agree with her too that my heart was now full of more justified hope, excitement and eagerness to forge ahead.

I was tempted to stop at the store and pick up a couple of bottles of elderflower fizz to celebrate with, but I knew that if either Melody or Kaya served me I wouldn't be able to keep what had just happened to myself, and I wanted Constance to be the first to know. After Carter, of course. And given that the happy news was down to him introducing me to Helen, his already knowing what had occurred felt perfectly acceptable.

'I must start another list,' I laughed happily, as I remembered that the first thing I needed to do was get the woods valued and then buy them!

Back at the house, I had to stop my car ahead of where I usually parked because there was something dumped on the drive. When I got out, I realised it was the for sale sign from the woods. The post had been snapped in half and the board was broken, too. Whoever had taken it down must have had Herculean strength because I'd tried to shift it and it hadn't budged an inch. I guessed Constance must have asked Rick to remove it now things were settled between us and the sight of it sent my spirits soaring even higher.

'Constance!' I called aloud as I rushed through the gate, which was unusually unlocked, with my trusty notebook clasped tight in my hand.

The sound of the piano drifted towards me and I knew exactly where to go to find her. I didn't recognise the tune, but she was playing it at a speed I wouldn't have thought her fingers capable of, and it wasn't the most delicate sound, either. In fact, the closer I got, the more it sounded like an assault, rather than a tender caress of the keys.

In my buoyed-up state, I thought I'd soon remedy her bad mood, assuming she was in one, and, throwing caution to the wind, I rushed straight through the doors that opened out to the garden and into the sitting room.

'Constance!' I said again, even louder that time, to make myself heard, and not at all concerned that I was about to out her as a musician when she'd made such a point of keeping it a secret. 'You're not going to believe what's just happened. Talk about serendipity . . .'

The words died in my throat as I came to a shuddering halt,

my heart beating a tattoo and my breath sharp in my chest. It was shock that had pulled me up so short, so fast, because I wasn't looking at Constance on the piano stool in the rather grand room, I was staring at the back of . . .

'James?' I frowned and he stopped playing and spun around. 'James!' I said again. 'It is you, but—'

'Tilly,' he gasped, cutting me off. 'What are you doing here?'

'What am I doing here?' I blinked, feeling utterly astounded. 'What are you doing here, more like?'

He looked as astonished to see me as I was to see him. I hadn't spotted his car, or indeed any car, on the drive, so there'd been no heads up that I was about to bewilderingly find him, rather than Constance, bashing seven bells out of her piano.

'I asked you first,' he said back, his former expression of amazement being replaced with one of suspicion and perhaps even a hint of anger, though why my presence should justify that, I had no idea.

I was every bit as shocked to see him, but I wasn't angry, was I? That said, the initial urge the sight of him had induced, that had me wanting to throw my arms around him and kiss the lips off him, had suddenly slunk off. Now, I felt a hard ball in the pit of my stomach that heralded something was seriously amiss. Now the initial moment of recognition had worn off I was feeling nauseous and unsteady on my feet.

'I live here,' I told him tentatively. 'Not in the house, but in an apartment that's attached to it.'

'You live *here*?' James repeated incredulously, and his eyes grew so wide they were practically on stalks. 'You live here, at Fernside?'

'Yes,' I confirmed. 'And I was just coming to find my friend.'

'Your friend being . . .'

'Constance Clarke,' I said succinctly. 'The woman who owns this house.'

James dropped his head and cradled it for a moment in his hands with his elbows resting on his knees. He appeared to be having as difficult a time processing what I had just said as I was trying to get my head around finding him so familiarly ensconced in Constance's sitting room.

'Please,' he said, when he eventually looked up again, and I could see the colour had completely drained from his face and that even his lips had turned white. 'Please don't tell me, Tilly, that you're the person who wants to buy Willowell Woods.'

'I'm the person who *is* buying Willowell Woods,' I said with emphasis. 'And now you can tell me how it is that you know about them?'

'How do I know about them?' he said with a grim smile that didn't suit his handsome features at all. 'We'll get to that in a minute, but first, I need to tell you that the woods aren't for sale.'

'Of course they are,' I said back as I tried to swallow down the rising feeling of panic that was starting to take over from the nausea.

Literally just a couple of minutes ago I had arrived at Fernside floating on cloud nine, but now I had fallen and was tumbling back to earth with no grasp on the straps that would open my parachute.

'I'm sorry, Tilly,' James said firmly. 'But they're not.'

'And that's you talking as Constance's legal adviser, is it?' I said, jutting out my chin in an attempt at defiance, even though on the inside I felt on the point of collapse.

My entire body felt consumed by an emotional cocktail of confusion, upset and shock.

'No,' he said as he fixed his gaze onto mine. 'This is me talking as her nephew, her exhausted adviser in all things financial and the person who now bitterly regrets ever going along with her suggestion to put the woods up for sale in the first place.'

'You're her nephew,' I whispered in shock, as I fumbled for the chair behind me and shakily sank into it. 'Oh my god, you're Grace's child.'

'Yes,' said James. 'I'm Grace's son. Constance is my aunt.'

'Constance is your aunt,' I repeated on an out breath.

'That's right,' he said bluntly, and I did then begin to feel angry myself.

'In that case, it's a shame you haven't looked after her better, isn't it?' I snapped waspishly.

'Sorry?'

James looked flabbergasted, but I felt furious with him and, for the moment, I forgot all about the woods and focused on the woman we were talking about.

'You reported her to Social Services, James! Don't deny it.'

'I wasn't going to deny it,' he fired back, sounding incensed himself. 'Did she tell you *why* I did it?'

'No,' I had no choice but to confess. 'But I know she was devastated that you did.'

James offered no explanation as to why he'd put Miss Lyons on his aunt's case and we were quiet for a moment, both of us lost in the shock of what was unravelling.

'Was it your mum who instilled in you your love for the outdoors?' I asked once my brain had calmed down enough to unscramble a few things. 'I know she was a keen gardener and a great plantswoman.'

'Yes,' said James. 'It was Mum. It was the greatest gift she ever gave me.'

And there went my heart, but my next question reined it in again.

'So, with that in mind,' I frowned, 'why *did* you go along with Constance putting the woods up for sale? I would have thought they'd mean even more to you than her.'

'They did,' he said. 'They do.'

'I heard a rumour that the house needs repairs and that's what prompted the sale—'

'Rumours,' James tutted. 'Gossip. All of which you know is untrue, because you've been doing the housework and found nothing amiss.'

'I haven't been doing the housework,' I said quickly. 'Constance has taken on a cleaner.'

James looked doubtful. 'But how has she funded that?' he said, more to himself than me. 'Because I know for a fact that she hasn't been spending any of the money I've been sending her . . .'

'You've been sending her money?'

James's gaze swung back to my face and his expression was stricken. So, that was where some of his salary was going every month, to Constance, to the house.

'Can you forget you heard me say that?' he requested. 'My aunt would be even more furious with me if she found out I'd alluded to her scant finances on top of everything else.'

'But if—'

I had been going to ask if there was any point in carrying on with doing work he didn't have the heart for if he'd realised that Constance wasn't spending the money he earned, but he cut me off.

'I mean it,' he said. 'Though however she is paying for a cleaner, it does feel wonderful that this place looks and feels more like home again.'

For the first time since I'd burst into it, I looked properly around the room. With its walls lined with bookcases, heavy sun-faded drapes, cushion covered squishy sofas, chairs and the piano that took centre stage, it was a beautiful and relaxed space and full of the bohemian charm which Constance had graced the supper parties with.

'She's funding it with the rent I'm paying her,' I told James, once I'd taken it all in.

'You're paying rent?'

'Of course I am. And we're planning to get the woods properly valued, too,' I said. 'What Constance was asking for them was absurdly low given there's a building on-site and proper parking next to the lane. So, going forward, you won't have to help her out with money because her finances will be far healthier.'

James looked mutinous again for a moment, but then his expression softened. 'I can't believe it's you,' he whispered.

His eyes met mine again and this time I could see that they were shining with tears.

'And I can't believe it's you,' I responded, feeling a mutual rush of upset.

'What are the chances?' He pressed the palms of his hands into his eyes.

'Constance only very recently told me that she still had a living relative,' I said quietly, 'and that she was estranged from them. Given the state of the house when I arrived and the fact that she wasn't eating properly, I was shocked to discover she had anyone at all, but then if you'd fallen out—'

'She wasn't eating properly?' James baulked and looked at me again, appalled.

'No,' I said, and given his shock, I felt bad for mentioning it, especially now the situation was so much improved. 'But she is now.'

'Well, that's a relief to hear.'

'Could you not have reached out before?' I ventured and James laughed, which made me jump. 'If it was me, no matter what had happened, I could never have left—'

'Is that what she told you? That I abandoned her?'

'Not in so many words, but—'

'Tilly,' he cut in again, 'I think we need to drop this. You don't know anything about what's gone on and right now, I have no desire to tell you.'

'Oh, well, if that's how you feel . . .'

'It is,' he said more gently. 'And discovering you here . . . it's all still so raw. I'd never forgive myself if I said things to you now that I'd later regret.'

'You don't feel that you can talk to me now?'

'I hate that you sound so upset.' He swallowed and ran his hands through his hair. 'But in this moment, I don't honestly know what I feel.'

Given what I'd discovered in the last few minutes, coupled with the fact that I was now going to have to fight a battle I couldn't in a million years have predicted to secure buying the woods, I could relate to that.

'Me neither,' I sighed and my shoulders dropped.

I felt as limp as a wrung-out dishcloth as I thought back

to the moment James and I had met in the lay-by not all that far away and I wondered if he had come to the house that day or been visiting the woods. And the time after that, when our cars had passed on the road. Had he been to visit Fernside then, too? Constance had told me she and her relative were estranged, but perhaps James *had* been trying to reach out.

I wanted to ask what he'd been doing in the area on those occasions, but there was a more pressing question to address first, and it landed just as I was trying to imagine how Constance was going to react when she discovered that her nephew was my meet-cute.

'Where is your aunt?' I frowned.

'In the garden.'

James stood up and went to look out of the door. It was then that we both tuned into the sound of a dog barking.

'Is there a dog out there?'

'Buddy!' James shouted and dashed outside. 'Aunt Constance!'

I quickly followed him towards the jetty where a large Golden Retriever was standing next to something on the ground.

'Aunt Constance!' James called again and I realised that the thing on the ground was his aunt. 'Tilly call an ambulance,' he shouted over his shoulder to me.

'No,' came Constance's reedy protest. 'I don't need an ambulance. I just need you to call this blasted dog off and help me get back on my feet.'

'Buddy,' James tutted and gently pulled the dog away.

The dog, whose name I recognised, looked extremely pleased with himself as he panted and his tongue lolled.

'I don't think you should try and get up,' I said, as I knelt next to Constance and gently laid a hand on her shoulder. 'Don't try to move her, James.'

'I wasn't going to,' he snapped. 'I'm not a total idiot.'

'Well, you've just made yourself sound like one,' I bit back.

Constance gave us both a look. 'If the pair of you could stop sniping,' she commanded, then winced as she tried to shift her position a little, 'we might be able to work out what to do.'

'Sorry,' James and I said together.

'How did you fall?' James asked. 'Buddy didn't trip you up, did he?'

'No,' she said. 'It wasn't him. I realised Tilly was back and I wanted to introduce the pair of you before she came across you with no idea as to who you are. I rushed to move and slipped over on the wet wood. Nothing to do with your fool of a dog, James, and I'm sure I'll be fine, once I'm up.'

'No way,' said James. 'As Tilly just said, we're not moving you.'

'If you've done some damage we can't see,' I said, offering an explanation as to why, 'then we'll do more harm than good.'

Constance didn't say anything.

'Right,' said James, to break the impasse. 'I am calling an ambulance.'

James made the call from nearer the house where he could pick up a signal and then came back with a couple of cushions and a blanket.

'I can't believe this is how the pair of you have met,' Constance tutted, while James gave me the quickest look and then solicitously made sure she was warm and as comfortable as she could be. 'I didn't expect you back so soon, Tilly.'

'I had good news,' I told her. My conversation with Helen in The Greenman felt like an age ago now. 'And I wanted to share it with you.'

'Go on then,' she said. 'It will pass the time.'

'It doesn't matter now,' I told her, having looked at James and the concern etched across his face. 'Let's just focus on you, shall we?'

'I'm all right,' she said, but I didn't think she was. 'You can get off if you need to, James. You're needed back in Cambridge, aren't you?'

'Yes,' I said, then faltered. 'How's that . . . journey? How do you find the journey from here?'

I went so hot, and my heart started to beat so fast because I'd already almost tripped myself up. I had been about to ask James how the case was going, but given that we were pretending we'd only just met, I shouldn't have known there was a case or even that he was a barrister!

'It depends on the time of day,' James blagged and I saw that his cheeks were burning as brightly as mine. 'And whether I'm needed or not, Aunt Constance, I'm not going anywhere now. Not until I know you really are okay.'

'I'm fine.'

'Well, whether you are or not,' he told her, 'we'll soon find out, because I can hear a siren.'

'I'll go and get my things,' I said and stood up.

'What for?' James asked.

'I thought I'd go with Constance, so you can stay here with Buddy.'

'I appreciate the thought,' he said, 'but I'm a blood relative, so it will make more sense for me to go, won't it?'

'Oh yes,' I conceded. 'I suppose it will. Shall I look after Buddy then?'

The dog bounded over at the sound of his name. I loved dogs, but I'd never been responsible for one and found the prospect a little daunting.

'If you wouldn't mind,' James said.

I put my hand out and Buddy plonked his paw in it.

'I don't mind,' I said bravely as the siren got louder. 'We'll be fine, won't we Buddy?'

He seemed happy enough with the arrangement and James looked relieved.

'Would you fetch my bag from the kitchen please, Tilly?' Constance asked me.

'I'll show the paramedics in and find it for you.'

Buddy willingly followed me up the lawn, said hello to the ambulance crew and then tagged along to the house, where I shut him in the sunroom after I'd found Constance's bag.

'She won't need this,' James said, when I handed it over.

His voice was a little shaky.

'Is she okay?' I asked. 'Are you?'

I went to lay a hand on his arm but then changed my mind.

'The paramedics think she's fine but it's standard practice to get checked over at the hospital in a situation like this.'

'That makes sense.'

'Can you tell her that?' James smiled. 'Because she's having a bit of a moan.'

'Your aunt, your problem,' I said, and he laughed.

It felt good to hear.

'I'll just go and say goodbye to Buddy.'

He gave the dog a fuss as the paramedics pushed Constance

in a chair up the lawn. I hoped she hadn't noticed the marks they were leaving in the turf.

'I need you to stay with, Tilly, okay?' James said to his dog. 'I won't be long.'

'You'll be hours,' I corrected him.

'Probably,' James said. 'But I can't tell him that.'

'Do I need to do anything with him?'

'There's some food in a container on the table in the kitchen. He can have two scoops of that around six and he'll let you know if needs the loo. He's good at asking and knows where to go.'

Constance obviously hadn't realised, but James had clearly been planning on staying as he'd brought Buddy along *and* some food for him. I wondered, given that James was mid-case in Cambridge, what the reason behind his surprise arrival was.

'Okay,' I said, knowing it was a question for another time. 'Well, you'd better go.'

I didn't expect him to, but he gently drew me to him for a hug and, with Constance now out of sight, I didn't resist. It felt both comforting and confusing to feel myself back in his arms. I had no idea how we were going to resolve the problems we now faced, but one thing I did know, was that I would be devastated to lose both him and the woods.

Chapter 19

There was nothing that I could settle to other than keeping an eye on Buddy and going repeatedly over in my mind what had occurred since I'd arrived back at Fernside after the most thrilling conversation with Helen in The Greenman.

Under different circumstances, such as those where I hadn't been confronted by my beau, Constance's only living relative and now the potential barrier to my blissful future, I would have been celebrating in style, booking a valuation and searching for a local solicitor, but I couldn't continue with any of that now.

'What's the matter with you, Buddy?' I frowned at the circling dog, when I came out of my reverie and noticed he was looking pleadingly towards the back door. 'Ah,' I guessed, and quickly jumped up to let him out. 'Go on then. And no peeing on your aunt's lovely green lawn. Or any of the plants!'

He shot off round the side of the house, and I hoped he was heading to where James had said he would go, rather than making a bid for freedom. It wouldn't bode well for us if I lost his dog, would it? The way James had fussed over and spoken to him suggested he thought the world of him.

'Wait for me,' I called to Buddy as I slipped on my shoes and followed him.

He'd found me before I spotted him and was looking much happier about life when he came tearing back, so I assumed he'd done what he needed to. I'd just started to tell him what a good dog he was when he ran off again, but this time to the garden gate. A loud woof alerted me to the fact that someone was there. I knew it couldn't be James because he hadn't been gone anywhere near long enough.

'Hello, you,' came the sound of Rick's voice. 'What are you doing here, you daft dog? Come on, let me through.' He appeared around the side of the house with the broken for sale board in his arms. 'Hey, Tilly. This was on the drive; I almost ran over it. What's going on?'

I realised then that James had doubtless been the one to pull it up and cart it back.

'Is this a friend of yours?' I asked, rather than answer Rick's question as Buddy capered about around him.

'Yeah,' he said, as he leant the board against the house wall and gave Buddy a fuss. 'Kind of. I mean, if it's who I think it is, I haven't seen him in a long time, but we were briefly acquainted once.'

'Right,' I said. 'I see. So, you also know James, then?'

'Same as the hound,' he shrugged. 'Our paths have occasionally crossed in the past. But never mind that, what has happened? Someone said they saw an ambulance turning onto the drive earlier. Is Constance, okay? And actually, what is her nephew doing here?'

'She slipped over on the jetty,' I told him, and his hands flew to his face. 'She seemed fine, but James called an ambulance

Walking on Sunshine

just in case and the paramedics wanted to take her to get checked over.'

'So, nothing broken or bleeding, then?'

'Not as far as we could tell,' I said, feeling suddenly emotional and a bit wobbly.

'And what about you?' he asked tenderly, rather than pursue the James topic. 'Are you okay?'

Buddy came over, sat on my feet and looked up at me with his big brown eyes. James had big brown eyes, too.

'Oh, I'm all right,' I said shakily, as I rubbed Buddy's domed head and tried to smile. 'I'm not the one who fell over, am I?'

'Perhaps not,' Rick frowned. 'But you do look a bit pale, Tilly. Let me make you a tea and you can tell me what's going on.'

I felt a lump form in my throat.

'Don't be nice to me,' I told him. 'I can't handle that today. Not from you or anyone.'

'Come on,' he said, and the three of us headed inside.

I sat quietly at the table while Rick bustled about and made me a mug of very sweet tea and watched me eat a couple of plain chocolate digestives. They were Constance's favourite, so I made a note to replace them on my next trip to the store.

'So,' he said, once I'd almost finished the tea, 'now you're full of sugar, do you feel up to explaining? What is James doing here? I'm dying to know.'

'Before we get into that,' I said rather crossly, the sugar having obviously made a difference to my recovery from the shock of it all, 'I want to know why you've never once mentioned to me that Constance has a nephew?' Rick puffed out his cheeks. 'I only very recently discovered she had an estranged relative somewhere out in the world and today I came back from a trip to the pub to find him playing her piano!'

'Is he good?' Rick asked. 'I bet—'

'Rick!'

There was a time and place for his silliness and here and now wasn't it.

'Sorry.'

'So, why has James never come up in any of our conversations?'

'Because when Constance and James had this monumental falling out a while back, she banned all talk of him,' Rick said sadly. 'Given her advancing age and the fact that she's on her own here, I did try and talk to her about it, but she said that if I persisted, or if I talked to anyone else about it, she'd find another gardener and it would be the end of our relationship, too.'

'Blimey,' I said. 'She was adamant that James was banished then.'

'You could say that. You know how stubborn she can be and I thought if I lost the gardening gig here, then I'd never have eyes on her. You might have realised, we don't share the same hairdresser.'

'But she wouldn't have known if you'd told me about him on the quiet,' I tutted. 'You could have filled me in on any number of occasions when she was out of earshot.'

'I could never break a promise to Constance,' Rick insisted. He sounded so genuinely appalled by my suggestion that I supposed I had to take him at his word. 'And anyway, as they no longer had anything to do with one another, I didn't think there was any need to talk about him. More than that in fact

... because it happened a while ago, James hasn't crossed my mind since you arrived, so it was never an issue.'

I wasn't sure I believed that Rick hadn't thought about him at all. He was as prone to admiring a handsome man as the rest of us, but I couldn't question his love for Constance. It felt more likely that his forgetfulness about James resulted from that.

'Well, as he's back now, I'm sure we're allowed to mention him,' I said. 'Do you know what it was that they fell out over?'

'Not in any detail. Constance has never gone into it. She's quite a private person where family is concerned . . .'

'You're telling me.'

'But I always assumed it was something to do with a conversation about selling the woods. The timing seems to fit, though it wasn't all that long ago that Constance asked me if I knew anyone who could put a board up for her, so she took a while after James became taboo to act on her decision.'

'I see . . .' I said, considering all of this information.

'I never knew James well,' Rick continued. 'He went to some posh private school and was only around in the holidays. I was really shocked when this ruckus first happened though, and he just walked away and disappeared from Constance's life.'

Clearly, I wasn't the only one who had assumed James had abandoned his aunt.

'I don't think the situation was quite as cut and dried as that, Rick.'

'Oh?'

'I don't know the details,' I said, as the conversation I'd had with Constance about monkeys and organ grinders popped into my head, 'but I don't think he'd completely disappeared.'

'Well, that's something, I suppose,' Rick accepted. 'And now he's back,' he added, with a nod to Buddy who was hovering in the hope of biscuit crumbs, 'perhaps things will turn out all right, after all.'

'Not for me.' I swallowed.

'How come?'

'James has told me that the woods are no longer up for sale.'

Rick's mouth fell open. 'You're kidding? No, of course you're not.'

'No,' I said shudderingly. 'Of course I'm not.'

'And has Constance confirmed this?'

'No,' I said. 'She hasn't. She was outside while we were . . . getting acquainted, so I don't know what she knows he's said at this point. And now the pair of them are at the hospital.'

'Given that James went with her, perhaps he's trying to patch things up between them. Though that's probably not much consolation for you right now . . .'

As much as I loved the thought of James and Constance restoring their relationship, I knew that wouldn't bode well for me. But in spite of that, I wasn't going to wish for their continued estrangement, just to get my own way over buying the woods, assuming Constance disagreed with James's desire not to sell.

And of course, if Constance and I did now forge ahead without James's blessing, that would doubtless sever familial ties again and end my relationship with James, romantic or otherwise. That is, if we still had one . . .

'Tilly?'

'Um . . .'

'Are you okay?'

'Not really,' I said dully, while trying not to cry. 'I was just thinking about my lost future.'

Rick didn't know it, but I wasn't only considering the woods. James was someone I could see myself being truly happy with for a very long time, maybe for ever, or he had been until a couple of hours ago.

'Oh, you poor love,' Rick said sympathetically and gave my hand a squeeze. 'I'll make another brew.'

I sat nursing my mug and further mulling things over. While Rick had made the tea, he'd told me how James used to help his mum in the nursery when he was back from school. It saddened me to think he'd just finished his A-levels and would have been able to spend more time with her than when he'd been away at school when he lost her.

'That is sad,' said Rick, when I aired my thoughts. 'But it doesn't justify him interfering over the woods. Though perhaps that's why he wants to hang on to them, because of the connection to his mum . . .'

That thought made me feel even worse about wanting to take them out of the Clarke family. Given that James had said the greatest gift his mum had given him was her passion for the outdoors then it was perfectly logical that he wanted to keep close the place where he had felt most connected to her.

'If that's the case, do you think Constance should hang on to them?'

That would make James happy, but at a huge cost to me. And us.

'I dunno,' Rick shrugged. 'But you should take comfort in the fact that, at the end of the day, Constance is her own woman and her say will be the final one. If she still wants to sell, she will.'

I wasn't sure if that was a comfort now. Whatever she decided had implications for both me and James, both separately and together, and not happy ones as far as I could currently see.

'You won't talk to anyone about any of this, will you Rick?'

'I won't mention it to a single soul.'

'Promise?' I asked.

I wanted a little extra confirmation because he'd felt no qualms about bringing up my date at the supper party.

'This is Constance's private business,' he said seriously. 'My lips are zipped. Scout's honour.'

I couldn't ask for a more sincere declaration than that.

Having eaten our respective dinners, Buddy and I sat in the garden as the evening slipped into night. It was much cooler thanks to the earlier storm, and I could see that the jetty was now completely dry.

Rick had told me that he'd warned Constance multiple times not to walk on it when it was damp and that he had wanted to cover it in chicken wire to give it some grip, but she hadn't liked the thought of how that would feel underfoot. He promised he'd now give some thought to coming up with an alternative.

I startled as my phone pinged with a succinct message from James, just as I was stifling a yawn.

'Now heading back,' I read aloud, but he didn't say how he was getting back or if he was bringing Constance with him.

It was then that I wondered where his car was. I had been about to take Buddy into the apartment but thought I'd wait it out in the sunroom and leave the back door open, so I didn't look too at home.

'Come on, Buddy,' I said. 'Let's head inside.'

I was just nodding off when I heard the garden gate open. It sounded louder than usual, but I reasoned that was because it was almost dark and I could only hear one set of footsteps. One set of human footsteps. Buddy had rushed off to see who it was and I could hear his claws scrabbling about on the path.

'Hello, mate,' James said tiredly, as he came into view and fussed his canine friend who was extremely excited to see him. 'Hello, Buddy, my love.'

What a warm welcome and wonderful term of endearment.

'No Constance?' I questioned, as I stood up and stretched out my back. 'Is she okay? Your message didn't say . . .'

'She's fine,' he said quickly. 'Physically all in one piece, but mentally furious at being told she's got to stay in overnight as it took so long before they could get to her in A and E.'

'Oh, dear.'

'She's hardly ever had a night away from Fernside,' he continued, sounding upset. He looked even more exhausted as he stared at the back of the house. 'And she hasn't even got her nightie.'

For a moment I thought he was going to cry and felt torn as to how to respond.

'Anyway.' He sniffed and the moment was gone. 'I'm back now and she can come home as soon as the doctor, or whoever's responsible, discharges her in the morning.'

'That's a relief.'

'It is.'

'How did you get back? I haven't seen your car, but I guess it's here. Did you ride with Constance in the ambulance or follow on behind?'

'I went in the ambulance. The car's in the garage. I had to get it under cover when I arrived as the sunroof has sprung a leak.'

'Not great timing given the weather earlier,' I sympathised. 'But thank goodness it wasn't an issue the day we met at the water meadows. Or was it?'

'No,' he said and his eyes met mine. 'It was fine then, so yes, thank goodness for that.'

I felt moved to say how much I'd enjoyed our impromptu picnic in my car, but with him looking so thoroughly worn out and me knowing that my emotions were still right at the surface, I didn't think it would be helpful to mention it.

'So, you came back in a cab, then?' I asked instead.

'No, Rick gave me a lift.'

'Rick?'

'Um. He said he'd called in here and then came to wait for me at the hospital.'

'That was kind of him.'

I hoped he hadn't mentioned the woods. He had promised he wouldn't talk about the situation, but I wasn't sure if that included saying anything to James.

'It was.' James nodded without elaborating.

'Well, I can go and pick Constance up tomorrow—'

'That won't be necessary,' he interrupted. 'But thank you.'

'It's no problem,' I insisted. 'And I'll keep an eye on her after that, too. Maybe do a bit more cooking for her. We already share breakfast most days.'

'That's kind, Tilly, but there's no need. My aunt and I will manage things between us from now on.'

Why was he being so stubborn?

'And how are you going to do that?' I asked. 'Surely you're needed back in Cambridge?'

'But I'd rather—'

'Look,' I said. 'I know everything's weird between us now, James—'

'Weird?' he snorted. 'Things are *weird*?'

'You find a better word then,' I said, feeling frustrated that the conversation had gone so far downhill so fast, 'but let's keep Constance front and centre, shall we? She's going to need help and as I'm already here and you're not going to be, I can offer it.'

'I don't know . . .'

'Okay, fine,' I snapped. 'Forget it.'

He looked at me again, and I looked at him, and I wondered if my expression now was as forlorn as his. I would imagine it must have been. After all, even though we'd both had a huge shock, I was also the one who'd had the rug with the pattern of my future printed on it pulled out from under my feet.

'I'm sorry,' he said, and distractedly shook his head. 'It's just . . . been a day.'

'You're telling me.' I swallowed. I could feel my bottom lip starting to wobble and it took every bit of willpower I possessed not to cry.

'Oh Tilly . . .'

'Don't,' I said and cleared my throat. 'It's fine. So, shall I collect Constance or not?'

He shifted his weight from one foot to the other. 'Yes,' he said finally. 'If you could bring her home, that would be helpful. We'll talk over what to do about everything else after that.'

'Great.' I nodded and made for the door. 'Let's do that.'

Chapter 20

For practically the first time since I'd arrived at Fernside, I barely slept. The combination of knowing that James was sleeping, or not, just a few walls away, and yet I hadn't been further from him since I'd known him was hard to bear, as was the fact that my business had felt within my grasp for less than an hour before it had been potentially snatched away.

Rick might have insisted that I shouldn't worry about what James had said and that Constance was the one in charge, but during the long watches of the night, his encouraging words were of no comfort because if she did still forge ahead then the consequences were going to be dire, and conversely, if James convinced her not to sell, I was going to be back to square one on the path of my adventure with limited chance of crossing the finishing line. Sites such as Willowell Woods were so rare, the chances of coming across another one was even rarer and it would be positioned nowhere near my beloved Willowell.

'Seriously, James,' I frowned as, at just after ten the following morning, my phone pinged with a message. 'Aunt Constance has been given the all clear,' I read aloud. 'You can pick her up whenever you're ready.'

It would have taken him all of two minutes to come and tell me that in person. Was this how things were going to be between us now? The situation might have been excruciatingly awkward, but I'd far rather talk to him in person than resort to succinct messages that were ripe for misinterpretation and likely to cause upset or an argument.

'Now on my way,' I typed back, refraining from saying more, and set straight off.

As I strode past the back of the house I sensed rather than saw that he was in the sunroom, but I didn't stop. He'd made it clear that he didn't want to talk, and I wasn't going to try and force the situation.

'Constance,' I smiled when I had finally tracked her down. 'Here you are. How are you feeling?'

She was sitting in a chair next to an already stripped bed and she looked rather pale. I made a point of making my tone brighter than I felt. She didn't need to know that I wasn't feeling like my usual sunny self or was concerned that she looked wan.

'Stiff as a board,' she muttered. 'And bruised all over. All over my side anyway, and on my . . . well, you get the idea. This has done nothing for my trick hip.'

I thought it was a miracle she hadn't broken anything, especially the alleged trick hip.

'Oh Constance,' I commiserated. 'Have you got any arnica? That's supposed to be good for bruises, isn't it? And a long soak in a deep bath might not be a bad idea.'

'I don't know if I'd be able to get in a bath,' she huffed.

She was clearly fed up, but with good reason.

'I don't mind helping you,' I told her. 'If you don't think it would be an imposition.'

'We'll see,' she said, which I took to mean, thanks for the offer, but not on your life.

'And who's this?' asked a nurse, who then arrived with some paperwork.

'My friend, Tilly,' Constance said.

'No nephew today?' the nurse said, looking around. 'My friend who works in A and E said I was in for a treat this morning.'

'Sorry to disappoint you,' I said pithily. 'But it's just me on chaperone duty today.'

The nurse did have the grace to blush, and I wondered if James was aware of the pretty privilege he wore. Probably not, given that he had felt no qualms about wearing that straw hat on our Cambridge date and making himself look comical. Not that I wanted to be thinking about that or indeed any of what had occurred since we'd met.

I'd always been a firm believer in fate and the expression *if something is meant for you, it will find you*, but now I wasn't so sure. What was the point in James and I finding our way to each other? All fate seemed to have in store for us was heartbreak and I'd had enough of that in my life and especially since losing Dad.

'Come on then,' I said to Constance as I determinedly shut that train of thought down. 'Let's find a wheelchair and get you in my car.'

Constance looked poised to object to the wheelchair suggestion, but didn't, which was a huge relief as it was a long way from the ward to the car and she never would have made it under her own steam.

'I was hoping it wouldn't be James,' she muttered. 'I can't imagine his car has dried out yet.'

'He did mention last night that the sunroof had developed a bit of a leak.'

'He turned up in a mood because of it,' she told me. 'And by the way, I hadn't known he was coming. He was the last person I expected to see standing at the sunroom door.'

'Here we are, look,' I said, changing the subject because it didn't feel like either the time or place to get into it. 'The nurse has found you a chair far quicker than I could have done.'

It took a bit of manoeuvring to get Constance installed and comfortable but, thanks to a passing and obliging porter, I was saved the long walk back through the car park with the wheelchair and we were on our way to Fernside sooner than I had expected.

'So, tell me,' Constance asked, 'how did your talk with Carter go yesterday? I didn't get a chance to ask you before. Have the pair of you had any more bright ideas?'

I could hardly believe that just twenty-four hours ago, or close to it, I had been on that cloud number nine and with my future so happily unfolding in front of me.

'Oh,' I said vaguely. 'It was fine, and no, not really.'

Constance shifted a little and turned her head to look at me. 'Fine?' She frowned.

'Yes,' I said again, keeping my eyes fixed on the road. 'Fine.'

'What exactly was it that you talked about that was so *fine*?'

'We didn't really get the chance to talk. The pub was rather busy because of the rain.'

I hoped that would get me off the hook, but it didn't.

'You must have talked to someone else while you were there

then,' she continued annoyingly. 'Why else would you have said you'd come back with good news? You did say that yesterday, didn't you?'

'Yes,' I confirmed. 'Yes, I did say that, didn't I?'

I could hardly say I hadn't and have her doubting her memory, could I?

'Well, if Carter wasn't responsible, who was?'

'A woman called Helen.'

'Not Helen Harper?' Had I for a moment thought Constance would know a Helen in the Willowell area, I would have picked a different name. 'The planning officer you mean? Did you talk to her about your business idea?'

'Yes,' I sighed. 'Yes, I did.'

'And what did she say?' I risked a glance at her and found she was still looking at me. 'Oh, don't worry,' she said. 'I'll just ring Carter later and ask him what went on. I'm going to need something to keep me occupied this afternoon.'

'Oh, Constance,' I groaned. 'You're incorrigible.'

She'd cleverly vetoed my chance to fob her off by remembering that Carter would have been privy to the conversation, too.

'And you're wasting time. I'm very uncomfortable here, Tilly,' she added, piling on the guilt, 'and I need a distraction, so distract me.'

'It's hardly worth mentioning now,' I began. 'But if you insist. I did talk to Helen about my idea and . . . she loved it. She thought there was an extremely high chance of the business being approved.'

'Well, that's wonderful news!' Constance applauded. She sounded genuinely delighted, definitely distracted and not at all uncomfortable. 'Why on earth would you think that was hardly worth mentioning?'

'Because of what James told me when I arrived back,' I said bluntly. 'You know the pair of us didn't exactly hit it off.'

'I assumed that was because you'd been so shocked to find him there and tackled him about who he was,' she said reasonably. 'It must have been a surprise to come across a man playing the piano in my sitting room.'

'Constance,' I understated, 'you have no idea.'

'So, what did he tell you then?' she frowned.

Given that they'd had such a wait at the hospital, James could have filled her in, but it obviously hadn't come up in conversation.

'Well,' I said. 'We very quickly got to the detail that I was the person buying the woods and he told me that the deal was off because they're no longer up for sale.'

'Tilly, what are you saying?' She sounded horrified.

'That, according to your nephew,' I repeated in slightly different words, 'Willowell Woods are staying in the Clarke family and I'm not buying them.'

'Good grief.'

'I take it you hadn't discussed that before he sat down at the piano and you went for a walk in the garden, then?'

'No,' she snapped. 'We had not.'

'So, what had you been talking about?' I practically demanded.

'Nothing of consequence.'

I knew I didn't have any right to ask, but I was curious to know more about their relationship. Much more. James hadn't gone into details, but he had inferred that the situation between him and Constance wasn't as clear cut as she'd made out when she'd told me she had one relative left in the world. And given that he'd then let slip he'd been sending her money to support her was proof that he wasn't a bad guy. Even though, given that he was hoping to stop me buying the woods, part of me wanted him to be . . .

'Well,' I sighed, 'the conversation we had when I got back from the pub was of the greatest consequence.'

'Yes,' she said, through gritted teeth. 'Wasn't it just?'

We drove the rest of the way in silence, but I could feel that she was seething and therefore decided to adopt the old-fashioned knock and run tactic as the gates at the top of the drive came into view.

'I won't hang about,' I said, as I pulled on the handbrake and took the car out of gear. 'There's some stuff I need to pick up from the store and look, here's James now. He'll help you into the house.'

His car was parked on the drive in the sunshine with the doors all open and he had been leaning inside it. Most likely inspecting the damp patches. He rushed over when he spotted us and, without so much as looking at him, I handed his furious relative over and dashed off again. I'd barely got the car back in gear before the sound of raised voices reached my ears and I thought I'd give it a while before I returned.

'So, she's really okay?' Melody asked as I added a couple of packets of plain chocolate digestives to my basket, which was already filled with carb-based treats.

'Bruised but nothing broken,' I confirmed. 'And now back at Fernside.'

'I can't believe I didn't know she had a nephew,' Melody continued. 'And Rick told me nothing about him, other than that he'd randomly turned up. How awful that Constance should have an accident on the very day that he came to visit.'

'Um,' I said. I wasn't going to tell her that it was mine and the nephew's fault that it had happened. 'I was in the dark about him until recently, too, and certainly wasn't expecting to meet him.'

'So, you were as surprised to see him as Constance, then?'

'Probably more so,' I said grimly, as I played out again the moment of recognition. 'Did Rick say anything else?'

'No,' Melody shrugged. 'He was too worried about Constance, but he did say that he didn't think she was in any danger. He was right about that, wasn't he?'

I was grateful that Rick had kept his word and the details of what I'd told him about James refusing to agree with Constance over selling the woods to himself. Really, I shouldn't have even mentioned it, but I put the indiscreet admission down to shock over both what had happened to Constance and the upset over finding out who James was.

'Yes,' I said. 'Thankfully, no danger at all. I don't suppose you've got any arnica, have you?'

'Tilly!' said Kaya, as she bounded in and dumped her basket of cleaning supplies on the chair Melody kept next to the counter for customers to sit on. 'I was hoping to see you!'

'Oh?'

'You must have seen this famous nephew,' she grinned. 'So, tell us, how handsome is he exactly? Rumour has it—'

'No gossiping please, Kaya,' said Melody, as she headed to the small but well-stocked health section.

Kaya rolled her eyes. 'Come on,' she said to me. 'Give me a clue, because I can't get anything out of Rick.'

'He's a good-looking guy,' I told her, because I knew she wouldn't give up asking.

'I knew it,' Kaya clapped. 'He's bound to do for one of us.'

'You're not planning a strategy to bag him yourself?' Melody teased.

'Not until I've seen him,' Kaya tutted. 'He might not be my type.'

'Well,' I told her. 'I wouldn't go getting your hopes up about seeing him, because I don't think he's going to be staying.'

I then realised that if I didn't get back to Fernside, James wouldn't be able to leave, and if he was needed in Cambridge, my continued absence wouldn't be appreciated. I knew he'd said he was going to find a way to support his aunt himself, but as I was already available, I was the most obvious choice of carer slash companion. For the time being, at least.

'I better go,' I said and quickly lifted my basket onto the counter, so Melody could ring up my bill. 'Constance will be wondering where I've got to.'

James was putting a holdall in the boot of his car when I arrived back, and when he straightened up, I could see his expression was strained. It didn't take a genius to work out that Constance had told him what I'd said he'd said.

'Now you're back,' was his opening comment, as I retrieved my bags from the passenger seat and set them on the drive, 'I'm going to get going. Are you sure you don't mind checking in with my aunt?'

'Good morning to you, too,' I sighed, rather heavily.

'I did wave when you set off to the hospital, but it looked like you ignored me,' he shrugged. 'I was on a video call to my furious boss, which was why I sent you a text to say the hospital had been in touch, rather than call round in person.'

'Oh right.' I swallowed. 'I assumed you didn't want to talk to me.'

'I did *then*,' he said and ran a hand through his dark hair in the way that still annoyingly made my fingers yearn to be his, 'but I'm not so keen now.'

'I had to tell Constance what you'd said, James,' I responded, guessing the reason why he didn't now want to chat. 'She'd already wheedled out of me what had occurred during my meeting about the woods in The Greenman—'

'Your meeting?' he interrupted. 'Exactly how far has this sale gone?'

I realised I had made my informal chat with Helen sound both scheduled and official.

'I'm sure your aunt has filled you in about that.'

'That's assuming she's told me everything,' he frowned.

'Nothing official has happened.'

'That's all right then.'

'For you perhaps,' I countered. 'James, we really do need to talk.'

'I know we do,' he said, sounding nettled. 'But there's no time now. I need to get Buddy to his sitter and I'm due in court this afternoon. I must refocus. My boss is already at the end of his rope with me.'

'The boss you don't really want to work for?' I reminded him.

He looked at me and shook his head. 'The boss who pays me enough of a salary to keep this place afloat.'

'I thought you said Constance hasn't spent any of your

money?' I said sneakily. 'She seems to be managing without the top-up as far as I can tell.'

'I wish I'd never told you that,' he said, sounding even more rattled. 'And that situation won't last for ever. She's going to need it when the weather changes in the autumn, if not before.'

'Or,' I suggested, 'she could give you back what you've sent her and make use of the money I'm going to pay her for the sale of the woods.'

'We're not selling the woods—' Buddy, who was loose in the garden, ran to the gate and started to bark. 'And I really do have to go.'

'I know,' I said. 'But before you do, will you promise me that you'll find some time for us to properly talk before you either get your own way or fall out with your aunt for ever because she's got hers? Not only does your refusal to get on-board with the sale—'

'You're still talking as if you think it's going ahead!' he remonstrated loudly.

'Not only does your refusal to get on-board jeopardise your relationship with Constance,' I continued as if he hadn't spoken, 'it also takes away the professional future I'd started to map out here, and it threatens . . . us . . .'

Our eyes met and he was the first to look away.

'We're doomed already, aren't we?' he tutted.

He sounded more upset than angry then. The question hung unanswered in the air and as well as the increasingly loud cacophony Buddy was treating us to, James's phone began to ring, too.

'For pity's sake!' he groaned and cut the call off without

answering it. 'Right, I'm going. Are you sure you're happy to look out for Aunt Constance?'

'You know I am.'

'And you won't put pressure on her about selling the woods while I'm gone?'

'Do you honestly think I'd do that?'

'Because,' he carried on without answering, 'she needs to make up her own mind.'

'Your aunt knows her own mind perfectly well,' I declared as his phone bleated again.

'Yes,' he muttered, and strode off. 'That's very much what I'm afraid of.'

Chapter 21

I hadn't meant to get into what had descended into a borderline row with James, and with my heart weighing heavier in my chest than it had for a long time, I headed around the side of the house and quietly slipped through the gate then locked it behind me. Constance was asleep in the sunroom, so I crept along to the garden apartment, unpacked my shopping, then pulled on my swimming gear and walked down to the river.

The water felt cooler than before, but whether that was because I was feeling tired or the result of the change in the weather, I wasn't sure and I didn't much care. I swam slowly along with the flow and then put in more of an effort to return. As I drifted along and powered back, I mulled over everything that had occurred during the last twenty-four hours.

My heart was breaking, not only for the potential loss of my new business, but also for the loss of the relationship I had so speedily become caught up in. I had never given love at first sight much thought, and admittedly some of that spark with James had also included a fair amount of lust, but there was something special there, too. It felt like a deeper connection, and it always had. Was it all now lost?

As I swam, I thought in more detail about some of the things James and I had talked about on our various dates. It had taken my brain until this moment in the river to properly process the shock of who he was and for me to be able to think a little deeper. That was often the case I found with swimming. The physical exercise and repetitive movement freed up some space in my brain and something James had said during our car park picnic was playing over in my head and turning some previously jammed cogs . . .

There's something precious that belongs in my family and by topping up the collective coffers, I'm helping to keep it there.

The 'something precious' was doubtless the much-loved Willowell Woods and James was chivalrously prepared to tether himself to a full-time and full-on job that didn't satisfy him to keep them in his family. Knowing he wasn't following his heart in order to keep hold of the place his mum had loved, especially when he'd been offered the chance to make his heart very happy indeed, further fractured mine.

'Good grief,' Constance tutted, once I'd bathed, changed and joined her in the sunroom. 'You look about as tired as I feel.'

'I didn't sleep well,' I told her. 'Do you fancy an éclair?' I was keen to divert her before she mentioned James, and cream cakes were her biggest weakness. 'I cleared Melody out and she had some arnica for your bruises, too.'

'Yes please, to the éclairs,' Constance said and stifled a yawn. 'Stick a few on a plate and I'll apply the arnica later.'

'And I've got a couple of other bits for your fridge, too, so I'll sort those now.'

'You're too kind to me,' she smiled, and I forced myself not to shed a tear.

James might have filled one spot in my heart, but his aunt had already bagged another.

'No notebook today,' she commented, once we'd both devoured an early and equal share of the cakes and washed them down with an entire pot of tea.

'No,' I said, as I wiped my fingers on a crumpled piece of kitchen towel. 'Not today.'

My hands felt empty without it, but since James's pronouncement, I couldn't bear to look at it, let alone flick through the pages I'd excitedly added to every time inspiration struck.

'You know, Tilly, what James said—'

'Yes,' I interrupted. 'I do. I haven't forgotten and, even though we haven't yet had the opportunity to talk properly about it, I'm also certain that he must have a good reason for not wanting to sell—'

It was impossible to tell her what I'd started to understand during my swim, because as far as she knew, we'd only talked for a few minutes in the Fernside sitting room and got no further than our initial argument.

'There's also an excellent reason for wanting to,' she interrupted me back. 'And at the end of the day, the woods belong to me and therefore so does the final decision about what to do with them.'

'Does that mean you aren't even going to listen to what has prompted him to ask you not to sell?' I questioned.

'I've already guessed what's prompted him,' she fired back, 'but more importantly, are *you* going to listen to him?'

'Of course I am.'

She looked surprised by my vehement response and then became suspicious.

'You aren't going to back out of buying the woods are you, Tilly?' she asked and narrowed her eyes.

'I'm sorry, Constance,' I said tiredly, 'but I don't think we should discuss this now. Personally, I feel I need to be in receipt of *all* the facts from James before we discuss it further. Is that all right?'

'I suppose it will have to be, won't it?' she said, rather belligerently.

She wasn't impressed that I was shutting the conversation down, but I wasn't going to keep it going, not when I'd promised James I wouldn't get into it. If Rick, of all people, could keep a promise, then I certainly could, too.

'Let's think of happier things,' I suggested, trying to sound brighter than I felt. 'Let's see if we can get you into a lovely bubble bath and feeling more comfortable, shall we?'

She sulked for a couple of minutes while I did some tidying up, then picked up the conversation as if we hadn't almost had crossed words and I was pleased about that.

'I don't know why I didn't think of it before,' she said. 'Probably because I never go in there, but we had a walk-in bath installed in Grace's bathroom when she got sick.'

'Do you think it will still be okay?'

I knew it was a long time since Grace had died and therefore the set-up would be old.

'I don't see why not,' she said. 'It cost enough to have it put in. It's not like those fancy ones that you see on afternoon TV now, but it'll do.'

'I didn't think you had a television.'

'There's one in the hairdressers.' She smiled. 'I watch it while I'm waiting for my appointment. I rather like the look of that *Downton Abbey*.'

I smiled at that.

'Shall we go and suss it out then?' I suggested.

'Yes,' she nodded. 'Let's do that.'

Despite how tired I was feeling, I was still excited to finally see more of the house, though I did wish it was under different and happier circumstances. It was then that the penny dropped, and I realised that the upstairs room Kaya hadn't cleaned was most likely James's bedroom. Had the situation been different, I might have taunted her about that.

'Help me up then,' Constance requested and held out her hands. 'Then you can go and check the bathroom while I make my way up there in the wretched stairlift.'

'No, it's okay,' I said as we made for the door to the hall. 'I'll go up with you.'

She was hobbling a bit, but eventually she reached the chair, which was parked at the bottom of the stairs.

'This confounded contraption takes so long,' she objected, giving it a whack with the end of her stick. 'Glaciers move faster.'

Personally, I thought she should have been grateful for it. Without it, following her fall, she might have struggled to access the whole of the house she loved for a while.

'You could have the bath ready in the time it'll take me to get up there,' she moaned.

Clearly her temporary loss of independence and mobility didn't sit well with her.

'There's no need,' I said as I pulled down the seat and helped her onto it. 'We're not in a rush, are we? And the slow progress will give me the chance to have a proper look at the hallway. This is the furthest I've been inside the house, and I must admit I'm full of curiosity to see what it's like.'

'Clean is what it's like.' Constance grinned, and I felt proud that my idea that she should take Kaya on had worked out so well. 'So, fill your boots, as they say.'

'I am.' I smiled as I looked around at the faded, but still beautiful, opulence.

'Feel free to have a look all over,' Constance offered kindly. 'Though don't go in James's room. That's the last door on the right at the top of the landing.'

'Right, I'll stay out of there,' I told her, but I was interested to see what the room was like. Had it been updated since he'd lived full-time at Fernside? I don't suppose I'd ever find out now and perhaps I shouldn't explore any of the place unchaperoned, in case James thought I was trying to get my feet under the table. Suddenly everything had a subtext, and I hated it. My carefree summer had left before the swallows. 'Let's get you upstairs then, shall we?' I said and focused on the task at hand.

'We can try.'

The large circular mahogany table in the hall which I'd previously seen was now polished to perfection, and it had an arrangement of fresh flowers at its centre. The strong scent of lavender and beeswax was wonderful and the whole space felt far fresher and lighter than it had the day I'd peeked through the door from the kitchen when Miss Lyons barged in. I guessed Kaya used the natural cleaning range that Melody carried in the store. The Fernside hallway was a fabulous testament to it.

'Here we go,' I said, as Constance began her regal ascent.

'Don't hold your breath,' was her sardonic response as she rose merely an inch. 'Blast,' she swore and I bit my lip. 'I think you have to keep the button pressed down.'

'It really is just as well we haven't got plans for the rest of the day, isn't it?' I laughed.

'I told you to go ahead of me,' she tutted. 'But as you're stuck here now, look at that painting.' She pointed with her stick. 'What do you make of that fella there?'

Having perused the paintings and then checked the bath in the stripy wallpapered bathroom that had once belonged to Grace was still fit for purpose, Constance then refused point blank to let me help her undress or get into it. However, once her modesty was covered in bubbles, I was allowed back into the room.

'How is it?' I asked, from my position on the dusky pink Lloyd Loom chair on the opposite side of the room.

'Heaven,' Constance sighed dreamily and splashed a bit. 'Absolute bliss.'

'I'm so pleased.'

'The only thing spoiling the experience is my frustration at not having used it years ago!'

'Well, that time's gone,' I said sensibly. 'So, there's nothing to be gained from fretting over it now. How do you fancy another cup of tea, only this time in the bath?'

'No, thank you,' she said and closed her eyes. 'But you could top the water up a bit.'

'All right, but just a little. It's almost full to the brim already.'

'This is one of life's pleasures that I'd forgotten about for far too long,' she said blissfully, once I'd turned the tap off again.

'A bit like playing the piano?' I risked asking.

She opened her eyes, looked at me and gave me a wobbly smile.

'Oh,' she said. 'I hadn't forgotten about that. I just . . .'
'Yes?'
She rested her head back against the bath pillow.
'Let's just say, you hit the nail on the head when you talked about your dad feeling guilty for having the opportunity to live more life than your mum.'
I had known that had been a moment for her.
'As I recall,' I gently reminded her, 'when I said that you told me we should make the most of our talents.'
'I did,' she accepted. 'And going forward, I am going to try. Grace would hate to know that I still wasn't playing on a regular basis after all these years.'
'Will you play for me?' I asked.
'Perhaps,' she smiled. 'We'll see.'
I wanted to ask if she had been James's teacher but given what I'd said earlier about not discussing anything related to him, I didn't bring him into the conversation again. That didn't stop me thinking about him, though.

A lot might have been said since I'd heard him playing when our unexpected connection to Fernside had been revealed, but I hadn't forgotten how accomplished, if a little robust, his playing had been. Perhaps I'd get the opportunity to ask him about his musical education when we'd finally had the chance to talk about the woods and other subjects were back on the table. That is, assuming they ever would be . . .

'I think I'd better get out,' Constance said after some time had passed and as she inspected her fingers. 'I don't really want to, but I'm starting to prune.'

I came out of a daydream which involved James and I sitting side by side at the piano, his fingers over mine as he taught me some simple tune, and I asked Constance if I could help. She refused my offer, even though I promised to keep my eyes closed, but she called me back in sooner than I expected.

'I can't get my slippers back on,' she tutted. She was sitting in the pink chair now, with the towel wrapped around her. 'I haven't got my shoehorn.'

'Well, that's all right,' I told her. 'I can help, but I was going to ask if you fancied a bit more pampering, so you might not want your slippers on yet. How about a mani-pedi to complete the spa experience before the slippers go back on?'

'How about a what?' she frowned.

'A manicure and a pedicure,' I smiled.

'The chiropodist does my feet,' she said, looking down. She had very nice feet. 'They look all right, don't they?'

'Perfectly serviceable,' I grinned. 'But no polish.'

'Tilly, really!' Constance gasped. 'In spite of my rather tempestuous youthful years, I've never had my toenails painted and I'm not about to start now. What would Mr Trotter think?'

I let out a bark of laughter. 'Please don't tell me that your chiropodist is called Mr Trotter!' I giggled.

'I know,' she said, looking minxy. 'Isn't it too perfect? It's his real name, too.'

'I don't believe it,' I laughed again, and pressed a hand to my stomach.

'It's true.' She grinned and looked at her toes again. 'What colour have you got? Anything subtle that might suit an octogenarian?'

I had a couple of shades of pink, and we settled on the darker for her toenails and the lighter for her fingers. I wasn't an expert in the field, but I'd had a few mani-pedi treats myself, so was able to give her a gentle foot and hand massage before applying the polish.

Carried out in the sunroom, once she'd applied the arnica to her bruises and was dressed, it felt like an intimate experience, and it tugged at my heartstrings and made me think even more of our friendship.

'I feel like I could sleep for a week,' she yawned lazily, as she inspected her fingernails again. 'I honestly can't remember the last time I felt so . . . unkinked.'

'That's a brilliant word,' I said, as I tidied everything away. 'Unkinked was the last sensation you might have experienced today, so I'm so pleased the bath's helped.'

'It really has.' She smiled. 'Thank you, Tilly. You're a dear, kind and thoughtful girl and I wouldn't mind making this a regular treat.' A flicker of upset crossed my face and unfortunately, she spotted it. 'But not if you haven't got the time, of course,' she said hastily, and I hated that she'd noticed. 'I'm sure I can manage the bath, if not the nails, on my own.'

'It's not that . . .' I started to say, thinking that I might not always be around now, but my words trailed off.

How could I possibly express that to her? In the end, I didn't have to because my phone started to ring, and James's name flashed up on the screen.

I jumped up to answer it, making sure the screen was shielded from view. Constance might not make anything of the fact that I had her nephew's number already keyed into my phone given that I was looking out for her, but then again, she might, and I wasn't about to take any chances.

'Hi,' I said briskly. 'Yep. Yes, it's me. Can you hold on a sec?'

I could hear him saying something as I turned to talk to Constance.

'I'll just take this outside,' I told her. 'The signal is better out there.'

'Is it Zack?' she asked loudly, as I lifted the phone to my ear again.

'Yes,' I said quickly. 'Yes, it's Zack, so I'd better hurry up. You know I don't get the chance to talk to him very often.'

'Say hello from me!' she cooed.

I rushed out of the sunroom and down the lawn towards the river.

'Tilly!' James's voice quacked. 'Have I lost you?'

The question felt like a punch to my gut.

'No,' I said shakily. 'You haven't lost me. I'm still here.'

He was quiet for a second and I wondered if he was thinking about the words he'd said, too. Had he asked, I would have told him he hadn't lost me in any way. Not yet anyway.

'Is Aunt Constance okay?' he asked. 'I rang the house phone a few times earlier, but no one picked up.'

'We were in the bathroom,' I told him. 'I thought it would help Constance's bruises if she had a bath before applying the arnica cream I picked up for her from the store.'

'Oh,' he said. 'I see. That was kind, Tilly. Thank you.'

'And then I gave her a bit of a pamper session, so we didn't hear the phone. Sorry.'

'You gave her a what?'

'A pamper session. I gave her a manicure and pedicure and painted her nails. Just made her feel nice after the fall.'

'That was kind, too.'

'She really enjoyed it,' I smiled. 'She told me she's never had her toenails painted before.'

I was still feeling surprised about that.

'You painted her toenails?' James echoed incredulously.

'Yep,' I laughed. 'A lovely shade of pink to surprise the chiropodist with. Did you know he's called Mr Trotter?'

'I don't believe you!' James laughed. 'You're having me on.'

'I'm not,' I giggled. 'Constance swore that was his name.'

'That's ridiculous, but hilarious.'

'I know!' I agreed.

'Oh Tilly,' James said, surprisingly, and the mood seemed to change in an instant. 'I do wish I was there with you.'

It had been wonderful to laugh with him, but the jovial moment had ended abruptly.

'I wish you were here, too,' I told him, as I looked back towards the house and imagined the pair of us snuggled up together on the apartment sofa. Not that that was likely to happen under the current circumstances. 'We could get our talk over with then,' I said, thinking of more practical matters. 'I think I've pieced together some of your reasons for not wanting to sell the woods.'

'Have you been talking to Aunt Constance about it?' he asked, rather sharply.

'No,' I said, feeling a little offended. 'Of course not. I promised you I wouldn't. This is stuff I've worked out for myself.'

And Rick's comments about James helping his mum in the woods in the school holidays and therefore wanting to hang on to them because of that had helped, too.

'Sorry,' James backtracked. 'I honestly didn't mean to sound so suspicious. I'm just so tired and narky.'

'You sound like you need to get outside for a bit.'

'That would be wonderful.'

'Can you maybe go for a walk when you finish work?' I suggested. 'Hug a tree or something.'

'No chance,' he sighed. 'I'm already going to be at least an hour late picking Buddy up from the sitter tonight.'

'Will they mind?'

'They won't, but Buddy probably will.'

I wondered how feasible it was for James to have a dog given the long hours he worked, but he seemed organised and Buddy was certainly a happy hound.

'Do you think there might be a chance that we'll get to talk soon?' I asked.

I hoped he didn't think that was a selfish question.

'If I keep putting these ridiculous hours in all week,' he told me, 'there's a chance I might be able to come up this weekend.'

My heart raced at the possibility of that. Before I had known he was Constance's nephew, that would have been solely because he was my new beau, but now it skittered with a little trepidation mixed in too because seeing and talking to him was going to potentially mean the end of something important for me. I was full of contradictions with one half of me craving the conversation, but the other wanting to put it off.

'Well, that would be great,' I said.

'Would it?' he asked. 'You don't sound so sure.'

'No, I am,' I tried to say more convincingly. 'But I'm scared, too.'

'If it's any consolation,' he confessed, 'so am I.'

'Are you?'

'How could I not be? This whole situation is just one big mess, isn't it?'

'Yes,' I agreed. 'It does feel like that at the moment, but hopefully everything will become clearer once we've talked things through.'

'My aunt still doesn't know that we'd met before, does she?'

'Not unless you've told her.'

'No,' he said. 'I haven't said a word, and I suppose that's something to be thankful about.'

I wasn't sure how to take that.

'Should I be offended that you've just suggested that keeping our relationship from her is a silver lining?'

'No,' James rushed to say. 'That's not what I meant at all, because had we not been at odds over the woods I'm certain she'd be ecstatic that we're a couple. She was full of praise for you that evening at the hospital.'

'Was she really?' I asked, noting that he'd referred to us as a couple in the present tense.

'It was all "Tilly this, Tilly that",' he mimicked, and I smiled and bit my lip because he'd sounded so funny. 'It was infuriating really.'

'Well, I'm sorry about that.'

'Um,' he said, 'you sound it. At least her not knowing is going to mean there's one less person in this situation with a broken heart.'

'Does your heart feel broken?' I whispered.

'It doesn't feel great,' he said back, softly. I heard a door noisily open and close and a man's gruff voice in the background. 'Oh Tilly,' James sighed. 'I've got to go. I'm sorry to cut this off. I'll see you at the weekend, okay?'

'Yes.' I swallowed. 'I'll see you at the weekend.'

Chapter 22

Had the situation between James and I been what it had been before I found him in the Fernside sitting room, I would have been excited about the prospect of seeing him again, but as I counted down the days, I became increasingly jittery and apprehensive.

It felt like the weekend was going to be the end of something, rather than the continuation of it, and I wasn't only talking about my new romantic relationship. My working life felt destined to receive its heftiest blow so far, too. Constance might have insisted that the decision to sell the woods started and ended with her, but I didn't think she could really ignore James's opinion, and I knew I certainly couldn't.

'What are you thinking about?' she asked me on Thursday morning. 'You look miles away. You're not still worried about this business over me selling the woods, are you?'

I'd had my usual early swim, and we were sharing breakfast in the Fernside kitchen. I had no idea how she could sound so blasé about the so-called 'business over her selling the woods' when it was keeping me awake at night.

'No,' I fibbed, covering my tracks. 'I was thinking about

whether to ask you if I could invite everyone around this evening, but now I'm not so sure I want to.'

'Why not? They might cheer you up a bit.'

'I'm sorry I haven't been the best company this week,' I apologised.

'It's hardly your fault, is it? Don't you want to see everyone?'

'Yes and no,' I said honestly.

Part of me was desperate to forget my troubles and enjoy a fun evening with them all, but the other part was worried that I wouldn't be able to pull it off. I hadn't talked to anyone other than Rick about what had really occurred when James turned up – that he told me he didn't want the woods to be sold – and I wasn't sure I'd get through an entire evening without letting something slip. I had promised myself that I wouldn't mention anything to anyone until James and I had had an opportunity to talk but with them all together, I might succumb to temptation.

'Well,' said Constance. 'I'd like to see them.'

'But you're not going to be here, are you? Unless you've changed your mind about going. It's that Women's Institute talk tonight, isn't it?'

'Oh yes,' she said. 'It is. We're being treated to a riveting talk about Doris's international tea towel collection. But you can still go ahead with your plan for here, I don't mind. And just think,' she added, 'this time next year, I could be heading to the hall in the village to hear you talk to the WI about your business venture, Tilly!'

'That really would be something, wouldn't it?' I attempted to enthuse but fell short. 'Shall I refresh the pot? This one must have stewed by now.'

In the end, Melody, Kaya, Rick and I decided on a night in the pub instead of a gathering in the garden. The weather still hadn't really warmed back up, so evenings were a bit chilly and going there meant Carter could join us for a chat, too. And of course, The Greenman served perfect pizzas, not that I currently had much of an appetite.

'Helen was in earlier,' Carter greeted me, the moment I walked in. 'She was wondering if you and Constance have got any further with things. She's so keen for you to—'

Aware that everyone else was right behind me, I vehemently shook my head.

'Do you mind if we don't discuss it tonight?' I asked urgently.

'Is everything all right?' he frowned.

'Yes,' I blagged. 'Totally fine, but I haven't told the others yet and I want to make a real song and dance of it when I do, rather than just dropping it into the conversation.'

Carter tapped the side of his nose and winked. 'Say no more,' he grinned. 'Mum's the word.'

'Thanks,' I smiled, but I hated the deception. 'I appreciate that.'

What should have been a relaxing evening left me feeling tense and stressed. Mindful that at any moment I might say the wrong thing, I resorted to asking Kaya to tell us about her most exciting overseas adventures – a topic she could wax lyrical about for hours – and that effectively stemmed all conversation for much of the night. And put me in everyone else's bad books because they'd heard it all before.

Early the next morning, I decided not to swim and was immersed in giving the apartment a thorough deep clean that it didn't really need, when I spotted Constance windmilling with her walking stick on the patio.

'Are you all right?' I shouted, as I simultaneously abandoned the vacuum cleaner, snatched open the door and turned down my music.

'I am,' she said. 'I just wanted to check that you are. What are you doing?'

'Cleaning,' I told her. 'I wasn't in the mood for a swim.'

She raised her eyebrows at that.

'I just assumed you must be running late following your trip to the pub as I hadn't seen you go down, but then when James said he couldn't get hold of you—'

'James has been trying to ring?' I quickly checked the call log on my phone. There were half a dozen missed calls registered and they were all from him. 'Damn.'

I looked back at Constance. My rather panicked reaction had made her eyebrows shoot up even higher and my face flushed in response.

'He must have been worried that something had happened to you, Constance,' I gabbled, to explain away my frustrated reaction.

'Well, if he was, I set his mind to rest when I picked up the house phone the first time he rang it, didn't I?'

'Yes,' I said and put my phone in my pocket. 'I suppose you did. So, how were the tea towels of the world?'

'Don't you want to know what he wanted?'

'Who?'

'James!' she said impatiently. 'What's the matter with you this morning?'

'Sorry,' I said, striking my forehead with my palm in a gesture I'd never used before. 'Yes, what did he want?'

'To let us know that he won't be arriving until after lunch tomorrow,' Constance informed me. 'He'd booked the whole of the weekend off, but he's out of favour with his boss, for some reason, and he's now got to attend a meeting in the morning.'

'I daresay his boss is still smarting over that extra pro bono case James has taken on,' I said aloud. 'I don't think he was happy about that.'

'He's told you about that aspect of his work, has he?' Constance asked, and I realised I probably should have kept that knowledge to myself.

Constance knew James and I had talked on the phone a little but had most likely assumed that what we'd discussed was her recovery following her fall and anything pertaining to Fernside, rather than what his work involved.

'Just briefly,' I shrugged. 'His work came up in conversation one day.'

'So, what else has come up?' she asked. 'Have you now told him about your plans for the woods?'

'No,' I said. 'Not yet. We decided it would be better to talk about all that in person.'

'Right,' she said, drawing the word out. 'I suppose that makes sense, but you won't let him talk you out of buying, will you, Tilly? He can be very persuasive.'

'I daresay that's part of his job,' I commented.

'I would imagine you're right, but you mustn't be swayed. My decision to sell the woods is solely for his benefit and the sooner he accepts that, the better it will be for everyone concerned.'

I was still adamant that I wasn't going to come between the

two of them, but I didn't want to get further into it with Constance while standing on the doorstep. We'd talk properly about it once I'd heard from James's own lips his reasons for not wanting her to sell.

'Duly noted,' I said briskly, cutting the topic off. 'Now, if you don't mind, I was hoping to get finished in here before breakfast.'

'Did the place really need such a thorough going over?' she asked and peered over my shoulder. 'It's sounded like you've been at it for hours.'

'No harm in keeping on top of things, and it's such a pretty place, it deserves to look its best.'

'An ethos, thanks to you, that I'm adopting for the rest of the house now.' She smiled. 'All right,' she accepted. 'Just don't work too hard. You need to save your energy for getting your business up and running.'

'Don't worry about that,' I told her. 'I've got plenty in reserve.'

The moment she'd gone, I closed the door and picked up my phone again. I was tempted to call James back but knew that if his boss was in the vicinity and James hadn't turned the ringtone down, that would be another mark blotting his copy-book.

'Zack,' I said, when I tried my brother instead, 'can you give me a call when you get this message? I could do with a chat. It won't matter what time it is. I hope you're okay. Love you.'

I went back to the vacuuming wondering which of the two main men in my life I was going to hear from first.

It was the sound of Buddy barking soon after lunchtime the next day that answered that question. I'd heard nothing from my brother yet, so James had beaten him to the punch. Assuming we talked before Zack called.

Had James not been Constance's nephew but rather simply someone I was dating who I had invited up for the weekend, I would have rushed outside to greet him and pulled him in close for the longest kiss, but that fantasy had long since flown. Now I stayed put and waited, with mixed emotions, for him to seek me out.

It was getting on for the end of the afternoon before he eventually knocked, and I felt my heart kick as I opened the apartment door and saw him standing there.

'James,' I breathed. 'Hello.' The sight of him prompted the strongest tug of attraction, and it was further heightened because he was wearing the same shirt he'd had on the day we'd met in Cambridge and had our first proper kiss. 'Would you like to come in?'

I opened the door wider, but he didn't move.

'Hey, Tilly,' he said, his voice thick in his throat and his hands shoved deep in his shorts pockets. 'Thanks, but I'd better not. Aunt Constance is waiting to continue our so-called conversation. I just wanted to let you know I'm here.'

'Is she giving you a hard time?' I asked quietly, in case she was in the vicinity.

'You could say that,' he said, as his gaze flicked towards the sunroom. 'She's in fine spirits and I blame you for that.'

'Me,' I frowned. 'But I haven't talked to her about our . . . situation. I told you I wouldn't.'

James shook his head. 'I know that,' he said quickly. 'I was trying to be funny. What I meant was you've aided her recovery so well that she's ready to step into the ring with me.'

'Oh.' I smiled sheepishly. 'I see. Sorry.'

'A bit of nail polish seems to have given her a new lease of life.'

'Shush,' I grinned. 'She might hear you and then you'll be in for even more of a battering.'

'I'll be all right.' He laughed quietly and I wished we could always be like this. 'I'm sure I'll survive long enough for us to meet later.'

Buddy bounded up and I bent down to give him a fuss and kissed the top of his smooth, domed head.

'Do you want to come here when you're done?' I suggested, as I straightened up again. 'We'll be out of earshot inside.'

'I was thinking we could meet at the woods,' James proposed instead, and it was a total surprise. 'Given that it's the place that's the cause of all our problems, it should be the woods, shouldn't it? And we'll definitely be out of earshot there.'

'Okay,' I agreed, but I wasn't sure my heart was going to be able to cope with the combination of him *and* the place I'd come to love as the setting for our talk.

'I'll see if I can find the key to the cabin,' James leant in and whispered as we heard the sunroom door open. 'And we can talk in there.'

'Your aunt has already given me the key,' I whispered back, and his face changed.

I wasn't sure how to read his expression. Obviously, he was relieved that he wouldn't have to sneakily look for the key, but he didn't appear thrilled that I already had it.

'That makes life easier then,' he said. 'Shall we say seven or thereabouts?'

'James!' came Constance's voice, making us both jump. 'Are you coming or not?'

'I'll meet you there at seven,' I told him.

He whistled for Buddy, who had run off again, and then headed back to the house for round two.

I had been sitting down by the river when I heard James and Buddy leaving Fernside and checked the time on my phone. It was only a little after five, so I guessed he must have had things to do before we met at the woods. Either that, or he was making a bid for freedom to escape Constance. I snuck back up to the apartment hoping she wouldn't now come and find me. She didn't, and a few minutes before the agreed time, I set off for the woods.

My heart felt heavy as I pulled up next to James's car. I hadn't visited the woods since he'd told me they were off the market, and I knew this could well be the very last time I saw them. I spotted James and Buddy on the other side of the gate and climbed out of my car.

'I came down early so we could have a look around,' James beamed at me and roughed up Buddy's coat.

They both looked thrilled to be there, and the tiredness James had carried with him back from Cambridge seemed to have all but disappeared.

'Are you making up for all the indoor hours this week?' I swallowed and tried to match his enthusiasm. 'You've come to the right place if you are.'

'Exactly that!' he nodded eagerly. 'Isn't it glorious here?'

The temptation to tell him that the feeling he was experiencing was exactly the sort of thing I wanted to offer to others as part of my business was almost overwhelming, but I reined myself in. These were James's family woods, so he should have the opportunity to tell me why he didn't want his aunt to part with them before I told him what I wanted to do with them.

'Utterly,' I agreed. 'I'll just get my jumper and climb over.'

I had my notebook in the car too, but I hadn't yet decided whether to take that.

'All right,' he said, 'but I need to climb back over first, because there's some things I need to get out of my car.'

'What things?' I asked.

'You'll see,' he smiled. 'Just a few essentials.'

The essentials turned out to be a blanket and some cushions I recognised from the Fernside supper parties, and a box full of picnic food and some elderflower fizz.

'I went to the store,' he said, and I wondered who had served him. 'I thought we could have a picnic in the cabin like Mum and I used to when the nursery was closed. What do you think? Are you up for that?'

'Beats sitting in my car,' I said, over the lump in my throat as I imagined him and his mum sharing simple but special moments together.

In my experience, it was the little things that made for the happiest and most treasured memories. I could still remember the upsurge of joy I had felt during a school Christmas performance when I spotted Mum sitting in the third row of the audience. Seeing her face smiling up at me and looking so proud gave me the confidence I needed to belt out my single line in the play, and I could still recall the blissful sensation of seeing her there, even after all these years.

'A definite upgrade,' he said and practically sprang over the gate while Buddy belly crawled back underneath. 'I take it the padlock's rusted shut. I'll get that sorted.'

I began to feel torn in two. It was wonderful to see the version of James I'd started to fall in love with putting in an appearance again, but the fact that the change in him was the result of time spent in Willowell Woods didn't bode well for me. I decided my notebook should stay in the car.

'I have been back to the woods quite recently,' James told me as I fumbled with the key in the cabin lock and wondered when exactly, 'but I haven't been in here because I haven't got my own key.'

'Well,' I said as I finally got the lock to turn, 'obviously, I haven't done anything in here other than have a look around.'

I shoved the door, which seemed to finally be getting used to being opened again. It barely protested and Buddy shot in ahead of us and began doing laps, his claws scrabbling for purchase on the wooden floor.

'Feel familiar, Buddy?' James laughed, as he followed me inside. 'Can you close the door again, Tilly? Just in case he decides to run off and we have to go and find him.'

I closed the door, spread out the blanket and cushions, which Buddy then ruffled up, then pretended to be engrossed in something on my phone while James reacquainted himself with the cabin.

'It smells just the same,' he said, when he came out of the office holding a plant catalogue with curled up pages. 'I can't remember the last time the fire was lit, but it made it so cosy in here in the winter.'

'I bet,' I smiled.

I hadn't thought about the cabin decorated for Christmas, and now, imagining how perfect it could be, didn't really want to.

'Shall we eat?' James asked. 'I'm starving. Arguments always give me an appetite.'

'Oh dear,' I said, as I joined him on the blanket. 'Was it really bad?'

'Yeah,' he said and looked far less happy than he had been. 'It was really bad.'

We sat close together and again my mind kept doing that annoying thing where it veered off and imagined that James and I were just a regular couple without this nightmare of a situation hanging over us. Consequently, I didn't eat much, even though the spread was wonderful and I knew it was tasty because Melody had baked much of it.

'Are you not hungry?' James asked as he wolfed down a sausage roll and shared a little of the filling with Buddy.

'Not really,' I confessed.

He looked at me for a moment, and his brow furrowed.

'Oh my god, I'm a total pig!' he then proclaimed loudly and I laughed in spite of myself. 'I'm so sorry, Tilly.'

'What for?'

'For being so excited to be back here, even though Aunt Constance has been chewing my backside off about it for the last few hours. I didn't consider for one second that this is the last place you would want to be when I suggested it. I'm an idiot!'

'At least you're self-aware,' I said teasingly, and he shook his head. 'In spite of the fact that you've been rowing with your aunt, does your excitement and happiness to be here mean that she's changed her mind about selling?'

'No,' he huffed. 'Not yet.'

Given his obvious pleasure to be back and the happiness the

woods had evoked in him, Constance digging her heels in didn't make me as happy as it might have done if he'd been a stranger whom I knew nothing about.

'In that case,' I said, as I shifted my position to get more comfortable and pushed my plate of food away, 'I think it's time for you to tell me why you want her to back down.'

'Well,' James sighed softly and I sensed a change in him, 'I get the feeling that you've guessed most of it.'

'Yes,' I nodded. 'I think I have, but I would like to hear the whole of it from you.'

'Okay,' he said and ran his hands through his hair. 'So, as you know, the cabin is here because my mum ran a woodland nursery from this site.'

'Yes, I have heard a little about that.'

'And Willowell Woods is the place that she instilled in me this passionate love to be outdoors that I've never set aside, not even when I've been in the city for weeks on end.'

He sounded as if he'd done far better than I had in the past at maintaining the connection.

'And this place is full of memories,' he continued. 'Such happy ones. All the best times Mum and I had together, we had here. Even when she got sick, we used to come here and walk among the trees and pretend she wasn't ill. I think the woods actually did stop her feeling poorly for a while. It felt magical then and it still does now, our own little bubble where time stood still and nothing could hurt us . . .'

His words trailed off, and I could see he was close to tears.

'Oh James.' I swallowed.

'It's my happiest place in the whole world and losing these woods would feel like losing Mum all over again, and this time, for ever. Even if Constance did sell and there was a possibility that I could come back and visit, it would be different. I know it would. It would be changed even if it looked the same and I couldn't bear that. I can't lose that.'

I could empathise on every level. I had been trying not to ever since I had started to piece together the reason behind why James didn't want to sell, but having heard him so heartbreakingly express it, I could no longer deny, either to him or myself, that I understood.

'Given that not buying the woods is going to have such an impact on me,' I said, as I stifled a sob, 'you might not expect me to say this, James, but I completely understand.'

'You do?'

'Yes,' I said. 'I might not want to, and I might wish that I didn't, but I do.'

'Can you tell me why?'

I finished my glass of elderflower fizz and when I put it down, James refilled it. I didn't want to recall the sadness and pain but as he was being so honest and because I thought it might help him if I shared, I then explained why it was that I could understand his desire to keep Willowell Woods in the Clarke family.

'A few months after Mum died,' I told him as I picked my drink back up, 'Dad decided that the best thing for all of us would be to move house. He thought that me and Zack and him would come to terms with what had happened so much sooner if we had a completely fresh start.'

'Oh no,' said James, and I smiled because he had understood instantly what came next.

'Our family home sold in a flash and by the time Dad

realised he'd made a mistake in tearing us all away from our memories, we were surrounded by packing boxes in a soulless new build, with no imprint of Mum to be seen, heard or felt.'

'Oh crikey, Tilly.' James sobbed and reached for my hand. 'Then you *really* do know, don't you?'

'Yes,' I said croakily. 'I do. When I sold that house after Dad died, I didn't feel any sense of loss because even though we'd been there a long time, it still didn't feel like home. I don't think anywhere will ever feel like home again.'

Other than Willowell and now Fernside, but I didn't verbalise that because I knew I was poised to lose both and couldn't bear to consider how that was going to feel in this moment. I might visit the village in the future, and even Constance, but it wasn't going to feel the same as it did now and had in the past.

'I'm sorry you lost that connection,' James said sincerely.

'I'm sorry about that, too,' I said before squeezing his hand and then letting it go. 'But having experienced that terrible trauma first-hand, it does now help me to understand why you aren't willing to lose these woods.'

'I appreciate that you're generous enough to accept what I've explained,' he said kindly. 'I had a feeling that you would be, but what you went through as a child has really solidified your understanding of the situation, hasn't it?'

'It has,' I confirmed. 'But I do feel devastated that the only way for you to keep the woods is to earn a high enough salary by carrying on doing work that you hate.'

'Hate is a strong word.'

'You hate it, James.'

'I hate eighty-five per cent of it,' he corrected me. 'The other fifteen per cent is great.'

'I thought your boss was supposed to allow you twenty per cent pro bono time.'

'He was, but not anymore.' He sighed and shifted to give Buddy, who was asleep on his back and snoring like a trooper, a belly rub.

'Is it going to be enough?'

'If the eighty-five per cent means we can hang on to this place because we don't need the money from selling it to keep Fernside afloat and my aunt in chocolate éclairs, then it's totally worth it.'

My eyes filled with tears and before I could blink them away, one rolled down my cheek.

'It's no wonder I started to fall for you, is it?' I sniffed. 'It would be really helpful right now if I could hate you, James. Why do you have to be so damn kind?'

'I'm that "one act of kindness every day", guy. Remember?' He smiled and leant over to brush the tear away.

That's what he'd told me the day he'd rescued Mum's hat.

'Yes,' I said. 'I remember. How could I possibly forget?'

I couldn't believe how much I wanted to kiss him. He had convinced me to relinquish my claim on Willowell Woods, and not by using clever barrister talk as Constance had warned me about, but by a truly heartfelt explanation, which I supposed was the reason why I still wanted to kiss him.

'Now I've told you why I don't want my aunt to sell, will you tell me what your plans were?' he asked. 'I'd really love it if between us we could come up with a way for you to set up somewhere else, Tilly.'

Having now thoroughly searched the area online, I knew there was nowhere else anywhere near Willowell that was even remotely suitable. In fact, I hadn't found anywhere easily accessible for sale in the entire country which offered the same scope.

'If it's all right with you,' I said, 'I'm not really in the right frame of mind to get into it at the moment.' James opened his mouth to no doubt coax me into sharing, but I was resolute. 'Besides,' I reminded him, 'you have something far more pressing to get to grips with right now, don't you?'

'What's that?' He sounded disappointed, but I wasn't going to back down.

'Convincing your aunt that not selling up is the right thing to do, of course,' I insisted. 'When I last spoke to her, she was still adamant that it's going to happen.'

'Having spent the afternoon listening to her telling me exactly that, *and* that I must beg to get my old job back, I am aware,' he said, rather sardonically.

'You haven't told her about the job offer?'

'Of course I haven't.' He grimaced. 'If she found out about that, she'd have an even stronger argument, wouldn't she?'

'That's true,' I said and bit my lip.

'What am I going to do?' he said and dropped his head into his hands.

'Nothing,' I shrugged.

'Nothing?'

'You don't have to do anything, James. I'll simply tell her that I'm no longer interested in buying the woods.'

'You can't do that!' he gasped loudly, which woke Buddy up.

The dog stood up, had a big shake and a long stretch, then plodded over to me and put one paw in my lap.

'Hey, Buddy,' I sighed. 'What do you think of my plan?'

'Tilly,' James said firmly, 'I don't want you to do that and not only because she'll blame me for your decision, but because the pair of you will be bound to fall out.'

'Rather me than you,' I said, giving him a wobbly smile.

'Please, don't,' James said. 'Give me some time to come up with something that will save your relationship. I know she thinks the world of you.'

'And I think the world of her,' I sighed.

'So, will you wait before you say anything?'

'All right,' I relented. 'I'll give you until lunchtime tomorrow but if you haven't come up with something by then, I'm telling her.'

James didn't look happy but accepted the tightly scheduled compromise.

'It's a shame tugging at her heartstrings hasn't worked,' he muttered. 'Though I do know she believes that selling is the right thing to do for me. I haven't lost sight of the fact that she's trying to make my life better by letting this place go.'

There he went, being kind again.

'You're right,' I agreed, as I looked out into the fading light. 'She's only thinking of what's best for you.'

If only there was some way we could *all* get what was best for us.

Chapter 23

It was getting dark by the time we'd packed away the picnic and locked the cabin again. As we walked back to our cars, I was delighted to hear the back and forth of tawny owls calling and then I wished I hadn't been so excited because knowing my favourite birds were living in the woods went no way to helping me disconnect from them.

'Are you heading straight back to Fernside?' I asked James, once he'd got the picnic things and Buddy packed into his car.

'I was going to,' he said, looking down at me, 'but I think I might just pop back to the store and pick up some flowers for Aunt Constance.'

'She does love the blooms from there,' I told him. 'But it will take more than that to get her to change her mind about selling the woods.'

'I know,' he agreed. 'But I don't like quarrelling with her. I never have and the falling out over the woods has been the worst. She's so stubborn. You know, she even refused to accept the weekly shopping order I always sent for her when she told me to stop visiting in person. I had to cancel it in the end because I kept getting emails of complaint from the supermarkets saying "delivery refused" or "no one in".'

'You used to send her food?'

'Every week. All her favourites.' James shrugged. 'To be honest, it must have killed her to turn away the pastries and baked goods.'

I suddenly didn't think that Constance had been quite fair to James. Neither to him in person or when she'd briefly talked about him to me. He'd clearly gone above and beyond to support her and yet she'd never done anything to stop me assuming he'd abandoned her. Perhaps she had hoped tough love and self-sacrifice would win him over but neither had triumphed and now it was a worse mess than ever because I was involved.

'I even tried leaving things at the house myself when I could drive up,' James continued, 'but then she started locking the damn gate!'

'And there's that blooming good guy again,' I whispered.

Without another word, the pair of us closed the gap between us and kissed. We didn't ease into it but went straight in with all the pent-up passion we'd both been feeling over the last few days. There was no gap between us and yet we pressed our bodies even closer, our hands exploring every inch we could reach over our clothes.

'James,' I gasped lustfully, as his lips found the tenderest spot on my neck and I wished we'd started this in the cabin. 'James,' I said more firmly, as in the next second, common sense kicked in. 'Stop.'

He immediately moved away and the air on my clothes and skin that replaced his proximity felt cold and I shivered.

'I'm sorry,' he said, his chest heaving. 'I'm so sorry.'

'It's not your fault,' I echoed. 'It was both of us who leaned in.'

'That wasn't perhaps the most sensible move, was it?' he said, once he'd caught his breath.

'No,' I agreed regretfully as I readjusted the neck of my top. 'Probably not.'

Now I'd had another taste of him, I wanted more. So much more, but given the current situation, I knew it wouldn't do to get carried away. Pursuing our personal relationship would only complicate the more pressing professional one.

'Even though I was wishing we'd started that in the cabin,' he said and gave me a look that was so full of desire that I was tempted to grab him again.

'Same thing crossed my mind,' I confessed.

He smiled and so did I.

'Right,' he said. 'I'm going to leave before we're tempted to do something we'll really regret.'

'Good,' I said primly. 'And don't come to the apartment tonight, because I won't let you in.'

'I wouldn't dream of it,' he grinned.

We didn't break eye contact, and neither of us moved.

'The store will be shut soon,' I told him.

'Yep,' he said and turned back to his car, where Buddy was patiently waiting. 'I know. I'll see you tomorrow.'

'And don't forget,' I reminded him, 'you have until lunchtime to convince Constance that your way is the right one. After that, I'm going in.'

I waited until he left, then climbed into my car. I didn't get in the driver's side but shifted my notebook, sat on the passenger seat and put my head in my hands. There was such a lot to think about . . . not only was I losing the dream location for my business, I now also felt compelled to convince Constance that she should keep it.

There was no doubt in my mind that task would fall to me because she obviously wasn't going to listen to James. She might have done him a disservice in letting me think he'd been the bad guy, and refusing his practical offers of support, but her desire to enable him to change jobs spoke volumes regarding what she really felt for him.

And now there was that kiss with James . . . or kisses . . . to consider. I jumped out of the car, switched seats and turned the engine over. With it all playing out in my head, I didn't have the bandwidth to process our embrace on top of everything else.

Back at Fernside, I parked slightly over on the drive, making sure I'd left enough space for James to put his car in the garage, should he want to. We hadn't got around to talking about his sunroof, but in the grand scheme of things it didn't really matter. I was just about to go through the garden gate, when I heard a car and decided to wait.

It was bound to be James and even though I knew it would probably be better not to see him so soon after our kiss, I reasoned he might need a hand with Buddy, the picnic things and the flowers. Who was I trying to kid?

However, as the car got closer, I realised it wasn't his. There was a light on the roof which told me it was a taxi. Constance hadn't mentioned she was expecting visitors, and I certainly wasn't. Maybe it was someone for James.

The car came to a halt a little distance in front of me and

I squinted at the light reflecting off the windscreen while whoever was in the back gathered up the bags they were travelling with and patted the driver on the shoulder. I recognised the friendly gesture immediately, but I also knew I must have imagined it because the person it belonged to was literally on the other side of the world.

Unless he wasn't.

'Oh my god!' I screeched, my hands flying to my face as the car door swung open. 'What are you doing here?'

I ran across the drive and flung myself straight into the arms of the person I had so longed to see but until that moment hadn't really wanted to admit it.

'Zack!' I shouted, as he lifted me up and spun me around. 'I don't believe it! Is it really you?'

'It's me.'

I squeezed him tight for the longest time and the strength of the returned embrace suggested that he needed the sibling hug every bit as much as I did.

'I can't believe you're here,' I sobbed, when I drew back a little and took his stubble covered face in my hands.

'Surprise!' He grinned and pulled me close again. 'A good one, I hope,' he said into my shoulder, his whiskers scratching my neck.

'The best,' I said back. 'Of course it is. But what are you doing here? I thought you were on sabbatical. I thought you were lying on a beach thinking things through.'

'I was,' Zack nodded, with the biggest smile lighting up his deeply tanned face. 'But all your talk of Willowell made me so homesick and I desperately wanted to be here to support you when you launched this fabulous adventure that you're about to embark on. So, I just thought screw it and booked a flight back.'

'God, I love you so much for that,' I said, as I kissed the back of his hand and squeezed it even tighter. 'And I'm so incredibly happy that you're here.'

Given that he'd travelled halfway across the world to see me set off on it, it was hardly the moment to tell him that the adventure was shelved. We'd get properly into it all once he'd had something to eat and some sleep.

'Thank goodness for that,' he laughed as he scooped up the huge rucksack and holdall which I guessed contained his worldly goods. 'Now come on. I'm in dire need of a decent cup of tea and an entire loaf of toast.'

'And Marmite?' I laughed, as I thought he was going to get on very well with Constance, the other toast lover in my life.

'Of course, Marmite! You have got some in, haven't you?'

'A brand-new jar.'

'I think that was your phone!' Zack called from his stretched-out position on the apartment sofa, while I was in the kitchen shoving yet more bread, in fact the last of the bread, into the toaster late that evening.

I rushed into the sitting room and snatched it off the coffee table. I hadn't wanted Zack to see James's name flash up on the screen, but my rush to grab it piqued his interest anyway.

'If that's a booty call,' he said in a sing-song voice, 'don't even think of abandoning me. Not when I've come all this way.'

'Of course it isn't,' I said and gave the suggestion the eye roll it deserved.

It was a message from James saying he hadn't yet come up with a plan, but he was going to sleep on it and see if anything appeared in his dreams. I vaguely heard the toast pop up, but didn't move to do anything with it.

'I'll see to the toast then, shall I?' Zack asked, as I stared at the phone screen and wondered if and how I should reply.

Maybe I could message James to meet me at the back of the house, so I could say goodnight in person . . .

'If you don't mind,' I said, and Zack looked surprised. 'I just need to check on something at Fernside.'

'At this hour?' he asked, making no attempt to move. 'Will Constance thank you for that?'

'Oh, for pity's sake,' I said, when I looked at my phone again. 'It's gone two in the morning.'

'I know,' Zack smiled. 'And we've not even started on your news yet.'

We had talked about his time in Bali and beyond and how he wasn't certain he'd be going back after he'd recovered from the unusual bout of homesickness that my time in Willowell had kicked off.

His declaration that he currently felt no desire to keep flitting rootless around the globe had come as something of a surprise, even though I had known he had been questioning things, and I was still processing the potential implications of that. The thought of him being in the same country as me full-time and therefore within regular hugging distance was blissful, but I wasn't about to get my hopes up in case the wanderlust struck again a week or so down the line.

'Aren't you tired?' I yawned, feeling a sudden wave of exhaustion wash over me now I had realised how late, or early, it was.

'Getting there,' he said, sitting up and having a good stretch. 'But still more hungry than ready for bed.'

'You're still a bottomless pit,' I tutted.

'I know,' he laughed and I thought how wonderful the sound was when it was in the same room.

'The last of the toast coming up then.' I smiled as I put my phone down again, screen down, and padded back through to the kitchen.

I'd message James when I went to bed, even if he might not see it until the morning. I'd rather that than rush a response and get it wrong.

'And maybe just one more cuppa before we turn in?' Zack requested.

Snuggled up on the sofa next to my brother, with a crumb covered plate and a pot of warm tea on a tray in front of us, it was finally my turn to talk.

'Crikey,' Zack said thoughtfully, once I'd found the words to explain that my plan to buy the woods had now been scuppered by James, along with the reason why. 'I can see your conundrum.'

'I knew you would,' I said and rested my head on his shoulder.

'We were devastated to leave our place, weren't we?'

'We were,' I said hoarsely. I'd talked so much in the last few hours, my voice was giving out. 'And even though James still has Fernside in the family, his happy place with his mum was the woods. That's where the memories are that he really wants to preserve and keep safe.'

'What did he think of your plans for the woods?'

'He asked what they were, but I didn't tell him.'

'Why not?' Zack demanded and gave me a nudge, so I had to sit up.

'He'd literally just told me about why he wanted to keep the woods,' I explained. 'So, it felt a bit raw. Also, I didn't think there was much point, to be honest. Going through it all would have only upset me, and it wasn't going to alter anything.'

'You don't think he'd be open to what you have in mind?'

'No. He wants Willowell Woods to stay just as they are and knowing we would have wanted to keep our house in a similar state if Dad had given us the chance, I wasn't about to try and make him think otherwise.'

'That's fair,' Zack accepted. 'So, what's the plan now? Aunt Constance sounds like a right firecracker to me, and I can't see her backing down.'

'Especially when she's got her nephew's best interests at heart.'

'Exactly.'

'I've told James that if he hasn't got her on-side by lunchtime, then I'm going to tell her I don't want to buy them anymore.'

'That's drastic action,' Zack puffed. 'She'll be peed off with you then.'

'Well,' I said, 'that's a risk I'm willing to take.'

'You really like this guy, huh?'

'He's okay,' I blagged. 'I'm just trying to see the situation from his point of view, rather than my own.'

'How very generous of you.' Zack nudged me again and stifled a yawn.

'Come on,' I said. 'I need my beauty sleep.'

'Bit late for that,' Zack scoffed and I biffed him with a cushion, almost upsetting the teapot. 'I meant,' he laughingly defended himself, 'because it's so late. The night is practically over. Why don't we just power through?'

'Because we're not teenagers anymore,' I told him, though it hadn't escaped my notice that was pretty much the age we acted whenever we were together. I stood up and pulled him to his feet. 'I'll take the tray; you move the cushions.'

I piled the dishes next to the sink, yawning as I did it, and when I looked at Zack again, I could see he was blearier eyed than he was willing to admit.

'You look like you need your beauty sleep, too,' I told him.

'I'm all right,' he said. 'I haven't got anyone to impress.'

'Neither have I,' I countered, perhaps a little too quickly.

'You sure about that?' he asked, narrowing his gaze.

'Oh, be quiet,' I tutted and he laughed. 'Come on, let's get this sofa bed set up and then you can get some sleep.'

I had wondered whether to mention my romantic involvement with James but figured the fewer people who knew at this point, the better. In typical tuned in fashion however, my brother had already sussed something was going on, so there was no need to spell it out.

Chapter 24

I was the sibling who ended up getting the most sleep and when I finally woke, rather late the following morning, with a thick head and an ache in my body that I couldn't account for, unless it could be associated with matters of the heart, there was no sign of Zack. The bedding I'd given him was neatly folded and the sofa bed was back to being just a sofa with its cushions neatly arranged.

My immediate thought, because he'd said he had a hankering to do it, was that he'd headed to the river for a swim, but I hoped he hadn't because if Constance happened to spot him, she'd get quite a shock – as would James for that matter – because I hadn't yet had the opportunity to tell either of them that Zack had turned up. However, when I rushed out to try and find him, it became immediately obvious he hadn't gone to the river because I could hear him talking in the house!

'Here she is, at last,' smiled Constance, when I joined the pair of them in the sunroom. 'Do close your mouth, dear.'

My mouth was open because I was so surprised to find them with their heads together and looking like they'd known one another for ever. Clearly, Zack still had the knack of falling into a friendship with anyone, anywhere.

'You'd run out of bread,' he said sheepishly. 'So, I thought I'd try my luck here.'

'And now *I've* run out of bread,' Constance grinned. 'Isn't your brother wonderful, Tilly? Did you know he was planning to visit? You never mentioned it if you did.'

'Yes, he is,' I said succinctly. 'And no, I didn't. You do know the pair of you will be so bloated from all that toast, you won't be able to move soon.' I smiled wryly.

'Then I'll be able to just float down the river and won't have to make any effort to swim at all,' Zack laughed. For someone who had just traversed the globe, he was remarkably bright-eyed and bushy-tailed, but then I supposed he was used to it. 'Will you be joining me, Constance?' he asked cheekily.

'No, not today,' she said primly, and Zack grinned.

'Is there any tea left in that pot?' I asked, stifling a yawn.

Zack lifted the lid. 'Not a drop. I'll make another, shall I?'

'Yes, please,' Constance answered. 'And there might be an éclair or two in the fridge if you fancy one.'

'You're my kind of gal,' Zack winked, and I rushed to follow him.

The last thing I wanted was James coming across a strange man in his aunt's kitchen and the pair of them getting off on the wrong foot. James however, and his lovable hound, were nowhere to be seen.

'Do you think Constance meant it about the éclairs?' Zack asked, while he waited for the kettle to boil.

'Yes,' I said. 'But we'll have them later. There are all these summer berries still to use up, so I'll make us a fruit salad instead.'

'I'm not sure she'll go for that.' Zack grinned as I lined the punnets up on the table and I realised he'd already got the measure of her.

'I'll splash a little cream on hers as a sop, then,' I smiled. 'Can you go and ask her if James has had his breakfast yet, please?'

'James has gone!' Constance called to me when Zack asked the question.

'Gone!' I shouted as I rushed back to the sunroom, still holding the knife I was using to cut up the strawberries. 'You mean for a walk or . . .'

'He set off for London after I'd gone to bed last night,' Constance explained. 'He left me a note and said he'd sent you a text.'

In my rush to find Zack I hadn't looked at my phone since I'd got up, and I then remembered that I hadn't messaged James before I went to bed, either.

'What did the note say?' I asked. 'Did he say why he'd had to go?'

I wanted to go back to the apartment and read his message, but as Zack already had an inkling that I might be harbouring more than friendly feelings for Constance's nephew, I didn't want to add to his suspicions. Things were already complicated enough.

'Something about his boss calling an emergency meeting with a celebrity client who has got themselves in some sort of bother,' she explained brusquely. 'Apparently, James is going to have to represent them, which is a far cry from the sort of work he should be doing. Did the pair of you have time to talk yesterday, Tilly?'

Zack had come back out to listen and gave me a look which I ignored.

'Yes,' I said, my mind racing. I needed to talk to James as soon as possible and clarify what our next steps were with regards to my telling Constance that I no longer wanted to buy the woods. 'Yes, we did . . . talk.'

'So, now you know why I'm so keen to sell you the woods,' she said and looked directly at me. 'The cash in the bank will mean he can look for another job which allows him to do the pro bono work he has a passion for. I've hated that he's currently having to shore things up here largely doing work he doesn't care for.'

I was shocked that she'd mentioned his diverted salary and bit back the comment that his efforts had been in vain because he'd discovered she hadn't spent the money he'd been sending her. Zack, I noticed, had discreetly retreated when he realised this was probably a conversation he shouldn't be privy to.

'Actually,' I ventured, 'I can see the situation from both points of view now. You want to give James the opportunity to follow the career he really wants, and he wants to keep Willowell Woods in the family because of the connection to his mum.'

Constance didn't look impressed that I sounded so reasonable and understanding.

'He'll still have his memories of the place,' she said, rather mutinously. 'And it's not as if selling the woods to you is going to put them out of his reach, is it? He'll still be able to visit and not have to worry about the cost of the upkeep.'

'But he doesn't want to see them changed,' I tried to explain. 'He doesn't want to lose the strongest connection to Grace's memory that he has.'

'You aren't going to change them though, are you?'

'But it's bound to feel different.'

'Are you siding with him over this, Tilly?' Constance frowned.

We had reached the point where I could say that yes, I was, and that I was withdrawing my offer, but I couldn't go that far without having talked to James first. On the trip back to London he might have come up with a plan of his own to convince his aunt to change her mind about selling, and if that was the case, he wasn't going to appreciate me causing a rumpus and a falling out by forging ahead with mine.

'Not siding exactly,' I hedged. 'But Zack and I lost the house that was full of memories of our mum because Dad, thinking he was doing the right thing and providing us all with a fresh start, went ahead and sold it, and we never got over it. Not really. And I'd hate to now be a part of the same thing happening to James.'

It was a rather gabbled explanation, but I think it got my point across.

'In that case,' Constance conceded, 'I can understand why you'd take his side.'

'I haven't taken his side—'

'You might think me harsh, but my sister is in the past and James's happiness now and in the future is my priority.'

'I know,' I sighed. 'I know it is.'

'So, we'll carry on as planned,' she pounced. 'Yes? He'll come round eventually.'

I could have screamed with frustration; I wanted to make them both happy but couldn't fathom how.

'Why don't we wait until James has seen this new case through?' I suggested cannily. 'With any luck, it will be so dire that it will be enough to make him change his mind and then we can go ahead with his blessing? I'd be far happier to do that.'

I knew I was playing for time and the look on Constance's face suggested she'd guessed what I was attempting, too. She opened her mouth to say something but right at that moment Zack rushed in and stood between us with a plate piled high with the éclairs he'd found in the fridge.

'There were loads,' he said, as he thrust them towards Constance. 'And look at the size of them. It'll take us ages to get through these.'

'I know I stepped in,' Zack apologised, when we later packed his bags into my car and got ready to head out. 'But I didn't think the pair of you were going to find common ground and it wouldn't have helped anyone if you'd fallen out.'

He was right of course and when I'd eventually had the opportunity to read James's message, which practically pleaded with me to give him a bit more time now he'd had to leave again, I was pleased Zack had. I'd sent a message back explaining what had occurred with Constance and that he was now in my debt. Unfortunately, I was still feeling too devastated about losing the woods to imagine all the ways I could get James to settle the bill.

'It's fine,' I said and gave Zack a hug before climbing into my car. 'More than fine because even though I'm not now going to buy the woods, I would hate to leave here under a cloud and with tainted memories. That would be the worst.'

Zack shook his head. 'You are going to buy the woods,' he said firmly, as he pulled on his seatbelt. 'And before you object, don't ask me how, but I just know it's all going to work out. There's no doubt in my mind that it will happen.'

I gave him a look. 'Is it like the time you had a feeling that you'd pass your mocks without revising?' I asked innocently. 'Or like the time you were completely convinced that Dad wouldn't find out about—'

'No,' he cut in, with a smile. 'It's nothing like either of those times.'

'Oh well, in that case,' I said and turned the engine over, 'perhaps on this occasion, you might miraculously turn out to be right.'

I didn't really think he would but I couldn't resist teasing him. My head and heart were still all over the place where James was concerned, but having my brother back in the country was stopping the feeling of overwhelm I might have succumbed to without him.

'This room turning up is a bit of luck, isn't it?' he said, effectively changing the subject. 'Did you know the landlord offered bed and breakfast?'

I laughed at that. 'I don't think Carter offers any such thing.'

'Oh?' Zack frowned.

'I think it's more a case of him offering you his spare room above the pub because he didn't want to upset Constance when she rang and asked if he could put you up. I know she would have offered you a bed in Fernside if it wasn't for the current turmoil, but as things stand, I do think this is a better option.'

'I get that, but I feel bad now,' Zack tutted. 'I hope Carter doesn't really mind. What if we don't get on?'

'You get on with everyone,' I reminded him. 'And Carter's an easy-going guy.'

'Someone else you've got your eye on?' Zack nudged.

'Don't you start,' I retorted. 'Just because we have a few things in common someone else has already hinted at matchmaking, but he's not my type.'

'He's not like James then?'

'A bit,' I said wistfully. 'Did I tell you James shares our passion for fresh air and green things growing?'

'No, you didn't, but you've clearly got things in common with him then.'

'He's a veritable tree-hugging type.'

'It must have been a long chat the pair of you had,' Zack laughed. 'You certainly seem to have got to know him rather well on the back of one conversation.'

'We've talked more than that.' I blushed. 'Don't forget I was looking after Constance following her fall and James checked in a lot to make sure she was okay.'

'Of course he did,' Zack grinned.

'Anyway,' I said. 'How are your bar skills? I hope you've pulled a pint since your uni days, because the arrangement is that you're going to earn your board by helping Carter out in the pub.'

'Luckily enough, I helped a mate in his bar in Bali just a couple of weeks ago. It wasn't quite a quaint country hostelry, but the experience got me back in the zone.' I rolled my eyes at that. 'What?'

'It doesn't matter where you are in the world, you always land on your feet, don't you?'

'Do I?' he laughed.

'You know you do.'

'I think you make your own luck in this world,' he shrugged. 'Is that the store your friend Melody runs?' he asked, as we drove by. 'That wasn't there when we used to visit, was it? It looks really nice.'

'It's more than nice,' I told him. 'Utterly idyllic and Melody's a real community champion. She supports local growers, makers and producers. You'll most likely meet her in the pub at some point. And she has a sister, Kaya.'

I already knew that Kaya and Zack would get along because they both loved to travel. I gave the pair of them less than five minutes before they were comparing favourite global locations.

'I take it the pub is a bit out of the way,' Zack said as I turned the car off the main lane and we started to bump along the smaller and considerably more pot-holed one.

'Just a bit,' I smiled, wondering how long my suspension would be able to handle it. 'I didn't believe it could be down here the first time I visited. But don't worry, you won't be stuck here. I'll come and pick you up, so we can spend lots of time together.'

'Maybe you could stick me on your insurance?' he suggested. 'That way, we could share your car.'

I wasn't sure that idea was a good one.

'Exactly how long is it since you've been behind the wheel?'

'Er,' he said, sounding affronted. 'About a week. I do drive when I'm out of the country, you know!'

'Um,' I said. 'Well, I'll think about it. Here we are.'

It was no time at all before Zack and Carter were chatting as if they'd known one another for ever. As soon as we arrived, we'd made a point of finding out if he was genuinely happy with the arrangement that Constance had facilitated and then Zack quickly got to grips with the set-up behind the bar.

While he was making his way along the pumps, I checked my phone again. I hadn't had a reply from James yet, but that was probably because he was talking to the celebrity who'd got themselves in trouble.

'Hello you!' said Melody, who bounded unexpectedly up as I put my phone away again. 'What are you doing here?'

'What are *you* doing here more like?' I asked. 'Shouldn't you be at the store?'

'I don't open on a Sunday, remember?'

'Of course you don't.' Given that there were no buckets of flowers on the pavement and the door was closed when I drove by, I should have remembered that. 'I've had no idea what day of the week it is since I moved to Willowell,' I told her.

The words caught in my throat, because I knew that feeling wasn't now destined to last. What I had been hoping would be a long-term, potentially for ever move had, despite what Constance and Zack still insisted, a fast-approaching expiration date.

Even though I entirely understood James's desire to convince his aunt to keep the woods in the Clarke family, it was still a huge blow to lose them and equally as vexing was the realisation that I had no idea where I would be heading when the day to leave dawned. With Zack behind the bar in The Greenman, I knew it wasn't going to be Bali.

'Are you okay?' Melody frowned.

'Yes,' I nodded and swallowed my upset away. 'I'm okay. Just feeling it a bit because I didn't get much sleep. My brother here kept me up all night chatting.'

'Your brother?'

She knew all about Zack of course, because we'd compared notes on travelling relatives when I'd first arrived in Willowell and stayed in Rose Cottage. What a long time ago that felt like now, though really it had only been a few weeks.

'Yep.' I smiled. 'Melody say hello to Zack. Zack, this is Melody, owner of the Willowell Store you were admiring on our drive through the village, and a fabulous friend.'

'So, this is your brother?' Melody repeated as Zack shook her hand over the bar. 'The brother who travels the world and is currently holed up somewhere in Bali.'

'The very one,' Zack laughed. 'Only now I'm holed up in Suffolk with no plans to go anywhere.'

I fell to thinking again that neither of us were likely to stay for long, but Rick walked in with Kaya hot on his heels, and the low moment passed.

'Hey,' Rick said to me, once introductions had been made, and while Carter was pouring everyone drinks and Kaya and Zack were staring at each other with identical lovestruck expressions written all over their faces. 'How's things?'

We moved to the back of the pub so we could talk without being overheard.

'Still messy.' I sighed heavily.

'Tell me.'

'Constance still wants to sell and James doesn't want her to,' I shrugged. 'Same problem, different day.'

'Not really a problem for you though, is it?' Rick pointed out.

'It is now I know more about why James doesn't want Constance to sell.'

'Ah.'

'Obviously, I don't want to lose the woods and the opportunity they're offering,' I told him, 'but I don't want to see James lose something he feels is so precious, either.'

'So, my guess about the connection with his mum, was . . .'

'Spot on,' I told him. 'Annoyingly.'

'And he's not willing to compromise? It's not as if he'd never be able to visit the woods if you and Constance went ahead, is it? What a shit.'

'He's not a shit.' I biffed him. 'And we haven't discussed what I had in mind. He did ask, but I didn't think there would be any point in explaining.'

'Um,' Rick said dreamily. 'So, he's gorgeous *and* a man who is willing to listen, even though you didn't feel like sharing when he asked. What a combination. No wonder you want to keep on his right side . . .'

'You're so shallow,' I tutted.

'Like you haven't noticed,' he shot back.

'The thing that I've noticed,' I told him as I looked over to the bar, 'is that he's Constance's last living relative. Just like Zack is mine, and I would do anything to stop them falling out even more, because when it comes down to just you and one other family member left in the whole of the world, you keep that person close.'

'I suppose, when you put it like that . . .' Rick said.

'There's no other way to put it,' I said and clapped a hand to his chest. 'Now, come on, let's have a drink before the others drain the bar dry, and remember, Melody, Kaya and Carter have no idea about any of this and until it's all properly resolved, I want to keep it that way.'

'You don't want your other friends to know?' Rick frowned.

'I don't want them to worry,' I amended. 'James, Constance and I can sort this out between us.'

At least, I hoped we could.

Chapter 25

Zack was exhausted by the end of his first day in Willowell, so I left him getting ready to go up to his room in the pub and headed back to Fernside. James called just as I walked through the garden gate, so I quickly walked down to the river to talk to him, but it was only a brief conversation because he was still in the office.

'It's gone nine, James,' I pointed out when he told me where he was.

'I know,' he yawned. 'Buddy's staying with his sitter overnight.'

I was beginning to feel sorry for that dog. He currently spent far more time with his sitter than his owner. I didn't voice that opinion though because I was certain it must have crossed James's mind, too.

'And I daresay he'll be in bed long before you,' I said instead. 'Are you sure you're going to be able to keep this up long-term? Not,' I then quickly added, 'that I'm saying that to try and make you change your mind about going along with selling the woods.'

'It won't be for ever,' he said, and I thought he sounded more hopeful than sure. 'As soon as I'm back in my boss's good books, things will settle down, and I'll get some balance back again.'

'Well, that's something to look forward to,' I attempted to enthuse. 'And in the meantime, what are we going to do about your aunt? Do you want me to tell her I'm pulling out of the sale?'

'Oh, crikey,' he sighed. 'I still don't know. The last thing I want is for the pair of you to fall out, but if you do say something, that's going to be inevitable, isn't it? What do you think?'

He sounded as though he was carrying the weight of the world on his shoulders.

'I think,' I said carefully, 'that if I tell her I'm not buying and why, then she will be cross with me, but she might also take your reasons for not wanting to sell more seriously.'

'Really?'

'Really. It's not that she doesn't care about your feelings, James. Far from it. The whole reason she wants to sell is to give you the opportunity to do the work you love, but if she—'

'That reminds me,' he cut in. 'Sorry to interrupt.'

'No, go on.'

'I've had an email from my former boss. He says he really needs an answer from me about whether I'm going back.'

'It is a long time since he offered you the job again, isn't it? And he must be really keen if he's still hanging on.'

'I know. And if it wasn't for the money and the memories . . .'

'The money your aunt hasn't spent according to you,' I reminded him. 'Again, not that I'm saying that to make you reconsider, but does she really need it?'

'I still can't believe she hasn't touched a penny of it. It's just sitting there in a joint account.'

'But if she can manage without it . . .'

'You know she can't,' James said. He was beginning to sound

frustrated. 'You said yourself she hadn't been eating properly when you moved in, and when the autumn comes she'll need to run the heating. Fernside is like a fridge at the best of times, but in the winter it can be glacial, and oil doesn't come cheap.'

That was a reasonable comment. I'd only been around for the hottest weeks of the summer and even then, the kitchen could be on the cool side. Come the first frost, the inside temperature in the whole house would doubtless plummet.

'So,' I surmised, 'you need the money, and you definitely want to keep the woods, so the only thing I can do now is go ahead and tell her I'm not buying. If she knows she's got to start all over again and find another buyer, it might put her off for a while, and you can work on her in the interim.'

James mulled that over. Given that his aunt had his best interests at heart, I wasn't sure it would put her off completely, but I felt he needed some hopeful thought to cling to.

'Don't say anything yet,' he said eventually, and I let out a long breath. 'Give me a tiny bit longer.'

'All right,' I agreed, though I wasn't sure I should. 'I won't say a word. Now, you'd better get back to work.'

'Yes, I suppose so, but Tilly, before I go . . .'

'Yeah?'

'I've been thinking it over and I'm even more sorry about that kiss. I know things between us are already difficult enough and—'

'Well, I'm not sorry,' I interrupted and cut the call off before he could respond.

My hands were shaking as I walked back up the lawn. Why did it feel like I was still falling for the guy who was going to deny me the perfect future I'd started to invest so much in?

My phone pinged with an incoming message as I reached the apartment door. Just four words – *I'm not sorry either*. Given the circumstances, I perhaps shouldn't have been pleased about that, but I was.

Knowing that, no matter what aunt and nephew decided, my halcyon time in Willowell wasn't going to last and that I still couldn't let anyone – besides Rick and Zack – know about it in case word got back to Constance, I decided to throw myself full tilt into what was left of the summer. I wasn't going to let James drag it out for too much longer, because I felt bad for Carter who was still enthusing about helping, but for the time being, I vowed to keep my promise and hoped a compromise could be reached.

Having Zack back in the country proved to be a wonderful distraction from my worries and his desire to look through my old holiday journals and relive our childhood memories helped, too.

'This house,' he said dreamily, early one morning after I'd driven to the pub to pick him up and we stood on the jetty looking back towards Fernside. 'And this river,' he added, as he turned around. 'I bet you still can't really believe you're here, Tilly, can you?'

'Not really,' I smiled, as I stripped down to my swimming costume. 'It's wonderful to be back in Suffolk, isn't it?'

'Absolutely,' he agreed wholeheartedly. 'And the opportunity to stay for ever is totally worth fighting for, you know.'

'Please, let's not start the day talking about that,' I sighed, as I piled up my clothes. 'Tell me how your date with Kaya went last night?'

'It wasn't a date,' he protested feebly, then gave the game away because he couldn't suppress the smile which went from ear to ear.

It was tempting to tease him when I saw him blushing beneath the deep tan that his many years working outside overseas had given him, but I resisted. He hadn't pursued the topic of my feelings for James after all and given that I snuck away to take calls from him and was often spotted staring into space after them, he had ample ammunition.

'What did you and Kaya talk about?' I asked, as I moved my towel closer to the edge of the jetty.

'Our travels, mostly.' Zack carried on smiling. 'And the deeper we got into it, the more we came to realise that we'd not just sometimes been in the same country, but the exact same area, literally a stone's throw from one another on at least half a dozen occasions.'

'No way,' I gasped, sounding as amazed as he did. 'What are the odds of that?'

'I know right?'

'And it took a trip to Willowell for your paths to finally cross.' I sighed dreamily.

'It's serendipity,' he said soppily.

'It's certainly something.' I nudged him and he shoved me back so hard I almost lost my footing and fell in.

'Don't be messing about near the river!' Constance called from her view in the sunroom the moment she heard me squeal. 'It's running quite fast today and the last thing we need is for one or both of you to get carried off.'

We both waved in response, shouted an apology and soon realised she was right. Neither of us had been swimming long, when we decided to cut the time short. It was tiring swimming against the strength of the flow and had I been on my own, I probably wouldn't have gone in at all. Once we'd climbed out again, we sat, wrapped in our towels and with our feet dangling over the edge of the jetty, our toes skimming the water as we watched the flotsam float by.

'Do you think he's still here?' Zack asked wistfully, with a nod to the bank on the other side. 'Dad, I mean.'

I had previously shown him the spot where I'd scattered Dad's ashes, and he had agreed that it was the perfect place.

'I don't know,' I sighed. 'I had been taking comfort in the thought that he was before, but now I know I'm going to have to leave in the not-too-distant future, I'm trying to change my feelings about it, so it won't feel like I'm leaving him behind when I do head off.'

'Nothing's been decided yet,' Zack tried to say softly, but I shook my head and felt rather cross that I'd unguardedly broached the topic again.

'This is one story that isn't going to have a happy ending,' I told him firmly. 'But before I try and find somewhere else to set my business up, there are a few more places I'd like us to revisit around here.'

I might have been certain that I wasn't going to start working in Willowell Woods, but I was still trying to keep faith in the plan that I'd come up with. The odds of me finding somewhere to make it come to fruition were slim to nothing given that I'd been scouring the internet and nothing currently for sale came close, but I was determined to keep searching.

'Where did you have in mind for us to go?' Zack asked, thankfully not suggesting I introduced him to the woods.

We took great delight in taking familiar walks and wasting

some time watching the river, playing Poohsticks, eating food cooked over the campfire Constance had given us permission to safely light at the end of the garden and staying out late to stargaze. I had wondered if Zack might have perhaps had his fill of constellation spotting, but he insisted the sky in Suffolk was as magical as any in the world and, given our location, which was completely free of light pollution, every bit as clear.

Immersed in the catch-up with my much-missed brother, I knew I had been neglecting Constance, but that wasn't all down to reforging family ties. The problem was, every time we were alone together, she brought up the subject of the woods, and it was getting harder not to blurt out that I wasn't going to buy them.

'I think we'd better give you a file and polish, Constance,' I suggested one day when I guiltily noticed how chipped the varnish was looking on her fingernails and realised how long it had been since we'd spent some time together. 'And how about a swim in the tub ahead of the supper party this evening?'

The weather had turned warmer again and the gang were all getting together to celebrate the return of the sun. Even Carter had managed to find cover for him and Zack so he could drive to Fernside in his car, meaning Zack could return mine. My former concerns about Zack's driving had proved unfounded, and having sorted the insurance we were now sharing my car as he'd previously suggested.

'That might be nice,' Constance said. 'But only if you've got time. I know you and Zack have lots of places to visit.'

'I can always make time for you, Constance,' I told her. 'I know I haven't been around much—'

'And with good reason,' she cut in. 'When a family member returns to the fold, it's something to celebrate.'

'I agree.' I nodded. 'And I'd love to see you and James back on a happier footing,' I added, feeling brave.

'We'll be fine once he sees sense,' she said crisply, and I bit back the temptation to remind her that he thought he already was. 'And on that note,' she continued, 'could you please pass me the folder that's on the worktop next to the egg safe?'

I kept my fingers crossed that it wasn't the file containing Grace's paperwork about the nursery, but it turned out to be something far worse.

'I'll go and run your bath, shall I?' I said, the moment I'd handed the folder over.

'Not just yet,' she said and pulled out a bundle of papers. 'First, I want you to have a quick look at these.'

I had no choice but to take the papers from her.

'What are they?' I frowned, then baulked when I saw a company name I recognised at the top of the first piece of paper.

'Valuations for the woods.'

'But when?' I spluttered. 'Who?'

'I picked three firms last week, all with decent reputations, and got them to go and value the site straightaway,' she told me briskly. 'I thought it was about time we did something. You've seemed to be dragging your feet since James turned up.'

My throat felt dry, and I could feel a tightening around my chest.

'I thought we were going to talk about sorting this?' I croaked, as I sat at the table and flicked through the pages without really seeing anything.

Two of the firms were the ones I'd been going to recommend, but I hadn't heard of the third.

'We had talked about it,' Constance pointed out. 'And now it's time to act. I know James still thinks I'm going to change my mind about selling, but I'm not.'

'I see,' I said and set the papers down.

'I hope the change of value doesn't take you too much by surprise,' she smiled. 'It did me, I'm not going to lie.'

'I told you, you'd seriously undervalued the site,' I reminded her.

'You did,' she said. 'And you were right. I'll always be grateful that you were honest with me about that.'

'Well, I'm an honest person,' I told her, but the words stuck a little because I wasn't currently being honest with her, was I?

'Indeed, you are,' she smiled. 'And once this sale has gone through and James can see the amount it's given us, he'll appreciate that, too.'

Now that was one thing I knew we would never agree on.

'Well, now,' Constance beamed, as we watched Zack and Kaya walk hand in hand down to the jetty that evening. 'Don't you two look a picture?'

She wasn't wrong. The pair looked made for each other. Kaya might have always had an eye for an attractive man, but she looked utterly besotted with my brother and he looked equally enamoured with her. I couldn't help wishing that James and I could have been enjoying as straightforward a relationship as they were.

'Thank you, Constance,' Zack and Kaya smiled, in perfect synchronicity.

'Aren't they a great match?' Constance remarked.

'Absolutely perfect,' I smiled in response. 'Is Melody here, too? I'll go and help her with the food.'

By the time Melody and I had crammed everything into the fridge, and Carter and Rick had carried down the tin bath Rick had found in the shed and filled it with ice for the drinks, I was feeling something akin to the excitement I'd enjoyed during our previous supper soirées.

Unfortunately, however the feeling didn't last. The evening went downhill from the moment I returned with a jumper from the apartment as the temperature had started to drop.

'Constance has just told us that she's had the woods valued,' Zack called to me as I walked back.

I appreciated the heads up and even though my steps faltered for a moment, I was able to carry on.

'That's great news,' said Carter. 'You can forge ahead now, can't you, Tilly? Assuming you're happy with the updated asking price.'

I knew everyone's eyes were on me and I took a moment to pick out a bottle of drink. I didn't really want anything, but I was trying to buy myself a second to decide how to play it. Should I continue with the pretence or come clean?

'Well,' I said, toying with the idea of saying I couldn't afford the new price but abandoning it because I knew Constance would immediately reduce it, 'I haven't had a chance to look properly through the documents yet, but it's a step in the right direction.'

'Cheers!' said Melody and Carter as they held aloft bottles and clinked them together.

'Cheers!' everyone else responded.

I knew I was slightly behind the toast and Constance noticed it, too.

'It is a step in the right direction, isn't it?' She frowned at me.

'I'm not sure,' I heard my voice shakily confess and suddenly you could have heard a pin drop. 'I would have been certain before . . .'

'Before James came along and made you doubt yourself,' Constance said crossly.

'I'm not doubting *me*,' I told her and everyone looked from one of us to the other. 'As we're truth telling, it's you I'm not sure about, Constance.'

'What's that supposed to mean?'

'I think we should—' began Melody.

'Stay where you are,' Constance commanded. 'Explain yourself, Tilly.'

'How can I buy the woods and happily set up a business in them knowing that my being there has broken James's heart?' I said in a rush.

She didn't ask why I cared for James's heart. Perhaps she'd simply assumed it was because I was trying to be honest, open and fair to everyone.

'So, you're not going to buy the woods then?' she demanded.

'No,' came a voice behind us and we all jumped. As one, we turned around to find James with Buddy, on a lead and quiet for once. 'Tilly isn't going to buy the woods.'

Chapter 26

Constance looked from her nephew to me and back again and I could see the colour rising in her cheeks.

'I see,' she said in a tone I hadn't heard her use before. 'I see. You've clearly talked in more detail than I realised, haven't you?'

'Perhaps we have,' James responded. 'And on every occasion, Tilly has come to further understand why I don't want to sell the woods, Aunt Constance. She can understand what they mean to me, because she herself—'

'Lost something precious,' Constance interjected. 'And she, and Zack,' she added, with a nod to my brother, 'have my every sympathy. And so do you, James, because I do appreciate what the woods mean to you, but in the long term, parting with them is going to give you so much more.'

James shook his head and Buddy strained on his lead. There were a lot of people he could be saying hello to, and he was becoming increasingly frustrated with being held back. As was his owner.

'You say you sympathise with me,' James fired at his aunt, his voice getting louder, 'but you won't accept that I know what's best for me. Along with how I feel about the woods, you won't accept what it is that I feel I need to do, either. You say you're doing this to help *me*, but I want to help *you*! I couldn't do anything to help Mum, when she was dying, but I can help you now and you won't let me!'

That declaration seemed to take the wind out of Constance's sails and caused a collective gasp and my eyes to fill with tears.

'Oh, James,' I said and, without thinking, reached for his hand.

Immediately after he'd said his piece, Constance's features had softened, but my making a physical connection with her nephew caused them to harden again.

'Oh my,' said Rick.

'Are these two—' Kaya began to say, but Melody cut her off.

'I know you were insistent that we should all stay before,' she said to Constance, 'but now I think we really should go. Come on, everyone. Let's leave.'

She stood up and everyone else followed.

'But I'd much rather stay,' Kaya said, and her sister gave her a nudge.

'As would I,' said Rick, as he looked from James to me, 'but now's not the time, Kaya.'

'Would you like me to stay?' Zack asked me.

'No, it's okay,' I said, 'but thanks, Zack. We'll catch up later and make proper introductions soon.'

'All right,' he said and offered James a smile, 'but I think I've already got the gist.'

Constance waited until everyone had walked through the gate, and once Carter had closed it behind him, she fixed James with a steely glare and then, while he let Buddy off his lead, she turned her hardened expression on me.

'Hello, Buddy,' I said, avoiding eye contact with her by giving him a fuss. He hadn't clued into the tense atmosphere and just wanted to play. 'Get down now.'

'Buddy,' James said, rather sharply, and the dog bounded off.

'Why do I get the feeling that there's more to this situation than either of you have chosen to share with me?' Constance demanded of us both.

James went to move, but before he could say anything, I stepped up and went for broke.

'James was my lay-by meet-cute,' I blurted out. 'He's also the guy I went on a date with that Rick announced at the first supper party and, prior to finding James playing the piano in your sitting room the day you thought was the first time we met, we'd got together on other occasions, too.'

I could feel James was looking at me, but I didn't reciprocate.

'And we've talked on the phone a lot,' I continued to gabble on. 'Both before and after it was revealed that the two of you are related.'

'Tilly . . .' James whispered.

'I know,' I said to him. 'But I couldn't keep it in any longer, James. It's such a relief to have everything out in the open now.'

'Well, I'm pleased you're feeling better, Tilly,' Constance said, sounding deeply upset, 'but I don't. If anything, I feel a total fool. You've both deceived me.'

'That was never our intention,' James was quick to say.

'So why haven't either of you said anything before tonight?' she asked. 'You've known for ages now who James and I are to each other, Tilly, and you've never said a word. Why?'

I took a moment to think how I could best frame my response in a way that wouldn't make her feel even worse because that was the last thing I wanted.

'Because once James was revealed as your nephew,' I said truthfully, 'I didn't know what that was going to mean for the two of us or our new relationship. Prior to that, I had been really falling for him, but then when I discovered who he was, and that he could influence my future in such a negative way, I had to try and call time on my feelings. Things were already so complicated that I didn't want to make the situation worse by telling you who he really was to me and throwing . . . love . . . into the equation.'

'Love,' I heard James say breathlessly.

'Love,' Constance echoed, then turned her attention to her nephew. 'And what about you, James?' she asked. 'Is this how you feel, too?'

'No disrespect, Aunt Constance,' he responded succinctly, and I wondered if I'd shocked him by uttering that four letter word that carried so much hope, comfort and promise, 'but I'll talk to Tilly about my feelings when the two of us are alone if that's all right with you? You and I have got plenty of other things to discuss.'

Buddy chose that moment to come hurtling back and almost knocked me off my feet.

'Come here, you daft dog,' James tutted and reached for his collar. 'Sorry, Tilly. Are you all right?'

'No,' I said, looking deep into his eyes. 'In spite of the cathartic moment, I'm not feeling all that great.'

'Me neither,' he puffed.

'I think we should continue this conversation up at the house,' Constance said and stood up rather stiffly.

James went to offer her his arm, but she waved him away.

'My two favourite people in the whole world have found

their way to one another,' she said, sounding wretched, 'and I should be thrilled, but I'm not. I can't be because all I can see coming from this connection is an unhappy ending . . .'

Her words, even though I agreed with them entirely, hurt me deeply, and when we reached the patio, I peeled off.

'I think it would be best if I left the pair of you to it,' I said hoarsely. 'Keep it in the family, for tonight at least.'

'You don't have to go,' James insisted. 'There's nothing I'm going to say to my aunt that I wouldn't want you to hear, Tilly.'

'And nothing that I probably haven't heard before,' Constance said rather cuttingly.

'I appreciate that,' I nodded to James, 'but I'm still going to call it a night.'

Constance didn't say anything further and as she turned towards the sunroom, James mimed that he'd talk to me in the morning and I gave him a thumbs up in response.

Once inside the apartment, I found I needed some comfort, so I warmed some milk, got undressed and, feeling the cool of the evening taking hold, climbed into bed. I had a WhatsApp message from Zack asking me to let him know if I was okay, which I did, and then I fell to wondering why James had turned up when he had. He hadn't mentioned that he was going to be able to visit so soon, and as I snuggled down for the night, I added that to the growing list of things I wanted to talk to him about.

Having spent much of the night tossing and turning, I woke late and with a thick head to the sound of my phone buzzing.

'James, hey,' I said tiredly. 'Are you okay?'

'That depends on your definition of okay,' he replied, sounding equally as tired. 'Can you meet me at the cabin in say, half an hour?'

I pictured him checking the time on his beloved timepiece, and even though the woods were the last place I felt like visiting, I made a concerted effort to push my feelings aside.

'Can we make it a few minutes longer than that?' I requested. 'I've only just woken up. I didn't sleep well.'

'Not to try to top trump you, but I haven't even seen my bed yet.'

'You've been up all night?'

'Aunt Constance and I were both up all night. She's just gone to her room.'

'Did you make any headway?' I asked, then immediately countered. 'No, tell me when we're together.'

'I'll see you down there.'

I didn't waste any time in dithering to get ready because I didn't want to think about the difficulty of making a return trip to the woods and I didn't want to catastrophise over what James might be going to tell me, either.

I did the bare minimum in the bathroom, piled my hair up into the messiest ever bun and pulled on a linen shirt dress I should have hung up because it was now deeply creased and crumpled. Moving fast and on autopilot helped me not to think too deeply, but I wasn't sure for how long.

I didn't have to creep by the house to avoid being spotted because I knew Constance had gone to bed and I was soon parked at the woods and feeling determined to take as little notice of the place as I could. That, however, turned out to be impossible.

It had only been a short while since I'd last visited, but looking quickly around, I could see how far the summer had moved on. Both the garden at Fernside and the lane that led to the woods were showing the very first signs of autumn, but I could feel them more keenly here. The bleached-out colours en masse gave a hint of what was to come and how quickly it was going to happen. There was no denying that I still loved Willowell Woods and the rapidly ripening sloes and hawthorn berries had me hankering to observe their changes through the next season and beyond.

'Just keep going,' I muttered to myself and strode more quickly towards the cabin.

A sudden burst of unexpected birdsong rang out, and I spotted a wren with its tail high in the air as it sang its heart out on a nearby tree stump. The sound was unexpected because the tiny bird had no need to draw attention to itself now that the breeding season was over, and I couldn't help thinking, as I watched it, that it was singing just for me. This was, without doubt, going to be my last visit to the woods, and the wren wanted to send me off with a happy memory.

'Tilly,' James frowned, when he spotted me approaching and opened the cabin door. 'Are you okay?'

I thought I'd swallowed my emotion away, but something about my expression must have alerted him to the fact that I was upset.

'I'm just feeling a bit overtired,' I told him. 'These last few weeks have been a lot, haven't they?'

'Yes,' he agreed, and closed the door behind me, so Buddy, who was currently engrossed in demolishing a chew of some sort, couldn't run off. 'They've been too much in so many ways.'

I wondered if he included us getting together in that statement.

'So,' I asked. 'What happened last night?'

James puffed out his cheeks and then a smile lit up his face. For a moment, I thought he was going to tell me Constance had changed her mind, but the alteration of expression was nothing to do with his aunt.

'Hey,' he said, taking a proper look at what I was wearing. 'I recognise that dress.'

'You do?' I frowned, glancing down at it.

'You were wearing it the day we met, weren't you?'

I tried to think back, but I couldn't in all honesty remember what I'd travelled to Willowell wearing, even though I hadn't had many options at the time.

'I remember the buttons.' James continued to smile.

'Then you've got a better memory than me!' I laughed, though when I came to think of it, I could remember every detail of what he'd had on that day.

'Oh my god,' he declared, before clapping loudly and running his hands through his hair. 'I think this is it! Yes, this is it! This is the moment!'

'What are you talking about?' I demanded. 'What's got into you, James? Are you so sleep deprived that you're becoming delirious?'

It was most likely exhaustion coupled with all the emotion that had shoved him off on a tangent.

'Tilly, do you believe in love at first sight?' His question stunned me. 'I didn't,' he quickly carried on before I'd answered. 'I thought it was nonsense, far more to do with lust than love, but then . . .'

'But then?' I frowned.

He took a step closer.

'But then I saw this woman jump out of her car in a dusty lay-by and chase down a hat with this determined look on her face,' knowing he was talking about me, I tried not to imagine how mad that must have looked, 'and I just knew . . .'

'Knew what?'

He took a deep breath and said, in all sincerity, 'That was what love at first sight felt like.'

I felt my own breath leave my body as he closed the gap between us and wrapped his arms around me.

'And there was me thinking it was lust,' I whispered, as I looked up at him.

'There was plenty of that, too,' he smiled. 'But after we'd gone our separate ways, I couldn't stop thinking about you and not only in a lustful way.'

My heart was racing, and I was sure he must have been able to hear it.

'And I even came back here on the off-chance of seeing you again after that first encounter where I'd made a random detour just to drive through the village because we were almost in the area,' he continued. 'Much to the annoyance of my colleague.'

'Your non-hat wearing colleague?'

'That's the one! And then when I did amazingly see you again the second time, by the time I'd driven up the road and turned my car around, you'd gone.'

'You came after me?'

'Of course I did.'

Ironically, he most likely hadn't been able to track me down, because I'd turned up the drive to Fernside.

'Well, thank goodness for dodgy air con,' I smiled.

'And business meetings in pubs,' he added.

I was beginning to think that my mention of love the evening before hadn't put him off me after all . . .

'So, what exactly are you saying, James?' I asked, even though I now had a pretty solid idea.

'I'm saying,' he said, as he rested his hands lightly on my waist, 'that I've fallen in love with you, Tilly, and it happened that very first day we met. That first moment I saw you, in fact. And I'm so sorry that I'm trying to deny you the future you were planning to establish here. Of all the people in the world I don't want to hurt, you're right at the top of the list.'

'Oh, James,' I breathed.

'Do you hate me?' he whispered.

'No,' I said and softly kissed him. 'Of course I don't hate you. I love you, too.'

I couldn't be sure how the next few minutes would have played out if Buddy hadn't finished eating his chew and nudged his way between us, but there was plenty of lust as well as love in the air when we finally broke apart.

'What do you want?' James pretended to tell his beloved dog off.

Buddy woofed and rested a paw on James's leg.

'The same thing as me, I daresay,' I smiled. 'Some attention from you. He must miss you when he's with the sitter.'

'Yes,' James agreed and squatted down to give Buddy a big fuss, 'I think he does.'

He got up and walked over to his rucksack and pulled out a bowl and bottle of water. Within a few seconds, Buddy was noisily drinking and James looked back at me and smiled. I realised then how tired he looked.

'Constance hasn't changed her mind, has she?' I sighed,

knowing we couldn't put off talking about the elephant in the room a moment longer, though I would have loved to.

James's unexpected declaration had made my heart soar with happiness but there were complications that came with it, too. I remembered Dad always said that love conquered all and that nothing else was as important. I hoped he was right. For the moment it seemed to be overriding my upset about losing the woods, but would that last?

'She hasn't changed her mind *yet*,' James amended. 'But I've asked her to give me time to prove that I can still make the current situation work. That's all I can do really, and it's why I drove up last night, to try and fix a date and get her to commit to it. I obviously didn't expect to find the two of you having a public showdown in the garden.'

'No,' I said wryly. 'I hadn't been expecting that to happen, either.'

'And you hadn't told me your brother was planning to visit,' he added.

'Because I didn't know. I did tell you how flighty he is though, didn't I?' I reminded him. 'He turned up with no warning, but I'm so excited that he's here and actually, I'm not so sure he is flighty anymore.'

'You look like each other, you know.'

'Do we?' I frowned.

'You do.' I'd have to look in a mirror to see if I agreed with that. 'And what about the others? I know Rick was there, and Carter, I think, but the other two . . .'

'We'll get to that,' I told him. 'Right now, I'm more interested in your plan to get Constance to keep this place. What exactly are you planning to do before this date you're trying to get her to stick to?'

He walked back over to where I was standing, and I pulled him close.

'First thing on the agenda is getting back into a decent work routine,' he explained thoughtfully. 'That will show my aunt that I can manage the workload. And if I stop taking the pro bono cases for a while, that will get my boss off my back and help with that, too.'

'I'm amazed he's given you time off to visit today.'

'The celebrity client you might have heard me mention before is refusing to work with anyone but me, so it's given me a bit of leverage.'

'That's a bit of luck.'

'You wouldn't say that if you knew who it was,' James grimaced. 'I'm not feeling lucky that I've got to work with them. Far from it. And my boss reckons if I win this case, there'll be more high-profile clients to come.'

'And will you have to deal with those, too?' I asked. 'That will be a far cry from doing the work you love, won't it?'

Given what James had just said about not taking more pro bono work on, I could imagine his boss capitalising on that and the percentage of time he'd previously allowed for it diminishing for good. My phone pinged with an incoming notification before James had given me his answer and opinion on the situation.

'Do you want to check that?' he asked.

'I suppose I should,' I said as I pulled my phone out of the dress pocket and unlocked it. It was an Instagram notification telling me that Woodland Adventures had just posted. 'Oh wow!' I gasped, as the images popped up.

'What is it?' James asked.

'Something stunning on Insta from the place I used to volunteer at.'

'Show me then,' James requested and I turned my phone around.

'Isn't that gorgeous?'

'Wow,' he smiled, 'that's absolutely beautiful. It's called a mandala, isn't it?'

'That's it,' I nodded and swiped to the next image, which was equally as impressive.

'Where is this place?' James asked, as we admired the images of different coloured leaves arranged in beautiful patterns. 'Woodland Adventures. I've never heard of it, but it looks right up my street.'

I looked at him and shook my head.

'And the prize for the most ironic statement of the day goes to!' I said, giving him a nudge.

'What?' James frowned.

'Never mind,' I smiled and turned my phone off again.

'No,' James insisted. 'Go on. Tell me.'

'Well,' I said, 'It's a place that offers outdoor wellbeing workshops and helps people reconnect with nature in all sorts of ways. Woodland Adventures was the inspiration for the business I wanted to set up here.'

James looked taken aback.

'You knew I was planning something outdoorsy,' I told him. 'We talked about that ages ago.'

'But we never got into the details,' he said. 'What else were you planning?'

'If I had my notebook,' I told him, 'I'd be able to give you *all* the details, but I've abandoned it now.'

'Then tell me what you can remember off the top of your head.'

'Why?' I shrugged. 'What would be the point?'

James pulled a picnic blanket out of his rucksack, spread it out, sat on it and refused to budge until I agreed to share each and every one of my business details. He even made me try and pull up the Woodland Adventures Insta account again, but the phone signal had dropped out, so along with my notebook, the visuals were absent, too.

None the more for that, I did an excellent job of explaining what I had been planning. I even remembered Carter, Rick and Melody's involvement and, of course, Helen's assertion that she was certain the plan would be approved.

'So,' I finished up as my tummy gave the loudest rumble and I remembered I hadn't eaten anything for breakfast, 'you can see why this place beats any other hands down. The woodland is perfect,' I reeled off, 'there's off-road parking, a building already on-site and there's been a business here before. It's a prime location and,' I added, getting completely carried away as I always had when I talked about it, 'it's in my favourite part of the world.'

James was staring at me intently and it seemed to take him a moment to realise that I'd stopped talking. When he did, he sprang to his feet and began to stride about.

'James—'

He put up a hand and shook his head, then continued to pace. Buddy, who had been sound asleep, suddenly woke up and, thinking this was some great game invented for his benefit, leapt up and began to scamper around, almost tripping James up on more than one occasion. I sat and watched them and wondered what source of entertainment was going to come next. I didn't have long to find out.

At the end of the next lap, James came over, pulled me to my feet and kissed me firmly on the lips.

'Tilly—'

Buddy's sudden barking cut him off and it made me jump. It wasn't his usual friendly sort of yap, but a protective deep rumble I wouldn't have thought him capable of. When James managed to quieten him, I cocked an ear and could hear a hammering sound.

'Can you hear that?' I asked James and he nodded. 'What is it?'

He quickly attached Buddy's lead.

'I don't know,' he said. 'Let's go and find out.'

We grabbed his things, locked the cabin and followed the noise to the car park. There we found a truck, two men, a ladder and a huge sign.

'Is that a for sale notice?' James bellowed, and the guys ignored him but carried on driving the posts into the ground that they were going to attach it to.

'Looks like it to me,' I shouted over the din, and Buddy started to bark again. 'And James, look! It says the site has already been sold!'

Chapter 27

Because we had driven to the woods in separate cars, we had to travel back to Fernside in convoy. James took the journey considerably faster than I did and by the time I pulled up behind him, he'd already parked, got Buddy out and was scowling at a muddy truck which was taking up most of the space in front of the house.

'Henderson,' he growled at it. 'Come on, Tilly.'

I almost had to trot to keep up with him and wasn't sure whether to follow him into the house, but he ushered me into the sunroom and then through to the kitchen.

'James!' bellowed a guy who I guessed was the owner of the truck. 'How on earth are you? It's been an age.'

He was standing at the side of the table, while Constance was looking though some sheets of paper. I didn't like how close he was to her and James's livid expression and Buddy's deep bark suggested they weren't impressed that he was crowding her, either. Sensing this, the guy took a step away.

'Hello, Tommy,' James said back and I noted he neither said how he was keeping nor returned the courtesy of asking how Tommy was.

'Constance mentioned that you were back,' Tommy nodded.

His huge bulk, both tall and wide, made the kitchen feel small. 'Not staying though, are you?'

Again, James didn't answer. His eyes were on his aunt.

'Hello, my dear,' Tommy said to me. I didn't appreciate the way his gaze seemed to take in every inch of me. 'I don't think we've met.'

'You're running the farm now, are you?' James finally spoke. 'I was sorry to hear about your dad.'

'He had a good innings,' Tommy sniffed, as he adjusted the waistband of his trousers. His belly was so large and the buttons of his checked shirt so strained, it didn't move far. 'And now I'm slowly bringing the place up to speed. Less farming, more . . .' he eyes flicked to the table and James's gaze followed.

'What's going on, Aunt Constance?' James asked, as her hand hovered over one of the pages with a pen in her hand. 'There's a for sale board going up down at the woods, and it's already got sold—'

'Just a formality,' Tommy interrupted rudely. 'My wife's agency is handling the sale, so we thought she might as well put a sign up. One that size will attract a bit of attention. Lovely bit of free publicity.'

'Constance, you can't have sold the woods already. I only told you last night I wasn't going to buy them,' I exclaimed, feeling bewildered. '*And*,' I added with emphasis, 'you know why.'

'I do,' she said. 'And you both know why I *am* going to sell them. Tommy's father had once expressed an interest and said if I was ever going to part with them, I should get in touch.'

I wondered why she hadn't just done that in the first place.

'And here we are,' Tommy said expansively.

'But Tommy's father is no longer with us,' James pointed out.

I had no idea how he could sound so calm because internally I was fizzing. 'And I'm sure his dad would have had different plans for the woods than his son.'

Tommy shifted from one foot to the other, which made Buddy growl.

'I can't believe this is happening so fast.' I swallowed.

I was beginning to feel dizzy and sick and not only because I was hungry.

'Nothing's happened yet,' James said, with a nod to the papers, which Constance hadn't yet signed. 'And no matter what it says on there, it wouldn't hold up in court anyway. With or without a signature.'

'Sometimes it's not what you know,' Tommy said and tapped the paper with a chubby finger. 'Just sign your name there, my dear, and that'll be enough to get the ball rolling.'

I frowned at Constance. This felt so completely out of character for her. I knew she had James's welfare at heart, but selling the woods to this guy just didn't add up, and how was James managing to keep so calm given what he was facing?

'So,' I said, as I forced myself to smile sweetly at Tommy, in the hope of trying to get some information out of him, 'what is it that you're planning to do with the woods?'

'Bikes,' said Constance as she held up one of the sheets and Tommy looked aghast. 'There's going to be a cycle route through the woods. Won't that be lovely?'

James and I exchanged a look and he took the paper from her. He read it for a few seconds and then his attention returned to Tommy.

'Motorcross.' He nodded. 'You're planning to set up a motorcross circuit in Willowell Woods, are you?'

I couldn't keep down the noisy sob that forced its way up and out of my mouth, but Tommy just shrugged and stuffed his hands in his trouser pockets as if the noisy, messy transformation of the currently idyllic woodland meant nothing.

'That sounds fun,' said Constance.

'Perhaps in the right place,' I said and gathered my wits enough to quickly search online for a video to show her what the woods could be reduced to, 'but I hardly think Grace's lovely plot should end up looking and sounding like this, do you?'

Constance covered her ears with her hands while she watched. The sound of the bikes as they blasted around on screen was deafening in the confined space of the kitchen. I didn't turn the volume down though because I wanted Constance to experience what it was both going to look and sound like.

'You'd never get permission for this,' I said to Tommy angrily when the video ended. 'Some of the trees there are ancient.'

'Hardly ancient,' he said patronisingly.

'But far older than us,' James put in. 'And that will count for something.'

'Not to mention the birds and wildlife you'll displace by wrecking the place.'

Tommy didn't look like he cared a jot about the birds, bees and possibly even badgers. Some farmer he must be!

'But like I said,' he shrugged carelessly, and James *still* didn't look rattled, 'it depends on who you know, and besides, we'll only take down the trees that are in the way.'

'You shouldn't be taking down any trees,' I objected loudly.

I knew for a fact that Helen wouldn't approve his awful scheme.

'Not the ideal alternative for the place considering what you had in mind, is it?' Constance said to me, and I began to get the first inkling of what her game was.

'It won't be that bad,' Tommy smiled. 'If the wind is in the right direction, you'll barely hear it from here. Now come on, let's have this signed.' He tapped the papers on the table again. 'I need to get to my solicitor.'

James gave the other paper back to his aunt and started to clap while Buddy slunk around the table to stand between Constance and Tommy.

'What are you doing?' Tommy frowned at James.

'I'm applauding my aunt,' James said. 'Can't you see that?'

'Congratulating her on her shrewd business acumen, you mean?' Tommy laughed.

'Not quite.' James grinned and turned back to Constance. 'This is all an elaborate attempt to get Tilly to change her mind about buying the woods, isn't it?'

That's what I'd guessed too, and the rush of colour spreading across Constance's face was proof enough that she'd been found out. It was a canny tactic on her part, but what was I going to do? Talk about caught between a rock and a hard place! Whatever option I chose, I was going to break one of their hearts and my own, too.

'You thought that if you set up some really vile alternative for the woods, I'd cave and not kick up as much of a fuss when you sold to Tilly, didn't you?' James continued.

Constance suddenly looked close to tears, rather than proud of her fiendish attempt at trickery.

'Don't say anything else, James,' I pleaded. 'You've made your point.'

'I'm just so scared that you're going to crack under the stress,

James,' Constance sobbed. 'You hear about it all the time, don't you? These apparently fit and healthy folk keeling over because they work too hard. I can't have that happen to you! You're all I've got left in the world.'

'Oh, Aunt Constance,' James cried when he realised the true depth of her fear for both his physical and mental health.

I quickly stepped aside so he could reach her and he knelt next to her chair and gave her the longest hug. She succumbed to a bit of a sob, and I was hard pushed not to cry myself when I heard her.

'Well, this is all very touching,' Tommy said uncertainly as he pulled his trousers up again, 'but what's the deal for me here? *Is* there still a deal?'

'Of course there's no deal, you buffoon,' James blustered as he stood back up. I noticed he was holding his aunt's hand. 'And there never was.'

Tommy began to turn red and lurched across the table to grab the papers, but I was quicker than him.

'We'll keep hold of those,' I said and snatched them out of his reach. 'We can shred them for you.'

'So, I've been tricked, have I?' he bellowed. 'And made to look a fool, to boot.'

'I think you've managed that yourself,' said Constance. 'Your dad would be ashamed of you and your current business dealings, Thomas. I've heard about it all and you should know, people won't put up with your bullying tactics much longer.'

She clearly had more intel on him and more of an agenda than I had realised.

'Yeah, well, Dad's not here, is he?' Tommy shouted. His colour had now reached a frightening shade of puce. 'So that's it, is it?'

James looked thoughtful for a moment.

'There is just one more thing,' he said and turned his attention to his canine companion. 'Buddy, see him off!'

Tommy tripped his way around the table in panic and shot through the kitchen door far faster than I ever would have thought he could move. Buddy, by comparison, stayed exactly where he was and scratched his ear.

'You think about what I've said!' Constance shouted after her unpopular visitor, as we heard him stumble and ricochet off the sunroom door, doubtless full of fear that Buddy was about to bite his backside.

James and I shared a quick look, and I wondered what was going to happen next. Life at Fernside was proving to be unpredictable of late and it was just as well I'd taken a leaf out of my brother's book and started to roll with the punches rather than rail against them.

'I have to tell you,' said James, as he sat next to Constance and I sat next to him, 'you needn't have gone to all that bother, Aunt Constance.'

'Oh?' she sniffed and blew her nose.

'Not that I didn't enjoy seeing my former school chum being wound up and made to look a fool,' James smiled wryly.

'You pair never did get on. Thank goodness,' she said, giving him a watery smile. 'I've heard a lot of talk about Tommy getting too big for his boots and I thought this plan I had devised would make you think *and* teach him a lesson, but why shouldn't I have bothered?'

James reached for my hand and held it before answering.

'Because,' he said, 'Tilly and I talked in the cabin earlier. She told me all about her ideas for Willowell Woods and I was just at the point of begging her to buy them when the sound of the for sale board going up interrupted us.'

'What?' Constance squawked.

'Oh my god, James!' I gasped and squeezed his hand so tight I could have cut his circulation off. 'Do you mean it?'

'Of course I mean it,' he laughed. 'What you've got in mind for the place is perfect and, what's more, I can't wait to help you set it up.'

'You're really serious?'

'Your business is going to give so many people the very thing Mum gave me.' He smiled at me. 'My love of the outdoors and all the benefits that comes with it. Of course I'm serious. I can't think of anything better to share than that, can you?'

'So, you won't mind people visiting and a few small things possibly changing?'

'I'm sure I'll get used to it in no time, but before we get into all that, I need to make a phone call or two. I have a new job to accept, don't I?'

'A new job?' Constance gasped.

'With my old firm,' he beamed. 'The offer came in a while ago.'

Constance's hands flew to cover her cheeks. 'You've got your dream job and Tilly is going to buy the woods!' she sobbed.

'Yes!' James and I said together and jumped up so we could kiss and embrace.

Suddenly, everything was right in my world again, everything was perfect in Willowell, and my heart felt full of love and joy!

'Perhaps,' said Constance through a rush of very happy tears, 'there will be a happy ever after for you two, after all.'

'A happy ever after for the four of us,' I said breathlessly as I swiped away a tear of my own. 'You,' I said, indicating her, 'me, James and Buddy.'

Buddy, picking up on the ecstatic mood, started to caper about and bark. Constance tore the paperwork Tommy had drawn up into tiny pieces while James and I exchanged another searing kiss. It was some minutes before the euphoria started to settle and, even when it did, it didn't dissipate completely because we were all so blissfully happy.

'Crikey,' laughed James. 'What a day! And I don't know about you two, but I'm absolutely famished.'

'I'm starving,' I said, hearing my stomach rumble again.

'I could probably manage something,' Constance joined in.

'Bacon sandwiches all round then,' said James.

He kissed my cheek before heading to the fridge.

'I thought you had important calls to make,' Constance laughed.

'I think I'd better eat first,' he grinned.

I'd just finished the last bite of mine when my phone rang. It was Zack, and I moved into the sunroom before answering because I got a better signal in there.

'Hey, Tilly,' he said when I answered. 'I hope it's not a bad time, but I wanted to check in. I've been worried about you. All of you, actually.'

I hated to hear the concern in his tone and couldn't wait to rid him of it.

'You are a love to fret,' I said, the words snagging because the emotion of the morning was catching up with me, 'but you don't have to worry.'

'You're okay?'

'More than okay.' I smiled. 'A million times more than okay!'

James popped his head around the doorframe and blew me a kiss which made me laugh.

'What's happened?' Zack asked. 'Something brilliant by the sounds of it. What is it?'

'I want to tell you in person,' I said, as an idea for how to make the future even more perfect popped into my head. 'Can you get to Fernside? Could you maybe borrow Carter's car?'

'I wish you'd tell me now,' he begged.

'I promise it's worth the wait. So, can you get here?'

'Carter's got to pick something up in the village in a bit so, if he doesn't mind closing the pub for an hour, I could ask him to give me a lift.'

'Brilliant,' I responded. The time would give me an opportunity to further mull over what I had in mind, gift Constance a hug and James another kiss. Or three. I don't think I'd ever felt so happy. 'That will be ideal.'

'Okay, I'll see you in a while.'

With the next round of hugs and kisses shared, James had important and exciting career calls to make. He'd already mentioned that working his notice wasn't going to be pleasant, but with the job he'd longed for as the light at the end of the tunnel, he'd be able to bear it.

'And while you're finishing up in the city and sorting out the tenancy on your flat, why don't you leave Buddy with us?' Constance suggested.

'Oh yes,' I agreed. 'No more sitter for Buddy. We can look after him while you're away, James. It will save you a fortune and I'm sure he won't mind.'

'What do you think, pal?' James asked Buddy. 'How would you like to stay here from now on?'

Buddy licked James's chin and that sealed the deal.

'Right,' I smiled. 'Now that's settled I'm going to go and wait for Zack and tonight we'll go to the pub and fill everyone else in, shall we, James? Unless you'd like us to tell them here, Constance?'

'No, no,' she said. 'You young things carry on. I've had quite enough excitement for one day. It will be an early night for me.'

'James?'

'All right,' he agreed, but he sounded nervous. 'As long as you don't think they're going to hate me.'

'Why should they?' I frowned.

'For making my life a misery, of course,' Constance said.

'Exactly that,' James said with a nod to his aunt.

'They'll be so agog when I tell them about our meet-cute *and* that my plans for the woods are back on that they'll forget all about that, and it wasn't all your fault,' I reassured him.

'Charming,' Constance tutted and I gave her a look.

'I'm trying to stop him fretting,' I told her.

'I know,' she chuckled. 'I'm only teasing. Of course they won't hate you, James. And you already know Rick a bit, and Carter, too.'

'So, we'll go?' I asked James again.

'We'll go.'

'Great,' I said, before he could change his mind. 'And now I need to get ready to talk to my brother.'

Chapter 28

I'd barely started to think about how I was going to word what it was that I wanted to ask Zack before he was messaging to say he was walking down the drive. I replied, telling him the garden gate was unlocked and that he could come straight to the apartment.

'Well, you certainly look happier,' he said, the moment I opened the door to him.

I knew I couldn't stop smiling and hoped he'd look the same soon, too.

'That's because I am happier,' I grinned and gave him a squeeze.

'So, come on then,' he said, as he disentangled himself. 'Tell me what's going on.'

I sat in the chair opposite where he was on the sofa, leaning forward with his elbows on his knees.

'Tilly, please,' he insisted. 'Spit it out.'

'Give me a minute,' I laughed. 'I want to savour the moment and say it right.'

He rolled his eyes, sat back and folded his arms.

'I'm going to lose interest at this rate.'

'No, you're not.' I smiled.

'No,' he said and leant forward again. 'You're right. I'm not. You're buying the woods, aren't you?'

'Stop!' I yelped. 'I don't want you to guess.'

'Hurry up then,' he groaned.

'Okay,' I said, bracing myself, and then took a deep breath. 'I'll start with the obvious.'

'Go on.'

'James and I are a couple.'

'I knew it!' Zack clapped. 'It was pretty obvious the other night, but I'd locked the pair of you in ages before that, hadn't I? Don't deny it, Tills.'

'You had,' I laughed. 'You were right when you guessed I had feelings for him.'

'Yes,' he said smugly and punched the air. 'I knew it.' Then his expression changed. 'But isn't he the bad guy in this whole *are you buying the woods or aren't you* saga?'

'Don't worry about that,' I told him. 'That's by the by.'

'I mean it,' he said seriously. 'Is he worthy of you?'

Despite the archaic way he'd worded the question, it felt so good to have my big brother close enough to look out for me.

'He's definitely worthy of me,' I said seriously. 'And there's so much more to our story than you already know.'

'Tell me then,' he said again.

I then proceeded to give him the run down on how I'd met this guy, thanks to Mum's runaway gardening hat, just seconds after we'd talked on the phone the day I arrived in Willowell and how, thanks to another fluke encounter, our relationship had since developed and we'd seen more of each other as a result.

'Nope,' Zack interrupted. 'Not a fluke. It was fate.' I grinned at that. 'Carry on.'

'So,' I said, drawing the word out, 'I was in pretty deep by the time I arrived back at Fernside one day with some good news for Constance, only to find it was James, *her nephew*, playing the piano in her sitting room, not her.'

'Fuck,' Zack exclaimed. 'Sorry, but damn. I knew that was coming, but how shocked were you?'

'I can't even tell you,' I laughed. 'But it's all water under the bridge now and our relationship is very much back on, as is . . . pause for dramatic impact . . .'

'Don't make me say it!'

'All right, all right,' I laughed. 'The sale is back on! I'm buying the woods!'

'Oh Tilly!' he said, as he jumped up and pulled me onto my feet. 'This is the best news! I'm so happy for you!'

We proceeded to hug, cheer and do a bit of a silly dance around the tiny sitting room before collapsing onto the sofa.

'And,' I said, giving him a nudge, 'I hope you're going to be happy for yourself, when you hear the next thing I have to say.'

'Go on,' he said and sat up straighter.

'Well,' I swallowed, 'I know I've been caught up here this summer with my love life and my *life* life, but it hasn't escaped my notice that you've been going through stuff, too.'

Zack started to look a little misty eyed.

'And it seems to me that your dream life isn't your dream life anymore,' I went on. 'I can't imagine how that must be making you feel because you've always been so content.'

I let a moment of silence settle and felt relieved when my brother opened up to me.

'It's made me feel . . . rootless,' he explained hoarsely. 'Homesick too. Hence the surprise visit. Willowell is working its magic on me and meeting Kaya and talking to her has made a huge difference, but I still feel like there's something missing. I know on the outside, it probably looks like I haven't changed, but I know I have on the inside and you've obviously picked up on that.'

'You're my brother,' I said softly, 'so of course I have.' He nodded but didn't say anything more. 'And with that in mind,' I carried on, 'I might have a suggestion that will help you feel rooted again.'

'Go on.'

'Well, there's still loads to do,' I pointed out before getting to the crux of it. 'I mean, I haven't even bought the woods yet, but when I have and when I've had permission to run the business confirmed, I was wondering if you'd consider becoming part of the team.'

'Crikey.'

'Of course, I appreciate that you and Kaya might have already made plans to leave once the summer's over, but I wanted to put this out there now, so you know you've got the option. Obviously, I don't expect you to answer before permission is granted, but what do you think?'

'What do I think?' he laughed. 'I think you're a legend!'

'You do?'

'I do. And Dad would be so proud of you.'

'You really think so?'

I'd talked to him less of late, but that didn't mean I didn't still think about him.

'I know so,' Zack said vehemently. 'You're finding your feet, finding your way and doing something so brave. He'd be thrilled!'

★

My brother's kind words and reaction to everything were the cherry on my day and I hoped my friends were going to be equally excited when I shared the news about the woods and my surprise relationship. I'd sworn Zack to secrecy about what was set to unfold and he was delighted to be in on it. I think he was relishing the opportunity to see the look on everyone's else's faces having had the benefit of a few hours to process it all himself.

'Don't look so worried,' I said to James, once I'd parked up at The Greenman and we were walking over to the pub that evening. He looked positively green himself. 'I told you; Zack was over the moon about everything and everyone else is going to be, too.'

'Given that until today I must have been branded the bad guy,' he winced, 'I hope you're right about that.'

'I am,' I insisted. 'Now, come on.'

'You go ahead,' he said and took a step away from where I was holding out my hand to guide him in. 'I just want to make sure Buddy doesn't need the loo.'

'Are you using your four-legged friend as an avoidance tactic?' I teased him.

'You know he's my support dog,' James smiled. 'Always here when I need him. We'll be two seconds.'

I shook my head, but left him to it.

'Hey, Tilly,' he called after me. 'Maybe you could tell them everything before I get in there. Let them absorb it all a bit before I walk in.'

'No chance,' I told him. 'We're doing this together.'

James took more than a couple of minutes to give Buddy the opportunity to delay the inevitable, but as the pub was busy, I managed to linger around the door without anyone inside spotting me.

'Believe it or not, I'm relieved you haven't gone in yet,' he puffed, when he finally joined me. 'You were right, Tilly. We're doing this together. From now on, we're doing everything together.'

I loved the sound of that and kissed him very thoroughly to make sure he got the message.

'I don't believe it!' came a shocked voice behind us. It was Kaya. She and Zack hadn't made it into the pub yet either. 'So, you are sleeping with the enemy, Tilly. I knew it the night of the supper showdown.'

'I can't believe you're calling it that.' I tutted and shook my head.

James looked as though he didn't know how to react.

'Did you know about this?' Kaya demanded of my brother and he nodded. 'And you never said a word. Oh well, at least I know you can keep a secret.'

'Always.' Zack smiled at me and then turned his attention to James. 'Hello, James,' he said. 'I'm pleased to meet you properly at last.'

'Likewise,' James said and the pair shook hands, which was something I'd never seen my brother do before. 'Tilly has told me so much about you.'

'Nothing good, I hope,' Zack laughed and bent to give Buddy a fuss.

'All absolutely terrible,' I confirmed.

'Brilliant,' Zack said, and together we headed inside.

The evening flew by and the explanations about mine and James's relationship and what was next on the agenda for the woods now I was definitely buying them were punctuated with delicious drinks, moreish pizza and trips outside with Buddy.

James's fears about being labelled the bad guy were soon quashed as everyone was firmly on his side once he'd explained why he'd changed his mind. They loved the sound of the new job he'd got lined up and roared with laughter when he told them how Tommy had reacted to Constance roping him into the situation. Clearly the guy was not liked, but his dad had been much loved.

'I'm going to help Aunt Constance to get the sale moving next week,' I heard James telling Zack as Melody and I went to order more drinks.

My heart skipped a beat at the thought. This time I knew it was *really* going to happen and I couldn't wait.

'Congratulations, Tilly,' beamed Carter, who, like Zack, had been splitting his time between chatting with us and serving. 'This round is on me.'

'That's so kind, Carter,' I smiled. 'Thank you.'

'What do you think of Tilly's new beau?' Rick, who was buying snacks, asked him. 'I think he's turned into a total dreamboat, but I can see he's off limits.'

We all looked across to where James and Zack were chatting with their heads together while Kaya made a fuss of Buddy.

'I can't say he's my usual type,' Carter laughed, 'but he certainly seems to be fitting in at last.'

'He does, doesn't he?' I sighed happily.

'The two of you look made for each other.' Melody nudged me and I blushed. 'It might have taken you a while to get back on an even keel, but I don't reckon anything will stop you now.'

Right on cue, James looked at me and smiled.

'You know what,' I smiled back. 'I think you're right.'

Chapter 29

One month later

'You weren't wrong about this, were you?' James beamed at me, as he swam back over to where I was treading water. 'It's utterly blissful.'

I had been astonished when he'd told me that he'd never swum in the river and had immediately set about rectifying that. He accompanied me every morning he could now and sometimes, if they were staying in the village, Zack and Kaya came, too. However, on the balmy September early start that day it was just James and I, and after such a hot and passionate night in the garden apartment, celebrating his last day working in London, the cool-down felt even lovelier than usual.

'I'm not often wrong about anything,' I smiled, as I drew him to me and wrapped my legs around his waist.

'Tilly,' he groaned, as I pulled him closer in. 'We can't be late, not today.'

Right on cue, the sound of Constance banging a wooden spoon on her ancient milk pan met our ears. It was her new way of summoning us without having to open the sunroom door and risk letting Buddy out. The dog loved to swim as much as we did, but we didn't always have time to dry him off, and on this particular day, we certainly didn't.

'Come on then,' I smiled, as I released James. 'Let's go.'

Ordinarily, I would have been disappointed to be interrupted, but with such an exciting time to look forward to, I didn't mind at all.

'Now then,' said Constance, as she waved us off a short while later. 'Are you sure you've got everything?'

'Even the kitchen sink,' I said, checking the list I'd jotted down in my new notebook.

I might have become a more carefree person since I'd left my old life behind and landed in Willowell, but there were certain things I would never part with, and my love of a good list was one of them.

'And I'll be back later to pick you and everything else for the party up around five, Aunt Constance,' said James as he readjusted his too small straw hat.

I, of course, was wearing Mum's so we looked like peas in a pod.

'I can't wait,' Constance said excitedly.

I couldn't wait either. The whole day was going to be the best fun. That said, I'd had to put a positive spin on what was going to occur ahead of our supper party that night, to ensure all my friends turned out to swell the numbers of the first Willowell Woods working party of the autumn.

The purchase of the wood was only just underway, but Constance had insisted that I should make a start on the remedial work that needed doing and we had agreed to split the cost. James, Zack, Rick and Carter had been keen to sign up for a day of path clearing and arboriculture assistance, but Kaya and Melody had needed some convincing. In the end, it was switching it to a Sunday so Melody wouldn't have to close the store *and* the promise of the first ever on-site supper party that swung it.

'Are you excited?' James asked, as I parked up next to Rick's truck and noticed Tommy's for sale board had been unceremoniously dumped in the back of it.

He'd been told to collect it but hadn't, so Rick was going to get rid of it for us.

'You know I'm excited,' I said, as I leant across to give James a kiss. 'I can't wait to get started.'

'No time for all that,' scolded Rick, as he opened my door and made me jump. 'Come on, let's get this gate open before the others arrive and then we can crack straight on.'

'Right you are, boss,' I laughed, and James gave him a salute.

'I'd love to see you in a uniform, James,' Rick teased him and James blushed.

'Any preference?' I asked, as I climbed out and released Buddy from his harness on the backseat.

'Don't encourage him,' James groaned, but with a smile.

'Arb assistant will suffice for today,' said Rick, as he thrust a large bag and a helmet and visor into James's arms. 'And there'll be no messing about on my watch. Tree work is serious business.'

'Right boss,' James said, rather meekly.

We made a great start on the work and even Kaya and Melody got into the swing of it, though the air was occasionally blue when one of us got snagged by a particularly brutish bramble or stung by a nasty nettle.

I had stopped a few times during the day to look at the trees, admire a plant I hadn't noticed before or tune into birdsong I hadn't previously heard. I was having fewer pinch me moments, but I was still in awe of Willowell Woods and extremely aware that I was poised to become the custodian of somewhere very special indeed.

I'd now had a more formal meeting with Helen – with Constance and James, who were still the current owners, in attendance – and she was even more enthusiastic about my proposal. In less than a year, I could be up and running and I couldn't wait.

And on that note . . .

'Hey, Tills,' said Zack, late in the day and as we started to flag. 'Have you got a sec?'

We'd all enjoyed a picnic lunch together next to the stinky pond, as Kaya had named it, but there hadn't been a moment to talk to my brother alone.

'Sure,' I said, as I pulled off my thick gloves and raked a hand through my tangled, sweaty hair. I'd returned Mum's hat to my car after lunch. 'Are you okay?'

'More than all right,' he nodded. 'Constance called me earlier—'

'She did?' I rummaged in my pocket for my phone. There were no missed calls. 'Was she okay?'

'She called me with an offer,' Zack carried on, ignoring my fussing.

'An offer?'

'I've been talking to her about the possibility of working with you here and she realised that if I did, I was going to need somewhere more permanent to stay than Carter's spare room.'

'Yes,' I said thoughtfully. 'I don't suppose you can stay there for ever, can you?'

'She told me that you're going to move into the house soon,' Zack carried on. 'You're having one of the bedrooms, aren't you?'

'That's right,' I confirmed. 'I'll be bunking in with James really, but she wanted me to officially have a separate room in Fernside, for appearance's sake.'

Zack grinned and I whacked him with my gloves.

'So that means the garden apartment will be empty,' he said and I began to join the dots. 'So, she's said I can move in there if I do decide to stay.'

'Oh Zack. That would be perfect. But, what does Kaya have to say about it?'

He still hadn't told me what they were planning to do, which was fine because I hadn't wanted to put pressure on either of them, but I didn't mind admitting that the offer of accommodation did make me hope that might encourage them to stay. For a while, at least.

'She's . . .'

'She's what?' I demanded and whacked him again.

I could now appreciate how frustrating he'd found it the day I'd had my grand reveal and dithered a bit.

'She's totally on-board,' he said in a rush. 'And she wants to move into the apartment, too, with Constance's blessing, of course! Settling into life in Willowell has quelled the wanderlust in both of us and we want to stay.'

'So, you're both staying put?'

'We're both staying right here,' he confirmed.

'Oh Zack!' I sobbed and flung my arms around him.

We were set to become one very happy family, indeed!

★

As we shared this thrilling development with everyone else, I noticed how hot and grubby we all looked as a result of the day spent felling, clearing and chopping and suggested we went back to our respective homes to get cleaned up ahead of the celebratory supper party.

Everyone thought this was a great idea and I made sure I was first back because there was some preparation I wanted to see to and I wanted it completed before James arrived with Constance, who was going to be visiting the woods for the first time in a very long time.

'Hey, Tilly!' I heard James call, just as I added the final string of solar lights that I'd had charging in the sun all day to the interior. 'Are you ready for us?'

'Yes,' I said, as I rushed outside to be greeted first by Buddy, and then by an emotional looking Constance. 'I'm here.' I swallowed as I smoothed down the shirt dress James loved so much. 'I'm ready.'

I linked my arm through the woman's who, in the space of just a few short months, had completely transformed my life. Or helped me to transform it would perhaps be a better description. It was high time I started owning my achievements and acknowledging that I was the driving force behind the brave life leaps I was making. Constance had contributed so much, but I had found the courage to step up to accept what it was that she was offering and then find ways to make it work.

'Welcome back, Constance,' I said softly, the words catching a little. 'Can we take you on a tour to show you what we've done today?'

'I'd like that,' she said, in a tone I'd never heard her use before, and I began to realise that this trip for her was every bit as significant as the journey James had been on. 'Let's have a look then, shall we?'

The sun was setting but it was still light enough for us to see how beautiful the woods were, and I very much appreciated the added ambience created by the pair of calling tawny owls as we walked along the freshly cleared paths.

'This all looks rather different to how I remember it,' Constance commented. 'I think it's been longer than I realised since I last visited and I can see what you meant about the state of the paths, Tilly.'

She sounded upset as she nodded to the stretch ahead of us that was still covered in brambles and meant we couldn't comfortably walk any further.

'But look how much we've cleared today,' James, who was standing behind us, pointed out. 'We'll have all the walkways reinstated in no time. Or Tilly will, I mean.'

'No, no.' I turned and smiled at him. 'It's a time-consuming job James, so I'm more than happy for you take on the responsibility of that and free me up to sort some other things.'

Constance chuckled and James rolled his eyes.

'I set myself right up for that, didn't I?' he laughed, his eyes shining in the fading light.

'Yes, you did rather,' Constance agreed. 'But now you've got some free time in the evenings, James, it'll do you good to get out in the fresh air. I know you've missed having the opportunity to regularly do that.'

'She has a point,' James winked at me.

'Come on,' I said, as I turned us back around again. 'Come and see what I've done in the cabin before everyone else arrives.'

We weren't all that close when we realised that the others had beaten us to it and my supper party set-up, with the added twinkling lights, was being much admired. My friends cheered as Constance, James and I crossed the threshold, and Zack handed me a glass of celebratory fizz and kissed my cheek.

'You've really arrived in Willowell,' he beamed and I willed myself not to cry as I remembered how we used to chant something similar in the back of the car when Dad drove us here for those treasured childhood camping adventures.

'And this time,' I swallowed, while Kaya poured and handed out drinks for everyone else, 'I don't have to leave and neither do you.'

After our endeavours, we were all hungry, so got stuck straight into the simple fare Melody and I had prepared. The set-up was like that which we'd enjoyed down by the river – I'd even got a comfy chair for Constance to recline in while the rest of us sprawled on blankets and beanbags – and as bellies were filled, the level of chatter escalated.

The topic of conversation that thrilled me the most was the discussion about what we had achieved that day. Despite the aches and scratches, everyone it seemed, even Melody and Kaya, had had the best time.

Carter noticed me smiling as he waxed lyrical about the safest way to fell a bramble.

'I know I did initially grumble when you changed the date because it was my only day off this week,' he grinned at me, 'but the working party has proved your point, hasn't it?'

'Yes,' I said, smugly, but good humouredly. 'It really has. And if I can make the visitors who come here feel even half as good as you guys, who were mucking in with the toughest jobs, then the business is bound to succeed.'

'We can already offer you glowing testimonials when it comes to appreciating the joy of being outdoors,' Melody smiled.

'As well as tasty snacks,' I reminded her.

It was good to know that mine wasn't going to be the only business to benefit from the new adventure being set up in Willowell Woods.

'And I'm really looking forward to creating and supervising bushcraft exercises for you to offer,' Carter added.

'And I've been thinking about Grace's nursery,' Zack shared. His words made Constance, who had been drowsing, sit up again. 'I've had a look around the outside of the cabin and can see quite a few plants that she would have put in. It would be wonderful to add some more to acknowledge her connection to the history of the woods as we move forward.'

'You could do that?' James asked.

'Easily,' Zack nodded. 'And Tilly tells me that you're quite the horticultural expert yourself, James, so you can help me if you like.'

'I'd love to,' he smiled. 'Thanks, Zack.'

'What do you think, Constance?' I asked.

'I think it all sounds wonderful,' she answered. She sounded so happy it made my heart fill with pride. 'But at this rate Tilly, we'll never see James at the house.'

'Oh, I'm sure he'll make time for us.' I smiled and went to sit next to her. 'I'm so grateful to you, you know.'

'I know you are,' she said, as she kissed my cheek, 'and I'm grateful to you, too. It's been a rocky path at times, but you've pulled my little family back together and helped me take a proper interest in things again that I'd set aside for far too long.'

I knew she was talking about playing the piano because she'd talked in even more detail now about how she had all but abandoned it after Grace had died. She had told me that the guilt she had felt whenever she lifted the lid and ran her fingers over the keys had been overwhelming.

Thankfully, she had moved away from that feeling now and was playing more often. And James's time at the keys was helping with that too, because the pair of them could become quite competitive when it came to playing a fugue from memory or composing something new. I had shed a few tears when James had told me that his aunt had been his first teacher, but they were very happy ones and I couldn't stop laughing when he said what a hard taskmaster she had been, even following up on his lessons when he was away at school.

'You're the granddaughter I never had.' Constance smiled shakily as she held my hand. 'Now, go and find my nephew. I saw him taking Buddy out a minute ago and you don't want to miss the opportunity to kiss under the harvest moon, do you?'

It took me a moment to recover from hearing her addressing me so fondly and then I stood up and slipped quietly out of the door. I closed it behind me so the cabin wouldn't be inundated with too many moths.

The air felt cool after the warmth inside, and as I set off, I could hear music. I looked back to see Constance being gently waltzed around by Rick while the others danced with varying degrees of abandon and shouted out the lyrics to 'Walking on Sunshine'. Given that it had been the catchphrase of our youth, it was doubtless Zack's choice.

With the fairy lights glowing, the place looked idyllic, the perfect supper party venue for nights when the weather let us down and we couldn't sit by the river back at Fernside but still wanted to enjoy a taste of the outdoors.

Fernside . . . my dream home come true . . . and there was another dream, just a few steps ahead of me.

'Hello, you,' said James when I joined him to watch the view of the moon rising between the trees.

'Hello, you,' I said back and wrapped my arms around his waist. 'Where's Buddy?'

'In the undergrowth somewhere around here,' James said, as he looked around.

I could hear snuffling nearby, so his pal hadn't wandered too far.

'I think it's a miracle he hasn't been in the stinky pond yet,' I laughed and felt James tense up.

'Don't even joke about it,' he shivered. 'That would be a disaster. Can you imagine the state his coat would be in?'

'Rather your car than mine to get him home,' I giggled.

'Buddy!' he called and made a grab for the dog's collar when he bounded over. 'Sorry mate,' he said as he reattached his lead, 'but I'm going to keep hold of you.'

'And what about me?' I asked as Buddy huffed and laid down. 'Are you going to keep hold of me, too?'

'I'll hold you if you want me to,' James smiled and pulled me into his arms. 'As tightly as you like. How's that?'

'Tighter,' I requested and he obliged.

'Better?'

'Perfect.' I sighed and rested my head on his shoulder.

'We're the perfect fit, aren't we?' James said and kissed the top of my head.

'We are,' I agreed. 'I thought that right from the moment we met.'

'Me too,' he nodded.

'I feel like I've known you for far longer than just a few summer months.'

'That's because we've gone through so much in such a short space of time,' he laughed. 'We've gone from perfect match to bust up and back again.'

He was right.

'And where are we now?' I asked, as I turned to look up at him.

His eyes met mine and I felt the tug of desire that always leapt into life whenever he was near.

'Now?' he asked.

'Um.'

'Right now,' he said, as he lowered his lips to mine, 'I'd say we're finally heading towards our happy ever after, wouldn't you?'

With Willowell Woods safely surrounding us, the sound of the party and the tawny owls providing a tuneful backdrop, and my arms wrapped around the man I'd fallen in love with the moment I'd seen him leap out of his car to chase down Mum's old hat, I felt inclined to agree.

'Yes,' I said, between kisses. 'A very happy ever after.'

Acknowledgements

I'm convinced that this part of the book-writing journey comes around faster every time I sit down at my desk to do it! It feels like only yesterday that I was trying to find the words to include at the end of my debut, *The Cherry Tree Café*, and yet here I am, doing it for the twenty-second time. Amazing!

I know I always say it but there really are a huge number of people to thank when a book heads out into the world and this time is no exception.

I have two editors to thank for guiding and encouraging me this time around. Clare Hey and I started this one together and Phoebe Morgan arrived literally just as I typed the final words of the first draft! Thank you both for supporting me while I created this new setting and got to know a whole cast of new characters. Let's raise a glass to us *and* Willowell!

And of course, hugest thanks to my wonderful agent, Amanda Preston. As always, you've been an absolute rock, but this year you've excelled yourself, my darling. Thank you for always being there and for saying exactly the right thing when I need to hear it!

I know I've kept my head down while I've written this one,

but I've always felt safe in the knowledge that family and friends have been just a message away if I've needed them and I've heard librarians, event organisers, content creators, bloggers and booksellers all supporting the Swainette cause, so thank you all so very much, too.

Wishing you all a truly wonderful summer and until the next time we meet, may your bookshelves – be they virtual or real – be filled with fabulous fiction!

With love,
H x

About the Author

Heidi Swain lives in Norfolk. She is passionate about gardening and the countryside, and collects vintage paraphernalia. *Walking on Sunshine* is her twenty-second novel.

You can follow Heidi on Instagram @Heidi_Swain or visit her website: heidiswain.co.uk

Best Summer Ever

Heidi Swain

Sunshine, love and happy ever afters . . .

Summer is in full swing when Daisy returns to Wynmouth in her clapped-out car, leaving behind both her job and the man her parents thought she was going to marry. Coming home could be just what she needs to move her life on.

At Wynbrook Manor, things are in disarray. Owner Algy isn't getting any younger, and Daisy's mum Janet, housekeeper at the manor, spends her days running around after him, while Daisy's dad Robin, the gardener, has been let down by the person he had lined up to take care of the new cut-flower garden.

As Daisy tries to find her place at Wynbrook and in the village, she's drawn to summer visitor Josh. But when he turns out not to be the person he appears to be, will the spark between them fizzle out? And with it, the chances of this turning into the best summer ever?

Available now in Paperback, Ebook & Audio

SIMON & SCHUSTER

London · New York · Amsterdam/Antwerp · Sydney/Melbourne · Toronto · New Delhi